I went to the path as I always did before return-ing. I liked to look down into the bushes far below and remember the thrill it used to give me as a child.

I gripped the rail and leaned forward and then suddenly it swung forward, taking me with it, so that I was clinging to it and hanging in mid-air. A startled bird flew up, brushing my face as it went past me. I had time to think: This is the end! before I fell.

I opened my eyes. I could scarcely breathe so fast was my heart beating. I looked down; far below were the tops of trees. I felt my feet slipping and I clutched at the bushes into which I had fallen.

For some minutes I was unable to do anything but hang on with all my might. I looked up and saw that the rail on which I had been leaning had come away on one side and that I had had a miraculous escape from certain death.

And now what must I do? One false move and I could go hurtling down. . . .

# VICTORIA HOLT

## Lord of the Far Island

A FAWCETT CREST BOOK

Fawcett Publications, Inc., Greenwich, Connecticut

# *Contents*

# Lord of the Far Island

# PART ONE

# The London Scene

# A Proposal of Marriage

The dream disturbed my sleep on the eve of Esmeralda's coming-out ball. It was not the first time I had had that dream. It had come to me periodically over my nineteen years. There is something vaguely alarming about these recurring dreams because it seems certain that they have a significance which one has to discover.

When I awoke from it I would be trembling with terror and I could never be entirely sure why. It was not exactly the dream itself, but the impression it brought of impending doom.

I would be in a room. I knew that room very well by now, for it was always the same each time I dreamed. It was an ordinary kind of room. There was a brick fireplace, on either side of which were chimney seats, a red carpet and heavy red curtains. Over the fireplace was a picture of a storm at sea. There were a few chairs and a gate-legged table. Voices came and went in the dream. I would have a feeling that something was being hidden from me; and suddenly there would come this overpowering sense of doom from which I would awake in horror.

That was all. Sometimes the dream would not come for a year and I would forget about it; then it would return. As time passed I would notice a little more in the room, for instance the thick cords which held back the red curtains, the rocking chair in one corner; and with these fresh details it seemed to me that the feeling of fear crept nearer.

After I had awakened and was lying in my bed I would ask myself what it could mean. Why should that room have become part of my sleeping life? Why should it be the same room every time? Why should I experience that creeping fear? My imagination had conjured up the room, but why should I have dreamed of it over the years? I had talked to no one of this. The whole matter seemed so foolish in the daytime, for dreams which are so vivid to the dreamer are almost always boring when retold. But somewhere deep in my thoughts was the conviction that this dream meant something, that a strange and as yet incomprehensible force was warning me of impending danger, and that perhaps someday I should discover what.

I was not given to wild fancies. Life had been too grim and earnest for that. Ever since I had been cast on the mercy of Cousin Agatha I had been encouraged to remember my place. That I sat at table with her daughter Esmeralda, that I shared the latter's governess, that I was allowed to walk in the park under the guidance of her nanny, were matters for which it appeared I should be eternally grateful. I must constantly remember that I was that most despised of creatures, a Poor Relation, whose only claim to have my existence abovestairs was that I belonged to the Family. Even my claim on that was a frail one, for Cousin Agatha was in fact my mother's second cousin, so the bond was very slender indeed.

Cousin Agatha was one of those women of immense proportions—everything about her was outsize—her body, her voice, her personality. She dominated her family, which consisted of her small husband—perhaps he was not so small but only seemed so compared with his wife—and her daughter Esmeralda. Cousin William, as I called him, was a man with wide business interests and wealthy; a power outside his home, I believed, though inside it he was completely subservient to his forceful wife. He was quiet, and always gave me an absentminded smile when he saw me, as though he couldn't quite remember who I was and what I was doing in his house; I think he would have been a kind man if he had the strength of will to oppose his wife. She was noted for her good works. There were days of the week which were devoted to her committees. Then ladies, not unlike herself, would be seated in the drawing room and often I had to help dispense tea and cakes. She liked me to be around at such times. "My second cousin's daughter, Ellen," she would explain. "Such a tragedy. There was nothing to be done but give the child a home." Sometimes Esmeralda helped me with the cakes. Poor Esmeralda! No one would have thought she was the daughter of the house. She would spill the tea in the saucers and once emptied a whole cupful into the lap of one of the charitable ladies.

Cousin Agatha would be very annoyed when people mistook Esmeralda for the Poor Relation and me for the Daughter of the House. I suppose Esmeralda's lot wasn't much better than mine. It would be: "Hold your shoulders back, Esmeralda. Don't slouch so." Or "Speak up, for heaven's sake. Don't mumble." Poor Esmeralda, with the splendid name which didn't fit her one little bit! She had pale blue eyes which watered frequently, as she was often on the verge of tears, and fine fair hair which always looked wispy. I did her sums for her and helped her with her essays. She was quite fond of me.

It was one of Cousin Agatha's regrets that she had only one daughter. She had wanted sons and daughters whom she could have commanded and moved about like pieces on a chessboard. The fact that she had only one rather fragile daughter she blamed entirely on her husband. The rule of the household was that good flowed from Cousin Agatha's actions and anything that was not desirable from other people's.

She had been received by the Queen and congratulated

on the good work she did for the poor. She organized clubs where such people could be initiated into their duty towards their betters. She arranged the sewing of shirts and the making of calico garments. She was indefatigable; and she surrounded herself with a perpetual haze of virtue.

It was small wonder that both her husband and daughter felt at a disadvantage. Oddly enough, I did not. I had long made up my mind that Cousin Agatha's good works brought as much satisfaction to herself as to anyone else and I believed that when they failed to do that they would cease. She sensed this lack of appreciation in me and deplored it. She did not like me; not that she was greatly enamored of anyone but herself; yet somewhere at the back of her mind she must have appreciated the fact that her husband provided the money which made it possible for her to live as she did, and as for Esmeralda, she was her only child and therefore must be given a little consideration.

I, however, was the outsider, and not a humble one. She must have noticed the smile which I could not keep from my lips when she was talking of her newest schemes for the good of someone. There was no doubt that she sensed in me a reluctance to conform. She would convince herself, of course, that it was due to the bad blood which I had inherited from my father's side, though she protested that she knew nothing else of that connection.

Her attitude was apparent in my first few years in her household. I was about ten years old when she sent for me.

"I think it is time, Ellen," she said, "for you and me to have a talk."

There was I, a sturdy ten-year-old—with a mass of almost black hair, dark blue eyes, a short nose and a rather long stubborn chin.

I was made to stand before her on the great Persian rug in the room she called her study, where her social secretary wrote her letters and did most of the committee work for which she took the credit.

"Now, Ellen," she said to me, "we must come to an understanding. We want to make clear your position in the household, do we not?" She did not wait for an answer but went on. "I am sure you cannot fail to be grateful to me . . . and to Cousin William Loring [he was her husband] for keeping you in our household. We could, of course, on the death of your mother have put you into an orphanage, but because you are of the family . . . though the relationship could scarcely be said to be a close one . . . we have decided that you must be given our protection. Your mother, as you know, married a Charles Kellaway. You are a result of this marriage." Her large nose twitched a little, which showed the contempt in which she held both my parents and their ensuing offspring. "A rather unfortunate marriage. He was not the man who was chosen for her."

"It must have been a love match," I said, for I had heard about it from Nanny Grange, whose aunt had been Cousin Agatha's nanny and was therefore quite knowledgeable about past family affairs.

"Pray," went on Cousin Agatha, "do not interrupt. This is a very serious matter. Your mother, against her family's wishes, went off and married this man from some outlandish place of which we had never heard." She looked at me very severely. "In something less than a year you were born. Soon after, your mother left her new home irresponsibly and came back to her family, bringing you."

"I was three years old," I said, quoting Nanny Grange.

She raised her eyebrows. "I did beg you not to interrupt. She had nothing . . . simply nothing. You and she became a burden to your grandmother. Your mother died two years later."

I had been five years old at the time. I remembered her vaguely: the suffocating embraces which I loved and the feeling of security which I did not recognize until she was gone. There was a hazy picture in my mind of sitting on cool grass, with her beside me, a sketchbook in her hand. She had always been sketching, and she used to hide the book from my grandmother. I sensed, of course, that she was in some sort of disgrace and it used to make me happy to think of myself as a kind of protector. "*You* love me, don't you, Ellen?" she would say. "No matter what I've done." Those words rang in my ears when I thought of her and I was always so impatient with myself for my five-year-old incompetence in not understanding what was going on.

"Your grandmother was scarcely of an age to bring up a child," went on Cousin Agatha.

No, I thought grimly. She had seemed incredibly old to me with her tight lips, her cold eyes and the little white cap without which I never saw her—a formidable old lady who struck terror into me when I realized that I was now alone and had lost that loving conspirator and companion and that in future I must extricate myself from the continual trouble which seemed to dog me. Fortunately I was naturally resilient and managed to cultivate a stoical indifference to reproaches and appeals to God as to what would become of me. I could not feel grief when my grandmother died and I made no attempt to pretend I did.

"When your grandmother died," added Cousin Agatha, "she asked me to care for you and so I gave her my solemn promise on her deathbed. I am determined to carry it out. You must realize that it is only because I have taken you into my house that you are not in an orphanage, training to give service in some household as a maid or, perhaps if you showed an aptitude for learning, a governess. However, I have brought you here and you share Esmeralda's lessons; you live as a member of my family. Pray remember it. I do not ask for gratitude but I expect it. Do not think that you will have advantages like those of my own daughter. That would not be good for your character. When you are of age it may well be that you will have to earn a living. I therefore advise you to take advantage now of the immense blessings which have come your way. You will have a governess to teach you so that by the time you reach your eighteenth birthday you will be an educated young woman. You will also learn the manners and customs of well-bred households. It is for you, Ellen, to profit from this. Learn all you can and always remember that it is due to my bounty that you are able to take advantage of these opportunities. That is all."

I was meant to go away and brood on these things, to marvel at my good fortune and to cultivate humility, that most desirable virtue of all for those in my position, and in which alas I seemed sadly lacking. I had at one time even thought briefly that Cousin Agatha regarded me with affection, for she would glow with satisfaction when her eyes rested on me, but I quickly realized that the satisfaction was in her own good deed in taking me into her household and had nothing to do with my progress. In fact she seemed to revel in the unsatisfactory defects in which I seemed to abound, and I came to understand that this was because the more of a burden I was, the greater her virtue in keeping me.

It will be seen that I had little love for Cousin Agatha. In character we were diametrically opposed, and I came to the conclusion that I was the only member of the household who ever contradicted her. When I was younger the threat of the orphanage hung over me; but I quickly learned that I should never be sent there because Cousin Agatha could never allow her friends to know that she had disposed of me in such a way. In fact my unsatisfactory character was a source of pleasure to her. I think she talked of me more often to her friends than she did of Esmeralda. Her own daughter was a nonentity. I was scarcely that. I often caught the comment after I was leaving a room: "Of course her mother . . ." And "It is hard to believe that poor Frances was an Emdon." Poor Frances being my mother and Emdon the name of the noble family from which both she and Cousin Agatha had sprung.

Of course I grew shrewd, "artful as a wagonload of monkeys" as Nanny Grange put it. "If there's mischief about, Miss Ellen will be in it. As for Miss Esmé, she's led there by her naughty cousin, that's what." I suppose in my way I was as much a force in that household as Cousin Agatha.

In the winter we lived in a tall house opposite Hyde Park. I loved the trees which would be growing bronzed and golden when we returned from summer in the country. Esmé and I used to sit at one of the topmost windows and point out the famous buildings to each other. From the north we looked right across the Park, but from the east we could pick out the Houses of Parliament, Big Ben and the Brompton Oratory. We used to listen for the muffin man's bell and watch the white-capped maids come running out with their dishes to buy his wares. Nanny Grange always sent for some and then we would sit by her fire toasting them and reveling in their soft buttery succulence. We used to watch the crossing sweepers—barefooted boys who made us unhappy because they looked so poor; and we both shed tears when we saw a man running behind a luggage-laden cab on its way to Paddington Station, where he hoped to earn a few pence by carrying the luggage. I made up a story of heartrending squalor which had Esmeralda weeping bitterly. She was very kindhearted and so easily touched that I had to amend my story and tell it the way Cousin Agatha would have done. He had come from a good family and had squandered his patrimony in gin and beer shops. He beat his wife, and his children went in terror of him. Poor sweet and simple Esmé! She was so easily swayed.

In the afternoons after lessons we would walk in Kensington Gardens with Nanny Grange. She would sit on a seat in the flower walk while we gamboled around. "And not out of sight, Miss Ellen, or I'll have something to say to you." She rarely had to worry on that score because I like to hang about and hear what she said to the other nannies.

"Esmé's mother. My word, what a tartar. I'd not stay if it wasn't for the fact that my aunt was *her* nanny, and it's right and proper to keep these things in families. Sickly little thing, Miss Esmé. As for that Miss Ellen, a real little madam. My patience, you'd think she was the daughter of the house instead of the poor relation. Mark my words, it will be brought home to her one day."

The other nannies would talk of their employers and their charges and I would make Esmeralda be quiet while we listened. Our companions shrieked, threw their balls to one another, spun their tops or cuddled their dolls and there would I be seated nonchalantly on the grass behind the seat on which the nannies sat, shamelessly listening.

I was obsessed with curiosity about my mother.

"My aunt says she was really pretty. Our young miss is the living image, I reckon. And we'll have trouble with her, I shouldn't wonder. But that's to come. Come home she did, said my aunt. She was in a state. Something went wrong—she never knew what, but back she came to her mother, bringing the child with her. My goodness me, it must have been jumping out of the frying pan into the fire. I heard they never let her forget what she had done. As for Miss Ellen's grandmother, she was another such as her cousin Agatha. Looking after the heathen and seeing he gets his soup and shirts and making her own daughter's life a misery . . . and the little 'un's too. Then Miss Frances goes and dies and leaves our Miss Ellen, who's never let forget that she's a burden. I mean to say an old lady like Mrs. Emdon and a lively young child . . . it didn't work! And when she died *she* took her in. Couldn't do anything else really. She's not likely to let the child forget what she's doing for her either."

Thus at an early age I gleaned the hazy facts about my beginnings.

They intrigued me. I often wondered about my father, but he was never mentioned and I could discover nothing about him. Contemplating my past, I felt I had not been exactly precious to anyone. Perhaps Cousin Agatha wanted me in a way, though, but only because I was a little check mark on her calendar of virtue.

I was not the sort of child to brood. For some remarkable and fortunate reason—or so it then seemed—I had an infinite belief in my ability to get the best out of life, and Esmeralda at least was glad to have me as a surrogate sister. In fact she was lost without me. I could never be alone long because she would soon seek me out; she had no desire for her own company. She was afraid of her mother, afraid of the dark and afraid of life. In being sorry for Esmeralda I suppose I could be glad to be my-self.

In the summer we went to Cousin William Loring's country house. What an upheaval that used to be. There would be packing for days and we would grow quite wild with excitement planning everything we would do in the country. We traveled in the brougham to the railway sta-tion and there followed the feverish bustle of getting into the train and debating whether we should face the engine or have our backs to it—an adventure in itself. We were accompanied by our governess, of course, who made sure that we sat erect on the plush seats and that I was not too noisy when I called Esmeralda's attention to the villages and countryside through which we passed. Some of the servants had gone on ahead and some would follow. Cousin Agatha usually arrived a week or so after we did, a blessed delay, and then she transferred her good works to the country instead of the town. The country estate was in Sussex—near enough to London to enable Cousin Agatha to go to town without too much effort when the worthy occasion demanded and Cousin William Loring could also attend to his vast business interests and not be altogether deprived of the fresh country air.

Esmeralda and I learned to ride, visit the poor, help at the church fete and indulge in the country activities of the gentry.

There was entertaining in the country as there was in town. Esmeralda and I were not as yet included in that, but I was vastly interested in it and I would sketch the dresses of the guests and imagine myself in them. I used to make Esmeralda hide with me on the staircase to see them arriving and watched with delight as they entered the great hall where Cousin Agatha, very stately, and Cousin William Loring, looking quite insignificant in com-parison, received them.

I would drag Esmeralda out of bed and make her peer through the banisters at the brilliant array, sometimes darting to the head of the stairs so that had any looked up I should have been in full view of them. Esmeralda would tremble with fear and I would laugh at her, knowing that I should never be sent away because above all Cousin Agatha must boast of her goodness to me. I would caper round our bedroom and make Esmeralda dance with me.

It was in the country that I became really aware of the great importance of the Carringtons. Even Cousin Agatha spoke their names with a certain awe. They lived in Trentham Towers, a very grand house on a hill—a mansion—and Mr. Josiah Carrington was a sort of squire in the neighborhood. Like Cousin William Loring, he had big interests in the City and had a London residence—in Park Lane in fact. Nanny Grange had pointed it out to us on several occasions. "That's the Carringtons' Town Place," she said in hushed tones, as though it were paradise itself.

They owned most of the Sussex hamlet and the surrounding farms, and Mr. Josiah Carrington's wife was Lady Emily, which meant that she was the daughter of an earl. One of Cousin Agatha's great ambitions was to live on terms of familiarity with the Carringtons, and as she was a woman who only had to want something to get it, she did, after a fashion. Cousin William's Sussex house was pleasantly Georgian with gracious portico and elegant lines. The drawing room was on the first floor and as it was large and lofty with a beautiful molded ceiling it was ideal for entertaining. Here Cousin Agatha "received" every Thursday when she was "At Home" in the country, and the dinner parties and the balls she gave were very well attended. She would be most disconsolate if for some reason the Carringtons were not present.

She was very gracious to Lady Emily and claimed great interest in everything that lady did while Cousin William and Mr. Josiah Carrington discussed "the Market" with equal passion.

Then there was Philip Carrington, who was about a year older than I and some two years older than Esmeralda. Cousin Agatha was very anxious that he and Esmeralda should be good friends. I remember our going to the country in the early summer and meeting Philip for the first time. Esmeralda had been formally introduced to him in the drawing room; I had been excluded. Then Cousin Agatha had instructed Esmeralda to take Philip to the stables and show him her pony.

I waylaid them on the way and joined them.

Philip was fair, with freckles across his nose and very light blue eyes; he was about my height and I was tall for my age. He looked interested in me, for I could see he had already decided to despise Esmeralda and was put out because he had been sent off with a girl, and a puny one at that.

"I suppose you ride ponies," he said rather scornfully.

"Well, what do you ride?" I asked.

"A horse of course."

"We shall have horses later on," said Esmeralda.

He ignored her.

I said: "We could ride horses just as well. They're no different from ponies."

"What do you know about that?"

So we bickered all the way to the stables.

He scorned our ponies and I was angry with him because I loved my Brownie passionately, but it is true that I never felt quite the same about the poor creature after that. He showed us the horse he had ridden over on.

"A very small one," I pointed out.

"I bet you couldn't ride it."

"I bet I could."

It was a challenge. Esmeralda trembled with fear and kept murmuring, "No, Ellen, don't," as I mounted his horse barebacked and rode it recklessly round the paddock. I must admit I was a bit scared, but I wasn't going to let him score over me and I had the insult to poor Brownie to answer.

Philip mounted then and performed some tricks for us to admire. He showed off blatantly. He and I sparred all the time, but there was no doubt that we enjoyed the sparring. It used to upset Esmeralda because she thought we hated each other.

"Mama wouldn't like it," she told me. "Remember, he's a Carrington."

"Well, I'm a Kellaway," I said, "and that's as good as a Carrington."

Philip had a tutor that summer and we saw a great deal of him. It was then that I first heard of Rollo.

"What a silly name," I said, which made Philip flush with fury.

Rollo was his brother, who was ten years older than he was. Philip spoke of him with pride. He was about twelve then, so Rollo was twenty-two. He was at Oxford and according to Philip could do everything.

"A pity he can't change his name," I said just to plague him.

"It's a great name, you silly thing. It's a Viking name."

"They were pirates," I said scornfully.

"They ruled the seas. Everywhere they went they conquered. Rollo was the great one who went to France and the King there was so worried he gave him a great slice of his country and that became Normandy. We're Normans." He looked at us disparagingly. "We came over here and conquered *you*."

"You didn't," I cried. "Because we are Normans too, aren't we, Esmeralda?"

Esmeralda was not sure. I gave her a little push. She had no idea how to deal with Philip. Not that either of us took any notice of her opinion in any case.

"We were better Normans than you were," said Philip. "We were the dukes and you were only the common people."

"Oh no, we weren't. . . ."

And that was how it went on.

Once Esmeralda said to me: "Mama would be cross if she knew how you quarreled with Philip. You forget he's a Carrington."

I remember when Rollo came down from Oxford. I first saw him riding in the lanes with Philip. His horse was white and as I said to Esmeralda after he had passed he ought to have had one of those helmets with wings at the side, then he would have looked just like a Viking. We did not speak to him. Philip called a greeting to us as he passed, making it clear that he had no time to waste on two girls with such a magnificent creature about. Rollo himself scarcely looked at us.

He was invited to the house of course and a great fuss was made of him. Cousin Agatha practically fawned on him. Nanny Grange said afterwards that you'd think he was some sort of a god and that Madam had her claws out to pick him up for Miss Esmeralda. "He'll be the heir of all those millions, I suppose," she said. "Though I reckon Master Philip will have his little picking."

When we returned to London that year I saw more of Rollo. When he was on vacation he called on us with his parents. I used to love those occasions when the carriages lined the street and pulled up outside our door. There would be red-and-white-striped awning for the guests to pass under and people used to line up to see them arrive. I loved watching from the nursery window.

They were enjoyable days. I used to wake up every morning with a delicious sense of excitement. The servants would chatter about the guests and there was a great deal of talk about the Carringtons. Sometimes Cousin Agatha and Cousin William Loring went to Park Lane to dine. We would watch them go and greatly regret that the dinner party was not at our house.

As I have said, I lived a great deal of my life below-stairs, and when possible I would secret myself at the servants' table and listen. If Esmeralda were with me they would be self-conscious; they didn't mind me so much, perhaps because my fate would one day be similar to theirs.

I heard one of them say, "That Miss Ellen, she's neither the one nor the other. I reckon when she's older she'll be sent out governessing. I'd rather be a housemaid. You do know your place then."

Such a thought alarmed me only briefly. I was sure that when the time came I would be able to take care of myself; but at the moment my lack of status gave me the glorious opportunity to hover between stairs. They talked quite freely in front of me. I quickly learned that Her and Him

were Cousin Agatha and Cousin William Loring and that
She was parsimonious, saw the cook's housekeeping accounts every week and relentlessly queried every item and
that He was frightened of Her and daren't raise his voice
against Her. She was all for social climbing. Look how
she ran after those Carringtons. Shameful! And they kept
a good establishment, my word they did, both in Park
Lane and in Sussex, and it had come to the cook's ears
that She had made Him buy that Sussex house just because
the Carringtons had their place there. Always plotting,
She was, to move up the ladder.

I learned through a series of subtle winks and nods
(which they thought I was not smart enough to interpret)
that She was determined to link the family with that of the
great Carringtons and them having boys and her having
a girl, the method was as easy as pie to understand.

I was amazed. They believed they were going to marry
Esmeralda to Philip or to the magnificent creature I had
seen on his white horse! It made me want to laugh as I
debated whether to tell Esmeralda. But there was no point
in scaring her completely out of her wits. She was not always in full possession of them as it was.

Life was full of interest: Upstairs in our nursery
quarters, where I could spy on what Cousin Agatha was
constantly reminding me were my betters, and downstairs
in the kitchen, where I could drink in secret information
when they all grew rather sleepy after finishing the joint or
the chicken pie washed down with cook's best elderberry
or dandelion wine.

I was pleased too that my origins were mysterious. I
would have hated to own Cousin Agatha for a mother, as
I would tell Esmeralda when I was feeling mean. Perhaps
Cousin William Loring would have been a kind sort of
father, but his subservience to his wife did not make me
admire him.

So there was the autumn and winter—roaring fires and
chestnuts popping on the hearth; the muffin man; hansom
cabs clopping by. Peering out to watch them and wondering about the people who were riding in them, I would

invent all sorts of stories to which Esmeralda would listen enthralled and then she would say: "How can you know who are in them and where they are going?" I would narrow my eyes and whistle. "There are more things in Heaven and Earth, Esmeralda Loring, than you wot of in your philosophy." She would shiver and regard me with awe (which I very much enjoyed). I would quote to her often, and sometimes pretend I had made up the words I spoke. She believed me. She could not learn as quickly as I could. It was a pity that she was so ineffectual. It gave me an exaggerated idea of my own cleverness. However, Cousin Agatha did her best to rid me of that; and perhaps, as I gathered from the servants' gossip and Cousin Agatha's manner towards me that I was of not much account, it was not so unfortunate after all, for I needed something to keep up my confidence.

I was adventurous and this gave rise to the speculation that I had a streak of wickedness in me. I loved the markets particularly. There were none in our district, but some of the servants used to go to them and I would hear them talking. Once I prevailed on Rosie, one of the parlormaids, to take me with her. She was a flighty girl who had always had a lover and had at last found one who wanted to marry her. There was a great deal of talk about her "bottom drawer," and she was always collecting "bits and pieces" for it. She would bring them into the kitchen. "Look what I've found in the market," she would cry, her eyes sparkling. "Dirt cheap it was."

As I said, I persuaded her to take me to the market. She liked to act outside the law too. She was rather fond of me and used to talk to me about her lover. He was the Carringtons' coachman and she was going to live in a mews cottage with him.

I shall never forget that market with its naphtha flares and the raucous Cockney voices of men and women calling their goods. There were stalls on which mounds of apples, polished until they shone, were arranged side by side with oranges, pears and nuts. It was November when I first saw it, and already holly and mistletoe were being displayed among the goods. I admired the crockery, the iron-mongery, the secondhand clothes, the stewed and jellied eels to be eaten on the spot or taken home, and I sniffed ecstatically at the cloud of appetizing steam which came from the fish-and-chip shop. Most of all I liked the people, who bargained at the stalls and jostled and laughed their way through the market. I thought it was one of the most exciting places I had ever visited. I returned with Rosie starry-eyed and wove stories around the market to impress Esmeralda.

I rashly promised that I would take her there. After that she kept asking about the market and I made up out-rageous stories about it. These usually began: "When Rose and I went to the market . . ." We had the most fantastic adventures there—all in my mind—but they had Esmeralda breathless with excitement.

Then the day came when we actually went there and what followed brought me to the notice of the great Rollo himself. It was about a week before Christmas, I remem-ber—a darkish day with the mist enveloping the trees of the Park. I loved such days. I thought the Park looked like an enchanted forest bathed in that soft bluish light, and as I looked out on it I thought to myself: "I'll take Esmeralda to the market."

Of course this was the day. There was to be a dinner party that night. The household could think of nothing else. "*She's* got the wind in her tail, that's what," said the cook, referring to Cousin Agatha. I knew what she meant. Cousin Agatha's voice could be heard all over the house. "Miss Hamer" (that was her long-suffering social secre-tary), "have you the place names ready? Do make sure that Lady Emily is on the master's *right* hand; and Mr. Carrington on mine. Mr. Rollo should be in the center of the table on the master's right-hand side of course. And have the flowers come?" She swept through the house like a hurricane. "Wilton" (that was the butler), "make sure the red carpet is down and the awning in place and see to it in *good* time." Then to the lady's maid Yvonne, "Do not let me sleep after five o'clock. Then you may prepare my bath."

She was in the kitchen admonishing the cook ("As if I don't know my business," said Cook). She sent for Wilton three times in the morning to give him instructions to be passed on to the other servants.

It was that sort of day. I met her on the stairs and she walked past me without even seeing me. And I thought again: "This is surely the time to go to the market." Nanny Grange was pressed into service with the goffering iron; our governess was to help arrange the flowers. So there we were "sans governess, sans nanny, sans supervision, sans everything," as I misquoted to Esmeralda.

"It's the very day when we could get away and be back before they noticed." The market should be seen by the light of flares and it grows dark soon after half past four in December. "The flares are like erupting volcanoes," I exaggerated to Esmeralda, "and they don't light them until dark."

I told Nanny Grange that Esmeralda and I would look after ourselves, and soon after afternoon tea, taken at half past three that day to get it over quickly, we set out. I had carefully noted the number of the omnibus and the stop where we had got off and we reached the market without mishap. It was then about five o'clock.

I gleefully watched the wonder dawn in Esmeralda's eyes. She loved it: the shops with their imitation snow on the windows—cotton wool on string but most effective—the toys in the windows. I dragged her away from them to look in the butcher's with the pigs' carcasses hanging up, oranges in their mouths, and the great sides of beef and lamb and the butcher in blue-striped apron sharpening long knives and crying "Buy, buy, buy."

Then there were the stalls piled with fruit and nuts and the old-clothes man and the people eating jellied eels out of blue-and-white basins. From one shop came the appetizing odor of pea soup, and we looked inside and saw people sitting on benches drinking the hot steaming stuff; there was the organ grinder with his little monkey sitting on top of the organ and the cap on the ground into which people dropped money.

I was delighted to see that Esmeralda was of the opinion that I had not for once exaggerated the charms of the market.

When the organ grinder's wife began to sing in a rather shrill penetrating voice the people started to crowd round us and as we stood there listening a cart on which there was a considerable amount of rattling ironmongery came pushing its way through the crowds.

"Mind your backs," cried a cheerful voice. "Make way for Rag and Bone 'Arry. Stand aside please. . . ."

I leaped out of the way and was caught up in the press of people who carried me with them to the pavement. Several of them called out to Rag and Bone 'Arry as he passed, to which he answered in a good-natured and pert manner. I watched with interest and found myself wondering about Rag and Bone 'Arry and all the people around me when suddenly I realized that Esmeralda was not beside me.

I looked about me sharply. I fought my way through the crowd; I called her name, but there was no sign of her.

I didn't panic immediately. She must be somewhere in the market, I told myself, and she couldn't be far away. I had presumed that she would keep close to me; I had told her to and she was not of an adventurous nature. I scanned the crowds, but she was nowhere to be seen. After ten minutes of frantic searching I began to be really afraid. I had charge of the money, taken with a great deal of trouble from our money boxes, into which it was so easy to put coins and so hard to take them out (the operation must be performed by inserting the blade of a knife through the slit, letting the coin drop onto the knife and then drawing it out). Without money how could she get home by herself? After half an hour I began to be very frightened. I had brought Esmeralda to the market and lost her.

My imagination—so exciting at times when I was in

control of it—now showed itself as a ruthless enemy. I
saw Esmeralda snatched up by some evil characters like
Fagin from *Oliver Twist* teaching her to pick pockets. Of
course she would never learn, I promised myself, and
would be arrested immediately and brought home to her
family. Perhaps Gypsies would take her. There was a
fortuneteller in the market. They would darken her skin
with walnut juice and make her sell baskets. Someone
might kidnap her and hold her to ransom; and *I* had done
this. The market adventure was so daring that it could
only have been undertaken when it was possible to sneak
into the house as we had sneaked out. Only on such a day
when there was to be an important dinner party had it
been possible.

And now Esmeralda was lost. What could I do? I knew.
I must go back to the house. Confess what I had done and
search parties would be sent out to find her.

This was distasteful to me, for I knew it was something
which would never be forgotten and might even result in
my being sent into an orphanage. After I had committed
such a sin Cousin Agatha would in her opinion be justified
in sending me away. I suspected that she only needed
such justification. I therefore found it difficult to leave the
market. Just one more look, I promised myself, and I
wended my way through the place keeping my eyes alert
for Esmeralda.

Once I thought I caught a glimpse of her and gave
chase, but it was a mistake.

It must be getting late. Coming here would have taken
half an hour and I must have been here an hour and now
there was the journey back.

I went to the omnibus stop and waited. What a long
time I waited! I was getting frantic. Silly Esmeralda! I
thought, finding some comfort in blaming her. Stupid little
thing! Why couldn't she have stayed with me?

At last the omnibus arrived. What was I going to say?
What trouble there would be! How could she have found
her way home? Oh, what had happened to Esmeralda!

I descended from the omnibus and made my way to the

house, intending to creep in by the servants' entrance. I saw with a shudder that the red awning was up and the red carpet down and that guests were arriving. I ran round to the back of the house. Rose was the one to find. She would be most sympathetic. She might well be in the mews, because the Carrington coachman would be there and she wouldn't want to miss a moment of his company.

I went to the mews. She was not there. Oh dear, the only thing for me to do was to go to the house and confess to the first person I saw. Cook? She would be blustering in the kitchen putting the last-minute touches to the dinner. Nanny Grange perhaps, because she knew that I had what she called reckless blood in me and wouldn't blame me so much for what I had done. "It's her blood," she would whisper knowledgeably.

I went in through the servants' entrance. No one seemed to be about. I made my way up the stairs to the hall and then I heard voices.

A policeman stood there, respectful, competent and re-assuring, and beside him, looking very small in compari-son, was a pale-faced Esmeralda.

"Found wandering," the policeman was saying. "Lost. We brought her home as soon as she told us where, Ma'am."

It was like a tableau and one I believed I should never forget.

Cousin Agatha, aglitter in a low-cut gown twinkling with emeralds and diamonds, and Cousin William Loring, immaculate in his evening clothes, had been brought down to the hall from the top of the staircase where they had been receiving their guests to receive instead their truant daughter brought home by a policeman.

Several guests stood on the stairs. The Carringtons were just arriving—Mr. Carrington, Lady Emily and the great Rollo.

I noticed the intense mortification in every line of Cousin Agatha's statuesque form; her emerald earrings quivered with passionate indignation. Esmeralda began to cry.

"It's all right now, Missy," said the policeman.

"My dear," said Lady Emily, "what on earth has happened?"

Cousin William began: "Our daughter was lost . . ." But he was immediately silenced by Cousin Agatha.

"Where is Nanny? What has she been doing? Esmeralda, go to your room."

Esmeralda saw me suddenly through her tears and cried: "Ellen."

Cousin Agatha turned and her basilisk gaze was directed straight at me.

"Ellen!" she said in a voice full of evil omen.

I came forward. "We only went to the market," I began.

"Wilton!" There he was, urbane, discreet in all his butlerian dignity.

"Yes, Madam," he said. "I will have the young ladies taken to the nursery." And to the policeman: "If you would care to follow me you will be refreshed and our appreciation shown to you. Ah, Madam, here is Nanny."

Nanny Grange appeared; she took me by one hand and Esmeralda by the other. Her anger was apparent in the grip of her fingers. I would have some explaining to do, I was sure, but at the moment I could only be relieved that Esmeralda was safe. There was one other thing that impressed itself on me. And that was the interested blue stare of the Great Rollo. His eyes were fixed temporarily on me. I wondered what he was thinking as Nanny hustled us up the stairs. Guests looked at us curiously. Some of them smiled. Then we were mounting the second stairs on up to the nursery.

"We only thought we'd like to see the market," I explained.

"This could well cost me my job," muttered Nanny Grange venomously. "And I know who was at the bottom of this, Miss Ellen, and don't you go trying to put it on Miss Esmeralda. She was led."

Esmeralda murmured: "I wanted to go, Nanny."

"You were led," said Nanny. "Don't I know Miss Ellen?"

"Well, it was my idea," I said. "And you shouldn't blame Esmeralda."

"What Madam is going to say to you, Miss, I don't know. But I wouldn't like to be in your shoes."

We were sent to bed without supper—not that we cared about that—and I lay in bed wondering what life was like in orphanages.

Rosie came in late that night just as the guests were leaving. She was bright-eyed—the way she looked when she had been enjoying the company of her coachman. She sat on the edge of the bed and giggled.

"You are a one. You didn't ought to have took Miss Esmeralda. She was sure to get lost or something."

"How was I to know she'd be so silly!"

"And to go off on your own like that. My word, you're in for trouble."

"I know," I said.

"Well, cheer up. Worse troubles at sea, as my first intended used to say. He was a sailor."

"What's an orphanage like?"

Rosie's face softened suddenly. "My cousin Alice was brought up in one. Quite the lady. Went governessing. No common housemaiding for her. Lots of company. There are a good many orphans in the world." She stooped down and kissed me. I knew she was trying to comfort me. She had been happy with her coachman and wanted all the world to be as happy as she was.

I supposed I'd be all right at the orphanage.

Cousin Agatha sent for me next morning. She looked as though she had had a sleepless night.

"Such conduct," she was saying. "Do you know I despair of you? I know that these inclinations come to you. It's in the blood, but as I said to Mr. Loring, what can we do with the child? Most people would send you away. After all we have our own daughter to consider. But blood is thicker than water and you are of our family. You try our patience sorely, Ellen—mine and Mr. Loring's. I must warn you that you will have to mend your ways if you wish to stay under our roof."

I said I hadn't known Esmeralda would get lost and if she hadn't no one would have known we had been to the market.

"Such deceit," she cried, "is intolerable. *I* am glad that Esmeralda *did* get lost—even though it ruined my evening. At least we know what a wicked child we have under our roof."

She had given Nanny instructions that I was to stay in my room until I had learned the Quality of Mercy speech from *The Merchant of Venice*. Perhaps that would teach me to be grateful for those who had—and let it be remembered that this could well be the last time—shown mercy towards me. I should have nothing but bread and water until I had *perfected* the piece, and while I was in seclusion I might well reflect on the havoc I had wrought. "What the Carringtons thought of you, I can't imagine. I shall not be surprised if you are not allowed to be with Philip again."

I was dismissed and learned my piece in a very short time. Later Cousin Agatha discovered that I loved poetry and it was no hardship to me to learn it; then I was given needlework to do, which was another matter. To read and reread beautiful arrangements of words delighted me; to cobble stitches was torture. But she had at that time to discover this.

Poor Esmeralda could not learn her piece half as quickly as I could and when she was obliged to say it before our governess I crept close to her and prompted her through it.

By Christmastime the affair of the market began to be forgotten. Philip appeared during school holidays and he was allowed to play with us in the Park. I told him about the market and how Esmeralda had got lost and in an excess of contempt he pushed her into the Serpentine. Esmeralda screamed and Philip stood on the bank laughing at her while I waded in and dragged her to the bank. Then Nanny Grange came along and we were all hustled back to the house to get our wet things off before we caught our deaths.

"I'll be blamed for that," I told Philip.

"Serve you right," he cried. He didn't care a bit if Esmeralda caught her death. He added to me: "You wouldn't. You're not so silly as she is."

When Esmeralda did catch a cold Nanny Grange reported the incident to some of the servants; I knew they were all of the opinion that I had pushed Esmeralda into the water.

Poor Esmeralda! I'm afraid we were very careless of her. It was not exactly that Philip and I banded together against her, but simply that she lacked our adventurous spirit and we were too young to respect the fact that she was different from ourselves. I remember how terrified she was of Dead Man's Leap. The very name was enough to strike terror into the timid and it certainly did to Esmeralda. This particular spot was not far from Trentham Towers. There was a climb up to it and at the peak the drop was considerable; it really was dangerous, for the narrow path was right on the edge of the steep drop and during wet weather was treacherously slippery. All along the path through the woods there were warning notices such as "At Own Risk" and "Road Unsafe"—just the sort of thing to spur on people like Philip and myself.

It was not only a dangerous spot, it was also uncanny, for it was said to be haunted because of the number of people who had committed suicide there. There was a saying in the neighborhood if anyone looked melancholy. "What's the matter with you? Thinking of jumping off Dead Man's Leap?"

This was therefore a favorite spot of ours and we jeered at Esmeralda if she showed any reluctance in accompanying us. Philip liked to stand on the very edge of this precipice to show how intrepid he was, and of course I had to do the same.

Once we were seen there and when this was reported to the tutor who was coaching Philip at the time, we were forbidden to go; but this naturally only made the place more desirable, and it became a meeting place for us. "See you at Dead Man's Leap," Philip would say casually, half hoping I would be afraid to go there by myself. I always went when thus challenged, although I was a little scared, for the place did have an eerie atmosphere, particularly when one was there alone.

Time started to pass very quickly, but there was one other incident in our childhood which brought me notoriety and I think I did give Cousin Agatha the justification to be rid of me. I was fourteen—at an age when I should have known better. Philip was fifteen and this happened in the country.

Philip wanted to have tea out of doors. We would make a fire and boil a kettle on it and live like Indians or Gypsies—he wasn't sure which it would be—whatever seemed best at the time. The great thing was to make a fire. We needed a kettle, which I had to bring.

"There are lots in your kitchen," said Philip. "There must be. Bring some tea and water in a bottle, and cakes. And we'll make a fire."

I made Esmeralda get the cakes from the kitchen and I got the kettle. Philip was bringing paraffin, which he said was fine for making fires.

"We'd better be Gypsies," he said. "We've kidnapped Esmeralda. She has been spirited out of her house and we'll tie her up and ask a ransom for her."

Esmeralda wailed: "Can't I be a Gypsy?"

"No, you can't," said Philip tersely. Poor Esmeralda! She was always cast for the victim.

The outcome of that adventure was that we had reckoned without the paraffin. Philip had collected some bracken and poured the oil liberally over it. The blaze first delighted us and then alarmed us. We couldn't get near it, and Esmeralda, both her ankles tied together, a gag over her mouth, very uncomfortable and longing to be allowed to play another part, was very near to it.

We tried to beat out the flames but they spread. I had the foresight to untie Esmeralda and by that time it seemed as though the whole field was ablaze.

There was nothing to be done but call for help. All the servants were busy trying to beat it out and to prevent its spreading to the cornfields.

There was great trouble about that.

"And on the Carringtons' land," said Cousin Agatha, as though we had desecrated some sacred temple. It was fortunate that one of the Carringtons had been involved but Cousin Agatha laid most of the blame on me.

I heard her say to Cousin William: "It is quite clear that Ellen is unmanageable. Into what disaster she will lead Esmeralda next I tremble to think."

I was given another lecture.

"You are now fourteen years of age. An age when many girls without means have been earning a living for some years. We do not forget that there is a family connection and for that reason we have *tried* to be good to you. But the time is coming very near, Ellen, when you will have to think of your future. Neither Mr. Loring nor I would wish to turn you adrift, and we shall do all we can to help you in spite of the manner in which you have so often repaid us. Yet this last disastrous escapade makes me feel again that our efforts have been wasted. You show a deplorable lack of discipline. You must be punished. The rod would be desirable. I have told Mr. Loring that it is his duty to administer it and he will be coming to your room to perform this painful duty. In addition you will begin a new sampler, which I myself shall inspect every week. The verse you learn will be 'Blow, blow, thou winter wind! Thou art not so unkind As man's ingratitude.' "

What she went on to say was even more depressing.

"I have been discussing your future with Mr. Loring and we agree that you must now be prepared to earn your own living. After all, you cannot expect to live on our bounty forever. You have been allowed to be a companion for Esmeralda—not a very good influence alas and one which I have so often thought she would have been better without—but in a few years a husband will be found for her and she will have no further need of your companionship. Mr. Loring and I do not forget that you belong to the family and therefore we should not throw you out into the world indiscriminately. We shall find the right post for you at the right time, for it is inconceivable that any member of our family should take a menial position. Governess or companion is *all* we would consider. Our circle of acquaintances is large and we hope in due course to find the right post for you. It is not as simple as you might think, for we would not wish you to be in a household which we might visit. That could be most embarrassing. So you see we shall have to choose the place with the utmost care. Meanwhile, you should prepare yourself. Study hard. Work harder especially with your needlework. I'll speak to the governess about that. Then when Esmeralda comes out and marries we shall hope to have the post ready for you. Now I trust you are in a contrite mood. Take your punishment, for you richly deserve it, and go to your room. Mr. Loring will come to you there."

Poor Cousin William! I was sorry for him. He came gingerly holding a cane with which he was to chastise me. He hated the task. I had to lie face down on my bed while he lightly tapped the cane about my thighs, which made me want to laugh.

He was red in the face and uncomfortable. Then he said suddenly: "There, I trust that has taught you a lesson."

It was comforting to be able to laugh at Cousin William, for I was feeling very uneasy about the future.

That night was one of the occasions when I dreamed again about the room with the red carpet, from which I awoke with the feeling of doom.

The years sped away. My eighteenth birthday came and went. The time when I must go into the world and earn my own living was coming nearer and nearer. Esmeralda used to comfort me. She would say: "When I'm married, Ellen, you shall always have a home with me."

I didn't envy Esmeralda. It would have been impossible to do that. She was so mild; it was true she had grown a little pretty, but I couldn't help noticing that when we were out together it was at me that people glanced. My black hair and dark blue eyes were striking and my "inquiring" nose, as Philip called it, made it seem as though I was asking a question. But at least her future was secure. We saw it happening all around us: Girls coming out into society, marriages arranged for them, becoming matrons with young children. It was all most carefully planned.

It was different for those who had to fend for themselves, as I should have to.

There had been one or two minor incidents when I had aroused the indignation of Cousin Agatha, but nothing so startling as the visit to the market or setting fire to Carrington land. When we were in the country we had to do more social work. We visited the poor and took them what Cousin Agatha called "delicacies"—usually something which she would not consider worthy of her own table; we decorated the church for harvest festival just before we left for London; we went to the gymkhana and church bazaars, where we had our own stalls. We played the parts of helpers of Lady Bountiful and in town we rode in the Row and at Cousin Agatha's At Homes we helped pass round the refreshments; we sewed for the poor; we worked for the Tories; we walked sedately in the Park and lived the lives of genteel young ladies. But then there was a subtle change. It was nearing the time when Esmeralda should come out and we were beginning to be segregated. Esmeralda was taken to the theater with her parents, and I did not accompany them. Often she went visiting with her mother now and I was left behind. The dressmaker who over the years had taken up residence in the house for several weeks at a time when there were functions ahead now settled in for a spell and worked on lovely new clothes for Esmeralda. There was nothing extra for me— only one spring, summer, autumn and winter dress—one new one per year.

I could feel that vague doom coming nearer. It was as in the dream.

Esmeralda was a little bewildered; she disliked going

anywhere without me, but I was rarely with her now except for those walks in the Park and the charity visits.

The Carringtons loomed large in our lives. They were Cousin Agatha's closest friends. Lady Emily's name was mentioned twenty times a day.

Philip was often a member of a family party and he, with Esmeralda, visited the theater with Cousin Agatha and Cousin William. The play was *Lady Windermere's Fan*, which had been produced for the first time in February at the St. James's Theatre. I had heard that although it was a light comedy it sparkled with wit and amusing epigrams. I guessed that Esmeralda would not see the point of it.

I watched them leave in the carriage and I saw them come back. When Esmeralda came up I waylaid her and made her tell me about the play. She gave me a brief outline of the plot and she said that Philip had laughed the whole way through. They had had supper afterwards and it had been very jolly. She looked quite pretty in a powder-blue gown and her blue velvet cloak. I longed for such a cloak, but most of all to go to the theater and laugh with Philip.

The next day we walked in the Park with Nanny Grange, who was still with us. She would probably go with Esmeralda when she married to look after her children, for Cousin Agatha felt it was good to keep nannies in the family. One could then rely on their loyalty. Besides, all the best people did it.

Now that we were older Nanny Grange always walked a few sedate paces behind us like a watchdog and if any young men came near us she would quicken her pace and be there abreast of us. It always amused me.

That day we met Philip in the Park. He fell into stride beside us. This was quite legitimate and did not need Nanny's attention. He was after all a Carrington.

Philip said accusingly to me: "Why didn't you come to the play last night?"

"Nobody asked me," I replied.

"You mean to say . . ." He stopped and looked at me. "No," he cried. "It can't be."

"But it is. Didn't you know I was the Poor Relation?"

"Oh, stop it, Ellen," wailed Esmeralda. "I can't bear you to talk like that."

"Whether you can bear it or not, my dear," I said, "it's true."

"When my parents return the visit to the theater I shall insist that you are included," Philip assured me.

"That's nice of you, Philip," I said, "but I wouldn't come where I wasn't wanted."

"Ass!" he said, and gave me a push just as he had when we were children.

I felt very pleased because at least Philip didn't see me as the Poor Relation.

There was going to be a grand dance. The folding doors of three rooms on the first floor were to be thrown open to make a fairly sizable ballroom which would be decorated with plants. It was in fact Esmeralda's coming-out ball. She was to have a very special gown in blue silk and lace. Tilly Parsons, the seamstress, thought it would take a week to make it. "All those tucks and frills, my word," she muttered.

I was to be allowed to go to the ball and for this I, too, was to have a new ball dress. I dreamed of deep blue chiffon which would heighten the color of my eyes; I saw myself floating round the ballroom and everyone calling me the belle of the ball. Esmeralda wouldn't mind that, being Esmeralda. She was very good-natured really and she had no desire for the role. She hated calling attention to herself.

Cousin Agatha sent for me. I might have known what it was about. After all, I was eighteen years old, and the threats which had haunted me all my childhood were not idle ones.

"Ah, Ellen. You may sit down."

I sat uneasily.

"You will realize of course that you are now of an age to go out into the world. Naturally I have done my best to place you and my efforts are now being rewarded. I have the post for you at last."

My heart started beating fast with apprehension.

"Mrs. Oman Lemming . . . the Honorable Mrs. Oman Lemming . . . is losing her governess in six months' time. I have spoken to her about you and she is willing to see you with the possibility of giving you the post."

"Mrs. Oman Lemming . . ." I stammered.

"The *Honorable* Mrs. Oman Lemming. She is the daughter of Lord Pillingsworth. I have known her well all my life. I had thought it would not be good for you to be in a house which we might visit, but these are very special circumstances. You will have to be discreet and keep out of the way if we should be there. Mrs. Oman Lemming will understand the delicacy of the situation, she is such a friend of mine. I have begged her to take tea with me, which she will do next week. While she is here she will have an opportunity of looking at you, and I trust you will, Ellen, be mindful of your duty, for if you should fail to please her it could be very difficult to place you. Such posts do not grow on trees, you know."

I was dumbfounded—quite unreasonably so. I had secretly never thought it could come to that. My absurd optimism would not let me believe it possible. But now here it was—my approaching doom. Six months away.

Cousin Agatha, who had clearly expected me to express my gratitude, sighed and lifted her shoulders.

"I should not wish you to go ill equipped and that brings me to the matter of your ball dress. I have chosen the material for you. Black is so serviceable and I am asking Tilly Parsons to make it in a style which will not date. There may be an occasion when you need such a dress. I should not like you to be without one."

I knew the sort of dress it would be. Suitable for a middle-aged woman. It was in any case a dress which was expected to last into my maturity. I felt uneasy.

When I met the Honorable Mrs. Oman Lemming my worst fears were realized.

Like Cousin Agatha, she was a large woman with

sweeping feathers in her hat and long tight gray kid gloves. A heavy gold chain descended the mountain of her bosom; a large brooch sparkled on her blouse. I could see a kindred spirit to Cousin Agatha, and my heart sank.

"This is Ellen Kellaway," said Cousin Agatha.

The Honorable Mrs. Oman Lemming raised her lorgnette and studied me. I don't think she was very delighted with what she saw.

"She is very young," she commented. "But perhaps that is not a disadvantage."

"It is so much easier to mold the young to our ways, Letty," said Cousin Agatha, and I thought how incongruous the name sounded for such a militant-looking female.

"That's true, Agatha. But is she good with children?"

"I have to admit that she has had little experience of them, but she has been brought up with Esmeralda and shared her education."

The Honorable Mrs. Oman Lemming bowed her head like some all-knowing oracle. I noticed that her eyes were too closely set together, and her mouth when she studied me was thin and cold. I disliked her on sight and the thought of becoming a member of her household in a certain menial capacity gave me no pleasure.

She turned to me then. "There are four children. Hester, the eldest, is fourteen; Claribel, eleven; James is eight and Henry, four. James will soon be going away to school and Henry will follow in due course. The girls will remain at home and it would be your duty—if I engage you—to teach them."

"I am sure," said Cousin Agatha, "that you will not find Ellen lacking in scholastic knowledge. Our governess told me that she was brighter than average."

Praise from Cousin Agatha for the first time in my life! But it only showed of course how eager she was to be rid of me.

It was arranged that in five months' time, one month before the present governess was due to leave, I should enter the Oman Lemming household and be instructed by the departing governess into my duties.

The thought depressed me more than I could say.

When we walked in the Park, Philip joined us. It was becoming a habit. The three of us walked together ahead of Nanny Grange.

"You look like thunder this morning," said Philip.

For once I found it difficult to speak and it was Esmeralda who got in first. "It's this wretched governessing."

"What?" cried Philip.

"Oh, you wouldn't know, but Mama is finding a place for Ellen. It's with the Honorable Mrs. Oman Lemming."

"A place!" Philip stopped short to stare at me.

"You always knew I'd have to go someday. It's time I earned a living. It seems I've been living on charity too long. Even members of the Family can't expect that forever."

"You . . . a governess!" Philip burst out laughing.

"If you find it amusing, I don't," I said tersely.

"The idea of your teaching! I could die of laughing."

"Very well, die! To me it is no laughing matter."

"Ellen really thinks something will turn up," said Esmeralda, "and so do I."

"Perhaps it will," I replied. "If I'm going to be a governess I'd rather find my own post and it wouldn't be with Mrs. Oman Lemming, I can tell you."

"Perhaps you'd find someone worse," soothed Esmeralda. "Do you remember old Miss Herron and that companion of hers?"

"I do and I can't believe she's any worse than the Honorable O.L."

"Never mind," said Philip, slipping his arm through mine, "I'll come and see you."

"That's kind of you, Philip," said Esmeralda softly.

"You'll forget all about me," I said angrily.

He didn't answer but he continued to hold my arm.

I became alarmed at the manner in which the days were flying past. There were sessions with Tilly Parsons while she fitted the ball dress. It was black, heavy velvet, and I had tussles with Tilly over the neckline. I wanted the dress low-cut and that was not according to Cousin Agatha's chosen pattern. By the time I had made Tilly pinch me in at the waist and recut the neckline the dress was slightly more presentable, but it was too old for me— as Cousin Agatha rightly said, it could be worn in twenty years' time and still be presentable because it had that one essential quality—it would never date. No, I had responded sharply, it had never had a date, that dress, and it never would have one, I imagined.

Nanny Grange was sad. This was breaking up with her charges, the fate she said which came to all of her kind. "They come to you as babies, you do everything for them and then they grow up."

"Well, Nanny," I said, "you don't expect them to stay children all their lives just so that you can carry out your duties."

"It's sad," she retorted. "Time passes though. And when Miss Esmeralda gets her babies I'll go with her. And that, if I know anything about it, won't be so very long. Poor Miss Esmeralda, she'll need someone to look after her."

It was through Rosie that I heard the gossip. She got it from her coachman.

"Oh, there's been some conferences going on over there as well as here. My word, they're planning an early wedding. Young people are impatient, they say. I laughed to my William. 'Impatient!' I said. 'Why, my Miss Esmeralda don't know what she's got to be impatient about!' "

"You mean they're planning Esmeralda's wedding?"

"To Philip," whispered Rosie. "Of course they would have liked the other one for her."

"You mean the elder brother."

"That's him. That Rollo."

"Why don't they try for him?"

Rosie pressed her lips together to indicate that she knew something which she was longing to tell me but was well aware she shouldn't. I calculated that a little persuasion was going to be necessary and that if I worked hard and long enough I would eventually discover what it was. I did.

"Well, it was about a year ago. . . . Such a to-do there was . . . in the family of course. Outside it was very secret. Oh, very."

"What Rosie, what?"

"It was like this: Mr. Rollo got married . . . runaway match, they say. There was a lot of talk, all behind closed doors and the doors are thick oak in Park Lane, I can tell you."

I nodded sympathetically. "But you did find out . . ."

"Well, little things came out. They ran away together . . . elopement and all that . . . and the family not too pleased. Then Mr. Rollo persuaded them that it was all right and they all got reconciled. But we never saw *her*. That was what was odd. It was just said that Mr. Rollo was abroad with his wife. . . . Very funny it was, for she was never seen at the house. Then we found out why. . . ."

"Why, Rosie?"

"It seems there was something wrong with the marriage. Mr. Rollo had made a terrible mistake. She's somewhere but she don't come to the house."

"Then he's still married to her?"

"Of course he's still married to her and that's why they've got to have Mr. Philip for Miss Esmeralda."

I thought a great deal about Rollo. I had always considered there was something unusual about him and that nothing ordinary could happen to him. It seemed I had been right.

A week or so passed. There had been a visit to the theater with the Carringtons and to my delight I was a member of the party. Philip had kept his word but Cousin Agatha was most put out. "I cannot think why Lady Emily should have included Ellen," I heard her comment. "It's really quite unsuitable, considering that she will soon be working more or less in our own circle. It could give rise to embarrassment. I wonder whether I should speak to Lady Emily."

How I disliked her, far more than I ever had before, and that dislike was largely because of my fear of the future.

I tried not to think about it, but my habit of thrusting aside the unpleasant and deluding myself into the belief that it would never happen was not quite so successful as usual.

The play was the second of Oscar Wilde's productions —*A Woman of No Importance*—and we went to the Haymarket Theatre to see it. I was greatly excited by the performance of Mr. Tree and between the acts I discussed the play animatedly with Philip and Mr. Carrington, for I was sitting between them.

I noticed that Cousin Agatha was regarding me with intense disapproval, but I didn't care. I thoroughly enjoyed myself. The mysterious Rollo was not present and Esmeralda on the other side of Philip said very little.

The next day Cousin Agatha took me to task.

"You talk far too much, Ellen," she told me. "It's a habit you will have to learn to repress. I think Mr. Carrington was a little put out."

"He didn't seem so at all," I couldn't help retorting. "He was most pleasant and appeared to be interested in what I had to say."

"My dear Ellen," said Cousin Agatha in a tone implying that I was anything but dear, "he is a gentleman, and therefore would not dream of expressing his disapproval. I really think Lady Emily was a little unwise to issue the invitation in view of your position. I must again ask you to remember to assume a more modest role in future."

Whatever she said she could not take the joy of that evening from me, and I was sure that Mr. Carrington had been rather amused by my comments and by the manner in which Philip and I disagreed with each other. As for Lady Emily, I had discovered that she was rather vague and she probably wasn't sure that I was the one who was having my last fling before I entered the gray world of governessing.

The night of the dance was fast approaching.

The three large rooms known as the drawing rooms on the first floor were opened up and made a rather fine ballroom. There were balconies in all rooms and these gave a view of the Park on one side and of gardens and some rather fine buildings on the other. Evergreen plants grew in elaborate containers on the balconies and when the rooms were decorated with flowers the effect was charming.

There was to be a buffet supper taken in the dining room, now equipped with little tables; and there was a group of six musicians who would play for the dancing and continue with soothing music during supper. There was to be no expense spared because this was after all Esmeralda's coming-out dance and Cousin Agatha wanted all to know, and in particular the Carringtons—as if they did not already—that Esmeralda's parents were very comfortably placed in life and a good dowry could be expected.

I was caught up in the excitement although I was not entirely pleased with my dress. Black was not one of my colors and the dress was severe and only just managed to creep into the ball-dress category. When I saw Esmeralda's beautiful concoction of frills and lace in a lovely sea blue that was almost green I was filled with envy. It was just the dress I should have loved. But of course it wasn't serviceable and would not stand up to the years as my velvet would.

The night before the ball I had dreamed once more of the room with the red carpet. There I was standing near the fireplace, and I heard the whispering voices as I always did. On this occasion they seemed nearer and then suddenly that feeling of doom overtook me and I was staring at the door—and this was new—it started to open. A terrible fear possessed me then. I could not take my eyes from that door. Very slowly it moved and I knew that whatever it was I dreaded was behind it.

Then I woke up. I was trembling and sweating with fear. It had been a very vivid dream. It always was but on this occasion the overtaking doom had come a little nearer.

I sat up in bed. How silly to be so scared by a dream and a dream of nothing really . . . just a room.

I saw then that the door of my wardrobe had come open and I fancied a figure swayed there. I felt the horror come sweeping back over me. Then I saw that it was the black ball dress hanging there. I must have omitted to fasten the door securely.

I lay back and admonished myself. It was only a dream. But why did I go on dreaming this same frightened dream year after year?

I tried to shake off that feeling of approaching disaster. How could I? It was six weeks since I had been interviewed by Mrs. Oman Lemming; the time was approaching.

But this coming night would be that of the dance. True, I only had a black gown which I didn't like, but it was adequate. I loved to dance. I was so much more adept than Esmeralda, who had little sense of rhythm. I would put the thought of Mrs. Oman Lemming from my mind.

During that morning a little box arrived, and to my amazement it was addressed to me. Rose brought it up; she had taken it in at the servants' entrance.

"Look at this, Miss Ellen,' she said. "It's for you. My word, admirers, is it!"

And there it was nestling into its protective box, a most beautiful and delicate orchid with a pinkish mauve merging tinge. It was just the decoration I needed to liven up my black dress.

I thought, It's from Esmeralda! and hurried to thank her.

She looked blank. "I wish I'd thought of it, Ellen. It is just right for your dress. I thought there'd be flowers for anyone who wanted them."

"But not for poor relations," I responded; I was not bitter with Esmeralda, who was always most kind, just happy because I had my orchid.

I enjoyed trying to think who had sent it to me. I thought

it must be Cousin William Loring because I had fancied he was a little uneasy at my going away to work for Mrs. Oman Lemming and Rose told me that she had heard him say to the mistress that there was no need for me to go.

"He rather suggested that when Esmeralda married she might like to take you with her as a sort of companion and secretary perhaps because once Philip gets into his stride he is going to have a very busy life and his wife will have to do a great deal of entertaining. I don't think he liked the idea of your going but *She* was firm about it."

So it seemed very likely that the orchid had come from kind Cousin William.

It was beautiful and there was no doubt that it transformed my dress. I no longer felt dowdy. Esmeralda gave me a pin with a small solitary diamond with which to hold it in place. I dressed with special care, piling my hair high on my head. I thought I looked quite elegant.

Esmeralda looked pretty in her magnificent gown but she was nervous, very conscious that she was the reason for the ball's being given and she was apprehensive at the notion of receiving a proposal.

"I wish we didn't have to grow up, Ellen," she said. It was clear that the prospect of a grand marriage appalled her. "They all think I'm going to marry Philip, but I never thought he liked me very much. After all, he did push me into the Serpentine."

"That was when we were children. Men often fall in love with girls they've not noticed when they were children."

"But he did notice me . . . enough to push me into the water."

"Well, if you don't want to marry him you can always say no."

"But you see, Mama wants it and . . ."

I nodded. What she wanted she usually got.

I comforted her. Her father would be on her side, so there was no reason why she should marry anyone if she didn't want to.

I had received instructions a few days before from

Cousin Agatha. "You will make yourself useful, Ellen. In the supper room make sure that people are well served. Keep your eyes especially on Lady Emily, and see that she is well looked after. I shall find one or two gentlemen to whom I shall introduce you, and perhaps they may ask you to dance."

I could visualize the evening. Ellen the Poor Relation —in somber black to distinguish her from the real guests. "Ellen, do tell Wilton we need more salmon." Or "Ellen, poor old Mr. Something is sitting alone. Come and let me introduce you. He may ask you to dance." And there would be Ellen stumbling round with rheumaticky old Mr. Something when her feet longed to be gliding over the floor with a kindred spirit.

How different it was. Not at all what I had dreaded. Right from the first Philip was beside me.

"So you received my orchid." he said.

"Yours!"

"No one else would send you flowers, I hope."

I laughed, for he and I had always been special friends.

We danced together. I wondered if Cousin Agatha noticed and hoped so. How well our steps fitted! I knew they did because we used to dance together in the country —jigs we made up as we went along.

"Did you know I was here tonight as the Poor Relation?" I asked.

"What does that mean?"

"That I have to keep my eyes open for neglected guests."

"That's all right. You keep your eyes on me, for if you don't I shall feel very neglected."

"And you . . . one of the Carringtons!" I mocked.

"But only a younger son."

"Is Great Rollo here tonight?"

"Great Rollo is far away. He's hardly ever here."

"That makes you the catch of the season, I suppose."

"Listen," he said. "Let's talk. I've a good deal to say to you. Where can we get away to be quiet?"

"There are one or two smaller rooms on this floor.

They have been set aside for private conversations."

"Let's go then."

"Ought you, or more important still, ought I? Cousin Agatha's eagle eyes will be searching for me soon if she has some aging gentleman who might care to amble round the floor with me."

"All the more reason why you should escape."

"Is this a game? We are not fourteen any more, remember."

"Thank heaven for that, and it's deadly serious."

"Is something wrong?"

"It could be quite the reverse, but I must talk to you, Ellen."

We sat in one of the small rooms in which were pots of plants, a settee and a few chairs. I sat on the settee and Philip was beside me.

"Ellen," he said, "I've been hearing things. Your servants talk to ours and ours to yours. These people know as much of our affairs as we do ourselves. More perhaps. The whispers indicate that you are indeed going away to be a governess to those odious Oman Lemming children."

"I've told you it's true."

"I didn't really believe it. You . . . a governess!"

"The only occupation for a young lady of some gentility, education and no money."

"But why . . . after all these years?"

"Cousin Agatha was doing her duty to the defenseless child. Now the child has become a woman and must fend for herself, so she is being given a gentle but very firm push into the cruel world."

"We'll put a stop to that. We're not having you governessing to that woman. She's poisonous."

I turned to him abruptly and my fear of the future suddenly enveloped me in earnest.

He took me by the shoulders and, laughing, held me against him. "Ellen, you idiot, do you think I'd ever let you go?"

"What authority would you have to stop me?"

"The best of all authority. Of course you're not going

to be governess to that woman's children! I happen to know they're terrors. I always meant it would be us two, Ellen. You and I are going to get married. That's the answer. I always meant we should."

"You . . . marry me! But you're going to marry Esmeralda. It's all arranged. That's what this dance is for."

"What nonsense!"

"That's where you're wrong. This dance is for Esmeralda, and I have it on good authority that during it or after it, they are hoping to announce your engagement to her."

"They say hope springs eternal in the human breast. But 'they,' by whom I presume you mean the Lorings, are going to find they have made a mistake. Engagement yes, but to Ellen not Esmeralda."

"You mean you'd announce your engagement to *me* tonight?"

"Of course. I always had a sense of the dramatic. You know that."

"What will your parents say?"

"They'll be delighted."

"To accept *me*! You're joking."

"I am *not*." He looked very serious. "My father likes you. He said you were amusing and he likes to be amused."

"And Lady Emily?"

"She'll like you too. She wants me to be happy above all else."

"Perhaps, but they can't possibly want me as your wife."

"That's where you're wrong. I've hinted to them and they're full of approval. They think I ought to get married soon."

I just did not believe it. I was quite bewildered. Philip had always liked to joke. Of course Philip and I had always been the best of friends, to the exclusion of Esmeralda; he had always expressed disappointment when I did not appear at the social gatherings Cousin Agatha arranged. I should have known; I wasn't in love with him. I couldn't be, because I had imagined his marriage to Esmeralda without any great sorrow. The fact was that Cousin Agatha had so impressed on me my inferior status and the glory of the Carringtons that I could never imagine myself marrying into that family—even to Philip. Now it excited me, not, alas, so much because of Philip—whom I liked very much of course—but because marriage with him would mean that I did not have to take up the post of governess with the odious Mrs. Oman Lemming and her brood, who, I was sure, were as unpleasant as she was. Chiefly perhaps I was savoring the triumph of being the chosen one. The sight of Cousin Agatha's face if our engagement were announced would compensate me for years of humiliation, and I would have been inhuman not to relish the thought. As for Esmeralda, for whom I had an affection, she would not be in the least displeased. She had never wanted a Carrington marriage and she had insisted that Philip despised her ever since he had pushed her into the Serpentine.

"Well," said Philip. "You seem at a loss for words. It's the first time I've ever known you so."

"It's the first time I have ever had a proposal of marriage."

"We'll have fun together, Ellen."

I looked at him and believed we would.

"I hadn't thought of you as a husband," I said.

"Why ever not? I thought it was obvious."

"You never mentioned it."

"Well, I'm mentioning it now." He took my hands in his and kissed me. "Well," he said. "What now?"

"Give me time," I said. "I have to get used to the idea."

"You're not getting coy, are you? That's not like you."

"Look at it from my point of view. I came here expecting an announcement of Esmeralda's engagement."

"To me!"

"Of course to you. Cousin Agatha had set her heart on a Carrington son-in-law. And what she sets her heart on she usually gets."

"She'll have to put up with one as cousin-in-law."

"Second . . . several times removed."

"Well, who cares about her anyway?"

"I'm liking you more every minute."

He put his arm about me. "It's going to be fun, Ellen. There's going to be no more of this poor-relation stuff. When I heard about that governessing project I knew I had to take action. The family want me to marry. They've been on about it for some time. I think what they want is grandchildren and it doesn't seem as if Rollo is going to have any sons or even daughters."

"Why not?"

"Oh . . . it's a bit complicated. His wife's a bit . . . strange. I'll tell you sometime. But it means the family is very anxious for me to marry."

"You'll be a young husband."

"You'll be an even younger wife."

I was getting used to the idea and liking it more. I had to start thinking of my old friend Philip as a husband. It was not difficult. I was beginning to enjoy myself.

Philip was telling me how he had always loved me although when we were children he hadn't thought of it as love. He had merely enjoyed being with me. When he came to the country the first thing he thought of was whether I would be there. "They were good times we had together, Ellen," he said.

He went on to talk of what our life would be. We would travel a great deal. It would be necessary for his business. Rollo did most of it, but he was going to help him. It would be great fun, he told me. We would go out to India and Hong Kong and stay there for a while. He was learning about his father's business and I could help him in this because when we were in London we should have to entertain a good deal.

He was opening out a glittering vista to me. We would have an establishment of our own in London not far from the parental home. He would see that I was introduced to the most exclusive dressmaker. "You'll be stunning in the right clothes, Ellen," he told me. "You're a beauty, you know, only it's never shown to advantage."

"Cousin Agatha insists on hiding my light under a bushel," I said. "I'm the sort to let it shine forth."

"So it should do. My God, Ellen, it's going to be wonderful."

"Yes," I said. "I do believe it is."

Then he held me against him and we laughed together.

"Who'd have thought it?" I murmured. "After the way you used to bully me!"

"It was latent love," he told me.

"Was it really?"

"You know it was. I must have decided years ago that I was going to marry you."

"One of those secret decisions . . . secret even to yourself," I said. "You were terribly critical of me."

"That was a symbol of my feelings."

"What would your praise be?"

"Wait and see."

I was happy. It was the old bantering relationship and the prospects he was offering me were brilliant.

"You know I shall bring no dowry."

"I'll take you without."

"You'd get a good one, you know, with Esmeralda."

"I'm not tempted. It has to be Ellen or no one."

I put my arms about his neck and kissed him heartily; it had to be at that moment that Cousin Agatha appeared.

"Ellen!" Her voice was shrill with mingled disbelief and righteous anger.

I broke away from Philip and stood up uneasily.

"What *are* you doing here? This is disgraceful. I shall talk to you later. In the meantime guests are being neglected."

"Not all of them," said Philip cheekily. He had always liked to disconcert Cousin Agatha and he invariably did, because she wanted to be indignant with him but how could she be so with a Carrington?

I said: "I'll go and see what I can do."

I wanted to get away because I still could not believe that Philip was really serious. He tried to take my hand, but I was away too quickly. I wondered what he said to

Cousin Agatha. Later he told me that she made a remark about the weather, which of course she would consider the very height of good taste and subtle diplomacy in changing the subject.

I was in a whirl. I caught a glimpse of myself in one of the mirrors. My cheeks were flushed, my eyes brilliant. I decided that the black gown was not so unbecoming after all.

Then Mr. Carrington asked me to dance with him and I did. I found him courteous and charming. We talked about the play we had seen together and I sat out with him afterwards. It was not long before Philip joined us.

"She's said yes, Father," he told Mr. Carrington.

Mr. Carrington nodded, smiling. He took my hand and pressed it. "I am very happy," he said. "You seem to me a remarkable young woman."

"We'll announce it at supper," said Philip. "You can do it, Father. Better not let Mother. She'll forget who's to be the bride and before I know where I am I'll be partnered off with someone most unsuitable."

Philip and I danced together. It was the waltz and our steps fitted perfectly. Had we not gone to dancing classes together?

"Your Cousin Agatha is glaring like a gorgon," he informed me.

"Let her," I answered. "That particular gorgon has now no power to turn me to stone nor even into a governess."

"Ellen, I fancy you're rather pleased with life."

"I know just how Cinderella felt when she went to the ball."

"I must make a delightful Prince Charming."

"He rescued her from the ashes. You've rescued me from Cousin Agatha and the Honorable Mrs. Oman Lemming, who are far more deadly."

"Remember it, Ellen. I shall remind you over the next fifty years."

"And after that?"

"I shall have brought you to such a state of gratitude

that you will never need to be reminded. That'll take care of the next twenty years."

"How odd to think of us . . . *old*."

"A fate to which we all must come, even my divine Ellen."

"Oh, Philip, I'm happy. Life is going to be so . . . amusing, isn't it?"

"Just imagine us together with no Nanny Grange hovering to observe decorum and silly little Esmeralda trailing on."

"Don't be unkind to Esmeralda. You're fond of her really, and she is very dear to me. Don't forget she's lost a bridegroom tonight."

"They couldn't have been serious about that."

"Why not? They wanted her married. Your parents evidently wanted you married. Two families governed by financial wizards! What could be better than a merger? And you have spoilt it all by preferring the Poor Relation."

"You're the one who's spoilt it. Who could look at Esmeralda with you around?"

When the waltz was over he took me to my seat and Philip talked about the future, but I was too absorbed in the glorious present to think very much about it. And when we went into supper, Mr. Carrington made the announcement to the company. He said how pleased he was to tell them all that this was a very special occasion for his family because his son Philip had confided in him that he had asked for the hand of a young lady who had promised to be his wife. He wanted everyone to drink to the health and future happiness of Miss Ellen Kellaway and his son Philip.

What a hush there was in the dining room, where the great table was so expertly dressed by Wilton and his minions, laden with cold salmon, meats of all descriptions, salads and desserts, and the black-gowned white-capped-and-aproned staff stood at intervals like sentries waiting to serve. All eyes were on me. I knew that some of the stern dowagers were thinking: But it was to be Esmeralda, and if not Esmeralda, were not their own daughters far more eligible than Agatha Loring's Poor Relation?

And there was I in my simple black gown made beautiful by Philip's orchid, just as I was made attractive because I was the chosen one. I knew my eyes were shining, my cheeks faintly flushed; and I sensed that Philip was proud of me. He gripped my hand firmly. Yes, I was happy as I had rarely been. It was a miracle. Mrs. Oman Lemming faded away as a nightmare does by day. She and her establishment were just an evil dream. No more humiliation. It was ironical. I, the despised, was to be one of the Carringtons. And there was Philip beside me, metaphorically fitting the glass slipper on my foot and proclaiming me as the one he had chosen.

Lady Emily wafted up to me and kissed me on the ear. I think she had meant it to be my cheek but she always missed the point; then Mr. Carrington took my hand and kissed it and his smile was warm and welcoming. Esmeralda came up and threw her arms about me. Dear Esmeralda! Even though she had not wanted to marry Philip she might have felt a little piqued to be passed over. Not she! She could see that I was happy, and she was contented too.

Philip and I sat together with his parents. Cousin Agatha and Cousin William Loring eventually joined us with Esmeralda. It was a kind of ritual—the two families together to celebrate the happy event. Cousin Agatha tried bravely to hide the fury in her heart and I had to admit she contrived to do so very well. But when I met her gaze once it was quite venomous.

Mr. Carrington said he thought there should be no unnecessary delay. Once two people had made up their minds and there was no reason why they should hesitate, they should marry.

When I said good night to Philip he said he would call next day. We had so many plans to make and he agreed with his father that there should be no delay.

I went to my room. I took off my serviceable ball gown. I would always keep it, I promised myself, even when I had magnificent *Carrington* ball gowns. I laughed to my-self remembering the awe in which this household had always held that name. And now it was to be mine.

While combing my hair the door opened and Cousin Agatha came in. She was breathing deeply and was clearly holding her emotions in check.

She looked magnificent in her way—massive bosom heaving and her jewels glittering. She ought to have had a bowl of poison in one hand, a dagger in the other, and asked me to choose. It was her eyes which were daggers; her voice from which the poison dripped.

"Well," she said, "you have made a fine fool of us all."

I was in my petticoats, my hair about my shoulders.

"I?" I cried. I could not resist adding a little ma-liciously: "Why, I thought you would be pleased. It gets me off your hands!"

"You have suddenly grown innocent. I will admit you have done very well for yourself. You must have known all this time, and poor Esmeralda has been thinking that it would be her wedding which would be announced."

"I don't think she is disappointed."

"Ingratitude! Not that you have ever shown anything else. From the moment you entered this house you caused trouble. You are wicked and I am sorry for the Carring-tons."

Why did I always want to incense her even further than I already had? But I did, and now I felt secure. I thought, I'll tell Philip about this. And then I was exultant because in the future I would have him to share things with. And I knew for the first time how very alone I had felt before.

"You have always led me to believe that the Carring-tons are the most important family in London," I said. "I scarcely think they will want your pity."

"They do not seem to realize the . . . the . . ."

"Viper you have been nursing in your bosom?" I sug-gested, rather insolently I'm afraid, but I was intoxicated with my success.

"Pray do not try me too far. You have betrayed our trust in you."

"I know such a marriage was not what you intended for me," I said. "And to be governess for the Oman Lemming children was not what I wanted for myself. Fate has intervened, and has raised me from the status of Poor Relation, which I can assure you, Cousin Agatha, has sometimes been hard to bear."

"When I think of all I did for you . . . I took you into my home. . . ."

"Because you made a solemn promise to my grandmother."

"Because you were of the family."

"Though the connection was not strong," I added.

She clenched her fists. She knew she was beaten. I was too flushed with victory that night.

She turned and said: "You are a schemer. I might have known it with such a mother!"

And with that she went out, which was just as well, for if she had remained, heaven knew what I would have said to her.

How life had changed for me! I had laughed in the past about the importance of the Carringtons and had imagined that Cousin Agatha had admired them so because they were more wealthy than she was and the leaders of a social set into which she wished to climb. It was more than that. Josiah Carrington was not only a banker and financier of great standing in the City, he was also adviser to the government and a power in diplomatic circles. His eldest son Rollo was following in his footsteps close behind and Philip was limping along in the right direction. Lady Emily, the daughter of an earl, was most highly connected and had before her marriage had a place at Court. Cousin William Loring, although comfortably off, was small fry in comparison; it was for this reason that marriage into the family had been considered such an advantage and even the younger son Philip a very ripe and desirable plum.

That I, the outcast, the Poor Relation, should have won the prize was almost comical. Rose told me that below-stairs the staff were "laughing their heads off." They were glad because they had never thought much of Cousin Agatha and they relished this "smack in the eye," as they called it, which Master Philip had administered.

I marveled at the knowledge of those belowstairs; there was little of what went on above that they missed, as I had reason to know. It was amusing to me to have Rose as a go-between.

Philip was a great favorite, Rose told me. He'd always been full of fun and mischief. Mr. Rollo was different. Very cold and aloof he was; and since that mysterious marriage of his had been very touchy, Rose reckoned. Mr. Carrington was a good master. He was always off here and there, always pulling off this and that big deal. And Lady Emily, she was well liked but seemed to be always in a dream. Never knew the housemaid from the parlormaid and the cook swore she didn't know the difference between her and the butler. Nevertheless, she was one of those mistresses who are not ill liked. You'd never find her poring over the household accounts or querying the price of this and that. Carringtons' was a good place to be in.

Philip and I would not be going into it, but we were going to have a house nearby and we would of course use the country mansion when we wanted it as all the family did.

There would be the fun of choosing the house and Philip said we would set about it right away. I had to keep assuring myself I hadn't imagined the whole thing. There was I, who had never been sure of my room, with a house all my own! The news had quickly come out and because Philip was a Carrington we were photographed for the society papers.

I felt as if I were indeed dreaming. There was a big picture of me in the *Tatler*. "Miss Ellen Kellaway, who is to marry Mr. Philip Carrington. Miss Kellaway lives with her guardians, Mr. and Mrs. Loring of Knightsbridge, and Mr. Carrington is, of course, the second son of Mr. Josiah Carrington."

I had taken on new status. Esmeralda was delighted. She

embraced me and said how happy she was, for she could see I was in my element.

"Of course," she said, "it was obvious all the time. He always liked you. You two were always the allies. Philip thought *I* was silly."

"He always really liked you," I said to comfort her.

"He despises me," she retorted. "Of course I wasn't adventurous like you. You two went so well together. You liked the same things. It's right, I know, Ellen. You'll be ever so happy."

I kissed her. "You are a dear, Esmeralda. Are you sure you don't really love Philip?"

"*Quite* sure," she answered emphatically. "I was terrified that he would ask me to marry him and I'd have to say yes because that was what Mama wanted. And then it all turned out this way!"

"I don't think your mother is very pleased."

"Well, I am," she said. "Oh, Ellen, I was dreading it."

Cousin Agatha had got over the first shock and was swallowing her disappointment. I wondered whether she was consoling herself that even a Poor Relation's link was better than none.

"Of course," she said, "you will have to have some clothes. We can't have people saying that we kept you short."

I said: "Don't worry, Cousin Agatha. Philip is not concerned in the least with my clothes and perhaps when I'm married he'll buy some for me."

"You talk like an idiot. Don't you realize that from now on you are going to be the cynosure of all eyes? People are going to try to discover what he sees in you." Her nose twitched to imply she could clearly not provide the answer to this conundrum. "You will have to be suitably clad. There will be functions . . . dinner parties and then of course the bride dress."

"We don't want a lot of ceremony."

"*You* don't want it. You forget you will be marrying into the Carrington family." Again that twitch of the nose. "It's true, he is only a younger son. But, of course, a Car-

rington. When you are married you will be required to
mix in certain circles. I doubt not you will wish Esmeralda,
who has been your companion since childhood, to stay
with you now and then."

I felt suddenly powerful. It was a marvelous feeling. I
couldn't resist smiling benignly on Cousin Agatha and
saying graciously that I hoped Esmeralda would be a frequent guest at my house.

I'm happy, I thought. I'm gloriously happy. Everything
has changed. Talk about Cinderella! Fancy Philip's being
my fairy godmother! I suppose this is being in love.

"I couldn't have people saying that we had not given
you of the best," she went on. "This strange thing has
happened and unless Philip changes his mind it seems that
you will marry into the family. You will always remember
of course your amazing good luck and whence it came.
No doubt you will feel gratitude towards those who cared
for you and but for whom you would never have been presented with this golden opportunity."

I let her talk on. Happiness had made me more generous, and it seemed a small compensation for her disappointment. Fortunately I was never of a vindictive nature
and could quickly forget the slights and indignities of my
childhood.

"I'm afraid Tilly will not be capable of coping with what
we shall need. She could make a housedress or so perhaps. Lady Emily may wish you to go to her couturière.
You will need a very elegant going-away dress and of
course there is the wedding dress. I was speaking to your
cousin Mr. Loring about it only a short while ago. He is
willing to foot the bills so that you may step into your
new life with grace. After all, as I said to him, it will reflect on us, and we have Esmeralda's future to think of."

I was scarcely listening. So many exciting things were
happening.

Philip was always calling at the house. We rode together
in the Row. I had a new riding habit—a present from Mr.
Loring, prodded no doubt by Cousin Agatha because rid-

ing in the Row made one very prominent. We were constantly being photographed.

"What a bore," said Philip. "Who wants all this? I just want us to get away together."

He was very happy and it was wonderful to know that he was so much in love with me. He teased me and bantered with me just as he always had; and we were constantly engaged, it seemed, in our verbal battle, which was a delight to us both. I was nineteen, he was nearly twenty-one, and life seemed good to us. I don't think he knew very much more of the world than I did, which was precious little. Sometimes, though, it is better to know little of what the future has in store.

It was pleasant to be welcomed by his family. Lady Emily's vagueness was rather charming and she confided in me once that she was looking forward to the little babies we would have. She liked to talk a great deal in a rambling fashion. There had always been boys in the Carrington family, she told me. She had had Rollo a year after her marriage and then there was a long gap before Philip arrived. Two very different boys they were. "Rollo used to frighten me sometimes, my dear. He was so clever. Philip was not like that."

It was a Carrington tradition to have boys, and in view of Rollo's misfortune in marriage Philip and I were to be the ones to produce the all-important male Carringtons. There was a certain implication that Philip and I should not delay too long before producing the first grandson.

The thought of having a baby thrilled me and there was not a cloud in my sky during those first weeks after the dance. I think I really believed it would go on like that forever.

We went down to the country for a week as the Carringtons wanted to celebrate our engagement among their friends there. I had always been attracted by the house from the first moment I had seen it, but now that I was to be a member of the family and it would occasionally be my home too, I was more than ever excited by it.

Trentham Towers was an old mansion dating back to Tudor times, although a great deal of reconstruction had been done on it during later periods. Built on a hill, it looked imperiously down on the countryside in what I had thought of as a true Carrington manner. But since I had been taken into the family I realized I had maligned them. It was Cousin Agatha who had given me my opinion of them. No family could have welcomed me more warmly, which was really very remarkable considering the circles in which they moved.

I told Philip I wanted to look over the house and, catching my excitement, as he often did about something which in the ordinary way would have been of little interest to him (it was one of his most endearing characteristics), he was delighted to show me. I was familiar with the gardens, which I had explored thoroughly during my childhood, and it was the house which interested me.

He took me through the great hall to the chapel, then to the dining room, where the portraits of his mother's family were displayed. After that he led me down a stone staircase and, throwing open a heavy oak door, he explained: "This is the old armory. It's now our gun room."

"What a lot of weapons!" I cried. "I hope they're just for ornament."

He laughed at me. "They're used now and then during the season. I'm a crack shot, I can tell you."

"I hate shooting things," I said vehemently.

"I don't suppose you mind partaking of a succulent pheasant now and then," he said. He had opened a case lined with red satin, in which was a silver-gray pistol and a place for another.

"Isn't that a beauty?" he demanded.

"I'd scarcely call it that."

"That's your ignorance, my darling."

"Where's the other one? There should be two, shouldn't there?"

"Oh, that's in a safe place."

"What do you mean by that?"

"What if I'm alone in a wing of the house? Stealthy footsteps creeping along the corridor. The door opens slowly and in comes a man in a mask. He's going to steal the silver, the pictures, the family treasure. What do I do? I feel under my pillow. I draw out my pistol. 'Hands up, villain,' I cry. And what happens? What can he do against me and my little beauty? The family treasure is saved and all because of this." He touched the pistol lovingly before he closed the case.

"You don't really keep a pistol under your pillow, do you, Philip?"

"Until we are married, yes. After that I shall have you to protect me."

"You are an idiot," I said. "And I don't like these guns and things. Let's continue exploring."

"Your wish is law," answered Philip. "Come on."

I loved the old butteries and storing houses. I was enchanted by the room in which Queen Elizabeth was reputed to have slept; there was even the four-poster bed which she was said to have used. The most delightful room was the solarium with its sunny aspect. It was here that I turned to Philip and said: "When shall I meet Rollo's wife?"

Philip looked uneasy. "We don't meet her. We don't even talk about her. It's the most unfortunate thing and so unlike Rollo. One couldn't imagine him involved in anything like that. He's always been so wrapped up in the business . . . finance and all that . . . every bit as much as my father . . . perhaps more. They're always dashing about the world, discussing the market. It seemed to me that they didn't think about anything else. And then to marry like that!"

"It was a hasty marriage then?"

"It must have been. I didn't hear anything about it until it was a *fait accompli*. Then after the honeymoon he found out."

"Found out what?"

"I never heard the details. I just knew she wasn't the

sort who could mix in society . . . his sort of society. She wasn't one of us. She would be a hindrance in his career. There was also a rumor that she drank too much."

"And this didn't come out until after?"

"I suppose so . . . or he wouldn't have married her."

"I should have thought some of it would have been obvious. Not being able to meet people, for instance."

"Well, he must have been infatuated with her. It's a common enough story. He married in haste and when all the excitement wore off he realized his mistake."

"It seems so odd that *that* should have happened to *him*. He seems the last person to be carried away by his emotions."

"People are often not what you think. You're sure you know someone and then you find they do the last thing you'd expect them to. That's how it was with Rollo. In any case it was a ghastly mistake and he keeps her out of the way. She lived in this house at one time. He engaged a companion for her. But it was difficult with the family coming down as they did. So now she's somewhere else."

"Where?"

"I don't know. We don't talk of it. It's Rollo's affair. He wants it that way."

"He must be very unhappy."

"You never know with Rollo. But don't speak of it to my mother. It upsets her. Everyone's upset by it . . . most of all Rollo, of course, but he doesn't show it much. He never did show his feelings."

"I wonder what she feels like . . . being kept away from the family . . . knowing that they're ashamed of her."

"She probably doesn't care. People like that can be insensitive."

"You said she was once in this house."

"Yes, for a while Rollo kept her here. There was a very good woman who looked after her . . . and then when it seemed impossible . . . they left here."

"I'd like to see the rooms she occupied."

"Whatever for?"

"I've just a feeling I'd like to."

"They're right at the top."

"Come on," I commanded. "Show me."

We mounted the oak staircase with its delicately carved banisters, and came almost to the top of the house. A spiral staircase took us right there. These lacked the lofty ceilings of the lower rooms and were much smaller. There were four of them together—a sort of apartment with connecting doors. Two of these were bedrooms. One for Rollo's wife, I thought. One for her companion.

I am sensitive about dwellings and as I stood savoring the atmosphere I fancied I could detect suffering in these. I shivered, and Philip said: "You're cold."

"No, just a shiver."

"Why are you shivering then?"

"Someone walked over my grave, as they say."

"Let's go down."

"Not just yet. I want to linger awhile. I wonder what she felt like up here. Perhaps she was trying to be different so that Rollo and his family wouldn't be ashamed of her."

"Come on. Let's go down. You're running on again. I can't tell you anything more about her. We don't talk of her. She's Rollo's affair."

"Hers too," I reminded him. I went to the bed and touched the quilt, then the back of a chair. She had lived with these things. I wanted to know about her, to see her. Perhaps I could talk to her, help her in some way.

We don't talk about these things, Philip had said. But that was the Carrington way of life. When something was unpleasant you pretended it didn't exist. I could never be like that and I couldn't stop thinking about Rollo's wife.

While we were in the country Philip insisted we go to Dead Man's Leap. We walked through the woods together and came to the spot near the path where there was a wooden seat. We sat down and Philip said: "It brings it all back, doesn't it? It'll always be one of my favorite places. You were a bit scared to come here alone, admit it, Ellen."

"Well, just a bit."

"I was a beast to make you."

"You were a horrid little beast quite often."

"But you were such a know-it-all that you had to be brought down a peg or two sometimes. It does seem a bit weird here, doesn't it?"

"I wonder how many people have sat on this seat and thought about jumping over."

"If rumor's true, quite a number."

Philip stood up to go to stand at the edge of the path as he used to.

"Come back," I shouted.

He obeyed, laughing. "Why, Ellen, you're really scared. You didn't think I was going to leap over, did you?"

"I thought you might show off once too often. There ought to be a rail of some sort up there."

"I'll speak about it. It's our land, you know."

I was surprised that he remembered to do so, and before we left for London an iron rail was put up.

Back in London, Philip and I liked to walk in the Park and talk about our plans. There we could often escape from people who wanted to come up and congratulate us and be quite alone, so we made the most of it. We would wander along by the Serpentine into Kensington Gardens and right across to the other side of the Park. It was in the Park that I was aware of a man watching us. There was nothing very remarkable about him except his unusually bushy eyebrows. He had come along very quietly, it seemed, and seated himself on one of the benches not far from us.

I don't know why I was aware of him, but I was. He gave me an uneasy feeling.

"Do you see that man over there, Philip?" I asked.

He looked about him. "On the bench, you mean?"

"Yes, he seems to be watching us."

"Well, he must be thinking how pretty you look."

"He seems interested in us."

Philip squeezed my arm.

"Of course he's interested in us. We're rather special people."

The man got up and walked away; and we forgot him.

# The House in Finlay Square

We went to see a house in a Knightsbridge square. I was so excited when Philip produced the key and we went in. It was a tall white Queen Anne house with a garden in front and four stories. There is something about empty houses which is almost personal. They can be welcoming or forbidding.

I don't think I have any special perception, merely an overcharged imagination perhaps, but this house affected me as the top rooms of the Carrington country house had done: It was the reverse of welcoming. There was something about it that was alien, and for the first time in my new-found happiness a coldness touched me. Was it because the house represented a reality and the rest had been dreams?

I was to spend my life with Philip—all the years ahead would be with him; we should grow old together, grow like each other. We should be the most important people in each other's lives. It was a sobering thought. I suddenly felt that I had been put into a cage—a pleasant gilded cage, it was true, but outside was the world which I had never yet explored.

I looked at Philip. He was saying eagerly: "Do you like it?"

"I haven't seen it yet. You can't judge a house by the hall."

"Come on then."

He took my hand and we went into the lower rooms; they were intimate—walls closing round me. No, I thought. No!

He ran up the stairs dragging me with him. The rooms on the first floor were light and airy. I liked them better.

"We'll give our parties here," he said. "Rather elegant eh?"

We went up again. There were more big rooms and on the top floor more, and above that attics.

"It's too big," I said, finding excuses.

He looked startled. By Carrington standards it was quite small.

"We shall need these rooms. There are the servants . . . to be accommodated, and we want a nursery. What's the matter? You want a nursery, don't you?"

"Yes, I do very much. But I just feel there is something . . . not quite right about it."

"What do you mean . . . ghosts or something?"

"Of course not. It looks so . . ." I floundered. "Empty!"

He laughed at me. "What do you expect it to be, you goose? Let's look all round. Come on." He was enthusiastic. "The right house is not so easy to find these days," he went on. "The sooner we get a place, the sooner we can get married. Let's look downstairs again."

"I want to stay here . . . alone for a bit."

"Whatever for?"

"To feel what it's like to be here by myself."

"You ass," he said, like the Philip of our childhood. But he went downstairs.

I stood there in the center of the room. I looked out of the long narrow window. There was a garden, small of course, with two trees in it, and a round flower bed.

I tried to imagine myself alone in this house.

It was a strange feeling. I just knew that I didn't want to come here. It was the same feeling that I had in the dream. How very odd, I thought, and disturbing, because I knew this could never be the house for me.

I went down the stairs to the room below and was standing at the window and looking out on the garden when there was a movement behind me. Hands encircled my throat. I gasped out in terror.

"Fe fi fo fum!" cried Philip. "I am the ghost of the last tenant. I was found hanging from the rafters."

He swung me round to face him.

He kissed me: and we were both laughing.

He took my hands and we raced down the stairs.

I couldn't shake off my uneasy feeling about the house in Finlay Square. I knew that Philip was eager to acquire it. He said we didn't want to spend months looking for houses. Buying a house was a lengthy matter at the best of times.

"We can always sell it if we don't like it," he pointed out. "We shall be wanting something bigger in due course, I daresay."

The house was to be his father's wedding present and I hated to curb his enthusiasm. It was not even that I could find anything definite to dislike about the place; but it was a fact that from the time we looked over it my happiness became a little clouded. Oddly enough I had the dream again, which was surprising because I had so recently had it on the night before the dance.

I became so obsessed by the house that one day I went to the house agent and asked if I could have a key to look it over alone. When they knew who I was they reminded me that Mr. Carrington already had a key. I explained then that I wanted to look it over by myself. So I got another key.

It was afternoon, about three o'clock, when I arrived at Finlay Square. It was warm and there were few people about. I stood near the gardens which formed the center of the square and looked at the house from across the road. Again I felt the odd misgiving. My impulse was to turn away at once, take the key back to the house agent and tell him that we had decided against the house. Philip would be disappointed but I could make him understand, I was sure.

Then it was as though some force was propelling me across the road. I didn't want to go, and yet the overpowering urge to do so was forcing me to. I would let myself in and go carefully through the house. I would make myself see that it was just an ordinary house. There was nothing different there from thousands of other empty houses.

As I opened the gate it gave what I thought of as a protesting whine; I was looking for omens, I told myself severely. Determined not to give way to such fancies, I went up the short path to the front door and let myself in. I closed the door behind me and stood in the hall. Then it came to me again—that strange feeling of foreboding. It seemed as though the house was telling me to go. It had no welcome for me. It had nothing to offer me but disaster.

I looked up at the tall ornamented ceiling and at the really rather beautiful curving staircase. It seemed to me as though the house was rejecting me.

I suppose I was a fanciful person, despite my firm intentions. Only such a one would have that recurring dream surely and try to read something into it. I supposed lots of people dreamed and forgot their dreams the next day. I was being foolish really.

I mounted the stairs slowly and deliberately and studied the rooms on the first floor—the entertaining rooms. They were elegant—long windows to the floor—typical of their period; the fireplaces were exquisite in their simplicity. Adam perhaps. I furnished it in my mind and imagined myself as the hostess—moving gracefully among the guests—a Carrington hostess, I thought with a curl of the lips. "Oh, good evening, Cousin Agatha. How *good* of you to come. Philip and I are delighted." And "Why, Mrs. Oman Lemming, how nice to see you and your daughters."

(There were two of them, weren't there?) They would all be so delighted to be received at a Carrington evening. I wanted to laugh at the thought of the imitation I would give of them later to Philip.

Then I went upstairs. Our bedrooms would be here, and there was a small room which had been made into a bathroom. "There wouldn't be a great deal to be done," Philip had said. "The house is ideal, Ellen."

"The house is ideal," I repeated aloud. Then I stood listening. I fancied I heard mocking laughter.

I went up to the rooms which would be nurseries and the attics where the servants would be housed. I pictured white walls and a blue frieze of animals, and a little cot of white wood with a blue coverlet.

I was looking very far into the future. But that after all is what marriage was for, wasn't it? That was why the Carringtons wanted it. Philip must marry young because it seemed as though Rollo would never have children. Odd to think of Philip and myself as parents.

Then I felt my heart leap in terror. In the silence of the house I heard something. I stood very still listening. All was quiet. Had I imagined it? It is strange really how sometimes without sound one can be conscious of a presence. I had the uncanny feeling that someone was in the house. Then as I stood very still in the center of the room, I heard a sound. I had not been mistaken. Someone *was* in the house.

My heart began to hammer painfully. Who? It couldn't be Philip. I knew where he was. He had told me he had to go to his father's London office that day.

I listened. There it was again. A muffled sound; the creak of an opening door.

Then I heard footsteps on the stairs.

I found it difficult to move. I was as though petrified. It was absurd. The house was for sale; we had not definitely bought it, so why should not some prospective buyer come to look at it?

The footsteps came nearer. I stared in fascination at the door. Someone was immediately outside.

As the door was slowly pushed open I gasped; Rollo Carrington stood there.

"Why," he said, "I thought there was no one here."

"So . . . did I."

"I'm afraid I startled you."

"I . . . I heard someone below and . . ."

He looked so tall and I remembered what Philip had said a long time ago about his being a Viking; he even had the appropriate name.

I had had a glimpse of him before but I felt I was seeing him for the first time. He exuded power and a sort of magnetism. I felt that if Rollo Carrington entered a room everyone must be aware of him.

I went on: "You are Mr. Carrington, Philip's brother. I am Ellen Kellaway, his fiancée."

"Yes, I know. Congratulations."

"Thank you. I didn't know you were in London."

"I arrived home last night. I had heard the news of your engagement, of course."

I wondered whether he had come home because of it.

"Philip has told me about the house. I said I'd look it over, so he gave me the key."

"I wanted to look over it on my own," I explained.

He nodded. "Naturally you are eager to see that it is suitable."

"Shall you advise your father to buy it?"

"I think it's very likely a sound proposition. I'm not sure yet of course."

He kept his eyes on me and I felt uncomfortable because it seemed as though he was trying to assess me, to probe my innermost thoughts; and I was not at all sure what he was thinking of me. As for myself, I could not stop thinking of him with that poor wife of his—a shadowy figure in my imagination—in those top rooms at Trentham Towers, and the decision which must have come to him that she must have a companion to watch over her.

It was impossible to imagine this man caught up in a passionate love affair, which there must have been to make him marry so hastily. I thought I detected a certain

bitterness about his mouth. He was no doubt reviling fate
for making his beautiful wife unsuitable and allowing him
to discover this after he had married her. So cool, he
looked, so much in command of himself—and I imagined
of everyone around him—that I could not reconcile the
story of his romantic tragic marriage with this man at all.

"Have you been round again?" he asked.

"Not properly."

"Shall we look at it together?"

"Yes, please."

"Come then, we'll start from the top."

He talked about the snares to look for. I was hardly
paying attention. I just wanted to hear his voice, which
was deep and authoritative; I wanted to know so much
about him—everything; he seemed so mature compared
with Philip and me; he talked of Philip as though he were
a mere boy and it was clear that he considered me very
young too.

"I've had some experience of buying property," he said.
"One has to be careful. *Caveat emptor*, you know."

We went through the house, then out into the garden.
We stood beneath one of the trees.

I looked back at the house. It seemed more menacing
than ever and I felt a great desire to run away from it
even though Philip's brother was beside me to protect me
from any evil that might befall me.

He started to walk back into the house and I followed.
It seemed to close in on me like a prison, and I found it
so hard to shake off this feeling of foreboding that I was
afraid I would show it. Rollo looked at me rather intently
as though he were about to say something, then he
changed his mind, or appeared to. He opened the front
door and as we stepped out of the house a great relief
swept over me.

"I'll call a cab," he said, "and take you home."

I don't know how to describe Rollo. There was something enigmatic and completely baffling about him. He
was not nearly as good-looking as Philip. His features

were more rugged, but he emanated power and a kind of magnetism. He was the sort of man who could slip quietly into a room and yet everyone would be aware of him and he gave the impression that whatever he did would be successful.

I could not get him out of my mind. Perhaps the venue of our encounter had something to do with it. I had been so terrified—ridiculously so—when I had heard his footsteps, which was simply because I had worked myself up about a presence in the house. And then he had appeared.

Ever since I had heard the story of his marriage, I had been thinking about him, and seeing those top rooms at Trentham Towers had set my imagination working. I pictured the hasty courtship, and Rollo's being swept off his feet. That was certainly hard to imagine. But she must have been very beautiful and had tremendous appeal for the opposite sex; perhaps she was greatly sought after—so Rollo married her. Then when passion had subsided he made the alarming discovery that she was not the woman he needed and there followed the terrible discovery that she was a secret drinker. I could imagine how horrified he must have been. He was a man, though, who would conceal his true feelings.

Perhaps in the years to come I should get to know him very well. After all, he would be my brother-in-law.

When Philip and I met in the Park I told him about my meeting with Rollo. He was amused.

"He came home from Rome only last night," he said. "Quite unexpectedly. Our mother had written to him about the engagement."

"Was that what brought him home?"

"Oh yes, he had to come at such a time."

"To inspect the bride?"

"He'd met you before. He knows your family well."

"And he looked at the house."

"Yes, as soon as he heard we were contemplating getting this one he wanted to see it. He thinks it's quite a good bargain. He suggests we make an offer for it."

"He doesn't object to our marriage . . ."

"Object! Why on earth should he?"

"Well, you're so rich and I have no money at all."

Philip burst out laughing. "What notions you get! As if they care about that. My mother was poor when she married my father and he was already a rich man then."

"She had a title."

"Well, look what you've got. You're beautiful and kind, and kind hearts are more than coronets. You should know that."

"And simple faith than Norman blood. Do I have simple faith?"

"You must have to love me."

He was so gay, jaunty, so sure that life was going to be good. I kept comparing him with his brother. How different they were.

"I think it's marvelous," I said, "the way your family have accepted me. Cousin Agatha is amazed."

"Cousin Agatha is a silly old woman. Forgive me, I know she's your cousin."

"Far removed, as I've told you before, and don't apologize. It gives me a certain gratification to hear this Carrington view."

"Why of course they're delighted. They want me married. They think it will be good for me. And they want some little Carringtons. As for Rollo, he's as pleased as he could be. It solves things, it makes it all so convenient."

"Very convenient," I said. "In fact, you could call this a marriage of convenience."

"It's most convenient for me."

"Still you might have chosen someone in your own set."

"Who could be more so? Whom did I tease and bully in my foolish youth?"

"I think you were teased and bullied by me as I ever was by you."

And so we talked; and I was fond of him; yet there was an uneasy feeling within me. I wasn't in love with him. He was kind; he was affectionate; and he was familiar. But I was suddenly afraid of the future.

I wanted to hear more of Rollo Carrington. Rosie was

a good informant by way of her coachman. "Harry says we'll get married next year," she told me. "The head coachman's leaving and he's having his place and that means a nice little mews cottage. Mr. Carrington has promised him. It's a good house to be in. I'll work in the house—it's expected. Harry says it's the best house he's ever been in. Mr. Carrington's away so much and Lady Emily's not one to interfere; and I'll see you now and then, Miss, because you'll be there on and off, I reckon. I can't say I'm well suited here. *She's* always poking and prying and never satisfied. Cook said if she had the angel Gabriel in her kitchen she'd be finding fault. It's different there, Harry says. They don't interfere. They don't want to keep reminding you you're a servant. They don't think of it. Mr. Carrington's too busy with what the Government's doing and Lady Emily's not the kind."

"What about the son?"

"Mr. Philip. Why, Miss, you know more about him than anyone else."

"I mean Mr. Rollo."

"Him. Oh, he's another like his father. All business, so they say."

"He did marry though."

"Oh, that!"

"Rosie, did you ever see *her*?"

Rosie was silent for a few moments. Then she said: "Harry did. He drove them once or twice."

"What is she like?"

"Harry couldn't say. He never heard her speak. She was just in the carriage with him."

"Did *he* speak to her?"

"Harry never heard him. Like two deaf-mutes, they were. Not that Harry drove them much. Then she went away and Harry never drove her again."

"What did she look like?"

"I've asked Harry that, Miss Ellen, but you know what men are. They never notice. He couldn't say. Just that there was something sad about her. He did say she was like a gray ghost. She was always dressed in gray."

"A sad gray ghost," I echoed.

"You're getting your fancies again, Miss Ellen. Don't I remember what a one you used to be. Nose into everything and what you couldn't find out you made up. I know you, Miss Ellen."

One of the maids came into the room.

"Now, Bess," said Rosie, "what do you want?"

"I only came to tell you Janet's looking for you."

"Tell her I'll be along soon. I'm engaged with Miss Ellen."

When the girl had gone she said: "These youngsters . . . they listen. They hear more than's good for them."

I wondered then what I was doing gossiping with one of the servants in my old belowstairs manner. I must remember to mend my ways, now that I was to be a Carrington.

I said a little abruptly: "Well, I won't keep you, Rose."

Lady Emily was a good informant. Strangely enough, she liked me, which was very comforting, since she could hardly have been delighted by my poverty. She encouraged me to visit her frequently and I often called at the house. She did a kind of tatting quite expertly and it was fascinating to watch her fingers working in an efficient manner while her mind wandered on inconsequentially.

She liked me to sit beside her while she talked.

"I always wanted a daughter," she told me. "I hope you'll have *some* girls. Of course they want boys . . . and the first should be one, I suppose, but girls are very charming. I always wanted a girl or two."

From her conversation I learned far more about the Carringtons than I had known before.

The house in Sussex had come to her. She had been an only child and Trentham Towers had been the home of her family for five centuries.

"It was a pity there were no boys . . . the title went to a cousin, you know. But I kept the house. I was so glad. At one time it seemed . . . and then I had boys, two boys and no girls. Isn't that strange? My parents longed for a boy and got me . . . I would have liked a daughter and had two boys. You are my new daughter, Ellen. I think we shall be fond of each other. You're a bright girl and you and Philip are so young. . . ."

"Perhaps you think we are too young," I said.

"I was seventeen when I married. It was a good match. We were so poor. Trentham was falling to pieces. Josiah has done so much for it. I used to shiver in my bedroom. So cold in the winter. Now we are in this house in the winter and we go there in the summer. So pleasant; and of course the servants . . . we had our faithful ones. Poor souls, they rarely were paid. So good; and the roof was a constant anxiety. . . . They were always talking of the fabric of the building. Such a strange term! And then there was Josiah. Of course it was not a family like ours . . . but so rich. He was ten years older than I. You wouldn't believe it, would you? The Carringtons wear well. It's all that energy. They are always doing something that's vital to something, some country, some business and of course to themselves. It keeps them alert and to be alert is to be young, they say. I was never very alert, but I did marry Josiah and that was the end of Trentham's troubles. I haven't heard the fabric mentioned for years. Josiah's people . . . builders and suchlike . . . take care of that. As soon as the fabric does what it shouldn't, it is rectified. Everything changed on the day I married Josiah. My parents were delighted with the match, and Rollo was born a year after our marriage. Perhaps this time next year, dear. . . ."

"I do hope I'm going to produce these babies," I said.

"You will, because you're in love. I believe that's very important. Philip adores you. He always did. He was always talking about you, you know."

"I thought it would be Esmeralda."

"Well, to tell the truth, my dear, so did I. You see, your cousin was certain of it but, as Josiah said, you are more vital and amusing and truthfully, my dear, much more good-looking and we are delighted that Philip and you chose each other."

I took her hand and kissed it suddenly. I was growing very fond of her.

"You are a dear girl. How I wish Rollo could have found someone like you. Ah, Rollo . . . !"

"You are not happy about him?" I prompted.

"My dear, how could I be . . . in the circumstances? He is his father all over again. He is going to be a power in the City . . . and of course with everything he touches. He needs a wife beside him though. Oh dear, it's *so* unfortunate. But of course we mustn't talk of it. It makes us all so unhappy and this should be a happy time. Tell me, have you and Philip decided on a date yet?"

"Philip thinks the end of June."

"That's a lovely month for a marriage. Josiah and I were married in June. Such a charming ceremony . . . at Trentham church of course. You should be married there . . . but perhaps London will be more convenient. What does the place matter when two people are in love? London will certainly be more convenient because your cousin will want you to have a grand wedding, I'm sure."

"I don't know. I have no income of my own, you know, Lady Emily."

"So much the better," she said. "I had none. All I brought was the house with its dilapidated fabric. I think it as well. A husband likes to be the sole provider, you know."

So we talked and the affection between us deepened. I think Philip was her favorite although she was proud of Rollo. Rollo was too clever for her, she confided in me. He takes after his father. He and Josiah got on like a house on fire.

Philip used to come and sprawl in a chair and look from one of us to the other. I could see he was delighted with the friendship between us.

One day he took me down to the mews to show me a new horse he had acquired.

I immediately noticed one of the grooms because I had seen him somewhere before. Philip introduced me and chatted with him in the easy way he had and which I was sure endeared him to everyone.

"This is Hawley," he said. "He hasn't been with us very long."

Hawley said: "Good afternoon, Miss Kellaway," and I continued to be puzzled.

When we left the mews I said to Philip, "I've seen him before. I wonder where."

"It may have been at someone's house. I forget where he was before he came to us, though he's not really a stableman. He just wanted any job that was going, I think my father said, and as he seemed a good man and there was this vacancy at the mews he took him. . . . I think we'll have the house in Finlay Square. It's the best we've seen. You must admit it."

"I'd like to look at it again, Philip."

"Oh come, Ellen, if we don't decide soon someone else might snap it up. Where are we going to live when we're married if we haven't a house? We'll have to be in my father's house for a while as it is, because I doubt everything will be ready by June."

I felt a little shiver of apprehension then. June. It was so near and I was very uneasy.

When I went to bed that night I remembered the man's face and where I had seen him before.

It was in the Park. He was the man I had thought was watching us.

We were going to a musical evening at the Carringtons'. Lady Emily had engaged a famous Italian pianist who would entertain us. Cousin Agatha was delighted to be going. "Half London will be there," she said. "At least anybody who *is* anybody will be."

"I suppose," I retorted, "everybody is somebody, and I doubt whether even Lady Emily's drawing room would accommodate more than seventy people in comfort."

I could never resist the temptation to be what she would have called "pert" in the old days. I shouldn't have been human if I could have resisted exploiting my situation a little. It was amusing how my stature grew daily, particularly since I had been such a frequent visitor to the house in Park Lane. In fact, my visits were quite informal.

This state of affairs I knew was a complete mystery to Cousin Agatha. Rose reported to me that she had heard her say to Cousin William Loring that I seemed to have bewitched not only Philip—which was understandable, for he was but a callow boy—but Lady Emily and Mr. Carrington too. Of course Lady Emily had always been oddly vague and Mr. Carrington *was* so immersed in affairs. . . .

Tilly was sewing all day long and far into the night making garments for both me and Esmeralda, because there was no doubt that Esmeralda was going to profit from the situation. I was determined that she should. I would give parties for her, I promised myself, and I would select the right sort of husband—someone kind and gentle and undemanding.

I said to her once: "All this fuss should really be for you." And she retorted: "How thankful I am that it is not. I couldn't do it half as well as you do. Mr. Carrington frightens me. He's so clever, isn't he? And I can never follow what Lady Emily's saying."

It was a relief to know she was not heartbroken.

I talked to her of the fun we should have in the country. She should come and stay and we'd have pleasant parties. We'd ride together just as we used to when we were children.

She said: "I'm so glad it's happened the way it has, Ellen. That Mrs. Oman Lemming is a dreadful person. Bessie told me that she is quite beastly to the servants there and particularly the governess. She can't wait to get away."

"What a miraculous escape I had!" I cried. "Thanks to Philip."

Somewhere at the back of my mind was the knowledge that I was trying to reassure myself. In the beginning it had all seemed so wonderful but now it occurred to me that everything had worked out too easily and that in itself was vaguely disturbing.

A few days later the Carringtons gave the musical soirée. I stood with Philip and people kept coming up to congratulate us. There was a photographer for the press. "Such a bore," said Philip, "but they catch my mother and she doesn't like to refuse them."

The recital was one of Chopin's pieces beautifully rendered by the Italian pianist. Dreamy, romantic, then militant and stirring.

"We're negotiating prices about the house," Philip told me. "They take their time, I can tell you. Lawyers and things. Rollo's most interested in concluding it all as soon as possible."

I nodded, scarcely listening.

"We'll go on the Continent. What do you think of Venice? Rome perhaps? Will you like that, Ellen?"

I said I thought it would be lovely.

"Perhaps the house will be ready by the time we come back. Rollo's taking over arrangements for it now he's in London for a spell. My father hasn't time. They seem to think I'm not capable of doing it, and they're probably right."

"It's good of Rollo."

"Oh, he likes doing that sort of thing."

The recital was over and there was a buffet supper to follow. Everyone was discussing the music, and Philip, having caught sight of an old friend, went over to have a word with him, leaving me temporarily alone.

A voice behind me said: "I've been wanting to meet you all the evening."

I turned sharply and looked up at one of the tallest men I have ever seen. I knew at once that I had not met him before at any of the Carrington gatherings because if I had I could not have forgotten him. It was not only his unusual height and broad shoulders, but there was something else about him—an aura of power. His eyes were dark, deep-set, heavy-lidded, but very bright and expressive, though what they expressed it was not easy to decide.

His nose was longish and arrogant-looking; his mouth could be either cruel or gentle, I was not sure which. All I can say is that even in those first moments I thought his was one of the most interesting faces I had ever seen.

"I haven't met you before," I said.

"I arrived just before the recital started. I have seen your picture in the papers. May I say that none of them does you justice."

"That's kind of you rather than truthful," I replied. "They are most flattering."

"Ah, I see you are modest as well as attractive. It's a nice combination but a rare one."

"Are you a friend of the family?"

"A connection."

"I hope you enjoyed the recital."

"I am enjoying it very much, thank you. Have you a date for the wedding yet?"

"Not exactly. It's to be in June. The actual day is not decided."

"I shall be there. I'm determined to be at your wedding."

"Lady Emily is giving my cousin a list."

Philip was looking across at me. "Ellen," he said, "we'd better go and speak to old Sir Bevis over there."

My companion bowed and turned away.

"Old Bevis is getting peevish," said Philip. "He always does if we don't make a fuss of him. Who was that, by the way, the tall fellow you were talking to?"

"I don't know. He said he was a connection of yours."

Philip shrugged his shoulders. "Must be one of my father's or Rollo's business friends. He looked it, I must say."

"Did you think so? I thought he looked the outdoor type."

"Probably been pulling financial wires in the Middle East. They do, you know. What I meant was there was that look of power about him. They all have it. I don't know how I shall get on because in me it's conspicuous by its absence."

"Perhaps they weren't born with it and it's something you develop," I comforted. "It comes with experience."

"Don't you believe it. These people were born wizards. Still, I've done better than they have in one way. I've got you."

"Oh, Philip, you say the nicest things. You make me feel more precious than a fortune, and that love is more important than the Stock Market."

"For a moderately intelligent young woman you are surprisingly foolish at times if you needed contact with the financial jugglers of the Carrington circle to bring that to your notice."

We talked to old Sir Bevis, who congratulated Philip on our coming marriage, but I could see that I was the one he was really congratulating. Like a lot of people, he just could not understand why the Carringtons were accepting a girl without money. The logical explanation seemed to be that they were so rich that another fortune wouldn't make much difference.

When we had left Sir Bevis I noticed the man Hawley, whom I had seen in the Park and later in the Carrington stables.

Philip noticed my interest in him and laughed.

"Oh, your man of the Park. Old Hawley. He's been pressed into service in the house. He seems to have a talent for most things. He's valeting now."

"For whom?" I asked.

"For us all really. My father's valet left recently and it seems Hawley knew the job. He valets for us all, as we have always shared. My father and Rollo are away so much that there is not much for a valet to do."

"I suppose *you'll* go away a great deal when you're older, and I shall see the world with you."

"That's how it will be," he answered; and I thought then how lucky I was. It was this sudden turnabout provided by the Carringtons and banishing the specter of poverty forever which had set my mind nagging over the suspicion that it was all too good to be true. It was all very well for people to say that the love of money was the root of all evil, but I had to admit that it would certainly be good to have enough so that I need not worry about the future any more.

During the rest of the evening I looked for the tall man who had spoken to me but I couldn't see him. I was sure that if he had been present it would not have been difficult to spot him, for he was not the sort who could be lost in a crowd. I wished I had had the presence of mind to ask his name.

"It seems," said Esmeralda, "that one of the Carrington servants is courting Bessie."

"Really?" I replied. "Well, I suppose she's quite attractive."

"There's Rose and her coachman and now Bessie and Hawley."

"Did you say Hawley?"

"Yes, I'm sure that was the name. There seem to be several bonds between us and the Carringtons."

"Isn't that what your mother always wanted?" I asked, and I was thinking: Hawley! The man in the Park, the valet who looks after them all. Philip might laugh at me because of my interest in him, but ever since I had fancied he had watched us, I had been aware of him.

The time was passing and we were halfway through May. The horse chestnuts in the Park were proudly displaying their candles, ready to burst into beautiful flower, and I should have been joyous, but I would often wake in the mornings and it was as though I were emerging from an uneasy world of dreams which left nothing coherent behind but a vague sense of uneasiness.

The Carrington offer for the house in Finlay Square had been accepted and the contracts were in the process of being drawn up. We still had a key apiece, Philip and I. I didn't want to give mine up because I still had the urge to go there, and I did so now and then, trying to reconcile myself to the place. I would stand in the rooms and try to discover what it was I disliked about it.

Once when I was coming out I met Bessie. It was her

half day off and she must have been walking near the square. She knew I went there because she had been talking with me when I took the key out of the drawer.

She looked at me shyly. "This is going to be your new home, isn't it, Miss Ellen?"

"Yes," I said.

"It's a beautiful house. I hope Hawley and me will be together one day. It's what he's said shall be."

"I daresay it will," I said brightly. "And Rose is going to marry the coachman. You'll all be together."

"You come here often, don't you, Miss Ellen? I would. To plan how things will be. I wouldn't be able to tear myself away."

Bessie went back to the house and I followed more leisurely.

Two days later I visited the house again. As I let myself in I was telling myself: It will look so different when it is furnished. I mounted the stairs. I was getting used to the place. I couldn't think what had possessed me to have the fancies I had. Was it really misgiving about the house or was it apprehension for the future and the life we would lead, Philip and I, in these four walls?

Did I want to marry Philip? Of course I did. I thought of the alternative. During the last few weeks I had forgotten how humiliating my position had been. I had ceased to think of Mrs. Oman Lemming waiting for her governess. What had the future held out for me before Philip had asked me to marry him? I had forgotten all that just because I had seen Philip's brother and realized suddenly that one does not necessarily want an old playmate— whatever the affection you have for him—for a husband.

I was marrying Philip to escape—and that was not really a good reason for marriage, I knew, yet how was it possible to back out now? But it's not too late. It was almost as though the house was telling me that. You could stop it now, negotiations are not complete and there has been no signing on the dotted line. You could escape now.

Escape? Where to? To Mrs. Oman Lemming?

Maybe. But to escape from her is no reason for marriage.

Then, I reproached myself, why didn't you think of this before? Why do you have to start plaguing yourself with it now?

It was just because I was afraid of the future. Mrs. Oman Lemming was looming up before me and there seemed no escape from the dreary life which I knew I was going to hate. And then Philip's proposal had been so unexpected and promised such fun; it was only at this eleventh hour that I realized I was plunging into marriage without much experience of life.

What nonsense! What experience of life do girls have? What has Esmeralda had? What does she know of life? She was once lost in a market. That was the nearest she came to knowing there was a world outside her tight little circle.

Yet there was this strange feeling creeping over me. The house was rejecting me. We don't want you here, it seemed to be saying. These rooms are not for you. We will never accept you. That was the message of the house.

I clenched my fists. Metaphorically I shook them at the house. If I want to live here, I will. It is my life and how could I possibly be a governess to that old tyrant and her loathsome brood now? Philip would never allow it.

It was comforting to think of Philip, his gaiety, his comradeship, his kindness. I did love him—in a way.

Then I heard it—or perhaps sensed it—the sudden awareness that I was not alone in the house.

The house was so quiet. One could imagine anything else. Then it was there again. The step on the stairs. The creak of feet on wood. Now it was distinct. Footsteps were coming up the stairs. I immediately thought of that other occasion when Rollo had come into the house. It's Rollo again, I reassured myself. As he is making the arrangements, he has naturally come to have another look at it.

The door opened slowly. I almost cried out: "Rollo!" Then my flesh started to creep, for it was not Rollo. It was a man who stood there smiling at me in an odd sort of way. I put my hands behind my back for fear he should see that they were trembling.

I knew this man. He was the tall dark one who had spoken to me at the Chopin recital.

I stammered: "How . . . how did you get in?"

He held up a door key.

"Where did you get it?" I demanded.

He laughed and answered: "The house is for sale, I believe."

"No, it's sold. I can't understand. I suppose the agent gave it to you. He shouldn't have done so. The house is sold . . . or all but sold."

"Oh, they can never be sure until everything is signed and sealed. They must go on trying to sell it."

As he spoke he kept his eyes fixed on me and I felt an uneasiness creeping over me. The fact that the house was empty and I was alone in it with this man struck me forcibly.

"So," I went on, feeling the need to say something even though it was obvious, "you came to look at the house."

He nodded and advanced into the room. I desperately wanted to get out through the door but I did not see how I could without passing him.

"This house is definitely off the market," I added.

"That's a pity because *I* quite like it."

"So you are wasting your time."

His hooded eyes regarded me intently. I wished I knew what he was thinking because I was sure there was something more in this than what he would have it appear.

"Perhaps," he said. "But while I am here I shall look round. You never know . . . if the sale fell through and I liked it particularly well, I could then jump into the breach."

I was nearly at the door but he had taken a step towards me. I said hurriedly: "I'll leave you to look round."

"Couldn't we look together? I know so little about houses. I should welcome your comments."

"I must remind you again that it is sold."

I thought cunningly that I would pretend to go round with him and when I reached the ground floor I would remember an appointment and before he had time to stop me I would open the front door and walk out.

"All the same," I went on, "if you want to look round, do. Let's start at the bottom."

"You are kind." He stood aside for me to pass and as I started to walk downstairs I was aware of him very close behind me. Why did I feel so scared? What was it about him? He seemed so large, so powerfully built that he made me feel helpless. Moreover, somehow I didn't quite believe he had come to see the house, and why should the house agent have given him the key when he knew the Carringtons were buying the house? It was all rather mystifying.

"A pleasant house," he was saying.

"My fiancé thinks so," I replied.

"And you don't?"

"I think it's adequate."

"Just look at this banister. It's rather elegant, don't you think?"

"Yes, it's well carved."

I took a few steps down. I had rarely been so frightened in my life.

Is he mad? I asked myself. Why is he here? I know it is not to see the house. Why did he follow me upstairs?

I prayed as I stood there on the stairs. Oh God, let me get away. I'll never want to come to this house again. But let me get away from this man.

"Did you say something?" he asked.

"Pleasant carving," I repeated.

"Oh yes, yes. And you are appreciative of that. Like you, I am appreciative of beautiful things."

I wondered whether I would dash down the stairs now. If I did he would follow me. Perhaps I could make it sound normal, something like: "Good gracious, look at the time. I had no idea. I have to hurry away. To meet my fiancé."

Why had he come here? He must have seen me come

in. Had he been lurking in the square? The agent had no right to give him a key. He had some motive for coming here and I could not think what.

Get down the stairs, I told myself. When you are in the hall make a dash for it. They say that when you are in danger you conjure up extra powers. You can run faster than you ever did before. It's nature's provision.

Could I open the door quickly enough? I tried to remember what the catch was like. Some doors were difficult . . . they had their little idiosyncrasies.

How frightened I was, and he sensed my fear I was sure. It amused him. Out of the corner of my eye I could see the curl of his lips, the glitter of his eyes.

I prayed again: Oh God, please help me.

And then my prayer was answered. We were on the stairs looking down onto the hall when I saw a dark shadow before the glass panel of the door. He saw it too. I heard his quick intake of breath as the door opened and Rollo stepped into the hall.

He could not have been more surprised to see us than we were to see him. He gazed at us in astonishment; then I saw his expression change as his eyes went from me to the dark man.

I had stood as though rooted to the stair. I heard myself explaining: "There's been a misunderstanding. This gentleman didn't know the house was sold. He came to look over it."

Rollo frowned. "Didn't the agent explain?"

"I think he wasn't completely sure," said the dark man. "There didn't seem to be any reason why I shouldn't look it over."

"He had no right to give you a false impression," said Rollo.

The dark man smiled. "I suppose he thought there was no harm in having a second string to his bow in case the first one broke. I shall have a word with him. I didn't realize negotiations had gone so far. There seems to be no point in my continuing my investigations."

He bowed to me and went to the door. There he turned

and looked straight at me before the door shut on him.

"What an extraordinary thing!" cried Rollo. "I can't understand the agent's allowing him to have a key when things have gone as far as they have, with the deal on the verge of completion."

"Who is he?" I asked. "He said he was some connection of yours."

"Of mine! I don't know him. A connection, he said?"

"Yes, he was at the recital. He told me then."

"So you'd met him before. I've no notion who he is. My father may know him. What's his name?"

"I never heard it. We weren't introduced at the recital. He was just beside me and addressed a few words to me. The next time I saw him was here."

"How very strange, and you seem a little upset."

"It was finding someone here . . . looking at the house."

Rollo nodded. "Oh well, we'll find out who he is. I am a little concerned about the dining-room ceiling. There's a certain amount of damp there. The surveyor pointed it out. I thought I'd come and take a look at it."

I was still feeling dazed as I followed him into the dining room. Rollo looked at the ceiling and said he would consult the builders and after that we went into the garden. He was very precise. "You should employ a professional gardener although it's small," he said. "Philip will be no good at it. Are you?"

"I doubt it," I said.

"Then a good gardener is definitely the answer. Get someone to plan it for you and keep it trim. It could be quite charming then."

We went through the house and out into the square.

"It's good of you to take so much trouble," I told him.

"For my own brother and his wife!" He turned to look at me, his eyes were appraising but warm. "I want you to know, Ellen, how very much we welcome you into the family."

I still felt uneasy. I just could not shake off the feeling.

Rollo called a cab. Clop-clop went the horse's hoofs, and Rollo sat beside me upright, looking satisfied as though something he had undertaken had succeeded very well.

As we turned into the square my heart gave a leap of terror, for standing on the pavement looking straight into the cab was the dark man.

He lifted his hat and bowed to me.

I glanced at Rollo. He had not noticed.

I could not get that morning's events out of my mind. I did not go into the house in Finlay Square again. I couldn't bring myself to. I did walk past it once or twice looking up at those long windows. I said to myself: Nothing would induce me to go there again.

The wedding was three weeks away. My dress was being made by Lady Emily's own dressmaker. Cousin William Loring was happy to pay for it. Mine was going to be one of the weddings of the year and even Cousin Agatha was growing excited about it, bustling about as if she had arranged it. Although it was the marriage of a Poor Relation everything must be perfect, because society must see the kind of reception the Lorings gave to their family. Her great sorrow was that all this fuss was for me, but when she convinced herself that it was a kind of rehearsal for Esmeralda's wedding she was reconciled. And of course Esmeralda was to be a bridesmaid.

"What a fuss getting married is," said Esmeralda. "I'm so glad I'm not the bride."

We had chosen a good many furnishings for the house and much would be done while we were away on our honeymoon, which would be for four weeks. Italy was the chosen place. Philip was delighted that I had never been and looked forward to showing me. Venice was to be our first call and there we should stay until we felt the urge to move on.

I should have been excited and happy, and yet I couldn't dismiss the feeling that I was on the edge of some disaster.

It's marriage, I thought. I'm not ready for it. I want to wait a while.

But how could I say to Philip: "Let's postpone our marriage. Let's get to know each other"? He would burst into laughter and say that if we did not know each other by now we never would.

It wasn't exactly what I meant. We didn't know each other because we scarcely knew anything of the world, either of us. If the genie of the lamp could rise before me and ask me what I wished I would have no hesitation in saying: Time.

I was frightened by the speed with which the time was flying past. Two more weeks, ten more days . . .

I wanted to stop time, to say: "Wait. I must think."

I was not sleeping very well and would lie awake during the night and my problem would niggle away at me. I fancied Rollo had changed towards me since that last encounter in the house. He seemed to avoid me.

Philip was exuberant. It was clear that he did not suffer from my doubts. I saw Philip afresh now. He was all enthusiasms for whatever obsessed him at the moment, and I thought again and again: He's very young. So was I for that matter, but it seemed to me that I had grown up since my engagement. Grown up, yes, and left Philip behind.

It was the Sunday before our wedding day. There were six more days to go. We were to be married at St. George's Hanover Square and then go back to the Lorings' house for the reception. In the late afternoon we should leave for Venice.

I should have been congratulating myself on my good fortune and at times I did, but not for long. Into my thoughts would creep an insidious notion that I was making a mistake, a mistake fraught with danger, and that I would never again be the old Ellen who, even as a Poor Relation, had enjoyed life wholeheartedly and had often been able to laugh at her own misfortunes.

In the afternoon Philip and I walked through the Park to Kensington Gardens. We skirted the Palace and watched the ducks on the Round Pond; then we walked back across the grass and sat by the Serpentine and talked.

Philip was gay. At least *he* had no doubts, capable as he was of complete absorption in the moment. I remembered that even as children when we would be doing something which would assuredly bring us some punishment, he had never thought ahead. I have never known anyone who had such a capacity for living in and enjoying the moment. It is a great gift. Darling Philip, I was to be grateful later that he possessed it.

"Six whole days," he was saying. "It seems a lifetime. I'll be glad when all the fuss is over. It won't be long, Ellen, before we're sailing down the Grand Canal with our gondolier soothing us with his beautiful song. Aren't you pleased?"

"Of course. It'll be wonderful."

"It was always *us*, wasn't it? As soon as I came home from school I'd ask if you were there. Of course we always had to have Esmeralda trailing on, but I wanted to be with you in spite of that."

"You're cruel to Esmeralda. In the first place you should have been kinder to her in your youth and in the second place you should have married her."

"As we're not allowed two wives in this country and I'd already decided on you, how could I?"

"You were always obstinate."

"And what of you? Ours will be a nice explosive union, Ellen. We shall argue and fight and make it up and love each other until the end of our days."

"Let's try to do that, Philip," I said.

He took my hand and held it firmly.

"I've no qualms," he told me seriously.

"It's not too late to get out of it even now. If you'd like more time . . ."

"More time! I want less time. A week's a hell of a long way off."

And so we chatted on that seat in the Park and afterwards I tried to remember every word that was said in case in that conversation there might have been some clue to what followed. Try as I might, I could remember nothing. It seemed to be the sort of conversation Philip and I had had a thousand times.

In the evening we went to church and afterwards I walked home with Cousin Agatha, Cousin William and Esmeralda. We retired early, for there was never entertaining on Sundays, and I sat by my window for some time looking out on the gardens and thinking that this time next week I should be married. Philip and I would be on our way to Venice.

I rose as usual without an inkling of what might have happened. Then Rollo rode over in the midmorning.

Rose, her face the color of chalk, came into my bedroom, where I was sorting out my clothes. Bessie was with her, peering from behind her back.

"What's wrong?" I said.

"There's been some accident. I don't know rightly what, but Mr. Rollo Carrington's here and he's asking to see you."

I went down to the drawing room. Rollo was standing by the fireplace.

"Is anything wrong?" I cried.

I saw his face then—pale, drawn and anxious. He didn't look like the Rollo I had known.

"Something terrible has happened," he said. "You must try to be calm."

"It's Philip," I said.

"Yes," he nodded. "Philip."

"He's ill. . . ."

"He's dead."

"Philip . . . *dead*! Oh no, that can't be. How could it . . . ?"

"Philip was found dead this morning."

"But he wasn't ill."

"He was found shot."

"Shot! But who . . . ?"

Rollo shook his head slowly and sadly.

"It appears the wound was self-inflicted," said Rollo.

I felt myself growing dizzy. Rollo caught me and held me for some moments until I regained my strength.

"There's a mistake," I said shrilly. "I don't believe it."

"No, alas. There is no mistake."

Everything was collapsing about me. It was like a bad dream. I'd wake up. I must. The world had become a strange place full of distorted nightmares. And the greatest of these was that with Rollo standing before me saying in a low tragic voice: "Philip is dead. He took his own life."

What did it mean?

# Dead Man's Leap

I lay on my bed. I did not want to move. I couldn't believe it. Philip dead! Philip who had been so full of life! It was impossible. And to take his own life. He, who had been so happy! Only the day before he had talked exuberantly of our future. What could have happened so suddenly to make him do such a thing?

Esmeralda came and sat by my bed. I wanted no one but I could just bear her. She was so quiet. She took a handkerchief soaked with eau de cologne and laid it on my forehead. I knew I should never smell that scent again without remembering this day.

I kept seeing Philip in scenes from the past. The day we set the fields on fire—that mischief in his eyes! He had wanted to let it blaze for a while before we gave the alarm. How his eyes had shone! How they had danced! We'd be punished for this but let us enjoy it while it lasted. Philip at the dance, proposing to me, serious suddenly, assuring me that he would always look after me.

And now he had done this.

"I don't believe it," I said. "It's not true. It can't be."

Esmeralda said nothing. What was there to say?

A great deal would be said of course and they would soon start saying it.

That very day it was there in the newspaper, the great headlines: "Suicide of Bridegroom-to-Be. Six days before he was to have married Miss Ellen Kellaway, Philip, son of Josiah Carrington, took his own life. What is the story behind the tragedy?"

Everyone believed that there was a story and that I was the one who held the vital clue.

Why should a young man who had every blessing shoot himself a few days before his wedding? It could only be that life had become too much for him to endure, so he had taken this way out. That he was to have been married in six days' time was the theme of the story.

I lay in my room, the venetian blinds drawn to keep out the sun. The sun that could not warm the coldness that invaded me. I could not eat; I could not sleep. I could only lie on my bed in shocked stillness and ask myself: Why? Why?

Esmeralda told me what had happened. I commanded her to and in the same way that she had obeyed my orders when she was young she did now: "He was shot with one of the guns from Trentham Towers. He must have brought it from there."

"It's not possible. That would mean that he had planned it."

She was silent and my mind went back to that occasion when I had been with him in the gun room at Trentham Towers. I remembered the satin-lined case and the silver-gray pistol which he had taken out and touched so lovingly. There had been an empty compartment in the case and he had talked, jokingly I had thought, about keeping a pistol under his pillow. What could he have meant? Was it really true that he had done this? Had he then been serious when he had talked of burglars? Even so, what could have possessed him to turn the pistol on himself? Was it possible that I, who had thought I knew him so well, had been mistaken? Was there a darker side to his nature which he had never allowed me to see? I could not believe it.

"He couldn't have killed himself!" I cried out. "He was talking to me only the day before. Imagine, Esmeralda, the despair a man must be in to take his own life! Can you imagine Philip ever in despair? *I* never saw him so. Did you? He wasn't the sort of man who could hide his feelings. He never attempted to. I *knew* Philip. Nobody knew him better, and I say it's impossible. I shall never believe it."

But it had happened.

Esmeralda said: "The newspaper people have been here. They want to see you. There'll be an inquest. You'll have to go."

I roused myself. "I want to go," I said. "I want to discover the reason for this."

It was like a dream. I saw faces . . . Mr. Josiah Carrington looking unlike himself; his face pale and distorted with grief, Lady Emily more bewildered than ever with a tragic look in her eyes. And Rollo grown cold and stern; his eyes like ice; they looked searchingly at me, making me shiver.

There could only be one verdict. Suicide. I wanted to cry out my protest.

Not Philip! He never could. Anyone who knew him must be aware of that. But that was the court's verdict.

There followed the funeral. I begged not to go. I just lay on my bed, weak from my emotions, lack of food and sleep.

"Mother thinks you should go to the country," Esmeralda said. "I'm to go with you. The press keep calling. She says it's better to go away for a while."

So we went and what a comfort Esmeralda was! I think in her mind was the belief that I had saved her from this ordeal and that she might so easily have been in my position if Philip had asked her to marry him as everyone had expected him to.

I felt a little better in the country, but I still could not sleep well. When I dozed I dreamed of Philip, the pistol in his hand and the blood on his bed. I dreamed too that other dream. I was in the room with the red carpet and the painting and Philip was with me.

He said to me: "You always felt the doom, didn't you, Ellen? Well, now here it is. I'm dead . . . I killed myself. I had to because I could not marry you."

I woke up calling out to him.

They were nightmare days.

I was in the country for two weeks and then Rollo came to Trentham Towers.

He walked over to see me. Esmeralda came to tell me he was there, and I went down into the small sitting room, and as he stood before me and bowed stiffly I thought how he had changed, as I must have done.

He insisted that we be alone that we might talk. He came straight to the point: "I want you to tell me why Philip killed himself," he said.

"If only I knew."

"Don't you know?" he asked harshly.

"How could I? If I had known what he was going to do I would have found some way of stopping him."

"There must have been something. . . ."

"I knew of nothing."

"Who else would?"

"It must have been something he kept to himself."

"He was not that sort of person." Rollo kept his eyes on me. "There was simply no obvious reason. He had no anxieties. It must have been something in his private life, for he was never deeply involved in our business affairs. Are you absolutely sure that there were no differences between you? Because there appears to be no other reason why he could have taken his life."

His eyes were cold and I believed he hated me because he actually suspected that I was somehow involved in Philip's death. It was more than I could bear.

I cried out: "It was a greater shock to me than to you. I was to be his wife."

He came close to me, his lips tight, and I noticed that he clenched his hands tightly together as though he were suppressing an impulse to do me an injury, so much did he blame me for his brother's death.

"I think you know something," he said.

"I have told you I have no idea how he could possibly have done such a thing."

"It must have been something to do with you. Perhaps you had deceived him and he had discovered this. You betrayed him and this shattered him. He was very inexperienced of the world and he killed himself rather than face the consequences of what you had done."

"You can't believe such nonsense. It's lies . . . wicked cruel lies."

"Who was the man I found with you in the house in Finlay Square?"

"How should I know who he is? He said he was a connection of yours."

"You know that's untrue."

"Then who was he?"

"He was a friend of yours presumably."

"I tell you, I don't know who he is. He was at the recital at your home . . . and then he came to the house to look at it. That's all I know of him."

Rollo looked skeptical. "How did he get into the house?"

"He told you. He got the key from the house agent."

"I know too much, Ellen. I have made it my business to find out. He met you there by appointment and I came in and surprised you."

"That's monstrous."

"I can only draw the obvious conclusions. You had one key, Philip had the other, which I used. There was no third key. I spoke to the agent and asked him why he had given that man a key and he said he had given a key to no one but ourselves. There was only one way that man could have got into the house. You let him in. Don't lie to me any more, but don't be surprised if when you refuse to tell me the truth I draw my own conclusions."

"This is nonsense," I cried. "I did not let him into the house. I was as surprised to see him as you were. He did have a key and the agent is lying."

Rollo rose. "I would have respected you more had you confessed the truth. You were obviously very friendly with this man. I believe that this is at the root of the mystery and you know the answer. Philip died because of something you had done to him and you are responsible for his death."

"How can you! How dare you! It's such lies. . . ."

"So many lies have been told, I can see. But Philip is dead now. I wish to God he had never seen you."

Then he went and I think that was the most unhappy time I had ever lived through.

I was desolate. I had lost Philip and with him everything. I could have borne this better if it were not for the fact that Rollo despised me and suspected me so cruelly and unfairly of knowing something, of doing something, of being something I was not. He would not believe that Philip's death was as much a mystery to me as it was to him.

I went for long walks but there was no comfort. There I had been with Philip. There was hardly any spot in the neighborhood which had not been one of our haunts. I rode out alone although Esmeralda always tried to accompany me, but then I would come to the inn where Philip and I—or perhaps the three of us but I suppose neither of us gave much thought to Esmeralda—had stopped for cider and a sandwich. There was the old smithy who had shoed our horses. He called a greeting to me as I passed, but his eyes were downcast and he did not know what to say. It was the same in the village where they had known us as children. They looked at me covertly and I knew the question which was in all their minds: Why had Philip killed himself? It was something to do with me. He would rather die than marry me. That was the inference everyone was putting on it.

I couldn't resist going to Dead Man's Leap. There I

would sit on the old wooden seat and brood over the many times when Philip and I had played in the woods from which we had emerged with a reluctant Esmeralda and forced her to witness our bravery in standing on the edge.

Dead Man's Leap! I thought a great deal about people who had found life so intolerable that they wanted to end it and I wondered what their tragedies had been to bring them to such a pass. One thing I was certain of. Philip had never been in that state. He could not have killed himself. But that had been the verdict. Why? Had I really known that boy with whom I had shared my childhood? Does one person ever really know another. I had always thought Philip was easy to understand. He said what was in his mind and rarely paused to think what effect his words might have. He was easygoing, good-tempered, a little lazy perhaps, eager for the good things of life but not liable to make any effort to get them, the son of a rich family who had never really lacked anything he wanted. That was how I had thought of Philip, but how much had I known of what lurked in the dark recesses of his mind?

A great melancholy would descend upon me as I sat on that seat. Esmeralda asked me where I had been and when I told her she was horrified. "You shouldn't go there," she said, "it's morbid."

"It suits my mood," I replied. "I can think of Philip there and in a strange way it comforts me."

"I'll come with you," she would say, but I always protested: "No, no. I want to be alone."

She was worried about me.

One morning when I was in the woods I had the strange feeling that I was not alone. I wasn't sure quite what made me think so. Perhaps I heard an unexpected noise —the dislodging of a stone, the rustle of leaves, the sudden scuttling of some disturbed animal. But as I sat on the wooden seat I sensed a presence. I thought: Is it true that the spirits of those poor souls who ended their lives abruptly cannot rest and come back to the last place they knew on earth? That was what was generally believed by those who said the place was haunted.

Oddly enough, instead of repelling me, this feeling attracted me. Perhaps I felt that I might be in touch with Philip and he would come back and tell me why he had died.

So every morning my footsteps led me almost involuntarily to Dead Man's Leap, and often I had the feeling that I was observed.

It was a hot sultry morning and I was glad to be in the cool woods. It was one of those still silent mornings when people say there is thunder in the air. More than ever I had the feeling that I was being watched as I sat on the seat and thought of Philip, wishing fervently that I could hear him whisper my name. I wished that I was young and carefree again when my chief desire had been to score over Philip and prove to him that girls were just as good as boys. I should have liked to go back to the time of our engagement that I might take less for granted and try to understand more about the man I was to marry. No matter what the evidence, no matter what the verdict, I could never accept the idea that he had killed himself. There must be another explanation.

I went to the path as I always did before returning. I liked to look down into the bushes far below and remember the thrill it used to give me as a child.

I gripped the rail and leaned forward and then suddenly it swung forward, taking me with it, so that I was clinging to it and hanging in mid-air. A startled bird flew up, brushing my face as it went past me. I had time to think: This is the end! before I fell.

I opened my eyes. I could scarcely breathe so fast was my heart beating. I looked down; far below were the tops of trees. I felt my feet slipping and I clutched at the bushes into which I had fallen.

Then I saw what had happened. By incredible good luck I had only fallen a few feet before my skirts had been caught in one of the thick clumps of bushes which grew on the steep hillside.

For some minutes I was unable to do anything but hang on with all my might. Then my heartbeats began to slow down and I was able to take stock of the situation. I looked up and saw that the rail on which I had been leaning had come away on one side and that I had had a miraculous escape from certain death.

And now what must I do? One false move and I could go hurtling down. I must remain where I was and hope to attract someone's attention. Few people came to Dead Man's Leap and even if they did they would not know I was here clinging to the hillside bush.

I shouted but my voice echoed back to me. I could feel pains in my legs and arms. My hands were badly grazed and I knew I should certainly be bruised all over. I felt faint but that was the last thing I must do. I must concentrate on clinging to the bush.

I shall never forget that terrible ordeal and how Esmeralda was my savior. But it was several hours before she missed me and then she immediately thought of Dead Man's Leap. What else she thought I was aware of, although she didn't mention it. She sent two of the grooms to look for me there and when they could not find me and noticed the broken rail they approached the place from below and that was how I was discovered clinging to the bush.

To bring me down was not an easy matter. Two expert climbers from the nearby town came with special equipment; there were quite a lot of spectators and my rescue was reported in the press. There was a piece about the danger of Dead Man's Leap and how the rail had apparently been faulty although it had been put up not very long before. Greater protection was needed and something would have to be done about it.

Esmeralda nursed me for three days. That was all I needed to get over the shock and my bruises and abrasions.

The fact that Philip was reputed to have killed himself raised certain speculation as to what had happened to me. No one stressed this, but it was there.

We could not stay in the country forever and Cousin Agatha recalled us.

I felt a quiver of alarm when I entered the house and was confronted by her. Her expression was one of mingled exasperation and veiled triumph: exasperation because I had managed to get myself "talked about," as she put it, through this unfortunate affair on the hill, veiled triumph because although she did deplore the fact that a member of her family had failed to climb into the Carrington oligarchy, yet at the same time she was gratified because after all the "tumult and the shouting" I had failed and had had to come back to the old familiar position of Poor Relation to be victimized at her will.

I went to Finlay Square and looked at the house. It was up for sale again but nothing would have induced me to go in. I wondered whether what had happened would affect its sale, because it had been mentioned as the future home of Philip and me. People might think it unlucky. That was, after all, how legends became attached to places.

As I stood in the square looking at it, it seemed as though the house mocked me. I had had the fanciful notion that it had never wanted me and had warned me to keep away; and I had failed to heed that warning while, without doubt, being aware of it.

I did not go out very much. The Carringtons avoided me. I supposed the very sight of me would be painful to them, and moreover, they were in mourning and did not entertain. When people came to the house Cousin Agatha, who was as completely indifferent to my feelings as she had ever been, suggested I keep out of the way. "We don't want all that gossip starting up again," she said with an unpleasant laugh. "It's most embarrassing."

Frustrated and unhappy, I lived from day to day, but I knew that the state of affairs would not go on.

I was right. Cousin Agatha summoned me to her sitting room.

As I stood before her she looked at me with distaste.

My brief glory was over and I had sunk back into the role of Poor Relation.

"I suppose," she said, "it will take us a long time to live down this very unfortunate affair. Of course I never really believed that marriage would take place. I always thought something would happen to prevent it. If I had had my way . . ." She shook her head, implying that she would never have given her consent to the marriage; perhaps she would have forced Philip to take Esmeralda.

She sighed. I had lost my spirit and made no comment. I no longer felt the irresistible desire to defy her.

"However, every cloud has a silver lining, they say, and it seems that in your case this may be so." I looked at her in astonishment and she gave me a wintry smile. I might have known her pleasure would be my pain.

"Mrs. Oman Lemming had decided to employ someone else but had not completed her search for the right person. Now that you are in need of a post she has decided in her kindness that she will ignore convention and give you a chance."

"Oh no," I protested.

"Yes. I know it is generous of her. All that fuss in the papers. Why, one might say you are a marked woman. However, she is of the opinion that in due course this will be forgotten and that it may have had a salutory effect upon you. I had to be honest with her and therefore considered it my duty to inform her that you could at times be pert and that your position in this family—and your connection with us—had given you certain ideas. Mr. Loring being absurdly tolerant—in fact, I have so often to restrain him—did not wish you to be made aware of your position. . . ."

"So you disobeyed him," I could not resist saying.

"I do not understand. I trust you are not being *pert* again, Ellen. One in your position should be especially contrite."

"Why? What have I done?"

"My dear Ellen," she said in a voice that showed I was far from dear to her, "when a man commits suicide rather than marry, people will always look askance at the woman who was to have been his wife."

"It had nothing to do with our marriage. Philip was in love with me. He wanted our marriage more than anything. And he did not kill himself. I am sure of it. Only the day before he died . . ."

"No hysterics, please. You must remember your place."

"Are hysterics reserved then for rich relations only?"

"I don't know what you are talking about. You are distraught and the best thing for you is to go to your new life as quickly as possible. There is nothing like work to help you over an unfortunate spell. Work, work, and then more work. So, as Mrs. Oman Lemming is prepared to take you, I have said that you will go to her at the end of the month."

I felt as though I were drowning in my misery. Philip was gone and there was no one to help me now.

I must prepare my trunk. I needed good serviceable clothes, said Cousin Agatha. I looked at my dateless black evening gown. There was a slight stain on it where the orchid had rested. I wished I had kept that orchid. It would always have reminded me of Philip on that night when he had astounded me and Cousin Agatha by asking me to marry him.

What I did have was a wardrobe of beautiful garments which were to have been my trousseau. I was sure Cousin Agatha would have liked to confiscate them but she could scarcely do that. They wouldn't fit Esmeralda, as I was much taller and thinner than she was. But what comfort were clothes when one was lost in a cruel world! My little craft—once so jaunty, once sailing with full honors beside the Carrington galleon of plenty—was now soon to be wrecked on the rocks of misery presided over by the Honorable Mrs. Oman Lemming, compared with whom Cousin Agatha might be considered quite charming.

There were times when I felt indifferent to my future. What was my misery compared with Philip's death? I had lost my champion and I felt even more sad because I had not appreciated him when he lived. It sometimes seemed of small moment that I was drifting towards the colorless existence of a governess in a household of which the servants spoke in distaste.

I awoke the next morning to the feeling of depression which had overwhelmed me so often since Philip's death, to find that there was a letter waiting for me. I did not know the writing on the envelope. It was big and bold in thick black ink.

The letter was headed Far Island, Polcrag, Cornwall. "Dear Miss Kellaway," it ran.

> *When you read this letter you will be wondering why I have not written before. The truth is that I only recently discovered your whereabouts. You will see that I live in this remote spot which was your father's home. When he died, about a year ago, he appointed me your guardian until you should reach the age of twenty-one. I know that you have not yet reached that age but will do so on your next birthday. It would give me great pleasure if you would visit the Island. I believe you have been kept in ignorance of your father's family and I am sure would like to know more. Do please come and visit us here. It would give me great pleasure if you would.*
>
>                                        JAGO KELLAWAY

I read the letter through several times. The Far Island. No one had ever mentioned it to me. My father's home! What had I heard of my father? Only that my mother had left him when I was three years old, taking me with her. I found a map and turned up the appropriate page. The Island must be off the Cornish coast but Polcrag was not marked on the map.

My first impulse was to find Cousin Agatha and ask her what she knew of my father, but I hesitated. She was so set on my becoming a governess in the household of the

Honorable Mrs. Oman Lemming that she would be capable of doing anything to prevent my going away. I was beginning to feel excited. There was something fateful about receiving a letter so fortuitously. The Far Island sounded romantic; and my father had been dead only a year. How tragic that he should have been living and I had never known him!

I said nothing about the letter, not even to Esmeralda, until by good luck I found an opportunity of speaking to Cousin William Loring. I showed him the letter and asked what he knew about it.

"Why, yes," he said, "your mother did marry and go off to this island. Something went wrong with the marriage and she ran away, taking you with her. Your father made no provision for her, which is not surprising, since she left him. When she ran away she forfeited everything—for herself and for you—apparently."

"Who is this Jago Kellaway?"

"He must be some sort of relation." He looked at me quizzically and I saw the compassion in his eyes. "Unfortunately I can tell you very little, Ellen, but I do remember that was the name of the island where your father lived. And if he is now dead and these people are asking you to visit them, perhaps they will make amends for his not bothering with you all these years." He laid a hand on my arm. "It is not my wish that you should take this post, Ellen. As far as I am concerned, you are welcome. . . ."

"I know. Thank you, Cousin William." I felt I wanted to stop his saying something disloyal about his wife which he might regret later. "What I wanted to be sure about," I went on, "is that this is truly my father's family. And you think I ought to go and see them?"

He nodded and I could see that he thought it might be a fortunate way out of my present difficulties.

That afternoon Mrs. Oman Lemming called. From my window I saw her arrive. I hated the angle at which she wore her overflowered hat as much as I hated the arrogant manner in which she ignored her footman as he handed her out of her carriage.

Soon I should be sent for and expected to go down and stand before them, eyes downcast, the Poor Relation to whom they were being so generous: Cousin Agatha, who had resented me all these years I had spent under her roof, and Mrs. Oman Lemming, who was so graciously forgetting the part they had decided I must have played in the recent tragedy and was giving me the unique opportunity to be bullied and humiliated under her roof!

And so I sat down without further delay and wrote to Jago Kellaway, telling him that I should be delighted to come to the Far Island and must indeed join members of my family and bridge the gap of years.

I had completed the letter when the summons came and the envelope lay sealed in front of me.

It was Bessie, knocking faintly as though she were sorry to have to bring such an order.

"Miss Ellen, the mistress wants you in her sitting room. That Mrs. Oman Lemming's there."

Defiantly I went down, my old spirits briefly reviving. I was not going to Mrs. Oman Lemming to be humiliated and treated with disdain. I was going to visit my relations in the Far Island off the coast of Cornwall.

# PART TWO

---

# The Island

# A Glimpse of Hydrock Manor

It was late afternoon when I arrived at Polcrag, for after leaving the main-line train I had had to make the six- or seven-mile journey on the small local one. There was a fly waiting at the station and I asked the driver to take me and my baggage to the Polcrag Inn. Jago Kellaway had suggested this procedure when he had written to say he was delighted that I was accepting his invitation.

"For," he wrote, "the Island is three miles out to sea, on whose pleasure I am afraid we have to wait. It may well be, my dear, that the boats can't come in when you arrive, in which case it is better for you to be at the Polcrag Inn, the landlord of which I know well, and I shall tell them to take especial care of you there."

My possessions—all I owned—filled three moderate-sized bags, and most of this was clothes which had been made for my trousseau so, ironically enough, now that I was leaving London society, I was better equipped for it than I had ever been in my life.

Esmeralda had bidden me a tearful farewell and Cousin

Agatha had made little attempt to hide her relief in being rid of me, while Cousin William had slipped a purse of sovereigns into my hand with a murmur: "I insist on your taking it, Ellen. You may need it."

As we clopped along from the station to the inn, I took stock of the little town which clustered below and yet at the same time seemed to climb the surrounding cliffs. Some of the houses were approached by steep slopes, others by steps cut out of the cliffside. They were made of gray Cornish stone and many of them had glassed-in porches undoubtedly for the dual purpose of catching the sun and keeping out the wind, which I imagined would blow in from the sea. The Polcrag Inn, a building of three stories with an archway at the side, stood in the main street, and we drove under this arch to the stables. Just as I was about to alight a man who wore a leather apron about his waist, and whom I guessed rightly to be the host, came into the yard.

"You'm Miss Kellaway," he said, "if I be not mistook."

I said that I was indeed Miss Kellaway.

" 'Tis a fine room I have for 'ee. I've been warned of your coming."

"I thought I should cross to the Island today," I said.

"Lord love you, no, Miss. The sea be proper treacherous today. Did you see the white horses out there, far out 'tis true but when you see them you know 'tis no time to take out the boat for the Island."

"So then I must stay the night here?"

" 'Tis the only thing, Miss Kellaway, and we'm prepared. Orders is you'm to be well looked after till the boat do come for 'ee."

Disappointed as I was not to reach the Island that day, I was comforted by the fact that my new-found kinsman had shown such concern for my well-being.

"Jim here will take your bags up and maybe tomorrow they wicked old white horses will go to stable."

I followed him across the courtyard to a door through which he led me. We were in a hall dominated by an oak chest on which stood a large pewter plate.

"Where be to, me dear," called the innkeeper, and a woman came into the hall.

"This be Miss Kellaway," said the innkeeper.

The woman's eyes opened wide as she looked at me wonderingly. "Be it so then?" she said, and dropped a curtsy. "I'd best be taking her to her room," she went on.

"I'd like to wash, please," I told her, "and change my blouse."

"So 'ee shall," said the innkeeper's wife. "If you will follow me, Miss Kellaway."

The innkeeper watched me as I ascended the stairs.

"This be the room, Miss Kellaway," said his wife, throwing open a door. " 'Tis the best in the inn. 'Twas to be kept for 'ee case you should have to stay a while. I'll have hot water sent up to 'ee."

"Thank you."

"Oh, 'tis a pleasure, Miss Kellaway. 'Twouldn't do to give you aught but the best. We'll have your bags sent up in a trice."

She hesitated. She had scarcely taken her eyes from me since she had seen me. I looked at her inquiringly, for I had the impression that she wanted to tell me something.

She did. After a second or so's hesitation she burst out: "I knew your mother. You'm like her."

"You knew my mother! How interesting."

She nodded. "I were maid to her before I married Tom Pengelly. I were with her . . . until she left."

"I'm so glad to meet someone who knew her. I was five when she died and one doesn't remember very much at that age."

She nodded. "Well, so you'm here. Little Miss Ellen! My word, you've changed."

I smiled. "I suppose I have since you last saw me. I could only have been about three years old then."

"Time passes," she mused. "It seems only yesterday, though much have happened since, I reckon. My boy's over there." She nodded towards the window. "He works for Mr. Jago. You look out for Augustus—though he be known as Slack."

"I will," I promised.

"I were married soon after your mother went off and Pengelly and I had Augustus. There be nothing wrong with him. 'Twere just that he was born too soon. He'm a good boy."

There was a knock on the door and a maid appeared with hot water followed by a boy with my bags.

"There be roast pig cooking in the oven," said Mrs. Pengelly as she went out.

I crossed to the window and looked at a magnificent view of the sea. I strained my eyes for a glimpse of the Island but all I could see were ominous dark clouds which were being scurried across a gray sky by that wind which was whipping up the white horses whose presence was holding me on the mainland.

There was a tap on the door and a girl with towels entered.

"Can you ever see the Far Island from here?" I asked her.

"If it be clear enough, Miss."

As I washed and changed my blouse I was becoming more and more excited, for now I should learn something about my parents. All I knew was that they had been unhappy together because my mother had left my father. I had often wondered about him and pictured him as a sort of ogre. I believed then that this adventure was going to prove exactly what I needed to take me away from a past in which I could only grieve for Philip's death and suffer a certain remorse because I had not appreciated him enough when he was alive.

I did not unpack very much since I hoped I should be leaving the next day when the white horses had "gone to stable." I wondered whether Jago Kellaway would come to meet me and what he would be like. There had been a very warm welcome in his letter and I was growing very eager to meet him.

As I descended the stairs the savory smell of roasting pork made me feel hungry for the first time since Philip's death. There were no other guests in the dining room and, seeing that I had noticed this, Mrs. Pengelly explained that it was early yet. "We thought you'd be ready for it after traveling," she added.

I assured her that I was and I was sure that she was glad, as I was, that we were the only people in the dining room because that gave us an opportunity to talk.

"You must have known my mother very well," I began, determined to make the most of that opportunity.

"Oh yes, Miss Kellaway. You too, when you was a little 'un. You was a lively one, you was. 'Twas one body's work keeping you out of mischief."

"Why did my mother leave the Island?"

Mrs. Pengelly looked taken aback. "Well, my dear, that were for reasons best known to herself. Reckon her and your father didn't get along so well."

The innkeeper came into the room saying that he wanted to know how I was enjoying the meal and when I told him it was excellent, he rubbed his hands together and looked pleased; but I did intercept a look he gave his wife and I wondered whether he had come not only to assure himself of my satisfaction but to warn her against talking too much.

"If there's anything else you'm wanting," he began.

I told him there was nothing and his wife asked if I would like coffee and, when I said I would, she replied that it would be served in the inn parlor.

"I'll bring it to 'ee," she added, with, I thought, a promise to continue our conversation, but when she brought it and I tried to ask her more about my parents, she clamped her lips together as though she was not going to let them say what they would obviously have liked to, and I guessed her husband had warned her against indiscreet talk.

Was there something mysterious about the Island and its inhabitants? I wondered.

I finished my coffee and went up to my room, where I sat by the window looking out over the sea. It was a beautiful sight, for the moon had arisen and was throwing a pathway of silver light across the dark water. I fancied the sea was calmer than it had been on my arrival and that the wind was less persistently strong.

They'll come for me in the morning, I told myself.

The great feather bed in the cozy room was warm, but I could not sleep very well and when I did doze it was inevitable that I should have the dream. This time it was vague and shadowy. Again I stood in the room which I just recognized by the red curtains, but as the objects, with which I had become familiar over the years—the rocking chair, the picture, the brick fireplace, the gate-legged table and the rest—began to take shape, I awoke.

My feelings as I did so were not so much of apprehension, which was the usual reaction, as of excitement and a great desire to discover, as though I were at last on the verge of learning the meaning behind the mists of my dream. For a few seconds after waking I could not remember where I was and I got out of bed to stand at the window and gaze out to sea in the direction where I knew the Island to be. I realized that my dream had reflected my feelings to some extent, for I was indeed about to embark on a voyage of discovery.

In the early morning the wind had risen again and the waves were now pounding on the shore. I was dismayed. Yesterday's white horses had not returned to their stables; in fact, more had come out to join them.

I went down to breakfast. Mrs. Pengelly shook her head dolefully. "There be quite a sea on," she said. "There'll be no boats this morning."

I ate her freshly baked bread hot from the oven so that the butter melted into it as I spread it, and drank hot coffee from a brown earthenware mug. The day stretched before me, and I said I would stroll out to look at the town.

There was not a great deal of the town when one left the main street, just a few shops and houses and very little more. I noticed people looked at me curiously and supposed they were unused to visitors.

The post office was the general store and I decided that I would go in and buy some stamps, for I had promised

to let Esmeralda know at the earliest possible moment
how I had fared on my journey.

When I arrived on the Island I would write to her at
length, giving her all those details which I knew she would
relish, but that would be later and she would be longing
to know something at once.

The postmistress and her husband, who was serving at
another counter, looked up when I walked in. I smiled and
said good morning, to which they replied cautiously.
While she was getting the stamps the postmistress, recog-
nizing me as a stranger, asked if I was visiting here.

"Yes," I replied, "although not on the mainland. I'm
waiting for the sea to grow calm enough."

"So you be going to the Islands then?"

"Yes. My family have asked me to stay with them."

"And you've never been there before!"

"Actually I was born on the Far Island but I haven't
been back since I was three."

"You can't be . . ."

"I'm Ellen Kellaway."

She stared at me in astonishment. "Well now," she said
at length. "That be something!"

"You apparently know my family."

"Everyone do know the Kellaways. There's been Kellaways on the Far Island for hundreds of years, 'tis said."

"Mr. Jago Kellaway has invited me to stay. You know
him, of course."

"Well, he be the Lord of the Island, as they do say."

I was aware that everyone in the shop was interested in
me and it suddenly occurred to me that I had been talking
too much and in a somewhat naïve fashion, so I hastily
paid for the stamps and went back to the inn, where I ate
a cold luncheon of ham, cheese and fruit.

The long afternoon had begun and the sea had not
changed for the better. The clouds were as lowering as
they had been the day before and the waves, edged with
white froth which the wind sent high into the air, were
thundering on the sands.

I could not stay in, so I decided to walk again. I turned

from the main street and went on towards the harbor. One or two little boats were tied up there. I read their names. *Our Sally. Jennie. Gay Lass. Bold Adventurer.* They danced on the water washing the quayside. I passed lobster pots, and a fisherman who was mending his nets looked at me curiously as I passed. I called a greeting. He mumbled a reply, and went on mending his nets. There was a big shed smelling of fish and in it was a great weighing machine. The fish market, I imagined, but silent and empty today. None of the little boats could go out. The gulls shrieked protestingly, it seemed, because of the lack of tidbits to which they would be accustomed when the catch came in.

I left the coast and took a winding path through some woods thinking of all that I was trying to forget. I found it so hard to shut out of my mind for any length of time the memory of Philip's face creased in laughter, gently mocking, but always ready to protect me; and as frequently I saw Rollo's accusing eyes. It was deeply wounding to know that he suspected me of having driven Philip to his death.

"Oh Philip," I said aloud, "I will never believe you did that. It is quite impossible; I know it is. But what happened?"

And there I was as close to the tragedy as I had been on the morning Rollo had come to tell me it had happened.

Because my thoughts had been far away in the past I had not noticed how deep into the woods I had penetrated and it occurred to me that I ought to retrace my steps and return to the inn, but I was in no great hurry to do this, as there was a lonely evening ahead of me.

I must not get lost, however, so I did turn and, as I thought, went back the way I had come, expecting I should shortly arrive at the spot where the trees grew less closely together and glimpse the sea again. But I did not and very soon I had lost all sense of direction and realized with dismay that I was lost.

I assured myself that I must eventually come out to the

sea, but after I had walked for half an hour I was still in the woods. At last I came to a gate and hopefully opened it and passed through. Here the trees grew less thick and I thought that if I went on I might come to a house and ask the way.

As I entered a clearing I heard the sound of horse's hoofs and a rider came into sight. It was a man on a gray horse and he hurriedly pulled up at the sight of me.

"Can you help me?" I asked. "I'm lost."

"You are in fact trespassing," he replied. "These woods are private because of the pheasants."

"Oh dear, I *am* sorry. I was really trying to find my way out of them."

"Where do you want to go?" he asked.

"I'm staying at the Polcrag Inn."

"You have come a long way."

"Longer than I realized, I'm afraid."

"The easiest way now is past the house. Actually that is even more private, but it's a shortcut."

"Do you think the owner would mind?"

"I'm sure he wouldn't," he said with a smile. "As a matter of fact, I don't and it's my house. I'm Michael Hydrock."

"Then these are your woods. I must apologize."

"Oh, strangers often stray in. It's so easy to slip into the private section. We should have more notices put up."

"If you will kindly show me the way I should be grateful."

"I will with pleasure."

I took a step forward and as I did so tripped over an old beech trunk and fell sprawling onto the grass.

He immediately sprang from his horse and helped me up. I noticed what a pleasant face he had, it was comforting to see that he looked really concerned.

"Are you hurt?" he asked.

"I don't think so." I stood up. Then I touched my ankle.

"You can stand on it, I see. Can you walk?"

"Yes. I think so."

"It might be painful later. You certainly can't walk all the way back. I tell you what we'll do. We're close to the house. We'll go in and see how badly hurt you are and I could send you to the inn in a carriage."

"This is too kind."

"Not at all. I'll help you onto my horse and I can walk it back," he said.

"That's quite unnecessary. I'm sure I can hobble."

"You might do some harm if you did," he insisted quietly.

"But I'm being such a nuisance. First I trespass and then you have to give up your horse for me."

"It's the least I can do," said the man.

He helped me onto his horse and, walking beside it, led it forward.

There is one thing I shall never forget—my first glimpse of Hydrock Manor House. We had come out of the wood and there before us it stood—this gray stone dwelling with its embattled gatehouse and the pointed arch at the entrance, the spandrels of the doorway decorated with Gothic patterns. On the smoothest and greenest of lawns I believed I had ever seen strutted a gorgeous peacock, brilliant and disdainful, followed admiringly by his comparatively drab little mate.

I experienced a deep sense of peace such as I had never known before. Places had always affected me deeply. For no reason I felt suddenly happy to be there in spite of the fact that I had hurt my ankle and was dependent on the kindness of a stranger.

There was a gravel path cutting across the lawn to the archway and we went along this and through the arch into a courtyard. Here, too, the sense of deep peace prevailed. Little tufts of grass grew between the cobbles, onto which latticed windows looked out.

The man called "Tom!" and helped me from my horse. Tom, obviously a groom, came hurrying out; he gave me a look as if surprised and took the horse.

"Come this way," said my host, and led me through a door.

We were in a hall—not large but beautifully proportioned, with a hammer-beam-type roof. The floor was paved in a mosaic design and there was a dais at one end and a minstrel gallery at the other.

"I think," said Michael Hydrock, "that I'd better call my old housekeeper. She would know whether the ankle is badly hurt or not. She's something of an authority on such matters. But first, do sit down."

He pulled a bell rope and I heard a bell clanging through the house as I sat down gratefully on one of the wooden chairs, which must have dated back to the sixteenth century, and looked up at the fine tapestry on the walls.

He followed my gaze. "It represents the events in the life of Bishop Trelawny, who is highly thought of here," he told me. "There you see him on his way to the Tower of London. And there you see the people of Cornwall marching. You probably know the old song. Most people do:

> *"And shall they score Tre Pol and Pen*
> *And shall Trelawny die . . ."*

I finished:

> *"Then twenty thousand Cornishmen*
> *Will know the reason why."*

"Ah," he said, "I see you do know it."

"Very well. I was wondering how many stitches have gone into all that fine work. It is very beautiful."

A manservant appeared. "Tell Mrs. Hocking to come here, please," said Michael Hydrock, and when the man had gone he explained: "Mrs. Hocking is my housekeeper. She has been with us all my life."

Before I had time to reply Mrs. Hocking had joined us. She was in her late sixties, I imagined, and there was about her the air of the servant who has been with the family for so many years that she regards herself as a privileged person.

Michael Hydrock explained to her what had happened and she knelt down and gently prodded my ankle. "Does that hurt?" she asked.

"A little."

"Stand up," she commanded. I did so. "Now step on it . . . put your whole weight on it." I did that too. "All right?" she asked, and I said I thought it was.

" 'Tis only a slight sprain," she announced. "I'd rest it today. Like as not it will be all right by tomorrow."

"I'll take you back to the inn in the carriage," said Michael Hydrock.

"Oh, surely I can walk," I protested.

Mrs. Hocking shook her head. " 'Twould be putting too much weight on it today."

"I don't know how to thank you both," I said.

"We're only too pleased to help, Miss . . . er . . ."

"Kellaway," I said. "I'm Ellen Kellaway."

The silence was immediate. Then Michael Hydrock said: "You must be related to the Kellaways of the Island."

"Yes. I'm on my way to them. I'm only staying at the Polcrag Inn until the weather permits me to cross."

Mrs. Hocking had pressed her lips together and I fancied that the fact that I was Ellen Kellaway had not exactly endeared me to her  I wondered why.

Michael Hydrock said: "I daresay you would like some tea. Mrs. Hocking, will you have it sent, please. We'll have it in the winter parlor. It won't be far for you to walk, Miss Kellaway."

I said halfheartedly: "I shall be giving you so much trouble . . ." and waited for him to protest that this was not so and was in fact a pleasure, which of course he did with a certain Old World charm.

Mrs. Hocking went away and he said: "Do you feel you can walk a little way?"

"Easily. In fact, I think I'm really here under false pretenses. My ankle scarcely hurts at all."

He took my arm and led me across the hall. We mounted a stone staircase which led to a room which was clearly the dining room. Here again there were beautiful tapestries on the walls and I noticed the big latticed windows at one end of the room through which I could see another courtyard. About six steps led from this room into the winter parlor, where I presumed the family took their meals when they were not a large company. In the center of the room was an oval gate-legged table on turned baluster legs and about it tapestry-covered chairs. It was an intimate room with one small window.

"Do be seated," said Michael Hydrock. "How does the ankle feel after that little walk?"

"I can hardly feel it, I'm sure it's nothing very much."

I said I thought the house was delightful, which clearly pleased him. "I think so too," he said, "but it is my home and has been that of my family for about four hundred years."

"It must be wonderful," I said, "to feel one belongs to such a place."

"One accepts it as a matter of course, I'm afraid. I was born here and I suppose I shall die here. And so have the men of our family for generations. The women usually marry and go off somewhere else. But every stone of this place is familiar to me. It's small as these manor houses go, but to me it's just as it should be. You're not a countrywoman, Miss Kellaway?"

"No, not really. Although we did spend several months of the summer in the country, I have always considered London to have been my home."

The tea was brought by a young girl. Mrs. Hocking accompanied her.

The tray with its Georgian silver teapot and kettle on a spirit lamp was set on the table, and there were little sugar cakes on a silver salver.

"Shall I pour?" asked Mrs. Hocking, and I was aware of the look of cold disapproval she directed towards me.

"Perhaps Miss Kellaway would like to," suggested Michael, and I immediately said I would.

I was glad when the old woman had gone, taking the young serving girl with her, and as I poured out the tea I felt that I was having a delightful adventure. There was something very relaxing about this room which made me feel completely at ease and I was liking my rescuer more every moment. He was serious—perhaps I was comparing him with Philip—yet warm and friendly; and suddenly I was talking—perhaps too freely—of my life in London and before I realized it I was explaining that I had been on the point of marriage and that my fiancé had died.

"What a terrible tragedy!" said Michael Hydrock.

I wondered whether he had heard the story. Heaven knew, it had been publicized enough. I realized that Michael Hydrock was the sort of man whose good manners would insist on his betraying no curiosity about such a delicate matter, at the same time not allowing him to mention the fact that he knew the story already, in case it should distress me.

"So," I went on, "when my relations wrote to me and asked me to come and visit them, I came. It's to be an indefinite visit. I thought that to be in fresh surroundings would help me to plan what I was going to do."

"It was wise," said Michael.

"As a matter of fact I didn't know I had this family until a few weeks ago." I told him about life with Cousin Agatha and Esmeralda. Looking back I found it all seemed rather humorous, as so many things do which are rather grim to live through.

"Yes, I'm longing to meet my relations," I added. "They seem to be very well known hereabouts."

"Everyone in the neighborhood knows Jago Kellaway."

"What sort of a man is he?"

Michael Hydrock smiled. "It's hard to describe him because there can't be another person in the world like him."

"I suppose I must wait until I see him. Do you often go to the Island and do they come here?"

"I do know some members of the household," said Michael gravely.

I could see there was a hint in his manner which meant

that he hoped I would not carry that inquiry further.

He told me about the countryside then, of the places to visit and the customs of the people. On feast days and holidays there was usually a wrestling match and the prize would be a fine hat made and presented by the town hatter or a buff waistcoat supplied by the tailor. There would be running matches and prizes for cooking for the women, for which they could win a holland shift or some such garment. There were dancing, throwing the hammer and indulging in all kinds of sport.

In May there was the furry dance—a welcome to the summer—which the gentry danced at midday—the children at ten-thirty and the servants later in the day; then there were the hurling matches, which were almost as popular as the wrestling. But Midsummer was the greatest feast of all. "It is the worship of the sun," said Michael Hydrock. "It has come down to us from pre-Christian days. You should see the people dancing round the fires. It's supposed to be a precaution against witchcraft. In the old pagan days they used to throw a living thing into the fire as a talisman against the evil eye. In some places now they throw in floral hoops and herbs, flowers of all kinds. Some of the old superstitions still prevail. And of course there are the midnight bonfires. You should see them springing up all over the moors."

It was all very interesting but finally it occurred to me that I was staying too long. So I thanked him for the hospitality and said I must be on my way. It had been such an enjoyable afternoon and I was glad I had been lost in the wood.

The pony trap had arrived and I was helped into it. Michael Hydrock took the reins and I sat beside him. His clean-cut profile was turned towards me and I thought what a pleasant face his was—not exactly distinguished but kindly. Here was a man whom it would be easy to understand: I felt he could be relied on to act in a predictable manner.

He said: "I fancy the wind is softening a little. It may

well be that the sea will be calm enough for you to go out to the Island tomorrow morning."

"I had no idea that I should be delayed so long."

"It's the geographical location of the Island actually. It's not so far from the land—only three miles—but this coast has its idiosyncrasies. It's a treacherous coast at the best of times and it's unwise to go out with anyone but an experienced boatman. There's a mass of rock just below the sea which has to be carefully skirted and there are quicksands about a mile or so east of Polcrag beach. It has been said that was why the Island was called the Far Isle. You see, it's not that it is so very far from the mainland, just that conditions so often put it out of reach."

"Is there more than one island?"

"There's the main one, which is moderately large as islands go. It's about ten miles by five; then there is a small one very close. There is only one house on that one. There is another, too, which is not inhabited at all and which is a sort of bird sanctuary."

We were almost in the town and I could see the beginning of the Polcrag street. I was sorry, for I wanted to go on riding with Michael Hydrock and hearing about the life of the neighborhood. I thought I might perhaps glean a little more information about my family.

"It was kind of you to take such care of me after I'd trespassed," I told him.

"I felt guilty because you'd tripped in my woods."

"Where I had no right to be! But I'm afraid I can't say I'm sorry. It's been such a delightful afternoon."

"One thing, it has shown you a little of our countryside. We shall meet again as you won't be far off."

"I do hope so. Do you often come to the Island?"

"Occasionally. And you must come to Hydrock Manor when you are on the mainland."

"I must pick a fair day if I don't want to get stranded."

"I think it may be possible for you to cross tomorrow. In fact the signs indicate that it almost certainly will be."

I felt excited at the prospect.

Now we were right in the town. One or two people

looked after the pony trap and I guessed they must be wondering who the stranger was with Michael Hydrock.

As we entered the inn yard Mrs. Pengelly, who happened to be there, looked at us in blank amazement.

Michael Hydrock smiled at her. "It's all right, Mrs. Pengelly. Miss Kellaway hurt her ankle in the woods and I've brought her back."

"My dear life!" she exclaimed.

Michael had leaped down and was helping me out.

"How is it?" he asked as I stood on my feet.

"Quite all right, I think. I can scarcely feel anything."

"Well sir," said Mrs. Pengelly, "would you come in and drink a tankard of ale or a goblet of wine or should I make a nice brew of tea?"

"Thank you but no, Mrs. Pengelly. I must be off now." He took my hand and smiled at me gently.

"Be careful of the ankle," he said. "And when you come to the mainland . . . or if you feel at any time you need . . . and you would like to, do call. I should be delighted."

"You have been most good to me," I said earnestly.

"It was nothing and has been a pleasure."

Then he was back in the trap and, smiling, turned the horse, who trotted out of the courtyard.

Mrs. Pengelly and I stood together watching him.

Then I went into the inn and up to my room, where I lay on the bed, my foot stretched out before me. I had not been there five minutes when there was a tap on the door and Mrs. Pengelly came in. Her eyes were alight with curiosity. I could see that she thought it very odd that I should have been brought back by Michael Hydrock.

She said: "I wondered if there was anything I could get you, Miss Kellaway?"

I assured her there was nothing I wanted but she lingered and I could see she wanted to talk and I must admit that I was eager that she should do so, for since she had known my mother and actually lived on the Island there was obviously a great deal she could tell me.

"It was strange that you should meet Sir Michael," she said.

"I had no idea that he was *Sir* Michael."

"Oh yes, the title's been in the family for years . . . one of the Hydrocks was knighted years ago . . . something to do with fighting for the King against the Parliament, and when the King came back, there was title and lands for the family."

"I gathered they had been at the Manor for generations. It's a wonderful old place."

"The Hydrocks have been the squires of these lands ever since they got the title and that's going back a few years—just as the Kellaways have owned the Far Island for about as many years."

"They own the Island?"

"Why yes, 'tis often known as Kellaway's Isle."

"There are surely not just Kellaways there."

"Bless you, no. It's a thriving community. Leastways it's been so since. . . . It's got its farmlands and shops and there's even an inn. People go there for quietness. You can feel really cut away from the world there."

"Mrs. Pengelly, what do you know about my mother and father?"

She spread her hands before her and gazed down at them as though looking for inspiration there. Then she raised her eyes and looked straight into mine. "She just couldn't abide the place," she said. "She was always saying she would leave. There were quarrels. Your father was not an easy man to live with. Then she just went away and took you with her. That's all I know."

"You were her maid so you must have lived close to her."

Mrs. Pengelly lifted her shoulders. "She came from the town. She used to hate the sound of the waves pounding on the shores. She said the cries of the gulls were like voices jeering at her because she was a prisoner."

"A prisoner!"

"That was how she felt . . . having left her home in London and coming down to Kellaway's Isle. . . ."

"So she left her home, her husband, everything . . . except me. She must have been unhappy."

"She was so bright and lively when she came here. Then she changed. There's some people Kellaway's Isle wouldn't suit and she's one of them."

"What of my father? Didn't he try to bring her back?"

"No, he just let her go."

"So he didn't care very much about either of us."

"He wasn't the sort of man to be very interested in children. And then of course . . ."

She trailed off and I said eagerly: "Yes, what?"

"Oh, nothing. I left then. There was no cause for me to be there when she was gone. I came back to the mainland. My father kept this inn then and I married Pengelly and he helped me to run the inn, and then my father died and it passed to us."

"Who is Jago Kellaway . . . what relation to me?"

"Now that's something he'll tell you. He wouldn't want me to be talking too much."

"You seem afraid of him."

"He's not the sort a body would want to offend."

"He's my guardian apparently."

"Is that so then, Miss?"

"That's what he said in his letter."

"Well then it be right and proper that you be under his roof."

"There seems to be a sort of mystery about the Island or the Kellaways. I notice a change in people when they learn who I am."

"They'd be surprised, I reckon. Hereabouts people know something about others' business and they'd know your mother went off with her child and you be that child. Stands to reason they're interested to see what you've grown up like."

"Is that all it is? I wish I knew more about the Island and my family."

"Well, Miss, that'll be something you'll soon be finding out, won't it? My dear life, I be forgetting I have work to do. Be 'ee sure there's nothing I can bring 'ee?"

I thanked her and assured her I wanted nothing. I could see that she was a little afraid that she might have said too much and that I might trap her into saying still more.

The evening passed quickly. I kept going over the events of the day and I told myself that I should not be completely sorry if the sea prevented my crossing to the Island for another day, for I might see Michael Hydrock again.

Next morning I awoke to a calm sea, glittering in the sunshine.

I was sure I would cross to the Island on that day and I was right. At ten o'clock in the morning the boat arrived.

# The Castle

I saw it from my window. A man and a boy alighted and two oarsmen remained in the boat. The man was of medium height, thick-set, with light brown hair; the boy slim and I imagined about fourteen years of age. I went downstairs. Mrs. Pengelly greeted me. "The boat be come, Miss Kellaway."

One of the men from the inn stables brought down my bags and by that time the man and the boy had come into the inn.

Mrs. Pengelly bustled around very eager to please.

"Oh, Mr. Tregardier, so you be come at last. I did see how 'twas. Miss Kellaway will be pleased to see 'ee, I know."

The man held out his hand and shook mine. He studied me with curiosity.

"I am so pleased to meet you at last," he said. "I'm William Tregardier, Mr. Kellaway's estate manager. He wants me to tell you how eagerly he is awaiting your arrival on the Island. Alas we have been at the mercy of the sea."

"It's calm this morning."

"Like a lake. You can be sure we set out as soon as it was possible to do so. We didn't want you to have a rough crossing right at the start. That would have given you a very bad impression."

He was smiling in a rather benign way and Mrs. Pengelly said: "You'd be liking some refreshment before you start out, Mr. Tregardier, I'll be bound."

"Well, it's a pleasant idea, Mrs. Pengelly."

"I'll be bringing you something. I've got my special bees wine if you'd care for it. There's my sloe gin too, a fresh batch of buns and a saffron cake hot from the oven."

"You know how to tempt me, Mrs. Pengelly."

"Why don't 'ee sit down and get acquainted with Miss Kellaway and I'll be back so fast you'll hardly known I'm gone."

She left us and Mr. Tregardier smiled at me.

"She's a good soul," he said, "and always ready to look after folk from the Island. She was once employed in the household and her son works for us, you know. Do let us sit down and, as she says, we'll get acquainted. First Mr. Jago wants me to tell you how pleased he is that you decided to visit us. The sea might not have been very hospitable but you will find your family very different. I trust there are no complaints about your reception at the inn."

"Complaints! Indeed I've been spoilt."

"That was what Jago wanted. I didn't doubt it would be so since he had given orders."

"I am longing to see the Island and my family. I'm afraid I know so little about them."

"Did your mother never talk to you?"

"I was only five years old when she died."

He nodded. "Well, Jago is in command of the Island. It's like a large estate. I work under him as chief estate manager, as it were. It's a large property really. It just happens to be an island. Jago's sister and his niece live with him. His sister keeps house. She has done so very many years."

"What relation is Jago to me?"

"He will explain all that. It's a little involved."

"It seems strange that all these years we have not been in touch with each other."

"That happens now and then in families, I believe. But better late than never."

Mrs. Pengelly brought in the wine and cakes and served us.

It must have been half an hour later when we set out for the Island. There was a light breeze blowing—just enough to ruffle the water—and the sun was now shining brilliantly. I felt my excitement rising and it was not long before the Island came into sight.

"There!" said William Tregardier. "That's a good way to see it. It looks fine, doesn't it—fine and fertile."

"It's beautiful!" I cried.

"The Far Island. More often known as Kellaway's Isle here."

A sudden pride took possession of me. After all, I was a Kellaway and it was thrilling to have my name associated with such a beautiful place.

"There's another island," I cried.

"That's the nearest. Known as Blue Rock for obvious reasons. It's not cultivated like the main island. It's more rocky and there's some sort of deposit on the rocks which in some lights gives it a bluish tinge. Now you can see that other island. It's just a hump rising out of the water. There's nothing there at all, but the choughs and sea gulls congregate there."

I turned my gaze back to the main island. The rock on one side rose in a stark cliff face beneath which was a sandy bay. I saw boats moored there.

"Are we going in there?" I asked.

"No," answered William Tregardier, "we land on the other side of the Island. It will look quite different from there. The water is very shallow here and there are certain rocks. One has to be careful. It's dangerous until you learn where the rocks and the currents are."

"How many people live on the Island?"

"I think the last time we counted the population was one hundred. It increases. People marry and have children. Many of them have been living here for generations."

The Island was now showing a different aspect. It was softer from this angle and I could see little houses with whitewashed walls and orange-colored roofs. There was a ridge of low hills running down to the sea—green and beautiful, brightened by purple heather and yellow gorse.

"It's lovely," I cried.

"It's almost subtropical where we are sheltered from the winds. We even have a palm tree or two growing on this side of the Island. Our fruit and vegetables are in advance of the mainland every year. But that's in the valleys where we are sheltered from the gales."

"I shall be so interested to explore and learn about the Island."

"That will please Jago, I'm sure."

We ran onto a sandy beach where two men were waiting—evidently for us—with horses.

"I trust you ride," said William Tregardier. "Jago was certain that you did."

'I wonder how he knew. I do, as a matter of fact. I've always been keen on riding."

"That's excellent. You'll be able to ride about the Island. It's the best way of getting around."

The slight breeze caught my bonnet strings and I was glad I had had the foresight to wear such headgear. Some of the smart hats from my trousseau would have been altogether useless and out of place. My baggage, which had been following in another boat, arrived at the same time as we did, and William Tregardier told one of the oarsmen to take care of it.

"I think you'd better try this little mare, Miss Kellaway," he said. "Later you will be able to select your own horse from the stable. I am sure that is what Jago will want. He keeps a very good stable."

I mounted the mare, which was a docile creature. Wil-

liam Tregardier took one of the other horses and we then
rode up from the beach.

"The castle is close by," he said.

"The castle!" I cried. "I had no idea we were going to
a castle."

"We always call it that. Kellaway Castle. It's very
ancient, so the name must have been given to it when the
family first came here."

We rounded a hill and there it was ahead of us.

It was indeed a castle with battlemented towers and
thick stone walls. It was a quadrangular edifice, its lofty
walls flanked by four circular towers rising above the cren-
ellated parapets of the roof. The stone gatehouse was
topped by yet another tower; it looked strongly formidable, as though defying intruders to approach. We passed
through it and were in a cobbled courtyard; from here we
went under a Norman archway into another courtyard
and as we did so a groom appeared as though he had been
stationed there to await our arrival.

"Take our horses, Albert. This is Miss Kellaway, who
has come to stay with us."

Albert touched his forelock to me and I said: "Good
day."

He took the horses and William Tregardier led the way
towards a heavy iron-studded door.

"I daresay you will wish to wash and perhaps change
before meeting Jago," he said. "I think the best thing is
to get one of the maids to show you to your room."

I was bemused. I had made up my mind that there
might be something primitive about a house on an island
three miles from the mainland. I had certainly been un-
prepared for such a castle. This was as grand as—no,
grander in its way than Hydrock Manor House and clearly
of an earlier period. We had entered by the side door and
passed along a passage into what seemed like a reception
room; sparsely furnished with a table and three chairs.
There was a suit of armor in one corner and shields and
weapons on the walls. I imagined it had once been part of
an armory or a guardroom.

It seemed as though everyone in the house was awaiting my coming, for no sooner had we stepped into this room than a maid came in from another door.

"Ah Janet," said William Tregardier, "there is Miss Kellaway."

Janet bobbed a curtsy.

"Take her to her room and see that she has everything she needs."

"Oh yes, sir," said Janet.

"Then in about . . ." He looked at me. "Say, half an hour?"

"Yes," I said, "that will do very well."

"In half an hour bring Miss Kellaway down."

"Thank you," I said.

"It's our pleasure to look after you well," he answered.

Janet said: "If you'd be pleased to follow me, Miss Kellaway."

I followed her, marveling. We went through several stone-floored passages and mounted a spiral stone staircase. Then we came to a gallery and were clearly in the more residential part of the castle, for the medieval aspect gave way to a somewhat more modern air of comfort.

"This way, Miss Kellaway."

She threw open a door and we entered a room on the walls of which were hung ancient tapestries in shades of red and gray. There was red carpet on the floor and curtains of red velvet trimmed with gold fringe. The four-poster bed had red velvet curtains about it, and the effect was luxurious.

The window—semicircular and cut out of an amazingly thick wall—had a window seat of stone around it. There were three stone steps to a window alcove. I mounted them and looked out. Although the castle was a little isolated standing on its incline, I could see that the Island was well populated. The little houses were picturesque and the orange roofs gave them a foreign look. There appeared to be a street in which were shops and what might be an inn. It was like a miniature town. I made out what must have been farmhouses surrounded by fields which had the neat patchwork effect of cultivated land. There were orchards and even a small forest and more houses. It appeared to be a pleasant, prosperous community. I could catch a glimpse of that other island, Blue Rock, which looked even nearer than the half mile distant that I had been told it was. Just a small channel of sea separated us. Then I gazed at the mainland and wondered what Michael Hydrock was doing now and whether he had given me another thought.

"It's magnificent," I said, turning from the window and surveying the room.

"Mr. Jago said as this was to be prepared for 'ee, Miss. 'Tis one of the best rooms in the whole of the castle."

"It is very kind of him."

She gave a little giggle. "Oh we've all been warned, Miss. We got to take very special care of 'ee."

It was indeed a warm welcome.

"If there's anything you do want, Miss . . ." She walked to the bell rope of red and gold. "You just pull this and I'll be with 'ee in next to no time. We did think everything be here but you can't ever be sure, can 'ee?"

At that moment a boy arrived with my baggage.

"Would 'ee like me to help 'ee unpack, Miss?" asked Janet.

"Thank you," I said. It was not so much that I wanted her to do that as to keep her with me that I might ask her a few questions. "There is not a great deal," I added. "It won't take long."

"I'll bring 'ee hot water first, Miss."

When she had left, I looked round the room at the oak settle, the big cupboard, the fireplace and the mantelpiece on which stood large candlesticks. The ceiling was lofty and ornately carved.

I opened one of my bags and took out a dress. It was one of those which had been made for my honeymoon and was in sapphire blue silk, which was particularly becoming. I remembered Philip's going with me for the last fitting. He had peeped round the door. "Why, Ellen," he had said, "I do believe I am marrying a beauty."

I felt suddenly wretched, and I could not stop myself thinking of the plans we had made for the honeymoon. "Venice," he had said. "Gondoliers. Serenades and the Grand Canal. Very romantic."

While I was standing there holding the dress Janet came in with the hot water.

"It's a beautiful dress, Miss," she said.

I nodded and laid it on the bed.

"Mr. Jago has just come in, Miss. He'll be wanting to see 'ee. I reckon you won't want to keep him waiting. He's just come in to the stables."

I said: "I will wash then."

Janet drew aside a curtain. Behind this was an alcove in which was a basin and ewer. She poured out the hot water for me and I washed while she hung up my dresses in the cupboard.

The blue dress was still lying on the bed.

I picked it up.

"You'll be wearing that one for dinner, Miss, will you?"

Before I could answer, there was a knock on the door and the boy Jim put his head in.

"Mr. Jago is in his parlor. He says Miss Kellaway is to go to him there."

Janet said: "All right, Jim. Get you gone. Come Miss, Mr. Jago don't like to be kept waiting."

I found that my hands were trembling. I was about to see this man of whom in the last few days I had begun to build up a formidable picture in my mind.

And so I went down to the parlor and my first meeting with Jago Kellaway. It was a magnificent room, that parlor with a deep bow window overlooking the sea. There was a big open fireplace with firedogs and a long stool in front covered with a tapestry which blended in with that which hung on the walls, and the ceiling was decorated with checkers and diapers in a pattern which incorporated the arms of the family. The name "parlor" seemed incongruous when applied to such a room. It was gracious and dignified, but all this I noticed much later.

Janet had knocked at the door and when it opened, as

if by magic, I advanced into the room. At first I thought there was no one there and then I heard a laugh behind me. The door was shut and he was standing leaning against it, studying me with amusement.

"You!" I cried. "You . . . Jago Kellaway!"

For the man who faced me was the dark man who had spoken to me at the recital and had been in the house in Finlay Square that morning when Rollo had come and found us together.

I felt a tingling sensation run down my spine. It was a mingling of horror and amazement.

"But I don't understand," I stammered.

"I thought you'd be surprised." There was laughter in his voice as he took my arm. I had forgotten how big he was. He drew me into the room and led me to the window. There he put his hands on my shoulders and looked into my face.

"Ellen," he said. "At last!"

"I should like to know . . ." I began.

"Of course you would. You are a very curious young lady and I'll agree with you that it must seem a little odd."

"A little odd! I feel as if I'm dreaming. Why did you come to London? What were you doing at the recital? What were you doing in the house in Finlay Square? Why didn't you tell me who you were, and who are you anyway?"

"You ask too many questions which I can't answer all at once. First, I want to welcome you to Kellaway Island and to tell you how very happy I am to have you here at last. You are indeed a Kellaway. You take after your father. He was a very impatient man."

"Will you please explain . . ."

"Certainly I will explain. Come, my dear Ellen. Sit down and I will answer every question."

He led me to a chair with carved arms and a tapestry-covered seat, and almost pushed me into it. Then very deliberately, as though he enjoyed my impatience and was not in the least eager to alleviate it, he drew up a chair for himself. It was like a throne, that chair. Large—it had to be, because he was a large man—it was ornately carved and there was an inlay of stone in the back which looked like lapis.

Now I could look fully at him. He was even more impressive than he had been in London. His hair was thick and dark; I noticed again those heavy-lidded eyes which I felt even then could hide so much; they were now surveying me with obvious pleasure. He wore a midnight-blue velvet smoking jacket and a white cravat. His hands, resting on the arms of his thronelike chair, were well shaped and slightly bronzed and he wore a signet ring on the little finger of his right hand on which I could make out the letter K.

"First," he said, "you ask who I am. I will tell you. I am Jago Kellaway. And what is my connection with you? you ask. Well, my dear Ellen, it is a little complicated. I had better tell you myself or you will not doubt hear garbled versions of the story. It's rather a common one." His lips twitched as though he were amused. "And perhaps a little indelicate for your ears. But no. You come from the sophisticated London world and will know that matters of this nature arise now and then in the most sedate families. Am I right?"

"I can't say until I hear it," I replied sharply, because something about him made me want to do battle with him. He knew how eager I was to know and he deliberately took his time in telling me. He had come to London and acted in a strange manner which had caused me a good deal of concern and it was clear that he thought that in itself was a great joke. I had imagined "my guardian," as he had called himself, to be quite different, and while I was all eagerness to understand the mystery which surrounded him, I felt irritated by him.

"The Bar Sinister comes into this," he said. "One of our ancestors—not so very far back, your great-grandfather—had a sister named Gwennol. Gwennol was beautiful and wild. There is a picture of her in the gallery. I must show it to you. The Kellaways were a great family. They owned the Islands and they lived here in some state.

A grand marriage would have been arranged for Gwennol, but one day she proudly announced that she was about to have a child. She would not name the father nor had she any intention of marrying. Her father, furious with her, threatened to turn her out of the castle unless she told him who was the father of her child. This she refused to do. She left the castle, taking with her several of the servants; whether they went through love or fear I don't know, for she was reputed to be a witch and it was said that the Devil was the father of her child." Again his eyes showed that flicker of amusement. "It may well have been true, for we Kellaways could be said to have some of the Devil in us. Does that aply to you, Ellen? But of course not! You're not of the Devil's strain. You come from the respectable side of the family. Well, this Gwennol went to the Blue Rock Island, which is only half a mile from here. You have seen it perhaps."

"I have. Mr. Tregardier pointed it out to me and I can see it from my window."

"That was where she went. She had a shelter built for herself there made of wood and grasses and she lived in it until her house was built. The house still stands. In it her son was born. He was my father."

"I begin to understand the relationship. We are a sort of cousin."

"Several times removed, but we are both Kellaways. I was quite young when my father died and I was brought to live at the castle with my sister Jenifry. Your father and I shared a schoolroom and played our games together. He and I managed the Island Estate together for some years; then he became too ill to do anything much and I took over completely. Last year your father died."

"And he never wanted to know where I was for so many years."

Jago looked at me steadily and shook his head. "But before he died he thought of you. He asked me to find you and to be your guardian until you reached the age of twenty-one."

"I'm not far off that now. He must have known that."

"Certainly he knew your age. It was not easy to find you. Your mother had determined to lose herself when she left the Island."

"She went to her own family, you know."

"Your father told me nothing of them. But when I saw the papers and learned that you were about to be married, I came to London."

"It seems strange that you should not have told me who you were."

"Ah, that was due to a little quirk in my nature. I have them, as you will discover. I like to surprise. I like life to be dramatic. I wanted to know you before you knew me. So I came to the recital."

"How? The Carringtons didn't know you."

"Shall we say I gate-crashed. It's easy enough—with a certain amount of aplomb. A quality which I possess in abundance. One didn't have to produce a ticket."

"What . . . impudence!"

"Yes, I have my share of that too."

"How did you get into the house in Finlay Square. You said the agent gave you a key, but it seems there were only two keys."

"That was what the agent told you. You know what these house agents are. They want to make sure of a sale and apparently there was some hesitation about this one."

"How was it that you were there at exactly the same time as I was?"

"I waited until I saw you enter the house. Easy to understand, eh? Let me tell you this: I had a duty. I am your guardian. I wanted to make sure what sort of family this was you were marrying into."

"You quickly discovered who the Carringtons were, I'm sure."

"Yes, I discovered a good deal about them. And then the tragedy happened and I asked you to come here. Is it becoming clear to you now?"

"Yes," I answered.

"I hope, Ellen," he said very earnestly, "that you will stay with us for a very long time."

"You are kind," I replied with a touch of asperity, for I didn't believe he was telling me the whole truth even now.

"I want you to like this place," he went on. "I feel strongly about it. It's been my home for so long. Your mother took you away but now you are back with us. You have come through a bitter tragedy and I hope that we shall help you grow away from it."

He looked sincere now. His heavy lids were lifted and his eyes seemed serene and very friendly. I think his was the most expressive face I had ever seen. A few moments before, he had looked so mischievous and I remembered that in the house in Finlay Square he had seemed almost satanic; now his looks matched his words and he had become the kindly protective guardian.

I was not sure of him but I did find him interesting.

"What shall I call you?" I asked.

"Jago, of course. That is my name and we're distant cousins. Don't let the fact that I am your guardian overawe you."

"Indeed I shall not. I have stood on my own feet most of my life and I certainly don't need a guardian at this stage."

"But you have one, Ellen, whether you want him or not, and as he is a man blessed—or cursed—with a very strong sense of duty, however much you object to his guardianship, he will feel obliged to honor his promises. So call me Jago and we'll be friends. It's the British form of James, you know, and it dates back to earliest times. As a student of the past—and I hope I'm going to interest you in some of our old customs—I make a point of knowing such things. James from the Latin Jacobus. It has no Spanish origin at all. Some people think it has because of the Spanish element along this coast. We were constantly raided by the Spaniards in Elizabethan days and then when the Armada failed, many of its seamen were wrecked here. But Jago is simply Old British . . . not English, mind you. What do you know of ancient history?"

"Very little," I answered. "I suppose I learned something from our governess, but I don't remember much."

"We're the pure British," he went on. "Uncontaminated by the races who made up the English. They didn't penetrate as far as the Islands, so we kept our characteristics . . . our old customs. You must discover something of this while you're here. It's Kellaway heritage. This Island has been in our possession for several centuries. It's a wonderful island; it's fertile, for the climate is conducive to growing things; we're protected by the rock formations on the east from the colder winds and on the west from the southwest gales, while the Gulf Stream keeps us warm. I'll show you the palms in my sheltered gardens. We have our township, our church, our cemetery, our inn, our thriving community. We are independent . . . almost . . . of the mainland; and it's all Kellaway land."

As he was speaking his manner changed yet again. Now he was glowing with pride of possession. I could see that he loved this Island and I warmed towards him because that fierce enthusiasm was infectious. I hadn't seen the place properly yet but I was beginning to glow with pride because *I* was a Kellaway and this was Kellaway land.

I waited eagerly for him to tell me more. He noticed my interest and remarked on it; it pleased him, I could see.

"I shall enjoy showing you everything, Ellen," he said. "We have our celebrations here—our mummers, our hurlers and wrestlers, our bonfires on Midsummer's Eve. All the old customs prevail here—more so perhaps than on the mainland—and some of these customs go back to pre-Christian days. But it is the family you must first get to know. There's Jenifry, my sister. She's a widow who lost her husband some years ago. That was during the typhoid epidemic which struck the mainland and filtered through to our Island. She's a few years older than I am and is the chatelaine of the castle, you might say. She's visiting one of the cottagers now who's bedridden. You'll learn how we care for everyone here. They look to us in their troubles. It's quite a responsibility, you know. Jenifry's daughter, Gwennol, will be company for you. She's about your age. She'll help look after you. Now tell me about yourself . . . and your life in your cousin's house."

I started to tell him and it seemed to amuse him, or perhaps I stressed the amusing side. I always seemed to do that when talking of Cousin Agatha.

"Oh come," he protested, "it wasn't very comfortable, was it? She had a daughter, didn't she, who wasn't half as attractive as you are? I saw that much. And she made you feel you were living on her bounty."

I was surprised that he had been so perceptive. "It's a common enough story," I said.

"And then," he went on, "this young man came forward —rich and indulgent. They wanted him for their daughter and he chose you—wise young man. And then he killed himself."

"He didn't. He could not have done it. If you had known him you would realize that was impossible."

"It's all over." His voice had become soft and soothing. "It's in the past. I mentioned it only because it had to be spoken of. Now we will not speak of it again. We have to think of the present . . . and the future. But before we dismiss the subject tell me what were your plans before you had my letter."

"I was going to be a governess to a friend of my cousin."

"And you were not looking forward to the prospect?"

"I hated it," I said vehemently.

"I should think so! You . . . a governess! My dear Ellen, it wouldn't do. You're too proud for such a menial task. You should be engaging governesses for your own children."

"But I am unmarried."

"An attractive girl such as you are will not remain single long."

I shook my head. "I have no intention . . ." I began.

"Of course you haven't until the right man comes along. As your guardian, I should like to see you happily married. Well now, I daresay you would like to go to your room and rest awhile. If there is anything you need, just ring the bell. Janet has been told to look after you."

I rose and he did the same, going to the bell rope and pulling it. Then he laid his hand on my shoulder and gripped it firmly. I could feel the strength of his fingers as we walked to the door.

Almost immediately a servant appeared.

"Take Miss Ellen to her room," he ordered, pressing my shoulder affectionately and smiling at me as he released me.

I went to my room in a strange mood. He was the most unusual man I had ever met. I was not at all sure of him and I could not rid myself of the feeling he had inspired in me when we had been alone in the house in Finlay Square. His moods seemed to change so quickly and his personality with them. Of one thing I was certain: I did not know what to make of my guardian-cousin Jago.

I certainly did not want to rest. I was too excited. There was plenty of time before dinner to explore the castle ground. I had been told very clearly that I was to make myself at home. Well, I would begin by looking round and taking stock of my surroundings.

I descended the staircase by which I had been brought to my room and came to the guardroom. Being there alone moved me in a manner I had not experienced when others had been present. Everything was so different from what I had imagined. A grand castle and a guardian who was not a middle-aged gentleman but a man not much more than thirty who behaved in an unconventional manner. There were his sister and daughter, whom I was to meet, and they were descended from that branch of the family which was reputed to have been entangled with the Devil. The prospect of the future, which I was sure in such a place dominated by such a man was going to be far from dull, stimulated me, and I felt more alive than I had since Philip's death. I wondered why my mother had left here so hurriedly and mysteriously. I was determined to find out. How different my life would have been if she had not!

And as I stood there the guardroom seemed to take on a menacing aspect, and it occurred to me that I had come here in rather a reckless fashion. Oh no, this was my family. I was just feeling uneasy because of the shock of finding that Jago Kellaway was the man who had frightened me in the house in Finlay Square. He was a sort of joker in an unconventional way. There were people like that. He had admitted he liked dramatic happenings. Yes, I thought, with him playing the leading swashbuckling role!

This apprehension was natural. Hadn't I always been impressed by atmosphere? I shuddered now to recall the repulsion I had felt when I had first entered the house in Finlay Square. This room—medieval in aspect—with the weapons on its walls—two swords crossed, an ax, something which was half spear, half battle-ax and which I believed was called a halberd—had subconsciously reminded me of the gun room at Trentham Towers where Philip had shown me the pistol, the fellow of which had been the weapon which had killed him. It was this shadowy memory which was tapping on my mind now, reminding me of hidden dangers. I fancied that just as I had sensed a warning in the house in Finlay Square, so I did now in Kellaway Castle.

I moved towards the door; my footsteps ringing on the marble paving stones seemed to fill the guardroom with sound. I stood still. What a silence! It is foolish to endow a house with a personality. But is it? When a house has stood for seven hundred years much must have happened within its walls. If those stones could speak what tales they would have to tell! And in houses such as this there would have been gaiety and sorrow, comedy and tragedy. I have the feeling sometimes that these emotions have been captured and held within stone walls and that there are times when they cannot keep them secret.

Stupid imaginings, but I was in an uncertain state. I was trying to throw off one life with all its unhappy repercussions and embrace a new one of which I was equally uncertain.

I stepped out into a courtyard and saw an archway

which appeared to be cut into the wall. It led into another courtyard slightly lower than the one I had just left and I crossed it and went down steps to an even lower one. A few windows looked out onto this courtyard; they were small and leaded. There was yet another archway and from this wound a pathway with stone walls on either side. I took this pathway.

As I walked along it I heard the sudden flutter of wings and the cooing sound of birds. I had come into yet another courtyard. This was where the cooing sound had come from, for there were several pigeons pecking at maize which was scattered over the stones.

As I approached, some of them fluttered up and perched on the little dovecotes which were attached to the walls; others ignored me and went on picking up the maize. Most of the pigeons were the bluish gray common color but some of them were brown. I had never seen pigeons that color before.

As I stood there watching the birds I was aware of a shadow at a lower window. Someone was watching me.

I turned sharply. The shadow was no longer there.

I looked back at the birds and waited. Now the shadow had come back. I could see it from the corner of my eye.

I called: "Are these your birds?"

There was no answer. I went closer to the window where I had seen the shadow, but it was no longer there.

There was a little door in the wall and I tapped on it. I wanted to ask about the brown pigeons. I realized that it had been slightly ajar and as I stood there it was quietly shut. Someone on the other side of the door was clearly determined to keep me out.

I fancied I could hear the sound of heavy breathing.

How strange! Well, if whoever was there didn't want to speak to me, I wouldn't disturb him . . . or her. Yet the impulse came to me to knock again on the door and I did so.

There was no answer.

I called out: "I only want to ask about the pigeons."

Still no answer.

How odd. How unfriendly. It was some servant, I supposed. I shrugged my shoulders, left the birds' courtyard and went back the way I had come.

Perhaps it was rather foolish to begin to explore the castle on my own. It would be far better if I had a guide to show me round. There would be someone who would be delighted to do so I was sure.

I found my way back to my room, where I must now dress for dinner. I decided I would wear the blue dress, which was extremely elegant, and I wondered if I should ever need the black serviceable one which I had worn on the night of Esmeralda's dance when Philip had proposed to me. If I had Philip's orchid it would look quite charming. . . .

Now I was back in the past again. Could I ever escape from it? Would I ever be able to thrust aside my memories? Even as I put on the blue dress I remembered how I had imagined wearing it dining with Philip on the Grand Canal.

I shook myself angrily.

How clearly that first night in the castle stands out in my memory.

A servant came to my room to conduct me down to the anteroom where the family were waiting for me. Jago was standing in front of the fireplace, his hands clasped behind his back, his eyes shining with pleasure, dominating the room. On either side of him was a woman—the older one about forty years of age, whom I guessed to be his sister Jenifry, the younger his niece Gwennol, who he had said was about my age.

"Come, Ellen," said Jago. "Come and meet the family. This is Jenifry, my sister."

My heart sank a little as she stepped forward to take my hand. She was almost as dark as Jago and had the same high-bridged nose which gave her the arrogant look which I had noticed in him; the family resemblance was strong.

Her voice was soft and warm. "We are glad you have

come, Ellen," she said; but there was something coolly appraising about her eyes which was in contrast to her words. I knew she was assessing me and I felt the same uncertainty about her as I did about her brother.

"It is good of you to be so welcoming," I answered.

"But of course we are delighted to have you at last. Gwennol, come and meet Ellen."

Gwennol was dark too. Her hair was almost black, her eyes dark brown, her nose a trifle retroussé, her mouth wide; and the entire effect was made striking by her soulful dreamy eyes and the alertness her nose and mouth seemed to betray.

"Hello, Ellen," she said. "Welcome to Kellaway Island."

"You two must be friends," said her mother.

"You must show Ellen the castle, Gwennol," said Jago, smiling from one to the other of us.

Almost immediately a servant came in to announce that dinner was served, and Jago put his arm through mine and led the way.

"As this is a very special occasion," he said, "we are dining in the hall. It is a custom reserved for feast days and special occasions, and what occasion could be more special than this one?"

I shall never forget the sight of the hall on that first night in Kellaway Castle. It filled me with wonder and awe which was none the less exciting because there was a strong flavor of apprehension mingling with it.

At one end of the vast room was a door leading to the kitchens through which the servants hurried back and forth; above these doors was the minstrels' gallery; and at the other end was a dais set at right angles to the main room. Antlers decorated the balustrade of the minstrels' gallery and the walls were partially covered with fine tapestries. There was something royal about this hall with its lofty roof, its thick stone walls and the weapons displayed there. Places had been laid at the long oak table and on the dais and already the long benches on either side of the table were occupied. These people, Jago told me later, were those employed on the estate—those who farmed the land, the managers of the various concerns, his clerks, and—I could scarcely believe this—there below the salt were those who worked in a more menial capacity. This was the manner in which kings had feasted in the old days.

The scene he had set was truly medieval and when the minstrels in the gallery began to play softly I was amused by this determination to create an atmosphere of bygone days, and I was touched, too, because I knew it had all been done to honor me.

All those at the long table rose as we entered. Jago led the way to the dais, his arm still through mine, and he stood there at the table with me beside him.

"I have great pleasure," he announced, "in introducing you all to Miss Ellen Kellaway, my ward and cousin, who has come to stay with us, I hope for a very long time. This occasion is to welcome her to the castle and the Island and I know that you are delighted to see her here—as I am."

There was a murmur of assent. I was not sure what was expected of me, so I smiled, and as Jago was holding out my chair for me, I sat down.

There was a shuffling of chairs and everyone did the same. Hot soup was served to us at the table and afterwards the huge bowl was carried to the long table and those there were helped from it.

"What do you think of it?" Jago whispered to me.

"It's incredible. I never imagined anything like it."

He patted my hand.

"It's for you," he said. "To show you how we can do things here—and to let you know how glad we are to have you."

"Thank you," I answered. "You are so kind to me. I have never had such a welcome in the whole of my life."

"Then our purpose is served."

The soup was excellent and followed by venison and as I listened to the musicians softly playing I thought that this hall could not have looked very different three hundred years ago.

Jenifry sat on Jago's left hand and Gwennol was beside me. I noticed several people from the long table taking surreptitious glances at me, and I wondered what they were thinking about all this ceremony. But it occurred to me that they were probably used to it. This was confirmed by Jago.

"Christmas is the time when we can really go back to the old ways," he said. "Then the hall is decorated with holly and ivy, and the carol singers and mummers perform here. It's been a custom of the family for centuries."

"I can see you enjoy carrying on old customs," I said.

"We all do, don't we?" he replied; and Jenifry and Gwennol agreed with him.

"We are trying to discover the exact age of the castle," Jenifry went on. "Of course the place has been added to over the years. It was originally merely a fortress to protect the Island, and very uncomfortable it must have been in those days, until it was made more like a residence. Gwennol's very interested, aren't you, Gwennol?"

"Living here, it grows on you," Gwennol explained to me. "You discover some new aspect of the place and then you start trying to find out during what period it had been put there."

"You'll be the same," Jago said to me, "once you start getting the feel of the place. I want to show you the Island myself. Tomorrow we'll explore. You ride, I know."

"Oh yes. We used to ride in the Row when we were in London. In the country, of course, I rode a good deal."

"That's good. It saves us the trouble of having to teach you. We must choose the right horse for you."

"I shall enjoy it."

"That's what we want, isn't it?" said Jago, appealing to the women. "We want you to enjoy being here so much that you won't want to leave us."

"It's early days to say that," I reminded him. "You know what is said about guests."

"No. You tell me."

"That it's wonderful to have them for a few days, but

if they overstay their welcome you can't wait to see them gone."

"You're not a guest, Ellen. You're family. Isn't that so?"

"Of course it is," replied Jenifry.

"Tell me more about the Island," I said. "I'm eager to explore it."

"You won't feel cut off," said Jago. "It's big enough to prevent that."

"There are times though," put in Gwennol, "when it's impossible to get to the mainland."

"And that," added Jenifry, "can last for days . . . perhaps weeks."

Jago cut her short. "Ellen knows that. Wasn't she held up at Polcrag Inn waiting for a boat? People here don't feel they're missing anything by not being able to reach the mainland. We can live without that. We have the local inn. People come and stay there to get away from the mainland."

"They only have four bedrooms for guests and they're rarely occupied," Gwennol said. "It's really a sort of public house where people go to drink and sing and find company."

"So much the better," said Jago. "We don't want the place spoilt with too many people."

I was learning how obsessed he was with the Island. He loved it; to him it was perfect. I could understand that. The Island was his and he was proud of it.

"Do you ever have any criminals here?" I asked.

"Hardly ever," he assured me. "I think I know how to keep the people lawful."

"So you don't have a prison?"

"There are dungeons in the castle which serve on the rare occasions they are necessary."

"And the law allows this?"

"I'm a Justice of the Peace. Of course in the case of a major crime . . . murder, for instance . . . the criminal would have to go to the mainland. But we can deal adequately with petty matters here."

"Is there anyone in the dungeons now?"

Jago laughed. "Why, you're not afraid that some desperate man will break out, steal to your room and demand your money or your life, are you? No, Ellen, my dear, there is no one in the dungeons now. There very rarely is. They're horrible, aren't they?"

Gwennol said: "Dank, dark and said to be haunted because in the past Kellaways put their enemies there and left them to die. The ghosts of those who didn't obey Kellaway law are said to stalk the dungeons. Naturally people think twice before doing something they shouldn't when it might result in a night or two in the dungeons."

"I'd like to see them," I said.

"So you shall," Jago promised me. "The whole place is at your disposal. Explore when you like."

"As a matter of fact I did explore a little before dinner."

"Did you then?" Jago looked pleased. "Well, what did you find?"

"I saw some pigeons, brown ones. I've never seen brown pigeons before."

"We've always kept a few brown pigeons at Kellaway," said Jago. "You tell her the story, Jenifry."

"It's simply that one of our ancestors was saved by a pigeon—a brown one," his sister said. "I think they originated in Italy. He was imprisoned after being captured in some battle and a little brown pigeon came and perched on his windowsill. They became friendly; the pigeon brought his mate and they shared the prisoner's food. He tamed them and used to attach messages to their legs, hoping that some of his friends would see them. It seemed a forlorn hope and when after a long, long time the message actually did reach his friends it was regarded as something of a miracle and the pigeon an instrument of fate. He was rescued and he brought back the brown pigeon and his mate with him. It was said after that that as long as there were brown pigeons at the castle there would always be Kellaways on the Island."

"A pretty story, don't you agree, Ellen?" asked Jago.

"Charming," I replied.

When the meal was over Jago rose and Jenifry, Gwennol and I followed him to a door at the end of the hall. The rest remained at table and I imagined how relaxed the company would be after we had gone, for they would surely be relieved that the ceremonial occasion was over and they would be able to talk naturally together.

We went to his parlor, where coffee was served.

The atmosphere there was decidedly more intimate. I sat beside Gwennol, who wanted to hear about my life in London, so I talked about the house near Hyde Park and how we took walks in Kensington Gardens, feeding the ducks on the Round Pond, strolling round the pleached alley which surrounded the Pond Garden.

"We have a pleached alley in our gardens," Jago told me. "And a pond garden too." It was as though he wanted the Island to compare favorably with everything I had ever known. Perhaps this was due to his pride in the Island, but I fancied too that he was anxious that I should be happy here and want to stay.

Gwennol was eager to hear more so I went on to tell her of the receptions at Cousin Agatha's and the Carringtons', of tea at Gunter's on winter afternoons, of the red carpet and awnings being put in place before the houses to receive the guests.

They all listened intently; then they talked more of the Island; and the life which I had known with Cousin Agatha seemed as remote as anything could be.

It was half past ten when Jago remarked that I must be tired.

"Jenifry will take you to your room," he said; and Jenifry took a candle from a table and asked me if I was ready.

I thanked Jago for a pleasant evening and said good night.

"In the morning we'll ride round the Island," Jago promised me.

Then Jenifry and I left them.

We made our way back to the hall. At intervals candles burned in the sconces fixed to the walls, making the hall look more medieval than ever.

Jenifry said: "This way to your room." And crossing the hall we mounted the stone staircase. "You will soon get to know your way around," she added, "but for the first few days you may get lost now and then."

"It's a vast place, this castle."

"There is a great deal of room and we are not now a large family. A place like this is meant to be populated by a large family."

We had come to the top of the staircase and we passed through a gallery. When we emerged from it and were mounting another staircase I recognized where we were.

She opened the door. The room looked different from when I had left it. Now there seemed too many dark shadows; it had become an alien room. The curtains had been drawn across the semi-circular window, shutting out the stone alcove with its window seat. The four-poster bed from which the curtains had been looped back seemed to dominate the room.

"Just a moment," said Jenifry, and she lit the candles from the flame in the one she carried. There were already two on the dressing table and two more on the mantelpiece. There is something mysterious about candlelight, and feeling overexcited by the day's events, I thought: I shall not sleep well tonight. A fatal mood when one is about to retire for the night.

Jenifry was smiling at me.

"I hope you'll be comfortable. You have been told, haven't you, to ring if you want anything." She indicated the red-and-gold bell rope. "That will ring directly to the servants' room and one of them will come immediately."

"I'm sure I have everything I want," I said. I was getting used to the candlelight. "You are all so kind."

She smiled at me, her expression benign as though I were a child and she a friend who was determined to look after me.

I glanced in the mirror and saw myself—rather elegant in the trousseau gown and my eyes unnaturally bright, my cheeks flushed. I looked like a stranger.

Then I caught a glimpse of Jenifry through the looking glass. Her expression had changed. Her face had changed; a different woman was standing there. Her eyes had narrowed; her mouth had hardened; it was as though a mask had slipped and revealed what was underneath. It was not pleasant to look at. I turned sharply. But her face had changed again and she was smiling at me.

"Well, if you are sure you have everything I'll say good night."

"Good night," I said.

She turned at the door to smile at me.

"Sleep well."

The door shut. I stared at it blankly for a moment. My heart was beating unnaturally fast. Then I looked back at the mirror and saw that it was a very old one—a little mottled perhaps—though the frame was heavy gilt and beautifully wrought. It had probably stood there for two hundred years. It was a distorting mirror, but how it had changed her face! Had she really looked like that at me? Speculatively, wondering, evil almost, as though she hated me?

I sat down and took the pins out of my hair. I shook it about my shoulders; it was dark and heavy and came to my waist.

The trouble is, I told myself, I am so used to being unwanted that I can't really believe in all this friendship and that was why I had imagined she looked at me as she did. But for the moment it had been quite terrifying. I brushed my hair thoughtfully and plaited it, trying to relax and get ready for sleep. I drew back the curtains and, mounting the steps, sat down on the window seat. The houses of the Island seemed as though they were sleeping, though here and there a light showed in the darkness; the sea was calm and beautiful, the moon's pathway of light shining clearly on the water. A peaceful scene. How different from my thoughts! Of course I must expect to feel wide awake. So much had happened today. I had met Jago Kellaway and had learned that he was not a complete stranger to me; I had expected to come to a humble house on an island and had found myself in a castle of which this Jago was the proud custodian; I had found my long-lost relations and was going to learn about my family. I wished it was daylight, so impatient was I to go on discovering.

The flickering candlelight was eerie; it threw long shadows about the room. I went to the dressing table and looked in the mirror and as I did so I seemed to see Jenifry's face suddenly distorted into an evil smile. It was all fancy, of course. I was overwrought. Tomorrow I would be laughing at myself, but this was tonight and there were several hours of darkness to be lived through before dawn.

As I looked in the mirror I heard a sudden sound behind me. I was so startled I knocked one of the candles over. Hastily I picked it up, splashing hot grease on my hands as I did so, and swung round, holding the candle high as I looked round the room.

No one was there.

I turned to the door. It was shut. Then I heard the sound again and saw that it was coming from the cupboard. I went to it and laughed aloud in derision at myself for the sound had come from the door, which was not securely fastened.

I opened it. My clothes were hanging up and as I stood there the blue dress which I had worn that evening slid slowly from its hanger and fell in a heap on the floor. I picked it up and in doing so I saw some writing on the wall of the cupboard. It had probably been scraped on the distemper by something with a sharp point.

I pushed aside the clothes and held the candle closer.

I read: "I am a prisoner here. S.K."

I wondered who S.K. was and what was meant by being a prisoner. I guessed it was a child because there was something childish about the lettering and it was the

sort of thing a child would scratch on a wall if it had been
sent to its room as a punishment.

I set the candle down again on the dressing table. The
incident had not made me feel any more sleepy, but I got
into the bed, which seemed very large, and I began to
think of all the people who had slept in this bed over the
last hundred years. S.K. had probably been one of them.

I did not blow out the candles immediately. I wanted
to retain a little longer the comforting light they gave me,
so I lay looking up at the ceiling with its ornate patterns,
which were difficult to make out in the gloom.

Suddenly I was wide awake. I fancied I heard footsteps
near my door. I sat up in bed, straining my ears.

You are fanciful tonight, I thought. It's nothing at all.
Why don't you lie down and go to sleep?

Esmeralda would say I was "working myself up." In
those days I used to make up stories about other people
and only if a role was a pleasant one did I imagine myself
in it. Now I was finding my imagination could work
against me as well as for me.

I slipped out of bed and noticed there was a key in the
door. I turned it and now that I had locked myself in it
was amazing what comfort I found, so I blew out the
candles.

I lay there for some time while scenes from the day's
events kept flashing in and out of my head; and finally I
was so tired, I suppose, that I slept.

It was inevitable that the dream should come.

There it was as vivid as it had ever been. There was the
room with the red curtains, the table, the window seat,
the firedogs . . . the china ornaments. The storm-at-sea
picture over the fireplace. I noticed that the wind was
blowing the curtains. The door was moving. Slowly it
opened. Now . . . that awful fear, that certainty that I was
in great danger.

I was awake, with the familiar sense of doom upon me.
At first I did not know where I was. Then I remembered
that I was in the castle on Kellaway's Island.

My heart was racing and I was trembling with fear.

It's only the dream, I soothed myself, but the doom seemed to have come nearer.

# Discovery in a Sketchbook

Sunshine filled my room and the terrors of the night had completely disappeared with the coming of daylight.

I rang the bell and Janet came in.

"Have 'ee slept well, Miss Ellen?" she asked.

I said I had finally.

" 'Tis always the same in a new bed," she answered, and went off to get my hot water.

When I went down I found Gwennol and Jenifry at the table. They asked how I had slept.

"Help yourself from the sideboard," said Jenifry. "There's ham, eggs and deviled kidneys. If there is something different you would like, Benham will see that it's brought for you."

I went to the sideboard on which were the breakfast dishes she had mentioned. I took some ham and eggs and sat down to eat them.

We were talking of the weather when Jago came in. His eyes went at once to me and he inquired solicitously if I had slept well and found all that I needed. He said that in an hour or so he would be ready to show me the Island. Could I be ready by then? I said that I could.

"Gwennol or I could show Ellen if you are busy," said Jenifry.

"Indeed you will not," he retorted. "I am determined to have that pleasure."

"Which mount will you give her?" asked Gwennol.

"Ellen will choose for herself in due course," he replied. "I was wondering if I'd advise Daveth for a start."

"She's a bit spirited," said Gwennol.

"Perhaps they'll be well matched." He was eyeing me with an expression I couldn't quite understand but it made me determined to ride the spirited Daveth.

After breakfast I changed into my riding habit—part of my trousseau. It was pale gray and very elegant, and I had a gray riding hat—tall-crowned like a man's top hat—which I was well aware suited me well.

Jago looked at me with approval when I met him in the stable yard. "You are so elegant," he said. "You put us all to shame."

I laughed. "This riding habit is part of my trousseau, and I can assure you I never had anything so grand before."

"At least then you got something out of it! But we made a pact, remember, not to talk of the past? The people of the Island will be enchanted with you and I am going to enjoy introducing them to you and you to the Island. I shall take you first to the highest peak, from where you can see all around you and for miles out to sea if the air's clear enough. You'll get the idea of the lie of the land, as it were. Then we'll go down to our little township. It's hardly that—but what's in a name?"

He was riding a white horse with a black mane and I had to admit that horse and rider looked magnificent; they suited each other. I found Daveth, as Gwennol had suggested, somewhat sprightly, but I was able to manage her. Jago glanced sideways at me on one or two occasions and I was delighted out of all proportion because I was a tolerably good horsewoman and, I believed, had his approval.

We paused at the top of the hill. What a sight lay before us! I had a wonderful view of the castle with its gray stone walls and battlemented towers. What an impressive edifice it was! It seemed impregnable, almost as though it were truculently inviting an enemy to come and try to take it and see what the result would be. In the past it would have been a perfect fortification against marauders. I could see the Blue Rock Island rising out of the sea.

Jago followed my gaze. "Blue Rock," he said. "It's a pity we allowed that to pass out of our hands. It belonged to the Kellaways at one time."

"What happened then?"

"Your grandfather sold it. He was in financial difficulties. To tell the truth, he was a bit of a gambler. I think the family have regretted the sale ever since."

"Is that a house on it?"

"Yes. It's Blue Rock House. The one built by that Gwennol I told you about."

"Does anyone live there now?"

"An artist. He inherited it from the man your grandfather sold it to. I think he's a nephew . . . or greatnephew or something."

"Does he live there alone?"

"Quite alone. He's not there all the time though. He travels around a bit, I believe."

"Is he a well-known artist?"

"I don't know enough about such matters to tell you. His name is James Manton. Have you ever heard it?"

"I can't say I have, although I don't know very much about painters either. My mother was an artist. I remember how she always had a sketchbook with her and she used to draw pictures to amuse me. Perhaps I shall meet this James Manton."

"He doesn't visit the Island. He and your father didn't like each other. Look. You can see the mainland. Can you make it out?"

I could. "It's a comforting sight," I commented.

"Comforting." A faint frown appeared between his eyes.

"One doesn't feel so cut off from the rest of the world," I explained.

"Does it bother you then . . . to feel cut off?"

"Not really, but I suppose one would always be aware of being on an island and therefore it's nice to know that the mainland is not far away."

"One is, you know, when the weather is bad . . . as you've discovered. There are some seas it would be folly to put out in."

"Yes, but there is always the knowledge that it will change and that the bad weather won't last forever."

He nodded.

"I will show you our community. It's complete in itself. We are a little kingdom, you might say. There is much of long-ago times left on the Island and I intend to keep it that way."

We cantered across a green stretch and had come to the shore.

He showed me a stake stuck in the sand. "At high tide," he said, "that will be covered with water. It's been there five hundred years. At that time the lord of the Island— it must have been a Kellaway—would order that a criminal should be tied to it at low tide. He would be given two barley loaves and a pitcher of water and left there. When the tide rose he would be drowned."

"How cruel."

"It was the justice of the day."

"You don't follow that practice now, I hope," I said jocularly.

"No, but I keep good order here, as I told you. Look! There is the old ducking stool. It is used even now. . . . Sometimes a man's friend will duck his nagging wife, or there will be someone suspected of being a witch."

"And that still goes on?"

He shrugged his shoulders. "Old customs remain and in a place like this more so than on the mainland. Come along, I want you to meet some of the people. I want them to know that you are my honored guest."

We had come to a group of houses surrounded by fields.

A man driving a cart was coming towards us. He touched his forelock and called out: "Good day to 'ee, Mr. Jago."

"Good day," responded Jago. "This is my ward, Miss Ellen Kellaway."

"Good day to 'ee, Miss," said the man.

"And a fine one, Jim, eh?"

"Aye, Master, 'tis indeed a fine one."

He passed on.

"All these people," said Jago, "are our tenants. Every bit of the land is Kellaway land owned by the family for the last six hundred years."

In the center of the houses was a shop, the window of which was crammed full of goods. It seemed to be a linen draper, hosier, tallow chandler, hardware man, grocer and baker all combined. I made up my mind that I would take an opportunity of visiting that shop as soon as possible.

From one house in the street came the cheerful sound of much merrymaking.

"I can guess what's happening here," said Jago, "because I know there's a new baby in the house. It's a christening party. They wouldn't like it if I passed by and didn't well-wish the baby. We'll dismount and join them for a moment." He shouted: "Boy! Come and hold the horses." And as if by magic a boy appeared.

"Take mine and the lady's," said Jago; and we dismounted and went into the house.

"Why 'tis the master," said a woman, dropping a curtsy.

We were in a small cottage in which several people were gathered, and there was hardly room for Jago and me—particularly Jago. It seemed like a doll's room when he stood in it.

" 'Tis honored we be," said the man who seemed likely to be the woman's husband.

"Where's the baby?" asked Jago.

"She be in her cradle, Mr. Jago. 'Twould be an honor if you'd bless the child like and take a piece of the cheeld's fuggan."

He would, he said, and I should too.

"And a glass of sloe gin, Master, to wash it down."

"I'll have it," said Jago.

The cake was cut, and both Jago and I had a piece and a glass of sloe gin, which burned my throat a little.

"Good luck to the child," said Jago.

"May she grow up to be a good servant to her master," said the baby's mother.

"Aye," said Jago, "so be it."

We came out into the street where the boy was patiently waiting with our horses. We mounted them and drove on through the cluster of houses.

"You'd find most of the houses similar," Jago told me. "They're what are known as Lives Cottages. They were put up in a night and therefore the owners have a right to live in them for a number of lives. For instance if a man builds it, it is his for his lifetime, that of his son and his grandson. Then the cottage reverts to the landowner. On the mainland there are Moonlight Cottages which have been built in a night but remain the property of the builder for evermore. The only condition is that they must be started after dark and finished before dawn."

"Can anyone build a cottage in that time?"

"If they are fully prepared and have their materials ready they can have the four walls standing and the roof on. That is all that need be. How did you like the cheeld's fuggan?"

"A little too yellow."

"Oh, that's the saffron—a great delicacy here. Don't let anyone hear you say you don't like it."

I had learned a great deal about the Island that morning. It was a community of fishermen mainly, although there was some agriculture. There were many little coves where boats were moored and we passed fishermen mending their nets as they sat among the lobster pots. They all called a respectful greeting to Jago and I felt a certain pleasure in their respect for him.

He told me that there was a fair once a month when traders came from the mainland. That was if the weather permitted. Then the islanders shopped and stocked up until the fair's next visit. Goods of all kinds and description were sold at the fair. It was an event much looked forward to.

He then began to tell me of other customs. "Fishermen don't like to land with their catch until daybreak. They think the Little People might carry them off if they did. There is a great fear of the Little People or the Piskies, who are said to have very special powers, not always kindly."

He went on to talk of their superstitions.

"When people are engaged in a hazardous way of life they become superstitious. When fishermen are at sea they never mention rabbits or hares or any wild animals. It's unlucky. If they meet a minister of the church as they are setting out in their boats they would turn back."

"How did such superstitions start? I wonder."

"It may have been that someone met a parson on the way to the boats and didn't return; and perhaps it happened a second time. That's all that would be needed with such people. And once a superstition is born it seems to live forever. In the old days these islands were also a sanctuary for those who wanted to evade the law. We here were a law unto ourselves. Many an outlaw settled here; some found political asylum and became subjects of the ruling Kellaway. You see, it's an interesting history this of our Island and we Kellaways have something to be proud of."

"And the line is unbroken all through the ages?"

"Yes. If a female inherited she was in duty bound to marry and her husband would then take the name of Kellaway."

"It's been a wonderful morning," I said, "edifying too. I feel I've learned so much and it's made me want to learn more and more."

He turned to me and laid his hand on my arm. "I want you to stay here, Ellen," he said. "I can't tell you how much I want you to stay. When I saw you in London it was the Devil's own job not to snatch you up and insist that you come down and get to know your family before you rushed into marriage. I can't tell you how much restraint I put upon myself."

"I still can't understand why you came like that. Why didn't you tell me who you were?"

"It was the whim of a moment. You were so immersed in the prospect of marriage . . . and then, when it fell through, I felt my chance had come. I wanted you to come here freely, because you wanted to. It's difficult to explain. Suffice it that I'm happy you are here."

I was touched by the emotion in his voice. I was finding his company stimulating. He had intrigued me from the moment I had met him at the recital; he had frightened me in the house in Finlay Square; but that moment on the Island I decided he was the most fascinating man I had ever met.

He seemed to make a great effort to curb his emotions. "Alas," he said, "we must now return to the castle. There is so much I want to show you, but perhaps you have had enough for today. Get Gwennol to show you round the castle but don't listen to too many stories about the ghosts."

"Are there ghosts then?"

"It would be strange if in six hundred years we hadn't managed to collect a few. Most of them are in the dungeons. There have been one or two over the centuries who have tried to wrest our heritage from us, for to rule an island is the irresistible longing of some men. I can understand it, can't you? It's a little world in itself, a little kingdom. Perhaps you begin to feel that, Ellen. Do you?"

"I certainly thought you must be rather proud when they show you such obvious respect, as they did this morning."

"Oh, they daren't do aught else." He laughed. "I will say, though, that since I've been in control we've prospered. Crops have been good. You might say that's in the hands of God. But it is a fact that it's in the hands of Jago Kellaway as well. I've introduced modern farming methods; I've discovered good ways of marketing. There is so much one can do with foresight on an island like this.

Your father and I didn't always see eye to eye with one
another, Ellen."

"Oh?" I said, wanting him to go on. Anything he could
tell me about my father was of the utmost interest to me.

"He was ill for a long time before he died. That left the
reins in my hands."

"And it was then that things began to improve?"

"People on the Island will tell you so. There! Now
you're not so happy. Don't talk about the past, Ellen.
You're here. Let's go on from there."

He smiled at me and I fancied I saw in his eyes that
which faintly alarmed me. But I was in a happy mood as
we rode into the stables. It had been an exciting and stimulating morning.

It was afternoon. We had had a luncheon of cold meats
and salad, Jenifry, Jago and I. Gwennol had gone to the
mainland. "She often gets one of the men to row her over
on calm days like this," Jenifry explained.

She asked how I had enjoyed the morning and where
we had been. She was very pleasant and I felt I had been
overfanciful about the image I had seen in the mirror on
the previous night.

Jago had to leave on some estate business and Jenifry
told me she rested in the afternoons, so I said I would
take a stroll round the castle alone. I should enjoy discovering things for myself.

It was about half past two when I set out—a beautiful
September afternoon with the sun picking out pearly tints
in the water. I passed between the battlemented bastions
to a courtyard and before me was a Gothic arch and two
stone steps considerably worn in the middle by thousands
of footsteps. I should never cease to marvel at the count-
less people who must have trodden the castle steps to
wear down the stone as it obviously was, and to wonder
about their lives. I was in another courtyard which looked
familiar and then I heard the cooing of the pigeons and
recognized this as the spot I had visited on the previous
evening.

Then I saw him. He was very small with a thatch of
hair so fair that it was almost white; his eyes were very
pale and the fact that he had fair sparse eyebrows and
lashes gave him a look of surprise.

He turned suddenly and saw me. I judged him then to
be about fourteen or fifteen although before I had seen
his face, on account of his being so small, he had appeared
to be younger.

He carried a bowl of maize in his hands and as he
looked at me a bird perched on his shoulder. A look of
fear came over his face and he started to walk towards
the outhouse where I had seen a shadow when I was there
before and which I now guessed to have been his.

I cried out: "Don't go, please. I've come to see the
pigeons."

But he continued to move towards the outhouse.

"If you go the pigeons won't be fed," I reminded him.
"Do let me see you feed them. I love the way they flutter
round you."

He paused as though he were giving a great deal of consideration to his next move.

I had an inspiration. "I think you must be Slack," I
said. "I met your mother at the inn."

He smiled slowly and nodded.

"I'm Ellen Kellaway. I've come to stay here for a
while."

"Do you like the pigeons?" he asked.

"I don't know much about them, but I did hear the
story of the brown pigeons taking the messages, and I
thought that was wonderful."

"These take messages," he said proudly.

"It's like a miracle. They just know where to go, don't
they?"

A smile crossed his face. "You train them," he said. He
took a handful of maize from the bowl and threw it onto
the cobbles. Several of the birds flew down and pecked
at it. Some remained perched on the bowl. They cooed
contentedly.

"I believe they know you," I said.

"Of course they do."

"How long have you been looking after them?"

"Ever since I've been here." He started counting on his fingers. It seemed something like five years.

"I saw you in there last night," I said, pointing to the outhouse.

"I saw you," he replied with a sly smile.

"I called you but you pretended you didn't hear."

He nodded and continued to look sly.

"May I look in now?"

"Do you want to?"

"Of course I do. I'm getting very interested in pigeons."

He opened the door and we stepped down three stone steps into a small room where sacks of maize and drinking troughs were stored.

"It's my pigeon house," he said. "But I've got to finish feeding them now."

We went back into the courtyard. He held out his arm and two birds immediately alighted on it. "There, my pretties," he murmured. "Be 'ee come to see Slacky then?"

I took a handful of the maize and threw it onto the cobbles. He watched the birds pecking at it. "You like pigeons, Miss," he said. "Her liked 'em too."

"Her?"

He nodded vigorously. "Her liked 'em. Her'd come and help me feed 'em. Then she went away."

"Who was that, Slack?" I asked.

"Her," he said. His eyes were bewildered. "Her just went away."

He was disturbed by the memory. I could see that he had almost forgotten my existence. He went on feeding the pigeons and because I could see that to question him further would only disturb him and make him less inclined to talk, I strolled off.

The next day Gwennol took me round the castle.

"Let's begin with the dungeons," she said. "They're really quite eerie."

We descended a stone spiral staircase clinging to a rope

banister and as we did so she warned me to take care.

"These stairs are so treacherous. You never really get used to them. A few years ago one of the maids fell down and wasn't discovered for a day and a night. The poor creature was nearly out of her wits when they did find her —not so much with pain as with fear of ghosts. She swore some ghostly hand pushed her down and nothing would convince her to the contrary."

We had reached a kind of enclosed courtyard, the floor of which was cobbled; it was surrounded by doors. There must have been about eighteen of them. I pushed open one and saw a cell which was like a cave in which it would have been difficult for a man of normal height to stand upright. Fixed to the wall on a chain was a heavy iron ring. I shivered, realizing that this would be used to prevent the cell's inmate from escaping. The walls were seeping with moisture and there was a damp noisome odor about the place. I shivered and shut the door. I opened another; there was a similar cavelike cell. I explored others. They were not all alike though equally dismal. Some were lofty with half windows high in the wall, glassless and barred. On one wall the sketch of a gallows was cut into the stone; on another an evil grinning face had been drawn. It was a dark gloomy place in which I knew many must have suffered utter despair.

"It's gruesome," I said.

Gwennol nodded. "Imagine yourself a prisoner here. You'd call and no one would hear you and if they did perhaps they wouldn't care."

"You can almost sense the suffering, the mental agony, the frustration and desperation that has gone on here," I said.

"Ugh! Morbid," she commented. "I can see you've had enough, but you had to have a look at them, of course. They're an important part of the castle."

We climbed the stairs to the upper regions and she took me through so many rooms that I lost count of them. We explored the towers—north, south, east and west; and we went along galleries and up and down staircases. She showed me the kitchens, the bakery, the buttery, the winery and the slaughterhouse; she introduced me to the servants, who bobbed their curtsies or touched their forelocks according to their sex and watched me guardedly and with obvious curiosity.

There was one room which led off the hall which interested me particularly because as we entered it she said: "I heard this was your mother's favorite room. Her name was Frances, wasn't it? Some of the older servants still call it Frances's room."

There was a step leading down to it and I followed Gwennol in. She seated herself on a settle which fitted exactly into an alcove.

"She used to paint, I heard," she went on. "She couldn't have used this room as a studio. It's not light enough. I don't think anyone has used it much since she went."

I looked round the room eagerly trying to picture her there. It was certainly not a bright room. The window was small and its panes leaded. It was furnished as a sitting room. There were a few chairs, a table, but little else apart from the wooden settle.

"I wonder if any of her things are still here," I said.

"Look in the cupboard."

I opened the door of this and cried out in triumph, for inside was an easel and some rolls of paper.

"These must have been hers," I cried, and as I picked up the roll of paper I saw a sketchbook lying on the floor. Written across it was her name: Frances Kellaway. This was indeed a discovery and I was so excited by it that my hand shook as I turned over the leaves. Gwennol rose from the settle and looked over my shoulder. There were sketches of the castle from various angles.

"She was quite an artist," said Gwennol.

"I want to take this book and look through it at my leisure," I said.

"Why not?"

"It's so exciting. You're amused, but I knew so little of my mother, and my father I can't remember at all. You must have known him."

"Nobody knew him well. I saw very little of him. I don't think he liked young people. He was ill for a long time and kept in his own rooms. I'd see him now and then in a wheelchair; Fenwick, his valet-secretary, looked after him. Uncle Jago would spend a lot of time with him discussing business. But he hardly seemed like a member of the household."

"It's strange when you come to think about it. I wouldn't be here if it wasn't for him and I never knew him."

"Console yourself that nobody knew him well either. Uncle Jago once said he was a loner. Fenwick could tell you more about him than anyone else, I daresay."

"Where is Fenwick?"

"He left when your father died. I think he lives somewhere on the mainland."

"Do you know where?"

She shook her head and seeming to find the questions about my father becoming boring, she changed the subject. "I wonder if there are any of her things in the settle. Look, the seat is the lid of a sort of trunk."

She lifted it and I went over to look inside. There was nothing there but a traveling rug.

"It was evidently used chiefly as a seat," said Gwennol, putting the lid down and sitting on it. But she jumped up almost immediately. "Let's go and see Slack," she said. "I want him to row me over to the mainland tomorrow. Would you like to come? I know you haven't explored the Island yet and you did spend some time on the mainland waiting, but I always like to take advantage of calm seas. I shall be visiting friends so perhaps you'd like to explore a bit. We could go to the inn and get horses there, if you liked. It's what I often do."

I said I would like to do that.

"Very well, though of course it depends on the weather."

"So Slack will row us over."

"Yes, he loves to and it gives him an opportunity to see his mother."

"He's a strange boy. I discovered him when he was feeding the pigeons."

"Oh, so you've already met Slack. They say he's 'lacking' but over some things he's quite bright. It's just that he's different from most people. He came to us when he was about eleven. Uncle Jago noticed him. He had found a baby robin and was looking after it. Jago thought he'd be useful to look after the pigeons, which at that time were being attacked by some disease, and you know there's a legend about when the pigeons go the Kellaways will lose the Island. Not that Jago would believe that, but he always says he's respectful about superstitions because other people believe in them. Well, he found out that Slack was quite knowledgeable about birds and nature generally, so he took him on. The pigeons thrived immediately. Poor Slack, he can only just read and write and when he was on the mainland he used to go away for days at a time. He drove his mother frantic. Then he'd come back. He'd been in the woods watching the birds. Now of course he wouldn't dream of going away. He has his pigeons to care for."

"When I stayed at the Polcrag Inn his mother mentioned that he was here."

"Yes, Slack's her only child. When he was a little one and showed himself not quite like other children she used to say there was nothing wrong with him but that he came before he was quite done. He was born two months before he should have been apparently. She said he was slack-baked and then people started to call him Slack. Few people understand him and I think they underestimate him. He's a good boy at heart and he made a magnificent job of the pigeons."

"I could see how he felt about them and oddly enough they seemed to be aware of it."

"There's no doubt he's got a way with him. Come on. Let's go and find him now."

He was in the outhouse nursing a pigeon; he scarcely looked at us as we entered.

"She have hurt her leg, see?" he murmured. "There,

my pretty, 'tis only Miss Gwennol and Miss Ellen. They'll not harm 'ee."

"Can you heal it, Slack?" asked Gwennol.

"Surely, Miss Gwennol. There be this power in me."

Gwennol looked at me and smiled. "I want you to row me over to the mainland tomorrow, Slack. That's if the sea's like it is today."

"I'll have the boat for 'ee, Miss Gwennol."

"Miss Ellen is coming with me."

He nodded but his attention was all for the bird.

"You know what to do, Slack?" asked Gwennol.

"Oh, aye, Miss Gwennol, I do know."

"And the strange thing is," said Gwennol when we had left him, "that he does, and in a short time that bird will be hopping around so that you won't know him from the rest."

We went back through the courtyards.

In the afternoon I went for a walk and explored various parts of the Island. During dinner I talked to Jago about what I had seen and found I was beginning to catch his enthusiasm.

When I retired for the night I was pleasantly tired. Each day, I promised myself, I would learn more about my family. I was looking forward to more conversation with Gwennol during the next day's trip and I thought I might have a further word with Mrs. Pengelly.

Then, as I was about to get into bed I noticed my mother's sketchbook which I had found that morning, so setting the candle down on the little table by the bed, I started to look through it.

How interesting it was to see parts of the castle reproduced. She had had undoubted talent. One could feel the antiquity of those gray stone walls which she had drawn so realistically. There was a lovely picture of the Blue Rock Island with just a hint of the mainland in the distance. There were some portraits too. There was one of a plump child looking out on the world with large inquiring eyes. I stared at it; then I saw the caption: "E. Aged Two."

Why yes, now I recognized myself. So that was how I had looked when I was two. I turned the pages. I was looking at Jago—two portraits of him, facing each other. How she had caught the resemblance! They were like two different men—and yet they were both Jago. Strangely enough, he was smiling in both of them, but in one the smile was benign and in the other . . . ? It was that one which interested me. It was painted so that wherever one looked the eyes followed one. I had seen him look like that. Had it been in the house in Finlay Square? The heavy lids had fallen slightly over the eyes and it gave them a veiled, almost sinister look; and there was a certain twist about the mouth as though he were plotting something which could brook no good to someone.

I looked at that picture for some time and the pleasant drowsiness which I had felt before I had picked up the book had completely disappeared.

What was my mother trying to say in those pictures? One thing was certain: Jago is not what he might seem to be at times. Could it be that she was saying: "Beware, there are two Jagos"?

I felt uneasy because I was beginning to enjoy his company more than I cared to admit to myself.

I turned the pages and there was another double portrait. My mother seemed to have a fancy for that kind of art, and these two pictures, although clearly of the same subject, were as different from each other as those of Jago. In one of these I saw a rather demure girl, her hair in plaits, one of which fell over her shoulder. She was looking upwards as though in prayer and she held a Bible in her hands. In the picture on the opposite page, the girl's hair was unbound. It fell untidily and her face peeped out from the curtain of hair; the eyes were wild and there was a look of strangeness in the face that I found hard to define. The expression was in a way tortured, the eyes pleading; she looked as though she were trying to tell some secret and did not know how.

It was a horrible picture.

Then I saw the initial under it. "S."

I was quite shaken. I got out of bed and opened the cupboard door to look at the immature scratching there. I knew this was the same "S" who had written her message on the wall.

Who, I asked myself, was S?

Sleep had deserted me. I turned over the pages and studied the peaceful landscapes, the colored parts of the castle, hoping they would soothe me; but I kept seeing the wild eyes of S and the picture of Jago had taken me right back to those moments in the house in Finlay Square.

There was a further shock from that sketchbook—and this was the greatest of them all. I was telling myself that my mother had just been amusing herself and that it might be she had conjured up pictures out of her imagination . . . taking a face she knew well and adding touches to it to show how a line here and there could change the character.

I didn't really believe that but the thought was comforting.

I turned a page and gasped in amazement. My first thought was that I had fallen asleep and was dreaming, that this was a new way of getting into the dream. There it was on the page and there could be no doubt of it: the room of my dream!

There was the fireplace, the chimney seat, the rocking chair, the picture over the fireplace . . . everything was there as I had seen it in my dreams.

I was too stunned to do anything but stare at it.

One thought kept hammering on my brain: The phantom room existed. My mother had seen it. Could it be in the castle? But I had explored the castle.

The sketchbook fell from my hands and lay on the bed coverlet. What did it mean? What *could* it mean? I almost felt that the spirit of my mother was in this room and trying to get in touch with me through her sketchbook.

What did she know of Jago? She had seen him as two different men. And who was S who could look so demure and so wild?

But it was the picture of the room which haunted me.

Where was that room? One thing I had learned: It must exist, for my mother knew it. She had sketched it in her book. It was there for me to see. It was no piece of imagination.

I tried to look back over the years to my grandmother's garden when we had sat together on the lawn and her sketchbook lay on the grass between us.

One thing I could now be sure of: The dream room existed. But where?

# On Sanctuary Island

I slept fitfully that night and oddly enough I did not have my dream. The first thing I did when I was awake was to pick up the sketchbook, for I had an idea, which I didn't believe for more than a moment, that I had dreamed what I had seen in the book.

No. There it was. The room which I knew so well. But the picture of Jago looked different in daylight. Perhaps it was the candlelight which had made it seem sinister.

When Janet came in with my hot water I opened the sketchbook at the page where my mother had painted the dream room.

"What do you think of this room, Janet?" I asked, watching her closely.

"Oh, pretty, ain't it?"

"Have you ever seen that room?"

"Be it a real room then, Miss?"

It was clear that she had never seen it.

After breakfast Gwennol came to my room to see if I was ready.

"I've been looking through my mother's sketchbook," I said. "It's very interesting. Look at this picture of a room."

She looked and nodded.

"Do you know that room?" I asked.

She was clearly puzzled. "Know it? Should I? It's just an ordinary room."

An ordinary room! How odd to hear it so described! I wanted to say: That room has haunted me for as long as I can remember. If I could only find it I might understand why it is I dream about it and always feel in such an ordinary room such an overwhelming dread.

But I found it difficult to talk of it, so I said: "I wondered if it was somewhere in the castle."

She shook her head as though vaguely surprised that I should make so much of such an insignificant matter. She was not very interested in the pictures and no doubt put my preoccupation with them down to the fact that they had been painted by my mother.

At that moment there was a knock on the door. I called: "Come in," and Slack entered.

"What's wrong?" asked Gwennol.

" 'Tis just, Miss Gwennol, that I thought we'd best get an early start because of the tide."

"You're right," said Gwennol. "And we're almost ready."

On impulse I took the sketchbook to Slack. I was determined to leave no stone unturned in my attempt to discover where that room was and how my mother had known it so well that she could reproduce it in every detail.

"Slack," I asked, "have you ever seen that room?"

He did not exactly change color—in fact, I never saw Slack other than very pale—but there was a change in his face. There was a tension about him and he kept staring at the page and did not look at me.

"You know it then?" I prompted eagerly.

" 'Tis a pretty room, Miss Ellen," he said slowly.

"Yes, Slack, but you've seen it before, haven't you?"

Was it my fancy or did it seem as though a shutter had dropped over his eyes?

"I can't tell 'ee about a picture room, Miss Ellen," he said slowly.

"Why not?"

"My dear Ellen," laughed Gwennol, "you're obsessed by this room. Your mother just painted a cozy homely place and that's all there is to it. What's so special about that particular painting?"

Slack nodded. A blank look was in his eyes. I thought: He is stupid after all.

"Let's be going," said Gwennol. "Is everything ready, Slack?" They exchanged a glance which seemed to have a meaning from which I was shut out.

"Everything be done and we'm ready to go," said Slack.

We went out of the castle and down to the shore where the boats were moored. The sea was calm that morning and the boat skimmed lightly over the water. There was a seraphic smile on Slack's face as though he loved the task. He looked very different from the way he had when I had asked him about the room.

I watched him—Slack-Baked—not finished off. It was an apt description of him in a way. His hands were strong and yet they looked like a child's hands; his eyes were childlike too, except when the shutters came down.

"If the sea's like this when we come back I'll row," said Gwennol. "Do you row, Ellen?"

"A little," I answered, and I immediately thought of rowing on the river near Trentham Towers where Philip and I had once overturned a boat. Philip's image was so easy to invoke.

"Then you should practice and do more than a little because you'll find it very useful to row yourself round the Island. There's usually someone available to row us but it's good here to be self-reliant."

Nearer came the mainland and in due course we ran ashore on the sandy beach. Slack took off his boots and rolled up his trousers before jumping out and with the water halfway up his spindly legs pulled the boat in and tied it up. We then made our way to the inn.

Mrs. Pengelly came out beaming a welcome and her delight was obvious when she saw her son.

"Why 'tis you then, Augustus my boy," she said, and for a moment I wondered who Augustus was and then I realized that a mother would not use such a nickname for her beloved son.

"And welcome to 'ee, Miss Gwennol, Miss Ellen. Would you like some refreshment? You'll be wanting horses, I reckon."

"I shall," said Gwennol. "Shall you, Ellen?"

I said I would, for the thought had come to me that it would be pleasant to call at Hydrock Manor. After all, I had been invited to when I should visit the mainland and here was the opportunity.

'Well, you go to the stables then, Augustus, and tell your father the ladies be here and what they do want. Then come to the kitchen where I'll have a tidbit for 'ee. We've pasties straight from the oven. And what would the ladies be looking for? A glass of wine while you'm waiting?"

Gwennol said: "Has anyone arrived at the inn yet?"

"No, Miss Gwennol. No one be here yet."

"We'll drink a glass of wine then please," said Gwennol.

We went in and she brought out her blackberry wine and the saffron cakes with which I was becoming familiar.

We had not been there long when there was a commotion in the innyard and it was obvious from the sound of horse's hoofs that someone had arrived.

Gwennol sat very still in her seat and a smile slowly touched her face, making it not only striking but beautiful.

"In the inn parlor," said a voice which I recognized with pleasure was that of Sir Michael Hydrock.

As he entered Gwennol rose and went to him, holding out both her hands, which he took. Then he saw me and a smile of delighted recognition lit up his face.

"Miss Kellaway," he cried. "Miss Ellen Kellaway."

Gwennol looked in astonishment from one of us to the

other. "You . . . you know each other. You . . . you can't."

"Oh, but we do," said Michael, dropping her hands and advancing towards me. I held out a hand, which he took and covered with both his. "How are you enjoying the Island?" he asked.

"I'm finding it enormously interesting," I told him.

"I don't understand this," said Gwennol rather impatiently.

"It's easily explained," Michael told her. And I added: "When I was waiting to come to the Island and had to spend a day at the inn I did a little exploring and got lost in Hydrock's woods. Sir Michael rescued me."

"I see," said Gwennol coolly.

"You must come to the Manor now," said Michael warmly.

"Thank you. I should love that. I found your house enchanting."

"Are the Pengellys' horses ready for you?" he asked.

"I've already ordered them," said Gwennol.

"Well, when you're ready perhaps we can go."

"Ellen may have other plans,' suggested Gwennol. "She said she wanted to explore the countryside."

"As a matter of fact," I answered, "it had occurred to me that I might call at the Manor." I turned to Michael. "You did say that I might call when I was on the mainland."

"In fact," he replied, "I should have been very hurt if you hadn't."

"I'm looking forward to seeing the Manor again."

"Ah, now you've lived in the castle. We're not as grand as that, I'm afraid."

"The Manor is beautiful," I said.

"It's the most beautiful house I've ever seen," added Gwennol fervently.

"Thank you, Gwennol," said Michael. "Do you know, I rather think the same myself."

We went into the yard where the horses were ready for us. Mrs. Pengelly, delighted to have her son with her for a few hours and pleased, I think, to see me again, watched us ride off. In a very short time we were in the drive leading to the Manor.

"I'm going to show you the house, Miss Kellaway," said Michael to me. "You didn't see it last time. By the way, how's the ankle?"

"I never felt any more from it. The next morning I shouldn't have known anything had happened to it."

"So you hurt your ankle then?" asked Gwennol.

I told her in more detail what had happened; she listened intently, but her expression was less pleasant, as though she were brooding.

We went into the hall with its refectory table, pewter ornaments and companion benches and I felt that sense of peace which I had experienced when I had last been here.

"There's something so friendly about this house," I commented.

"We all feel it," said Gwennol shortly.

"Yes," added Michael, "there's a saying in the family that the house will either welcome or reject you and that one knows it almost as soon as one enters it. It certainly seems to welcome you, Miss Kellaway."

"That is endowing a house with a personality," I replied. "I do that. I didn't know many people did."

"Rather a fanciful notion, you think. But as you are so impressed by the house I should like to show it to you. You don't mind, Gwennol? Gwennol is a very old friend," he told me. "She knows the house as well as I do."

"I'd love to see it," I assured him, and Gwennol put in: "You know very well I can't see enough of the place."

"Look at that armor on the walls. Those breastplates were worn by ancestors of mine during the Civil War. These pewter vessels have been used by the family for hundreds of years. I like to keep everything as it was as far as possible."

"Jago is like that too, isn't he, Gwennol?" I said, for I was anxious that she should join in the conversation. I realized by this time that she had been expecting Michael at the inn and that he was the friend whom she was proposing to visit. She had not therefore been very pleased that I had already met him and was joining them. I fancied too that her feelings towards him were warmer than those of ordinary friendship; there was something about the manner in which she looked at him which betrayed it and the softness of her eyes and mouth was rare with her, I was sure.

"Jago would like to go back to feudal days," said Gwennol sharply. "He'd like to be not only the lord of the manor but lord of us all."

"He's very proud of the Island," I said, defending him, "and justly so. I've been talking to some of the people on my walks and it's easy to see how they respect him. He's done a great deal for the place."

"My dear Ellen, they're afraid to say a word against him. If he's not entirely their lord and master he's at least their landlord. He could turn them out of their homes tomorrow if they offended him."

"I am sure he would do no such thing," I said warmly.

She raised her eyebrows and smiled at Michael. "Ellen has a great deal to learn," she said.

In his easy manner he diverted the subject from Jago and said: "Come and look at the chapel."

Our footsteps rang out as we crossed the stone flags of the hall and he led us up a stone spiral staircase to a heavy oak iron-studded door.

"Many a drama has taken place here. There's a priest's hole in this chapel I'll show you. There's also a lepers' squint. One can imagine the terror when the priest had to be hidden away at a moment's notice. One of my ancestors married a Spanish lady and she was the one who was reckless enough to have a priest in the house. Someday I intend to compile a history of the family. There are lots of documents in the vaults under the chapel."

"That sounds exciting."

"It's the sort of occupation which is fun if you share it with someone. Gwennol has promised to help me."

"There's nothing I should like more," she said, becoming animated. "Particularly with a family such as yours,

Michael. Ours is rather different." She grimaced. "We're more the brigand type. You are the aristocrats."

"There are skeletons in the cupboards of most families," commented Michael. "Who knows what we shall unearth in these documents."

"What an exciting thought!" cried Gwennol, and she looked as though she would like to suggest they get down to the task immediately and leave me to wander round on my own.

The floor of the chapel was paved with small square stones set in a mosaic pattern. There were about twelve pews with linenfold ends. On the altar was a very fine cloth worked, he told me, by his grandmother, so comparatively recent. "There are two squints," he went on, "one is the lepers' squint from a small room beyond where lepers might come and look through into the chapel without contaminating or distressing those who were there. The other . . ." He pointed upwards. "That comes from a little alcove from above where the ladies used to congregate when they did not wish to come down to the chapel, perhaps through sickness or some incapacity. Now I'll take you to the solarium and show you the other squint."

"You see how wonderful it is," said Gwennol, "to belong to such a family."

"It's rather like a chain coming down through time," said Michael. "From each link springs another and so on. Luckily we have always had boys in the family, so the name has been preserved. I want my sons to have sons and so the name will be carried on."

"Have you sons?" I asked.

He laughed. "I haven't married so far."

"But you will," I said. "You will regard it as a duty to do so."

"I should like it to be something more than that."

Gwennol was looking at him intently and I thought: Yes, she is in love with him. I'm in the way. I shouldn't be with them. I ought to have seen that and said I wanted to go off on my own. She shows it clearly and just because he's too polite to show he doesn't really want me, I imagined he was eager for me to come.

"The solarium is a bright room—naturally," he was saying. "The room built to catch the sunshine. It does too. I believe it was used as a ballroom at one time. There is a screen across it to make it into two rooms but it is rarely used now. I like it to be as it was originally intended." He led the way. It was necessary to pass through the punch room, where I had been on my last visit, and we mounted some stone stairs, passed along a passage and were in the solarium. The sun streamed through the wide windows onto the deep blue of the tapestry which adorned one side of the wall and which depicted the Civil War. There were the battlefields—Naseby and Marston Moor—and on the opposite side of the room Prince Charles in the oak tree and being welcomed in London on the Restoration.

I examined them closely and was enchanted by the fine workmanship and the subtle colors. He watched me, obviously pleased with my absorption.

"Here you see the squint," he said. "Come into this alcove. This is where the ladies sat and as you see they look right down into the chapel. Let us sit here for a while. I want to tell Miss Kellaway about our ghost, Gwennol."

Gwennol nodded. "You'll like this one, Ellen. It's the nicest ghost that ever was."

"There were three sisters at the house," said Michael. "They each wished to marry and their father would not give his consent. One ran away and left the family forever; the two others remained; they grew more bitter every day; their lives were a misery to them and all around them. They never forgave their father and the story is that when he was dying he begged their forgiveness and they refused to give it. And he is our ghost. He is said to be a benign one. He roams the house trying to earn forgiveness for his selfishness by making everything go smoothly for lovers."

"That certainly is the most pleasant ghost story I ever heard."

"It was in this room he died," he said. "This room is

supposed to be good for lovers. In those days there was a bed in the far end which was divided off by the screen. That was his bedroom. It is said that all Hydrock marriages are happy ones now because of his influence."

"Well, he has certainly earned forgiveness for his sins."

"Indeed he has. But it's a pleasant thought don't you agree? Brides come to this house with the feeling that their marriages must be happy because old Simon Hydrock will not allow them to be otherwise."

"It must be a very comfortable thought for a Hydrock bride."

He was smiling at me. "I assure you it is. My mother used to tell me the story often. She was a happy bride. 'When you have a bride,' she used to say, 'tell her that she will have special care.' "

"And she herself did?"

"It was her way of looking at life. Isn't that what happiness is? You could put two people in the same set of circumstances and one would think him- or herself happy while another would be full of complaints. When I was ten years old she knew she was suffering from an incurable disease. She lived exactly ten months in that state. She told me about it because she wanted me to know the truth and not listen to garbled stories. 'I'm fortunate,' she said. 'I've had such a happy life and now that I'm ill I shall die before I'm in pain.' And she did. She did not suffer at all, though had she lived longer she inevitably would."

I was deeply moved by the story, so was Gwennol. Her eyes never left Michael as he talked.

"Now," he said, "we'll go to luncheon. I'm sure you are ready for it after your sea trip."

"How kind of you," I said. "I didn't expect to be invited to luncheon. Perhaps I . . ."

They were both looking at me and I went on: "I think Gwennol was expected but I . . ."

"We're delighted to have you," said Michael warmly. "Yes, Gwennol was expected. I had the message," he told her. "It never fails." He turned back to me. "It's an excellent method of communication. With all that water between us we can never be sure when messages will reach us. Slack sends them over by carrier pigeon. He trains the birds, you know. He has a magical touch. We have pigeons here, too. After luncheon we'll show Miss Kellaway the gardens, won't we, Gwennol?"

I enjoyed sitting at the table in the dining room with its window looking out over smooth lawns, I loved that aura of brooding peace and I thought it emanated from the spirit of the old man who had ruined his daughters' lives and had tried to atone ever since. I sat in my chair, which was covered in dark red velvet, and looked across the table at Michael Hydrock and it seemed to me that he was a man who was completely contented with his lot, which is a rare thing. I could not help comparing him with Jago —that restless spirit, those changing moods, the unpredictability which I could not help finding half attractive, half repelling, but always intriguing.

After luncheon we strolled through the Manor grounds. They were beautifully kept and conventional. There was the fashionable Italian garden, the English rose garden, the shrubbery, paddocks and well-kept lawns. There were several gardeners at work who touched their forelocks as we passed. Michael Hydrock was, I was sure, a highly respected and benign master.

When it was time for us to return to the inn, Michael accompanied us and there was Slack waiting to row us across.

"Come again soon," said Michael, and there was no doubt that I was included in that invitation.

Gwennol was silent as we rowed back. She scarcely looked at me. I sensed that there was a change in our relationship, for whereas before she had been inclined to want to make me feel at home, now she was suspicious of me.

When we reached the Island we left Slack to tie up the boat and made our way to the castle.

Gwennol said: "How strange that you should have met Michael and did not mention it."

"I suppose there were so many other things to talk about."

"And you hurt your ankle in the woods."

"Yes, just as he appeared, I tripped and fell. Then he took me to the Manor House and brought me back to the inn."

She gave a little laugh. "You apparently didn't hurt your ankle very badly."

"It was just a temporary twist. It was all right the next morning."

"Just a convenient little twist," she said, and before I could give expression to my indignation she had turned and run into the castle.

I went up to my room. The pleasant day had been spoilt. I should have to be careful now and stay away from Hydrock Manor.

Jago looked at me reproachfully. We were at dinner that night and he had asked how I had been spending the day. I told him I had been to the mainland.

"What, Ellen, deserting us already?"

"It was only for a few hours."

"There's so much on the Island you haven't seen yet."

"I shall appreciate it all the more for having been away for a day."

"You have what we call here a silvery tongue. You say the right thing, doesn't she, Gwennol?"

"I'm sure she does . . . on every occasion," said Gwennol shortly.

"Well, where did you go?" asked Jago.

"To Hydrock Manor."

"Both of you?"

"I'd met Michael Hydrock before."

Jago put down his knife and fork and gazed at me. I was aware of Jenifry's eyes on me too. Gwennol kept hers on her plate.

I repeated once more the account of my meeting with Michael in the woods and how I had hurt my ankle.

"You were hurt!" cried Jago. "Why didn't you tell us?"

"It was nothing. In fact, the next day I had forgotten about it."

"It was one of those temporary twists," said Gwennol, and I detected a note of sarcasm in her voice.

"And what happened then?" asked Jenifry.

"He took me to the Manor and a Mrs. Hocking—the housekeeper, I think—looked at it and said I shouldn't walk on it for a while and then Sir Michael drove me back to the inn."

"A very perfect gentleman," commented Jago.

"I thought so," I retorted.

I realized that this information had disturbed both Jago and Jenifry.

Jago said: "Tomorrow I will show you more of the Island. There's a good deal you have to discover yet, you know."

"Thank you," I replied.

"I was telling Ellen," said Gwennol, "that she should practice rowing."

"Have you ever rowed?" asked Jago.

"Yes, but not at sea, on a river, which I suppose was different."

"It's the same really," said Gwennol, "only you have to be more careful at sea—mostly because of the weather. When it's calm it's perfectly safe."

"Just practice going from bay to bay," said Jago, "and at first always have someone with you. I'll take you out tomorrow. Slack will always take you where you want to go. But just don't go alone at first."

I said I would like to try.

"First lesson tomorrow," said Jago.

I was very tired when I went to my room. It had seemed a long day. I had very much enjoyed visiting the Hydrock Manor even though the day had been spoilt by Gwennol's jealousy. It meant I should have to be very careful in future, which was a pity because it had been rather comforting to have such a pleasant friend on the mainland.

I lighted the candles on my dressing table and was sitting there plaiting my hair when there was a knock on the door.

I started up in dismay. I wasn't sure why, but always when the candles were lighted in this room I felt uneasy.

For a few seconds I merely looked at the door. Then there was a further knock and the door was quietly opened. Jenifry stood there holding a candle.

"I thought you might be asleep when you didn't answer," she said.

"I was just about to say 'Come in' when you did," I replied.

"I wanted to have a word with you."

She set down the candle and drew up a chair, so that we were both sitting at the dressing table.

"It's about Gwennol and Michael Hydrock," she said.

"Oh?"

I caught her reflection in the mirror. Her eyes were downcast and it was as though she did not want to look at me.

"He's one of the most eligible bachelors in the neighborhood," she went on. "He and Gwennol have always been good friends, in fact. . . ."

"More than friends?" I suggested.

She nodded. "The general opinion is that they will in due course make a match of it . . . providing there are no obstacles."

"Obstacles?" I repeated.

I watched her reflection. Her mouth twisted and for a moment she looked quite ugly. It's the distortion of the mirror, I told myself hastily.

"A great family like that . . ." she said bitterly. "There are some who wouldn't think Gwennol quite suitable. They're so proud of their ancestry." Her lips curled in contempt. "That Mrs. Hocking . . . she doesn't think anyone but the daughter of a duke or an earl is good enough for him."

"Surely she wouldn't have any say in the matter."

"She's a sly one, planting doubts and suchlike. You know the sort. A woman in that position can have great influence. She was his nurse. She looks upon him as her child still. Clucks over him, pampers him. . . . Nobody's good enough for her dear Michael."

"He strikes me as a man who would make up his own mind."

"I reckon the Kellaways are good enough for anybody, but there's the story of our bastard branch . . . having something of the Devil in us."

"He wouldn't believe such a legend, I'm sure."

"People are superstitious and although he might not believe it, he'd be aware of what people were thinking and the effect it might have on future generations and all that. They were getting along very well and she was going to help him with his book. Now she comes back . . . a little upset."

"Why?" I asked boldly.

She moved closer to me. I just could not bring myself to look at her face then. If I did I knew I should see the evil expression there which I had caught in the mirror on my first night.

"You know, don't you?" she said. "He was very taken with you, wasn't he? All that play about a twisted ankle."

"It wasn't play. I really did hurt my ankle."

"Well, it made a romantic beginning, didn't it? I daresay he found you different from most of the girls he meets. Ambitious mothers of neighboring squires are constantly bringing their daughters forward and they are country girls . . . all of a piece. And then you come—different, already having lived, as some would put it. Naturally his interest is aroused and although you're a Kellaway too, yours is the pure strain. Your branch escaped the Devil's taint, didn't it?"

I felt exasperated. "Listen," I said almost fiercely. "I met a man when I arrived. I was lost in his woods and he took me back to the inn. I met him again with Gwennol and lunched at his house, and you are suggesting I am trying to snatch him from under the noses of ambitious mothers with marriageable daughters. I've met him; I like him; I like his house. There's nothing more in it than that."

"Gwennol seems to think . . ."

"Gwennol is in love with him and sensitive. I can assure you I am not desperately looking for a husband and ready to take the first man I meet."

She rose and picked up her candle and as she stood there I shivered slightly. She was holding the candle in front of her, below her face, and it had the effect of lighting it up while the rest of her was shadowy, so that it seemed like a disembodied face there in the mirror. There was a faint color under the skin and her eyes were half closed. She looked malevolent.

"Perhaps I have said too much." Her voice was a whisper. "But, *please*, do not try to take Michael Hydrock from Gwennol."

"My dear Jenifry, from what I know of him he will not be a man to be taken. He will make his own choice."

"It is Gwennol," she said. "It *was* Gwennol before you came."

"Then," I answered, "you can rest assured it is still Gwennol."

"Good night," she said. "I hope you understand a mother's anxieties."

"I understand," I told her.

The door shut on her and I saw her back looking at my reflection. I was certain that there was something more than the fears of an anxious mother for her daughter's happiness. She filled me with apprehension, for it was as though she were warning me.

As if enough had not happened on that day, before I slept that night I found the first of the notebooks.

I was so disturbed by Jenifry's visit that I knew it would be foolish to try to sleep, so I decided I would write a letter to Esmeralda. She would be longing to hear about my first impressions of the Island and it would be soothing to write to her of the more peaceful aspects. I would tell her about the small farms and pretty houses with their orange-colored roofs, the Lives and Moonlight Cottages and the rest.

There was a rather charming little desk in my room, small, its sloping top covered with leather and inlaid with ivory. I had already noticed it, admired it and put my writing materials inside it. I tried to open it but it was difficult and I imagined the paper had become jammed in some way. I forced it open with all my strength and as I did so a flap which I had not noticed inside the top compartment fell open and the notebook came out.

I picked it up and saw that inside was written in a childish hand: "S.K. Her Book." This, I guessed, was the one who had scratched those words in the cupboard and whose picture my mother had painted.

I flicked through the book. Some of the pages had been written on and sentences caught my eye.

"I hate it here. I wish I could escape." And then: "My father hates me. I don't know why. But then I don't think he likes anyone very much . . . not her . . . nor Baby." I turned to the front page. It was headed "Life on an Island."

This was only a child's exercise book, I realized, but it had clearly belonged to the mysterious S.K. "I am a prisoner in this room" would most likely have referred to her being sent to her room as punishment for some misdemeanor as most children had been at some time. But the two portraits had fascinated me and I wanted to know more of her. I decided to ask someone at the first opportunity. Gwennol was the obvious one, but I thought it might be advisable to avoid Gwennol for a few days.

I looked down at the large scrawl on the page.

"I am supposed to be writing an essay," I read. "It is to be called 'Life on an Island.' Miss Homer said I shall stay in my room until it is done, but I am not going to write an essay. I'm writing this instead. It is a secret and I shall not show her. She wants me to write about crabs and jellyfish and tides and scenery, but I don't care about those things. I'm going to write about Them and Myself in a way I can't talk because there is no one to talk to. It will be fun to write it because then I can read it afterwards and remember it all afresh. My father hates me.

He always did. My stepmother doesn't like me very much
either. Nobody likes me except Baby and she's too young
and silly to know. My stepmother loves Baby. She said to
me: 'Look at your little sister. Isn't she a love?' I said:
'She's only a half sister. That's not a real one. I'm glad. I
don't want a silly baby for a sister.' Baby cries for what
she wants and then she smiles when she gets it and everyone comes and looks at her and says how lovely she is
and what a good baby, although she has been screaming
for something a minute before. I suppose I was a baby
once. I don't think they said I was wonderful though."

There were blank pages after that, and then the writing
started again.

"I have just read what I wrote when Miss Homer sent
me up to do my essay. It made me laugh so much I'm
going to do some more. It reminds me how cross she was
when she found out I hadn't done my essay. She said: 'I
don't know what will become of you.' That's what they all
think. I can see it in their faces. What will become of her!
I am rather naughty really, although I can be good for a
while. 'Butter wouldn't melt in her mouth today,' they say.
I wish I could *see* my father. He doesn't want to see me
although he sees Baby now and then. Even he likes to see
her. It's something to do with my mother, I think . . . I
mean the reason he doesn't like me. He didn't like her. I
was the reason, I heard one of the servants say. It's funny
to be a reason for something and not know it. Then she
died. I was seven then. I remember it was just before my
birthday and everyone forgot it—my birthday, I mean.
She was buried in the cemetery. I go to her grave sometimes. I cried a lot because she loved me and I didn't
really know until she died that nobody else did. Miss
Homer doesn't. Nor does Nanny. They say I'll come to a
bad end with my tempers and tantrums. My mother used
to hide my birthday presents. There was always more than
one. I suppose that was because she knew no one else
would give me anything and she wanted to make it seem
as though they had. But there was always a mystery
present. She never said who that came from. I said she

gave it to me like the rest but she said she didn't. But after she died I looked for the mystery present and it never came, so that shows it was hers too. I became worse after she died. I do terrible things, like the time I threw Miss Homer's hair dye over the floor when she didn't want anyone to know she used it.

"Then my stepmother came and it all changed and was better for a while. Stepmother used to have them dress me in my white embroidered dress and she gave me a lovely blue sash to wear. I had to go and talk to my father but I knew he didn't like me and only spoke to me because Stepmother asked him to. Baby came then and everybody made a fuss of her and nobody cared about me. My stepmother only cared about Baby and gave up trying to make my father like me.

"Oh dear, this is silly. What's the good of writing down what I know already?"

*I* wanted to know more, but the pages at the end of the book were blank except one on which she had done a few sums. She had written at the bottom of that page: "I hate arithmetic."

I put the notebook back into the desk. I was in no mood for writing to Esmeralda now.

I took the oars and Jago sat opposite me in the boat. We were going to row to the bird sanctuary, which he was eager to show me. It was not very far from Kellaway Island, he told me, and it would be good practice for me.

It was a beautiful day with a pellucid sea as still as a lake and with that pearly tinge which I had noticed before and which I had thought so attractive.

"It's the best time of the year," said Jago, "before the October gales set in."

"Are they very wild?"

"They can be. On the other hand, they might not come at all. There's only one thing that's certain about our weather and that's its unpredictability. You row very well, Ellen. I can see you're going to be quite a champion."

"I realize that if I'm going to stay here for a little while it's something I have to learn to do."

"*If* you're going to stay. My dear Ellen, I hope you are going to stay here a very long time." I looked up and was a little disturbed by the intensity of his gaze. "Why not?" he went on. "You are fitting very well into our way of life. You are beginning to love the Island, confess it."

"I'm finding it all very interesting, yes. I don't need to have to confess that, do I? Isn't it obvious?"

"It is and it pleases me. After all, you are a Kellaway."

"There is something about a place which has been the home of one's ancestors for generations. I think that, when I was in Cousin Agatha's house, I was, without realizing it, dogged by the notion that I didn't belong."

"You belong here," he said earnestly.

I was silent, concentrating on rowing. The island sanctuary lay before us, a green hump in the ocean. "Run her up to the beach here," he said.

I was proud that I was able to do so with a certain competence because I had an absurd childish desire to shine in his eyes.

He helped me out of the boat, tied it up and we started to walk up a slope to a kind of plateau. Birds rose all around us, gulls mostly, screaming their indignation at being disturbed.

Jago produced two bags containing scraps of food, one of which he gave to me.

"I always bring them something when I come," he explained. "It's a sort of apology for coming at all. This is their sanctuary and they need some compensation for receiving unwanted visitors."

"Do you think they are as inhospitable as that?"

"Undoubtedly. Look at those choughs over there. There are hundreds of them. We get the occasional stormy petrel. She just lands to lay her eggs and then departs. I saw a beauty once. It was quite an occasion."

"I'm surprised that you find time to be interested in these things."

"I find time for anything I want to do, don't you, Ellen?"

"I suppose so."

He put his arm through mine, ostensibly to help me up the slope, but I felt he was conveying the fact that he was going to find a great deal of time available to spend in my company.

"You'll become more and more absorbed in the life of the Island," he said. "You won't really want to go on trips to the mainland very often. It was interesting that you went to Hydrock's place. Pleasant, isn't it? But very conventional. Gwennol has a romantic attachment to the place. Poor girl, if she ever married Michael Hydrock she'd be bored for the rest of her life."

"Why should she be?"

"Because of the life she would lead. Imagine it. Social occasions. Hunt balls, good works, one day very like another and the same thing going on year after year."

I didn't answer.

"Let's sit down here," he went on. He had brought a traveling rug with him and spread it out on the grass for us to sit on. We looked over the sea. The main island looked beautiful with its gentle green slopes and sandy bays and the sun glinting on those orange roofs. And not far off was the Blue Rock Island. The rocks looked very blue today because of the clear air, and I thought I could make out the house which someone had told me was there. It was sheltered by tall shrubs and was not far from the beach.

"Tell me," I said suddenly, "who is S.K.?"

He wrinkled his brows. "Who?" he asked.

"I think she must have occupied the room I am now in. There are scratchings on the cupboard wall and the initials S.K."

He continued to look puzzled, then he laughed. "You must be referring to Silva."

"Silva? Was she Silva Kellaway?"

"Yes, she was your half sister."

"Then I'm the Baby referred to. Oh, you see, I found one of her notebooks in the desk and she had written something in it about her stepmother and a baby. How strange! My sister!"

"Your half sister."

"We shared the same father and the stepmother she mentions is my mother.

"Poor Silva, her life was tragic."

"*Was*? She is dead then?"

"It's almost certain that she was drowned."

"*Almost* certain?"

"Her body was never found, although the boat was. It was washed up on the shores of the Island . . . without Silva."

"How very sad. How old was she when this happened?"

"It happened about eighteen months ago. She would be well into her twenties. Twenty-eight perhaps."

"And she lived at the castle . . . in my room . . . until then?"

"Yes. She was a difficult girl. No one knew why she should take a boat out on such a night as she did, but that was what happened. It was a crazy thing to do, but then she was crazy."

"You mean she was . . . *mad*?"

"Oh no, just unbalanced. She'd be very docile for months on end and then suddenly she would create scenes. She was a queer creature. I had very little to do with her."

"Do tell me all about it. I'm longing to hear everything about the family."

"There's not a lot to tell. Your father married twice. His first wife was Effie and she had Silva. Effie and your father didn't hit it off together and they used to quarrel violently. Your father was not an easy man to live with, obviously. He was not even fond of his daughter. It might have been that he was disappointed because she wasn't a boy. I don't know. In any case, he had little time for the child and could hardly bear to look at her."

"Poor Silva!" I said. "She noticed it and it made her very unhappy. No wonder she was unbalanced as you say."

"Then Effie died of pneumonia and after a year or two

your father went to London on business and came back with your mother. That seemed another mistake because she couldn't settle down either. Then you were born and that seemed to reconcile them, but only for a little while. Your father was not meant to live peaceably and they quarreled and she eventually went off, taking you with her. That was a surprise. She left no warning. She just went off. So you see he couldn't have been an easy husband to live with."

"I think poor little Silva must have been very unhappy."

"I wish we could have known why she left, where she was going, and indeed could have some proof that she was drowned."

"If the boat she went in was washed up empty isn't that proof enough?"

"It is to some, but you know what people are and there never were people more like those around here to see the unnatural hand even in the most ordinary happenings. They say that she was 'taken by the Little People,' who, as you have gathered, are a supernatural colony who inhabit these parts. She was always 'fey,' they said, and in fact 'one of them,' and they just took her back where she came from. Some say she was discontented with her lot and asked the Devil to take her. As you know, the Devil has played quite a big part in our family saga."

"So you told me."

"Well, you'll hear people tell you that on wild nights they can hear Silva's cries mingled with the sound of the wind and the waves. Some of the servants think she haunts the castle."

"Do you think she haunts my room?"

He burst out laughing. "I hope I haven't alarmed you, Ellen. My dear girl, we'll change your room."

"No, I shouldn't want that. I'd like to meet Silva, so if she should 'walk,' as they say, she'd be very welcome. She was my sister. That's what I can't forget. All those years of my childhood when I longed for a sister and had to do with Esmeralda, I really had one. I wish I'd grown up in the castle."

He leaned towards me suddenly and gripped my hand.

"So do I, Ellen. Then you wouldn't have to get to know me now, would you? We'd be firm friends already, but then we soon shall be."

A gull shrieked overhead as though he were mocking us. Jago did not seem to hear. His expression had grown tender.

We were silent for a while. I was thinking of my sister growing up lonely in the castle while I was the unwanted one in Cousin Agatha's house. Those few sentences in the notebook had built up a picture in my mind. The unwanted child who was so poignantly aware of her aloneness. Nobody could understand that better than I. I had been singularly lucky to be blessed with a resilient nature, and perhaps having a companion like Esmeralda, who was meek and suffered so much more from circumstances than I had done, so that my lot always seemed better than hers. But poor Silva, living in that vast castle with no one in whom she could confide! I was sure my mother had been kind to her but she had run away when I was only three years old. Silva could not have been so very old then. How old? I wondered. Perhaps twelve years old.

Jago was surrounded by birds, for he was throwing tidbits from his bag. I joined him and shared his pleasure in the rising and swooping of the graceful creatures.

"Aren't they beautiful?" he cried. "Do you know those biggest birds weigh only a few ounces? Wouldn't *you* like to fly like that, Ellen?"

"What a glorious feeling it must be. I wonder why they make such mournful cries."

At that moment I was aware that we were being overlooked. I turned round sharply and saw that a man had climbed onto the plateau and was standing behind us. Jago had seen him too.

"Why, it's James Manton," he said. "Good day, Manton. Are you working here?"

We rose to our feet as the man advanced. "Ellen," said Jago, "let me present James Manton, Manton, this is my ward, Miss Ellen Kellaway."

"Why, you're the artist," I cried.

He bowed and looked pleased, no doubt thinking I knew his work.

"I'm glad to meet you," he said. "I just rowed over here to make a few sketches."

"So you'll be painting our Island, will you?" said Jago.

"Yes, and the birds. This is one of the spots where one can get the best view of your Island. The light's good today. Just look at the color of the sea."

We agreed that it was even more beautiful than usual.

"Difficult to capture," said the artist, "but I'll have a shot. I hope you're enjoying your visit to the Island, Miss Kellaway."

I said I was finding it fascinating.

He watched a bird soar away into the distance and then with a nod said: "Good day to you!" and went back the way he had come.

"Now he is the one who lives on the Blue Rock Island, isn't he?" I said to Jago.

"Yes. He's lived there for a good many years. He paints a lot of bird pictures. He's rather good with them. I expect that's why he likes it here. He came for a few weeks, so the story goes, and he stayed here. He goes away now and then though. To London to arrange about the sale of pictures, I imagine."

"Yet he doesn't come to Kellaway Island."

"Not since this quarrel with your father. We're polite when we meet but we don't visit. What do you think about getting back now? Are you sufficiently rested to row us?"

"I don't feel in the least tired."

He sprang up, threw the rest of the contents of his bag to the birds—and I did the same—picked up the traveling rug and, taking my hand, ran down the slope with me to the spot where our boat was moored.

"Jump in," he said. "I'll push her out."

He did so and I took the oars.

"You don't need practice," he said. "You're an expert oarswoman."

We reached the Island and tied up the boat.

"Before we go back," he said, "I'm going to take you to old Tassie, the wise woman of the Island."

"A sort of lady witch doctor?"

"Not a bad description. She'll tell your fortune. I know you like having your fortune told. All women do."

We walked up the incline and came to a small cottage which stood in the center of a garden; among the herbs which grew there I recognized rosemary, parsley and sage; but there were plenty of others which I did not know. As we approached, an old woman appeared at the cottage door.

"Good day to 'ee, Master Jago," she said.

"Good day, Tassie," he returned. "I've brought my ward along to see you. This is Miss Ellen Kellaway."

"Good day to 'ee, my lady," she said. I returned her greeting while I studied her. Her face was very wrinkled and her bright black eyes reminded me of a monkey's, sharp and shrewd in her aged face; she wore a gray crocheted shawl about her shoulders and the black cat who rubbed himself about her skirts, with his bright green wary eyes, fitted the scene perfectly, as no doubt he was meant to.

We stepped into a room cluttered with objects and in which there was a faint pungent odor. The hearth was large enough to take a chimney seat on either side and the cat, who had followed us in, leaped into a basket and lay there watching us. I noticed the various pots and pans full of mysterious contents which stood on the table and the bunches of herbs which hung from the beams.

"So you have brought your young lady to visit me, Master." She almost smirked. " 'Twas what I would have expected of 'ee."

"She's anxious to learn about the Island, Tassie, and she couldn't know much until she'd visited you."

" 'Tis so. I've lived in this dwelling all my life, my dear. My mother lived here before me and my grandmother. It were her mother who had it when married. Moonlight

Cottage it were, built in a night, though it have been added to since."

"That must have been in my great-grandfather's day," said Jago.

She nodded. "And a man he were for scattering his seed far and wide. There be a saying on the Island that there's scarce a family that hasn't got the Kellaway blood in it somewhere back."

"It binds us together," said Jago. "What have you got to tell Madam Ellen?"

"Let me see for 'ee, my dear. Come close and do 'ee sit down near me."

She took my hands but did not gaze into my palms but into my face.

"Oh my life, I do see much here for you. There's good and there's bad."

"Doesn't that apply to all of us?" asked Jago.

"To some more than others." Jago was watching her intently and I was as much aware of him as of her. "You've had trouble . . . tragedy in your life. You've lost someone close to 'ee. That was a black time, and now there's a choice for 'ee. There's two roads open to 'ee. You must be sure and take the right one."

"Tassie has special powers," said Jago. "She is greatly respected on the Island."

"How shall I know which is the right one?" I asked.

"You'll be guided, my dear. There's one right beside 'ee to guide 'ee. You'm come home to your family and 'tis a good thing you've done, for that's where you belong to be."

The black cat rose from its basket, stretched itself and came to rub itself against her skirts.

"I see happiness for 'ee, me dear, if you do take the right turning and I see trouble if you don't. You'm facing the right way now but a little while back 'twasn't so."

"You'd better listen to Tassie's advice," said Jago. "The girls of the Island all come to her and they'll tell you she's never wrong."

" 'Tis so. A love potion they'll be wanting and I give it

to them. They wants some young fellow to fall in love with them. You won't want that, me dear. Your fate be settled. 'Twill be soon, for 'tis right at hand."

Jago laughed, evidently pleased with her.

"Go on, Tassie," he commanded.

" 'Tis for the young lady to take the right course and she'll be happy for the rest of her days. She'll have fine sons and a daughter or two to bring comfort to her. She's had a long journey but she's home now."

"There, Ellen," said Jago smiling at me, his eyes gleaming, and I thought: He is really falling in love with me!

The prospect excited me and at the same time made me feel a little apprehensive. I knew that his emotions would be fierce, for there were no half measures about him. He was young; he could not be much more than thirty; he was unmarried—I wondered why he had remained so, so long —and right from the moment I had seen him at the Carringtons' I had been aware of him . . . physically.

Tassie seemed to have come to the conclusion that she had settled my future. All I had to do was to be guided, presumably by Jago.

She started to tell me what she did for the young people of the Island. "I'll charm the warts off their skins, the sties from their eyes, and when they'm choking for breath I'll give ease for that. There's many who have more faith in Tassie than any doctor. And I'll look into the future too. My great-grandmother was hanged for a witch. We don't hang them now. People has more sense. They know a white witch from a black 'un and we're the white sort in our family. Pellar families we be. Long ago a mermaid were stranded on this Island and one of my ancestors helped her back to the sea. For that she gave the family special sight. And we've had it ever since."

"So if you see a mermaid about, Ellen," said Jago, "help her back to the sea. You'll probably be rewarded."

" 'Tis true," said Tassie. "The seventh child of a seventh child and pellar into the bargain." She came close to me. "I can help you to lift a spell that be cast on you, to turn aside an evil wish. So come to me, young maid, if you be in trouble."

"That's more than an invitation, I must tell you, Ellen," said Jago. "It means that Tassie accepts you as an Islander."

He placed several coins on the table and I saw an avaricious gleam in Tassie's eyes, for she couldn't help watching and, I was sure, counting them as he laid them down.

We came out into the autumn sunshine.

"You must admit she gave you a pleasant fortune, Ellen," said Jago.

"And it seemed to me that she was well paid for it."

He looked at me sharply. "Well, she deserved it, didn't she?"

"If clients are going to pay according to what they're told, isn't that a temptation to the seer to be overoptimistic?"

"I don't think she was about yours. In fact, I know you're going to have a good one."

"Don't forget that rests with me."

"But you're a wise woman, Ellen. I knew it from the moment I saw you. But joking aside, she's a colorful character, our white witch, don't you think? She provides quite a bit of entertainment for our young. They think it's a great adventure to visit her at night in secret to get a love potion which they can administer to a lover."

"Is she really the seventh child of a seventh child?"

"So she tells us and whether her ancestor in fact found the mermaid, I'll leave you to guess. Old Tassie has always been there as long as I can remember."

"And people really believe in her!"

"Some do. If their wishes are granted they think Tassie has helped them. If they aren't, they think it's due to something they have failed in. It couldn't work out better than that from Tassie's point of view."

"And what about you? Do you believe her?"

He looked at me steadily. "I'm like the rest. If I get what I want, I do."

"And if you don't?"

"My dear Ellen, I always make sure I do."

We returned to the castle and I was preoccupied all the rest of the day thinking of this new aspect in our relationship and asking myself if it had really been there or I had imagined it; and when I retired to my room and lighted my candles and the shadows began to form I remembered Silva, and it seemed to me that her spirit brooded over the dimly lit room.

"My sister," I whispered; and I seemed to sense a response about me. It was fancy, of course. Jago would laugh at me. He laughed at so much—at Tassie (and how much had he commanded her to say?), at the manner in which he had behaved in London both at the recital and the house in Finlay Square. The disconcerting aspect was that when I was with him I could accept these things in the light he wished me to; it was only when I considered them calmly that they seemed, at the least, exceedingly unconventional. But then he *was* unconventional; he was also unpredictable. I could not understand him; yet he had betrayed something during the afternoon. He did not want my friendship with Michael Hydrock to grow any more than Gwennol and Jenifry did; but was I right in thinking it was for a different reason?

He had enjoyed listening to Tassie, the wise woman who gave her clients what they wanted whether it was something to cure their warts and sties or wedding bells.

Could it really be that Jago Kellaway wanted to be my husband!

It was a disturbing thought, but if I was honest I must say that it was one which excited me. Yet what did I really know of him? What did I know of anyone here?

"Silva," I whispered into the gloom. "Are you there, Silva?"

I listened. The curtains moved lightly in the breeze but there was no sound but the distant murmur of the sea.

The next day I went to find Slack.

He was in the courtyard feeding a sea gull which stood on the cobbles and was eating fish from a saucer.

"Her can't fly, Miss Ellen," Slack told me. "Found her on the cliffs I did. Her wings be all clogged with oil. Cowering on that ridge she were and I reckon had had no food for days. 'Twasn't only that—the others was pecking at her. Birds be terrible cruel one to the other. If one be maimed or different-like, they peck it to death. People be like that sometimes. They don't always like them as are different."

He spoke without sadness, merely as though he were stating a simple fact, although I knew he was likening himself to a bird who was "different." He accepted what life had given him. He was content to be different and never forgot that God had given him the Power, as he called it.

"What a good thing you found it," I said.

"Her's frightened yet. But her's calmer when I speak to her. When I picked her up first her tried to flutter and fight me but when I spoke to her and told her it was only Old Slack, who knew what to do and make her well again, her was quiet. See, I'm getting the oil off her wings. But I don't want her flying yet. I want to feed her . . . slow-like at first. Mustn't gobble up too much yet. There now, my pretty, Slack 'ull look after 'ee, you see."

"What happened to the pigeon with the injured leg?"

"Bold as brass now. He have forgot he were ever hurt."

"And suitably grateful to Slack, I hope."

"I wouldn't want that, Miss Ellen. 'Tis thanks enough to see him there, pecking at his maize, sitting on my hand, head cocked on one side as though to say: 'Hello, Slacky. I'm myself again.' "

"Slack," I said, "I've come to ask you something. Will you come out in a boat with me. I shall do the rowing. I just want you to sit with me. I've promised Mr. Jago that I won't take a boat out alone . . . yet."

He was pleased to be asked. His great pleasure in life was looking after people, and the fact that I trusted him enough to ask him to go with me delighted him.

I rowed round the Island.

"You be proper good with the oars, Miss Ellen," he

said. "And you soon get to know where the rocks are. 'Tis safe enough if you don't go too far out to sea though there'd be little danger on a sea like this one. But you do know how quick a breeze can arise. The sea can be smooth like a sheet of silk; then in fifteen minutes she can get all angry and ruffled up. That's what 'ee've got to watch for if 'ee be going to the mainland. Rowing round the Island be easy enough. There be many little bays where you could land if need be."

"Do you hear of many people drowning?"

I was watching him intently and I saw the shutter come down over his eyes.

"There have been," he said.

"There was my half sister Silva," I suggested.

He was silent.

I went on: "You knew her, of course, Slack."

"Yes, I did know her."

"Just think. She was my sister and I never knew her. I was three years old when I left here and I believe she must have been about twelve then . . . perhaps thirteen. I should love to know about her. Tell me what you know."

"She were fond of birds," he said.

"Ah." So there had been a sort of bond between them. I had guessed that.

"Did she often come to the dovecotes and help you feed them?"

He smiled and nodded. "Yes, her did. And they knew her too. They'd perch on her shoulder. She were terrible fond of birds and little things. Kind and gentle she were to them."

"So you and she were great friends. I'm glad of that."

He looked suddenly happy and I knew he was seeing pictures of Silva there with the pigeons or perhaps cradling some hurt animal in her arms while she discussed with him what should best be done.

"Did she talk to you much, Slack?"

"Oh yes, Miss Ellen. She'd always talk about the birds."

"And about herself? Did she tell you whether she was happy or not?"

"She'd talk and talk . . . like I wasn't there and then she'd look up and smile and say, 'I do run on, don't I, Slacky? That's because you're such a good listener I forget you're there.'"

"And was she very unhappy?"

He looked frightened and nodded. "Yes, her used to cry and that was terrible . . . I never saw anybody cry like Miss Silva did. It was laughing and crying all at once and she'd say she hated the castle and Mr. Jago and all of them."

"Why did she take the boat out that night? Do you know, Slack?"

"It were wild and stormy."

"I know. But why?"

I saw his lips press together. I believe he does know something, I thought.

"And she was drowned they say?"

He nodded, his lips still tight. "The boat were washed up," he said as though with a sudden inspiration.

"Did she go out in that boat because she was unhappy, because she was tired of living at the castle? Was she running away from something? You know, don't you, Slack?"

He nodded. "You might say she were running away."

"But to go away in a heavy sea . . ."

"There was a storm that night she left the castle," he said. "I remember the thunder and lightning. They do say that be God's anger. Do you think they'm right, Miss Ellen?"

"No," I said. "If she went out on a night like that she must have deliberately tried to kill herself. No boat could survive in a sea like that, could it?"

"You can never be sure, Miss Ellen, what can happen to boats on the sea."

"But this was washed up some days later . . . without her."

"Aye," he confirmed, "without her. I pray she be happy in the new life. 'Tis all we can do."

"Some of the servants say she haunts the Island, Slack."

"Aye, 'tis so."

"Do you believe that?"

"I do think she be still with us."

"So you believe that the ghosts of people who were unhappy in this life or met violent ends still live on."

"I'm not clever enough to say, Miss Ellen."

His pale face was impassive; the shutters were down over his eyes. I was convinced that he knew more about my half sister than he had betrayed and that I had not yet won enough of his confidence for him to tell me.

Perhaps in time he would. In the meanwhile I was obsessed by my curiosity.

# The Ellen *Is* Lost

I had now become a good oarswoman and was as capable
of handling a boat as Gwennol or Jenifry, both of whom
had not referred again to Michael Hydrock and seemed
to be trying to convince me that their outbursts on the subject had never taken place.

Jago was busy on the Island. He personally supervised
the farms and arranged the Island's business transactions,
which meant that he was constantly going back and forth
to the mainland. He usually managed to spend some time
of the day with me and liked nothing better than for us
to ride round the Island together, when he would introduce me to the farmers and shopkeepers, the innkeeper,
the parson of the little church, the doctor and all those
who made up the life of the Island. We were growing
closer and almost against my will I was being drawn into
that magnetic aura which seemed to surround him, so that
I was beginning to feel that I needed a strong dose of his
society every day.

He was delighted with my progress in rowing and one

morning he took me down to the cove and there was one
of the boats freshly painted with "Ellen" written on the
side of it. I was very proud of that.

After that I used to take the *Ellen* out by myself but I
never went far out to sea. I liked to skirt the Island and
put in at some bay which I had not visited before; there
I would lie and think of what had happened to me and
wonder what the future held. There was so much I had to
learn and it seemed to me that those about me were inclined to be overreticent, which in itself suggested a mystery. I believed that if I could discover what had really
happened to Silva I would have a key to the whole situation. Why had Silva gone out in a flimsy boat during a violent storm? If she had really done that there was only one
answer: Because she was tired of life and saw that as a
way out of what had become intolerable.

Had she determined to end it all? My poor sister, how
unhappy she must have been! "I am a prisoner in this
room." Oh, but she had been a child when she wrote that,
shut in her room and told to do some task before she was
released. It happened to most children at some time, but
she had overdramatized the situation. She was unbalanced,
Jago had said; and he did not want to talk of her. He
had not been interested in her and had dismissed her as
unbalanced. The foolish girl had been unable to adjust
herself to life and had found a dramatic way of ending it.
So the boat was washed up . . . without her. That was an
obvious answer to what had become of her.

My father—who was hers also—had hated her, she said.
Perhaps he disliked children generally. He was not emerging as a very pleasant person. He had quarreled with one
wife, and another—my mother—had left him. I did know
a little of her and my memories were of love, care, security, all that a child looks for in a mother. If she had
loved her child and left such memories, could it be her
fault that she had failed to make a happy marriage?
There could be all sorts of reasons, of course. Good
mothers were not necessarily good wives. Oh, how I wished
they would tell me what I so desperately wanted to know!

Then I remembered something I had heard. My father had kept to his room a good deal but he had had a valet-secretary, Fenwick. What had I heard of him? That he had left the castle and gone to the mainland. Now if I could have a word with Fenwick, I might discover something about my father. I decided to try and wondered how best to tackle the problem. If I asked Jago he would say: "What can Fenwick tell you that I can't?" Perhaps he was right but all the same I could not discover what I wanted to know from him and a second person's opinion was always valuable. Secretary-valets often knew more of their employers than a close relation. I couldn't ask Gwennol or Jenifry because there was too much restraint between us.

While I was pondering this, letters came from the mainland. One of the boats went over each day—weather permitting—to collect mail. In this bag I was delighted to find one from Esmeralda. I had written to her from the mainland about my journey and again from the castle, giving her my early impressions. I seized on her letter and took it to my room to read.

She was glad that I was finding life with my relations interesting. The castle sounded wonderful. She longed to see it. Her parents had given several balls for her and she had met a very pleasant young man named Freddy Bellings. He was a second son but the Bellings were wealthy and her mother was not displeased at the friendship between them. There was a good deal about Freddy —the color of his eyes, the kindness of his manner and the way in which he could make jokes without hurting anyone's feelings in doing so. I could see that Esmeralda was delighted with Freddy and that pleased me because I had always had a conscience about Philip, who had been intended for her.

"Mrs. Oman Lemming's governess has a bad time, I think. She looks such a poor frightened creature. Oh, Ellen, you would never have done it. You were lucky to escape that.

"We see a great deal of the Carringtons," she went on.

"Lady Emily has started to give parties again. No one mentions Philip but Lady Emily looks a little sad at times. She asks me how you are getting on and hopes you are happy. There is someone else who asks about you. Rollo. He wanted to know where you had gone and whether you were settling down. I had just received your letter about that exciting island and castle and everything. He was most interested."

I dropped the letter. I was so glad Esmeralda had found her Freddy and it seemed too good to be true that she should feel as she obviously did about him and Cousin Agatha also approved. I was surprised though that Rollo should be interested in what I was doing. Perhaps he repented of his harshness to me. It was an indication of how far I had grown away from the past when my thoughts were almost immediately back with the problem of the moment. How to find Fenwick and talk to him about my father.

The Pengellys were knowledgeable about what was going on in the neighborhood and would be as likely to know the whereabouts of Fenwick as anyone. I decided I would go to the inn and see what I could discover.

I would rather enjoy rowing myself over, and as the sea was very calm and I was now well practiced, I thought it would be a good opportunity to do so. Once I had rowed to the mainland and back I should feel competent enough to do it often.

I set off in the *Ellen* and when I, in due course, reached the mainland I went straight to the inn, where I found Mrs. Pengelly and asked her if she could spare a few moments, as I had something I wished to say to her.

She brought out the inevitable homemade wine and saffron cakes, and over them I asked if she had any idea where I might find Mr. Fenwick.

"You be thinking of him who worked up at the castle for Mr. Charles Kellaway."

"Yes, my father's secretary-valet."

"Well, he did leave, you know, when your father died."

"That's not very long ago. Where did he go? Did you hear?"

"Why yes, I did. He retired to a little cottage down in Fallerton."

"Where is that?"

"Oh, 'tis but six or seven miles from here. I did hear he were a market gardener of sorts—growing vegetables and flowers and suchlike."

"I want to go and see him."

She looked alarmed.

"I want to talk to him about my father."

She shook her head. "Your father were very ill at the end, Miss Ellen. 'Twould only distress you, maybe, to hear how very ill."

"I naturally want to hear about my family. It seems so difficult to get people to tell me."

"Well, I can't tell 'ee much, Miss Ellen. I was away seventeen years ago. When your mother went, there weren't nothing for me to stay for."

"I understand he was rather an unhappy man. My mother left him. . . ."

"She couldn't abide the Island, that was what. She used to say she was like a prisoner there."

"You must have known Silva."

"Oh yes, Miss Silva. She were a strange girl."

"How old was she when you left?"

"Well, I reckon she were about thirteen years old. I couldn't be sure, but it seemed so. There was no doing naught with her. She were wild-like—used to go out in the wind and lose herself for hours so we'd think something had happened to her. Seemed like she wanted to put all in a turmoil. We did our best, your mother and I, and when you came along we thought she'd be better. She were, in a way. She were fond of you. But your father wouldn't see her. He wouldn't have her near him. I never knew such a thing. Sometimes I'd hear her sobbing and I'd go and try and comfort her. Then she'd get up and dance around and laugh at me. She'd shout: 'Do you think

I care for him, you silly old woman!' My dear life, that were a time!"

"It was very strange that she should go off as she did."

A wary look came into Mrs. Pengelly's eyes and I was reminded forcibly of her son. I realized that even if she knew something about Silva's strange disappearance she was not going to tell me and in any case I was obsessed at the moment by the thought of finding Fenwick.

"I'll have one of the horses and go to Fallerton," I said. "What was the name of his house, do you remember?"

"I can't tell 'ee that, Miss Ellen, but Fallerton be naught but a village. If you get there and ask, someone will be bound to know."

As I was about to leave the inn, Michael Hydrock rode in.

"Hello, Miss Kellaway, what a pleasant surprise!" he said.

"I'm just off to Fallerton," I told him.

"Fallerton! That's on my way. I'll come with you."

"I thought you were going into the inn."

"Just for a little refreshment, which I can well do without."

"Please don't let me interrupt your morning."

"My dear Miss Kellaway," he said with a smile, "even if it were an interruption there couldn't be a more pleasant one."

He had turned his horse and walked him up to mine.

"I know a shortcut to Fallerton," he said. "I'll be able to show you."

It would have been churlish not to accept his company, which, had it not been for those unfortunate scenes with Gwennol and Jenifry, I should have been very happy to do. Well, they would both be on the Island today, so I could give myself up to the pleasure of Michael's company.

"Where do you want to go in Fallerton?" he asked. "It's only a small village."

"So I heard. I want to find a Mr. Fenwick."

"Fenwick. . . . There was a Fenwick who worked at the castle at one time."

"That's the Fenwick I'm looking for. I want to talk to him about my father."

"I believe he was a secretary-valet to your father for many years and your father left him enough to get this place at Fallerton. At least that was what I heard."

"I find so few people ready to talk about my father and naturally I want to hear. It seems so odd not to have known one's own father when he was alive. He never seemed to take any interest in me."

"Your mother had taken you away, hadn't she?"

"Yes, but it still seems strange that he should never have tried to get in touch with me. After all I am his daughter."

"I have heard that he had rather an unforgiving nature."

"What I hear of him is not very pleasant."

"Would it therefore be better to let sleeping dogs lie?"

"I don't feel like that. I have a burning desire to know."

"Well, let's see if we can find this place in Fallerton."

It was very pleasant riding across the country which he knew so well. All his life this had been his home ground. Fallerton was just outside his estate, he told me, otherwise he could have given me more information about Fenwick.

We soon came to Fallerton. It was, as Mrs. Pengelly had said, a small village. There was merely a short street in which a few houses clustered together, and one or two outlying cottages.

We saw a man with a horse and cart which was filled with hay. He was fixing his horse's nose bag and as we passed Michael called to him: "Do you know a Mr. Fenwick hereabouts?"

The man looked up and immediately showed that respect which Michael inspired on all occasions.

"Well sir, if you do mean John Fenwick as took Mulberry Cottage, he have gone."

"Now where would Mulberry Cottage be?" asked Michael.

"Just follow the street and turn right for a hundred

yards and you'll see Mulberry. A bit of land there is to that place. He took over the market garden. The vegetables was good and the flowers fine but he just took off and went. Told some of 'em 'tweren't his line at all. He'd been working up at Kellaway Castle for years and he weren't cut out for it, he said. So he sold the place and went off."

"Do you have an idea where?"

"No sir. I ain't got no idea."

"I wonder if anyone round here would have."

"I dunno. They might know at the inn. He'd been there pretty often, so I'm told."

We thanked our informant and went to take a look at Mulberry Cottage. The grounds seemed flourishing and a rosy-faced woman came to the door. Yes, Mulberry Cottage had belonged to Mr. Fenwick. They'd bought it from him and they been here this last six months. They'd taken the market garden which she understood he'd taken over from the previous owner. No, she had no idea where he had gone. All she knew was that he wasn't there now.

Michael thought it would be a good idea if we went to the inn where we could refresh ourselves and ask questions.

We found the inn with the old sign creaking over the door: The Corn Dolly. We went inside; there were no other guests and we ordered cider to drink and whatever they had to offer us to eat. There were pasties, of course, and squab and lammy pies as well as cold meats.

When the innkeeper's wife brought us hot pasties and cider Michael asked her if she knew the whereabouts of a Mr. John Fenwick.

"Oh, you do mean him as was up at Mulberry," she said. "He didn't stay long. 'Tweren't the life for him. He was more of a clerk like."

"He used to come in here quite a lot, I believe."

"Oh yes, he were a regular. He reckoned our cider were the best he ever tasted. Had a fancy for my pasties too, the same as you be having now . . . he did."

I said I was not surprised, which pleased her; but she

couldn't help us over Mr. Fenwick as she had no idea where he had gone.

"Not a very profitable morning," said Michael ruefully. "Never mind, we'll find him in time. I'll make inquiries. It shouldn't be too difficult. What do you think of the old Corn Dolly?"

"It's charming and what an odd name."

"You saw the sign as we came in?"

"Yes, it looked like a bundle of corn tied up to look like a doll."

"That's exactly what it is. At the end of the harvest they make these corn dollies and hang them around the place. Did you see the one in the hall as we came in? They're supposed to bring a good harvest next year."

"It reminds me in a way of the Polcrag Inn. The open fireplace . . . the oak beams."

"They haven't an earthenware lamp like this," said Michael, picking up an object from the center of the table. It was shaped like a candlestick. "See this hole at the top?" he went on. "A cupful of oil can be poured through that and then they insert a wick which they call a purvan. I like to see them keeping up the old customs. You don't see many of these Stonen Chills about now."

I picked it up and examined it. I said it was quaint but my mind was really on Fenwick and I was bitterly disappointed that our search had been fruitless.

He leaned across the table and patted my hand.

"Cheer up," he said. "I promise you I'll find Fenwick for you."

"Thank you. It's good of you to be so helpful."

"Nothing of the sort. It will be a pleasure. Leave it to me. I'll tell you what I'll do. When I find something I'll send you a message by carrier pigeon. How's that?"

"That would be fun," I replied. "And I'm sure Slack would be delighted."

"Gwennol and I often send messages like that."

"Yes, she told me."

We left the Corn Dolly and when we came in sight of

the sea I was dismayed to see that a little way out the white horses were putting in an appearance.

"It's an offshore wind," said Michael. "Nothing much. They'll get you back all right, but it would be advisable to set out without delay."

"I rowed myself over," I said.

"Oh." His expression changed and became anxious, but he said no more until we reached the inn.

By that time I could see more of the white-crested waves.

"I'll row you over," Michael announced.

"That's not necessary."

"But I shall insist. It might be hard going. You need a man's hands on the oars in this tetchy kind of sea."

"And I was so proud of myself for rowing over alone!"

"It was fine coming. That's always the trouble though. Changes come too quickly."

Michael had arranged everything. He would hire a slightly stronger boat than the *Ellen* and in it he would row me over and row himself back. He would arrange for the *Ellen* to be taken over by one of the inn men. It was a very simple matter.

I felt uneasy as he rowed me to the Island—not of the elements but of the construction Gwennol and her mother would put on this if they discovered that I had spent some time on the mainland with Michael Hydrock and that he had rowed me back. It seemed almost certain that they would.

As we drew farther from the mainland the wind seemed to drop a little.

"I could have managed by myself," I said.

"Perhaps you could," he replied, "but I shouldn't have been very happy letting you go."

We got out of the boat and stood together on the shore.

"You'll come to the castle?" I asked.

"I don't think I will. I should get back. The *Ellen* should be here soon."

"It's been so kind of you."

"It's been the greatest pleasure for me."

He jumped back into the boat and I pushed it out. He waved and took the oars.

As I went up the incline towards the castle I met Jenifry. I knew by the manner in which she looked at me that she had seen our arrival, had watched him hold my hand on the shore when he said goodbye and had seen him go off in the boat.

I wondered whether Jenifry told Gwennol what she had seen. I found myself watching them furtively, which, if they noticed this, might have made me seem guilty.

The next day Gwennol went to the mainland and I stayed on the Island, and it occurred to me that I might go and call on Tassie. Perhaps she would have a different future for me if Jago were not present.

She was sitting at the door of her cottage and her wrinkled old nutcracker face screwed into a smile as I approached. The black cat came out from under her skirts and glowered at me.

"Come in," she said, and I followed her.

Some logs were burning in the fireplace and the pungent smell of herbs seemed stronger than it had on that previous occasion.

"So you be all alone today, Miss," she said with a smirk. "I hope I see you well."

"Yes, thank you, and I hope I see *you* well."

That made her laugh, implying I supposed that she who could charm away other people's disabilities should certainly not be expected to have any of her own.

"And what can I do for a young lady like you?" she asked. "Tell me that. Do you want the cards read, would you like me to look into the crystal ball or would you be wanting me to read your palm?"

"You gave me a very good fortune last time I saw you," I replied. "I'll be content with that one—after all, what you see today might not be so good."

That seemed to amuse her. "Ah, I see you was well content—and not you only."

"I want you to tell me about someone else."

"Oh?" She cocked her head on one side and looked like a mischievous monkey. "No, Malken," she went on, addressing the cat. "We ain't used to that are we, my poppet?"

The cat mewed as though to answer her.

"It's someone who may . . . or may not be dead," I said.

"Ghosts don't have futures," she retorted sharply.

"But if you can see into the future perhaps you can also see into the past. I want to ask about my half sister Silva."

"Oh you do, do you? Poor maid! Hers was a sad life."

"Did she ever come to see you?"

"She often came. Especially at the end. She had reason to then."

"What reason?" I asked excitedly.

"She was anxious about the future."

"People don't seem to want to talk about her."

" 'Tis natural . . . where she be. She could be lying at the bottom of the sea, the fishes her only companions. Poor maid, poor sad maid!"

"Can you see her at the bottom of the sea?"

She looked at me shrewdly. "I might see her there one day and I might see her somewhere else the next."

"But if you can really see what you say you can, you must know whether she's dead or not."

"There's many as swear they can hear her crying when the wind do howl."

"Are you telling me she was really drowned?"

"The boat came in, didn't 'un? Where could she be if the boat she went in come in empty?"

"So you don't know," I said.

"I didn't say that, Miss. I said there's some as hears her ghost, and the boat came back without her."

"Why did she visit you?"

"To see into the future."

"What was she like? Did she look like me?"

"Different as chalk from cheese."

"They can sometimes look not unlike."

"Nay, she had a lot of yellow hair. She took after her mother. There was nothing of the Kellaway in her."

"Did she come to you because she was unhappy?"

"She was born to be unhappy perhaps and knew it."

"Why should she be?"

"Can 'ee keep a secret?"

"Yes," I said eagerly, "I promise to."

"Her mother come to me afore she was born. She wanted to do away with her."

I caught my breath. "Why?"

"I reckon she had her reasons."

"What was her mother like?"

"Oh, Madam Effie didn't belong to these parts. Your father always chose them from far afield . . . leastways your mother didn't belong here either. Then he'd wonder why they was always pining for somewhere else. He went away a lot on business. The sort of business Mr. Jago does now. And she came to me and she said: 'Tassie, I'm with child. I can't bear this child.' And I looked at her and I said: 'You'm too late, Madam Effie. Should have come to me two months ago. I dursen't do anything for you now.' "

"Poor child! So even her mother didn't want her."

" 'Tis sad to be an unwanted child. She knew it from the moment she knew anything."

"You must remember me as a baby."

"Oh, I remember you all right. Sun shone right out of your eyes for Madam Frances."

"Was it a happier family then?"

"There's some as is doomed never to be content. Your father be one of them, me dear."

"Tell me what happened during the days just before Silva went away."

"She came to see me . . . twice she did . . . in the week before she went away."

"Did she seem unhappy?"

"You could never be sure with her. She laughed and laughed and you could never be sure whether her laughter was tears. She said: 'Everything's going to change now. I shan't be here much longer, Tassie.' Then I talked to her and she wanted me to read her palm and I could find little for comfort there. But I didn't tell her that. Sometimes I don't tell the bad." She stared over my head as though she were watching something. "If I see darkness hovering there, I don't always say so. What I say is: 'You be watchful.' For who can say when the dark shadow of danger ain't hovering over us all, me . . . you . . . yes, you, Miss Ellen. That's what I say."

I looked uneasily over my shoulder and she laughed at me. Then she said: "That's what I tell 'em to be, me dear. Watchful . . . ever watchful. And there's nothing more I can tell 'ee about Miss Silva."

It was the signal to go. I had, however, gleaned just a little more about my half sister.

I put several coins into the bowl on the table and, as when Jago had done the same, her shrewd eyes watched and counted.

"Come to me again, me dear," she said. "Come whenever you do feel the need."

I thanked her and went on into the sunshine.

Two days later, as it was calm, I rowed over to the mainland once more. On this occasion I intended to go to the inn for a glass of wine and to look at some of the shops, for Christmas was not so very far off and if I were to be on the Island during that season I should need to find some presents for everyone.

I should not stay long this time, I promised myself, and being near the coast would be watchful for a change in the weather.

After having tied up the boat I went first to the shops, where I bought one or two little items, and then I paused before a window, for displayed there was a picture which caught my eye. It was a seascape—a clear summer's day with a sapphire-blue sea and waves edged with white frills rolling gently on a golden shore; but what was so arresting was a cloud of white sea gulls rising and swooping above the water. The contrast of white birds and blue sea was dazzling and I was fascinated. I thought I must have that picture. It was so evocative of Sanctuary Island and I knew that, wherever I was, when I looked at that picture I would be back there.

Then it occurred to me that it would be an ideal Christmas present for Jago, and no sooner had that thought occurred to me than I was even more delighted at the prospect of giving it to him than keeping it for myself.

I went into the shop and told the man behind the counter that I should like to have a closer look at the picture entitled "The Gulls." It was brought from the window and was, I thought, reasonably priced. The more I saw it, the more I liked it. I would have it, I said.

While this transaction was taking place a man came from the back of the shop. I knew him immediately. He was James Manton, the artist who lived on Blue Rock and whom I had met when I was with Jago on Sanctuary Island.

His eyes shone with pleasure and for a fleeting moment I thought he was expressing his delight at seeing me. Then I understood. "The Gulls" was his work and he was merely showing an artist's appreciation for someone who appreciated his work.

"Why, it's Miss Ellen Kellaway," he said.

"I remember you too," I told him.

"So you are buying 'The Gulls.' "

"I was completely fascinated by it when I was passing the window and I just felt I had to have it."

"What was it you liked about it so much?"

"The color of everything struck me most. And the birds . . . they're so alive. They seem as if they are going to fly right off the canvas. And the sea . . . it's so calm and beautiful. I don't think I've ever seen such a perfect sea but I know I shall, and I shall wait for it."

"You have given me great pleasure," he said. "It is such a joy to talk with someone who sees what one is trying to express. Are you taking the picture with you?"

"I thought I would. Though I suppose I could have it sent."

"Did you come over alone?"

"Yes. I'm keeping an eye on the sea though. I don't want to get caught."

He laughed. "I have an idea," he said. "They can pack up the picture and you and I will go and drink a cup of tea at the inn. Then I shall carry the picture to your boat. How's that?"

"It's an excellent idea."

So that was how I came to be sitting at the Polcrag Inn opposite James Manton drinking Mrs. Pengelly's strong brew and eating scones with jam and clotted cream.

He asked me how I liked the island life and I replied that sometimes it didn't seem like being on an island, although it would when the sea made one a prisoner there.

"You're on a bigger one than Blue Rock," he commented. "It makes a difference, you know."

"You knew my father, I believe," I said, for I was determined to discover all I could and this seemed a heaven-sent opportunity.

His face hardened. "Yes, I knew him."

"I can see that you did not like him very much."

"I would prefer not to talk about him to you, Miss Kellaway."

"But I want to talk about him and nobody seems to want to."

"You could hardly hope to hear what you obviously want to from one whom he regarded as his enemy."

"He regarded you as such? I am sure he was wrong."

"Your father was a man who thought he was never wrong."

"I know his first wife died. . . ."

"He was cruel to her. Had he been different . . ."

"You're not suggesting that he killed her!"

"There are more ways of killing people than driving a knife through their hearts or dropping poison into their soup. You can kill with cruelty, and that's what he did. Her life was so wretched with him. He was a jealous and vindictive man."

I shrank from the vituperation in his voice; he had

seemed so placid before, a mild middle-aged man mainly interested in his art. Now his hatred of my father seemed to endow him with new life, a greater vitality than he had shown before.

"So you knew her well," I went on.

"I knew her and I knew your mother, too. Your mother was an artist. She could have been a good one but he despised that. She and I had a good deal in common naturally."

"I see. And she too was unhappy with him."

"She was and finally left, taking you with her."

"Did he care very much?"

James Manton laughed ironically. "Care! He was probably glad."

"What did he feel about his daughters?"

"Poor Silva. He hated her. She might have been so different. . . . I wish . . ." He shrugged his shoulders. "Silva was never given a chance. That was why . . ."

"She disappeared," I put in, as he did not appear to want to continue. "Her life seems to have been a very sad one. She was unbalanced, I gathered."

"Who wouldn't have been in such an atmosphere? She wasn't very old when her mother died . . . and to be brought up in that place . . ."

"I remember so little, being only three years old when I left. Did he hate me too?"

"He wouldn't have had time for children."

"Do you know what happened after my mother went away with me?"

"He didn't try to find you. He would never forgive your mother for running away just as he never forgave Effie. . . ." He shook his head. "I shouldn't be speaking to you like this about your own father."

"What I want is to get at the truth. If it's unpleasant I have to face it. I'd rather know it all and see it clearly than have it dressed up to look pretty to please me."

"You must forgive me," he said. "I was carried away. Your father and I were not on speaking terms. When he was alive he wouldn't have had me on the Island. If I had put a foot there someone would have been ordered to throw me into the sea."

"Well, I hope that unhappy situation is over now."

"Oh, these family feuds get carried on for generations. They exist when the families don't know the original cause of the quarrel. Did we ever know what was the start of the trouble between the Montagues and Capulets? I wouldn't go to Kellaway Island now—just wouldn't dream of it. I'm content to stay at Blue Rock."

"You enjoy your little island all to yourself."

"It suits me. I paint most of the time I'm there and then I go up to London to arrange exhibitions and see other people's. I come to the mainland and put my pictures in shopwindows hoping that art-conscious, beauty-loving young ladies will come along and buy them."

"I'm glad I saw 'The Gulls' and I'm glad it's yours. I hope my appreciation of your picture has done something to break through a little of the feud."

He smiled at me. "It's miraculous," he said, "that you could be his daughter."

It had been an interesting afternoon, and after I had rowed myself back with the picture I set it up in my room and studied it.

Then I put it away, for if I was going to give it to Jago it would have to be a secret until Christmas.

It was a golden October and people were talking about an Indian summer. The days were warm and hazy and there was no sign of the gales. Jago said it was hardly possible that we should avoid them altogether and that they had probably delayed their visit until November.

I took the *Ellen* out every day. I loved to row round the Island. The place was growing on me. Jago used to talk to me about the troubles of the various people and I was beginning to know a few of them. They accepted me and I was gratified when they appeared to like me, and I felt especially delighted when they hinted what a good landlord Jago was.

"Stern," said one old woman, "but just. You've got to

keep your cottage neat and clean and the garden ship-shape, then he'll see your roof's mended if the need arises."

It was a lovely afternoon with a rather hazy sun visible through the slightly misty atmosphere. My thoughts were with the people of the Island—not so much those who lived there at this time, but those vague figures of the past whom it was so difficult, on the flimsy evidence available, to bring to life.

Why was I so anxious to know about the lives of people who were gone?

"Idle curiosity," Philip would have said.

"Oh, you always want to know everything," I could hear Esmeralda telling me. "Particularly about people."

Yes, it was true. But there was something more. I could not help feeling that my life was interwoven with those of the people who had lived here and that there was some reason why it was important to me to know what had happened to them.

Never far from my thoughts was Jago himself. My feelings for him were so varied that he was of perpetual interest to me. I often looked at the pictures in my mother's sketchbook, from which I would not be parted. She, too, had been aware of a dual personality. But then she had felt the same about Silva. Perhaps she had meant to convey that there were two sides—and often more—to everyone's character. My father, for instance. He seemed to have been very difficult to live with and yet both my mother and Effie must have been in love with him at one time to have married him.

I shipped the oars and drifted on the tide. It was so beautiful with the faint cool breeze on my face and that benign reddish sun up there. The clouds drifting slowly in the wind were taking on weird shapes. There was a face up there—a woman's face, a nutcracker of a face—and I immediately thought of Tassie. Dark shadows hovering over all of us, she had said. "Be watchful." Had that been an oblique reference to some danger threatening me, or was it just the fortuneteller's jargon? When I was with Jago it had been all the "happy ever after if you take the right turning" theme. Wouldn't that apply to anybody? Wasn't there a "right turning" in everybody's life which if taken at the flood leads on to greatness . . . or happiness, which was more to be desired? I was misquoting and mixing metaphors but truth was there.

I had drifted nearly a mile out from the Island, I should think. Perhaps I ought to go back.

As I moved the oars I stared at the bottom of the boat in sudden consternation. Water was seeping in.

I bent forward and felt with my hand. The water was very shallow so the boat had only just started to leak. I touched the bottom of the boat. There was something sticky on my hand. It looked like sugar.

Even as I looked the water started to come in faster. The whole of the bottom of the boat was covered now. I seized the oars and started to row for the Island as fast as I could.

The *Ellen* had sprung a leak. There was no doubt of that. How far off the Island seemed! The boat was going to sink at any moment and I was not a strong swimmer.

It was sooner than I expected. The *Ellen* tipped to one side and I was in the water.

Frantically I sought to get a hold on the boat. By great good luck I managed to clutch at the keel as she turned upside down. She was floating and I was clinging to her with all my might. Temporarily I was safe . . . but it could not last, I was well aware.

Could I swim to the shore? I could feel the water saturating my skirts and making them heavy. They were dragging me down. I had swum very little; Esmeralda and I had bathed in the sea at Brighton when our governess had taken us for holidays there, but then we had gone into bathing machines set up on the beach and emerged from them straight into the water and just let the waves toss us about as we hung on to the ropes. I could manage a few strokes but could I reach the Island, hampered as I was by my clothes?

My hold on the boat was precarious. I shouted: "Help!" My voice sounded feeble. Overhead gulls wheeled, screeching in what seemed to me a mocking fashion.

"Oh, God," I prayed, "let someone find me." And into my mind there flashed an image of Silva in another boat. They never found her but the boat was washed up.

Oh, this treacherous sea! How powerful it seemed even in its present moderate mood.

Should I try for the shore? I could feel my wet skirts wrapping themselves around my legs and I knew it would be disastrous to attempt it, and yet with every passing second my hold on the *Ellen* was becoming more and more slight.

My hands were growing numb. I can't cling much longer, I thought. Is this the end? It was strange that it should all have led to this. No, no. Someone would come. Jago would come. Yes, it must be Jago. If only I could will him to be taking a stroll along the cliffs.

"Jago!" I called. "Jago."

I'm slipping, I thought. I can't hold on much longer. What is it like to drown?

I would make an attempt to swim. Who knew, I might manage it. It was said that when one was in danger nature provided extra reserves of strength. I wouldn't die, I was going to fight for my life.

I heard a shout and it was as though my prayer had been answered, but I dared not turn to look towards the shore for fear I should lose my grip on the boat.

The shout came to me over the water. "Hold on, Miss Ellen. I be on the way."

Slack!

He was near to me now. I knew that he swam like a fish; I had seen him twisting and turning in the water, as much at home there as he was on land.

" 'Tis all right, Miss Ellen. I be here now. . . ."

How small he was! How fragile! He had the body of a child, but of course he was not much more.

"There now. Here I be." His voice was soothing, comforting, as though I were a wounded bird.

"Now now, I be taking 'ee to the shore."

I still clung to the boat.

"I . . . can't swim . . . very well, Slack."

"Never 'ee mind, Miss Ellen. I be here."

I released my grip on the boat and for a moment was submerged. I was on the surface again and I felt Slack's hand under my chin holding my head above the water.

The boat had moved away from us and the shore seemed a long way off.

How can this delicate boy bring me safely ashore? I wondered.

Then I heard Jago's voice.

"I'm coming."

Then I knew that everything was going to be all right.

I remember vaguely being brought onto the land. I remember Jago's strong arms about me as he carried me to the castle. I remember being laid on my bed and soothing drinks being brought to me. I was wrapped in blankets and hot-water bottles were placed round me. I was told I was to stay there for a day or two. I had had a shock which was greater than I would realize at the time. I had come near to death by drowning.

As I lay in my bed I could not stop thinking of the terrifying moment when I had noticed that the boat was leaking. I knew that could have been the end of me if Slack had not been there—and later Jago. I still wondered whether little Slack could have brought me in; and I rejoiced that Jago had come. The moment I had heard his voice I had ceased to be afraid.

Jago came and sat by my bed.

"What happened?" he asked. "Do you feel you can talk about it, Ellen?"

"Of course. Everything seemed all right until suddenly I noticed that the boat was leaking."

"That should never have happened. You must have struck something when you brought her in. The boats ought to be thoroughly examined before they are taken out."

"It was all right at first. I had been in it for about ten

minutes. I was drifting away from the shore when suddenly I noticed."

"It has happened on other occasions. Thank God I came along when I did."

"Slack too."

"Yes, he's a good boy but he's a weakling. He might not have been strong enough to bring you in."

"I felt my wet clothes dragging me down."

"Yes, that was where the great danger lay. My dear Ellen, if anything had happened to you . . ." His face was distorted with real emotion. "It's a lesson to us though. We have to be very careful in future."

"Are you going to suggest that I give up rowing alone?"

"It mightn't be a bad idea. At the moment I'm going to suggest that you stay in bed for a while. The effects of this sort of thing can be greater than you realize."

"I haven't said 'Thank you' for saving my life."

He rose and bent over me. "All the thanks I need is to see you safe. Don't forget I'm your guardian."

"Thank you, Jago."

He stooped and kissed me.

I was glad that he went out then for my emotion was hard to hide. I am in a weak state, I told myself. Anyone would be after such an adventure.

Gwennol came to see me.

"You had an unpleasant experience," she said. "And you don't swim very well, do you?"

"How did you know?"

"You told me. My mother made me take swimming lessons. She said that living on an island everyone should."

"I was fortunate."

"Perhaps you were born lucky."

"I'd like to think I was."

"Well, you'll be more careful in future, won't you?"

"I really didn't realize I was being careless. Who would have thought a boat like the *Ellen* would have sprung a leak?"

"Any boat might. She hasn't come in yet. I expect she's drifting out to sea. I wonder if she'll ever come back. If we had a gale she would no doubt be broken up. Perhaps one day a spar of wood with just the word 'Ellen' on it will turn up."

"And people will say: 'Who was Ellen?'"

"They'll know it was part of a boat and therefore the name of it."

"Oh, but they might wonder who the Ellen was for whom the boat was named."

There was restraint between us which we were trying to pretend did not exist. I sensed that she was longing to ask me if I had seen Michael recently. She would want to know what had happened on that day I had spent on the mainland in his company, for I was sure Jenifry had seen us together and would have told her daughter. But Gwennol couldn't bring herself to ask. The rift between us made us both uneasy and she didn't stay long with me.

Jenifry came, her face puckered into an expression of concern.

"How are you feeling, Ellen?" she asked. "My goodness, you gave us all a turn. I couldn't believe my eyes when Jago brought you in. For the moment I thought you were dead."

"I'm very healthy," I said. "It would take a lot to kill me."

"That's a comforting thought," she replied. "I've brought you a drink. It's a concoction of herbs and things and is said to be very good for shock. My old nurse always gave it to me when she thought I needed it."

"It's kind of you to bring it to me now."

"Come, drink it. You'll be surprised how well you'll feel afterwards."

I took the glass and then I looked up and saw her eyes on me and I had the same uneasy feeling which I had experienced when I had seen her face in the mirror.

"I couldn't drink anything," I said. "I feel sick."

"This will make you better."

"Later," I insisted, and set it down on the table beside my bed.

She sighed. "I know it will make you feel better."

"I'm so tired," I said, half closing my eyes but so that I could still see her through my lashes. She looked at me for a few seconds in silence.

"I'll leave you then," she said. "But don't forget—do take the tonic."

I nodded sleepily and she went quietly from the room. I lay listening.

There was something stealthy about her, something which had made me feel uneasy right from the first day I had seen her. I heard her footsteps going down the corridor and I picked up the glass and sniffed the liquid. I could smell the herbs and they were not unpleasant. I put it to my lips. Then I thought suddenly of old Tassie and I heard her voice saying: Be watchful.

Why should I have thought of that now? Thoughts were beginning to stir in my mind and I was too tired to consider them now. You have come very close to death, I reminded myself. It has made you fanciful and . . . suspicious.

Suspicious I was, for I rose from my bed and went to the window, taking the glass with me. I tipped the liquid out of the window and watched it trickle down the castle walls.

I climbed back into my bed and lay there thinking.

# The Island Necklace

The next day I felt fully recovered and the strange ideas which had beset me on the previous night receded. The first thing I wanted to do was to go to the dovecotes and thank Slack for coming to my rescue.

He was there as though expecting me.

"Thank you, Slack," I said, "for coming to my rescue."

"I could have brought you in on my own," he said.

"I'm sure you could, but Mr. Jago happened to be there."

"I may not be big but I have the Power. I could have saved 'ee, Miss Ellen, like I save the little birds."

"Thank you, Slack. I know."

"It bothers me . . . what happened."

"Boats do spring leaks sometimes, I suppose."

He shook his head and said: "What did 'ee see, Miss Ellen?"

"See? Well, I suddenly noticed that the water was coming in. I thought there was something sticky there . . . like sugar . . . and then I didn't have time to think of anything but how I was going to get to the land."

"Sticky." His brows were wrinkled. "Like sugar, did 'ee say? I wonder what sugar could have been doing at the bottom of the *Ellen*?"

"I expect I was wrong. I was frightened, I suppose."

"Little bits of seaweed, perhaps."

"Perhaps. But I'm safe and I can tell you, Slack, how pleased I was to hear your voice calling me."

" 'Twas the Power. I had this feeling. Go along down to the shore. I heard the voice telling me. You be needed there. 'Tis sometimes so when some little bird or some animal do need me."

"Well then, I have to thank the Power as well as you, Slack."

"Aye, Miss Ellen. Don't ever forget the Power. Miss Ellen, you say you did see sugar then?"

"Well, that's what it looked like to me then . . . a few grains of sugar."

" 'Tis a strange thing. Don't 'ee fret though. I be going to look after you, Miss Ellen. If you do need me, I'll know."

The pale eyes had changed. There was a look about them which was almost fanatical.

The servants tapped their heads significantly when they spoke of Slack. I had heard the whispered comment: "Not all there."

But there *was* something there, I was sure. Dear Slack. I was glad he was my friend.

The incident of the boat had brought me closer to Slack. Understandably for a week or so after the accident I had no desire to go to sea, certainly not alone. There had been no need for Jago to warn me against that. So I stayed on the Island and I took to going to the dovecotes when Slack was feeding the pigeons.

He would give me a bowl filled with maize and we'd stand together with the birds fluttering round us.

Once he said: "Did 'ee say sugar, Miss Ellen?"

I wondered what he meant for a moment, then I said:

"Oh, you mean when the boat started to sink. I didn't have time to consider very much. I thought I saw what looked like a few grains of it on the bottom of the boat where it hadn't, at that time, been touched by the water. And then as the water swelled up there seemed to be some grains floating in it. I was too upset though to think much about it. It just flashed into my mind. You understand. It was a horrible moment, Slack."

His brow was furrowed. "Sugar takes a little time to dissolve in cold water. Now salt would dissolve quicker."

"How could it have been sugar? How could that have got there?"

"Couldn't have got there if it hadn't been put, Miss Ellen."

"Slack, what do you mean!"

"Where be the boat? If we had the boat and her weren't broken up."

"You wouldn't find the sugar now."

"No, but we'd see the hole it come through."

"We know that must have been there."

"But how did it *come* to be there? That be what I want to know."

"Slack, what are you thinking?"

"What if the hole were put there by someone as filled it with sugar? There's the Demerara kind . . . brown and coarse grained, the kind that takes time to dissolve . . . specially in cold salt water. I've heard it said hereabouts more than once that it would hold a leak for a while if you happened to be not too far out to sea and supposing you had a packet of such with you . . . which is hardly likely." His eyes shone with the intensity of his feelings. "You wouldn't see it when you started out and when it did dissolve you have a hole, don't 'ee, what the sugar was bunging up. And the water could get in, couldn't it, where it couldn't when you started out."

"You're suggesting that someone . . ."

"I don't rightly know what I mean, but terrible things can happen. I do know that. It don't do to forget it. I reckon we don't want to laugh at it and say . . ." He floundered and tapped his head, implying that I might be thinking as others did that he was "not all there."

What he was suggesting seemed absurd. Did he really think that someone had tampered with the boat—*my* boat, which no one took out but me—knowing that sooner or later I should be at sea in it . . . and almost certainly alone!

It was too farfetched. Who would possibly do such a thing!

Gwennol was jealous because Michael Hydrock had been friendly towards me. Jenifry was angry on her daughter's account. I had always felt uneasy about Jenifry since that first night. I had often laughed at myself about that. Just because her reflection in an old mirror had looked momentarily malevolent I had started to endow her with all sorts of sinister motives. And now of course there was this aspect of my friendship with Michael Hydrock. But no. It was too flimsy. It was not as though Michael had asked me to marry him and I had accepted. I could understand that there would have been acute jealousy then. But it was not so. I liked him and it was quite obvious that he liked me. He was just a very courteous and kindly gentleman who had been helpful and hospitable. Gwennol had no reason to be jealous on my account.

And yet our relationship had changed since she had discovered that I had met him before I came to the Island. She had been prepared to be very friendly before that discovery; now she was cautious as though she were trying to trap me into admissions. I imagined that every time I went out she wondered whether I was going to meet Michael Hydrock. As for Jenifry, she had no doubt set her heart on Michael as a son-in-law and indeed he was undoubtedly the most desirable party in the neighborhood—a man any mother might have been expected to want for her daughter.

So this matter of the sugar was the wildest conjecture and I wished I hadn't mentioned it to Slack.

"You must be careful, Miss Ellen," he said very seriously.

"I shall. I shall examine any boat thoroughly before I attempt to go out in it."

"Mightn't be a boat next time."

"Next time?"

"I don't know what put that in me mouth, Miss Ellen. I want to look after 'ee, you see . . . like I looked after Miss Silva."

"How did you look after her?"

He smiled slowly. "She always come to me. She used to get fits, Miss Ellen. Oh, not so she'd lie down and do damage to herself . . . not they sort of fits. Fits of sadness and fits of wildness when she wanted to do things that would hurt herself. Then she'd come and talk to me and the Powers would show me how to soothe her."

"You must have known as much about her as anybody did."

"Reckon so."

"And that night when she went away. . . . It was a stormy night and yet she took a boat and tried to cross to the mainland."

I saw the shutter come down.

" 'Tis something all marveled at," he agreed.

"Did you know she was going?"

He hesitated, then he said: "Yes, I knew she was going."

"Why didn't you try to stop her? You must have known the chances were against her reaching land safely."

" 'Tweren't no good trying to stop Miss Silva when she were set on doing something. Her were like a wild pony. There were no reasoning with her."

"Something must have happened to make her want to leave so hurriedly."

" 'Twere so."

"What, Slack? You must know."

He was silent for a moment.

"She was my sister," I went on. "Just think of that. We had the same father, though different mothers. We should have been brought up together."

"Her weren't like you, Miss Ellen. There couldn't have been two ladies who was so different."

"I certainly wouldn't have gone out to sea on a stormy night."

"Her came to me afore her left. She fed the pigeons with me just as you be doing now. Fluttering round us they were, making their lovely cooing noises, and she said to me: 'Slack, I be going away. I be going to some place where I'll be happy as I never could be here.' "

"Oh, Slack, do you think that she was so unhappy that she deliberately went out like that?"

He was thoughtful. "Her gave me something, Miss Ellen. Her said: 'Keep these, Slack. Someone might want them someday. Perhaps I will myself if it don't all go according to plan.' "

"What did she give you?"

"I'll show 'ee."

He took me into the outhouse and in the cupboard there was a box. He took a key from his pocket and opened it. Inside were two notebooks—exercise books like the one I had found in the desk.

A great excitement seized me. Could it be that these exercise books held the clue to Silva's disappearance? I held out my hand but Slack was regarding me in a puzzled fashion.

"I were to hold 'em," he said.

"And not show them to anyone?"

"Her didn't quite say that."

"Have you read them?"

He shook his head. "They be too much for me, Miss Ellen. I can read only little words. Her was frightened . . . frightened of someone in the castle. I reckon it's in here."

"Slack," I begged, "let me read them."

"I been pondering," he said. "I have said: 'Show 'em to Miss Ellen.' And I'll tell 'ee this, I've been on the point of doing that time and time again. Then when you said about the sugar it was as though Miss Silva spoke to me. 'Let her read 'em, Slack. Might be they'll be of help to her.' "

He put the books into my hands.

"I shall go to my room and read them immediately," I said. "Thank you, Slack."

"I hope I be doing right," he said uneasily.

"I shall never forget what might have happened to me but for you," I told him earnestly.

"Master Jago were there, were he not? He just happened to be there. I be mighty glad I were there too."

I did not think about what he meant by that until later. I was so excited about the exercise books, and lost no time in going to my room and shutting myself in there.

It was still the same scrawly untidy handwriting though a little more mature than that in the first exercise book.

"I found that notebook I wrote in years ago and it made me laugh and cry a bit. It brought it all back so clearly and I thought it would have been interesting if I had written more of it and had a whole stack of such notes, recording my life, my miserable uneventful life. Those were good days in a way when my stepmother was here with Baby, and when they went I was terribly lonely. At first I thought my father might have liked me a little more if there was no competition. How wrong I was! Of course I was a difficult child. Governesses came and went. They always said the same. They despaired of me. What I do remember from those days was my father's sending for me.

"It was soon after my stepmother had gone. I must have been about fourteen. I remember how excited I had been when the summons came. I had let myself imagine that he was going to tell me he loved me after all and we were going to be friends from now on. It's amazing what pictures the imagination will conjure up without having any sound reason for doing so. I saw myself in his study, toasting muffins on winter evenings or sitting on a footstool at his feet while we talked. I could hear the servants whisper: 'There's nobody who can soothe him like Miss Silva. The moment he comes in you know he's going to shout: "Where's Miss Silva?" '

"What a silly little thing I was. As if my stepmother's

going would have softened a nature like his. The reality
was that I stood before him, my hopes blighted by his
withering gaze. My best dress—crushed-strawberry color
with a matching sash which I had thought so becoming—
seemed to hang on me awkwardly. I was seeing myself
through his eyes. All he wanted to tell me was that my
latest governess had given notice and he didn't feel inclined to engage another, and if I wanted to be ignorant,
which I obviously did and was, I could continue so. I was
lazy, stupid, useless and he was going to wash his hands
of me. He wondered why he had bothered to do as much
as he had. But as he could not allow people to know that
he had a little savage in his household he had decided,
after long consideration, to engage a new governess, and
if he had any complaints from her, she would be the last.

"I returned in abject misery, but I reminded myself: At
least he had actually sent for me and talked to me. I didn't
remember when he had done that before. Then it occurred
to me that if I worked hard and tried to be the sort of
daughter he could be proud of he might, in time, grow to
love me. It was a comfort and my imagination was my
friend because it started to supply those cozy scenes for
me to brood on. He and I together on the mainland
doing business. 'My daughter? She is my right hand.' 'My
daughter Silva, yes, she is growing into a most attractive
girl.' 'Marriage. Oh, I hope not yet. I don't want to lose
her. I shall insist that if she does marry, her husband lives
in the castle.'

"How stupid can one be! I knew in my heart it was
never going to be like that.

"But those days when I lived between ridiculous dreams
of personal glory and the depth of depression, when I
hated everyone, and most of all myself, are past and I'm
wasting time writing about them, because I can only write
in retrospect and I'm probably not giving the real picture,
which can only be seen clearly at the time it happens."

There was a blank page and I guessed she had aban-
doned the idea of writing for a while and continued later.
The girl she had been in those days was the one who, find-

ing herself confined in her room, would have scratched 'I am a prisoner here' on the wall of the cupboard. She had been a prisoner because she had been shut in by her own nature, I guessed; but perhaps those about her had helped to make her what she was.

The writing began again.

"There is nowhere one can go without being aware of him. Since my father's stroke he has taken over completely. Of course he was always there and people were more aware of him than they ever were of my father. He just has to command people and they obey him. They have to. My father was not like that. He would get angry with them and be vindictive too. He never forgave anyone who did him an injury. Jago isn't like that. I don't think anyone would *dare* do him an injury, so one couldn't really know how long he would bear resentment.

"Yesterday I was in the rose garden picking roses when Jago came to me. I turned suddenly and he was beside me. He always seems now as though he is assessing me and that makes me nervous.

"He said: 'My sister Jenifry is coming to the castle with her little daughter. They'll be company for you.'

" 'Are they going to live here?' I asked.

" 'It'll be their home. You'll like that.'

"Jago has a way of telling you what you are going to like and almost daring you not to.

" 'What does my father say?' I asked, because I always wanted to know what my father was saying and doing. The only time I saw him was when he was at his window and I was in the gardens. I'd look up hopefully but he was always turning away then. I would see Fenwick pushing him about in his bath chair. I always had to keep out of the way then, and if he did catch sight of me he would behave as though I were invisible to him. I can feel the hot tears coming to my eyes now when I remember such times. I always wanted to shout out to him: 'What have I done? Tell me that.'

"Fenwick was always very discreet. Jago said that my

father couldn't do without Fenwick, nor Fenwick without my father.

"Now I am eagerly awaiting the coming of Jago's sister and his niece."

Another blank page which indicated that some time had passed.

Then: "Gwennol is about eight. She is bright and pretty. Baby would be about her age. I took a dislike to Jenifry. I think she resents my being the daughter of the house. The idea of anyone's being jealous of me is comic! But she is always trying to push Gwennol forward. Not that she need worry. Gwennol is so much more attractive than I could ever be. I'm glad they're here though. Gwennol shares my governess. She is much brighter than I ever was.

"Why did I start this writing? There's nothing to write about really. Every day is like another. I shan't do it any more."

There was no more writing in that book although there were many blank pages. I picked up the second.

"I was clearly not meant to be a diarist. My life is so dull and I'm getting old now. Most girls have parties and eligible men around them. My father, I have been told, has said that he will not waste money on bringing me out. Jenifry sees that Gwennol has a certain social life. She has become quite friendly with Michael Hydrock, who is the most eligible bachelor in the neighborhood. Gwennol is excited by the fact that he has been particularly nice to her.

"She came to my room last night. She had just been rowed back from the mainland. Her eyes were bright and there was a lovely flush in her cheeks which goes beautifully with her dark hair.

" 'It was a sort of garden party at the Manor,' she said. 'Oh, what a beautiful house; peacocks on the lawn and that lovely lovely house. I hate this old castle. Don't you, Silva?'

" 'Yes,' I said. 'It's too full of the past. When I go near

the dungeons I fancy I hear the screams of souls in torment.'

" 'You would,' said Gwennol. 'People must have laughed here and been gay sometimes. There must have been feasting and revelry in the hall. Why do ghosts always have to be horrible? Why can't they be nice . . . like the ghost of Hydrock Manor? A benign old gentleman who says people have to be happy in the house. Michael told me the story today. It applies particularly to brides.'

" 'You're in love with him,' I said.

" 'Everybody's in love with him.'

" 'That must make life a bit complicated for him.'

" 'Why? Wouldn't it be nice to have everyone in love with you?'

" 'As not one single person has ever been in love with me, I can't say.'

"She said: 'Poor Silva! I'm going to take you to Hydrock Manor. You know, *you* might meet someone there.'

"It's night and I can't sleep. There is something about this room which I don't like. It seems full of shadows. Perhaps because I've been so unhappy in it. Somebody said once: Life is what you make it. If that's true, I've made a very bad thing of mine.

"I'm sitting at my desk writing. It's no use lying in bed when you can't sleep. I have just been to the cupboard and seen that silly childish scrawl. I wish I could obliterate it. I remember the day I wrote it. Sent to my room for two days and nights because I had committed some crime. I can't even recall what now.

"I'm introspective tonight and because of Gwennol. Gwennol is in love and watching her has shown me clearly what has been wrong in my life. No one ever loved me— except perhaps my mother and when she died there was absolutely no one else. That's what I want more than anything—just someone to love me. Because nobody does, I do wild things. I suddenly lose my temper and scream. I just want someone to hate me if they won't love me. At least they're taking notice of me then.

"I'm thinking of Jago as I write this. He has changed

towards me. He is being very kind. Not that he was unkind before. He just didn't notice me. Two days ago he rode round the Island with me and talked about things in that way he has—as though it's just about the most important thing in the world.

"I was excited when we came back to the castle. Why is Jago suddenly becoming interested in me?

"Yesterday Fenwick was in the garden sitting on the wicker seat by the pond. I went up to him because it is unusual to see him without my father.

" 'Where is my father today?' I asked.

" 'He's having a day in bed, Miss Silva.'

" 'Is he . . . less well?'

" 'He's a very sick man, Miss Silva.'

" 'I know he had a stroke some time ago.'

" 'It's crippled him and now . . .'

" 'I'm sorry,' I said. 'I wish he would see me.'

"Fenwick shook his head. 'Don't come to his room whatever you do, Miss. That would just about finish him, the state he's in now.'

" 'Do you know why he hates me so?' I asked.

"He shrugged his shoulders.

" 'I suppose he wanted a son,' I suggested. 'Most people seem to.'

" 'Maybe he did,' said Fenwick. 'But he's not one for children.'

"Fenwick was anxious, I could see. I wondered whether he was asking himself what he would do if my father died. My father couldn't do without Fenwick, as Jago had said. But what would Fenwick do without my father?

"I wouldn't *say* this to anyone, but I can write it. Oh, how careful I shall have to be with these notebooks. It's a good thing no one is interested in what I do. I think Jago is contemplating asking me to marry him."

I put down the notebook. I didn't want to read about Silva and Jago. It was prying into his life and hers. Well, I had already done the latter. What I really felt, I suppose, was that I was going to read something which I was not going to like.

Jago and Silva! I hadn't thought of that.

I stared at the book in my hand. I shouldn't be reading this. Why had Slack given it to me? Why had Silva given the books to Slack?

There must be a reason.

"I met him today. I went over to the mainland and he came to the inn. He is so distinguished and handsome. I couldn't believe he could be interested in *me*. We had wine and saffron cakes and we talked so much. Why didn't we hire horses and go riding together, he said.

"What a day it was! We had a snack at the Corn Dolly Inn. A beautiful romantic place with those lovely Stonen Chills on the table and the corn dollies hanging about the place. Cider and pasties. I had never known them taste so good.

"He said: 'We must do this again.'

"Is it possible to be in love so soon?"

She is in love with Michael Hydrock, I thought. Was he in love with her? Or was he merely being his charming, courteous self? Oh poor Silva. I hope she was not badly hurt.

I turned the pages.

"Who wants to write when one is happy? He loves me. He said he does. It is all so exciting. He says we shall be together and everything is going to be different. I talked to him about my father and life at the castle.

"Life is wonderful."

There was a further gap. Then I read:

"The artist was on the mainland today. He asked us to Blue Rock and he was very kind and hospitable. He showed us his studio full of his paintings of birds and pictures of the sea and the islands. He said he hoped we'd come again.

"It was a lovely day. It always is when we are together."

Another gap. Then:

"I wish I hadn't started writing all this now. It seems pointless, I think that before I was just brooding on my unhappiness, enjoying my misery if that's not a contradiction, but it fits the case. Now it's all over. I'm so happy I just love everybody.

"Today I looked up at my father's window and he was there. He looked very ill and I thought: 'Shall I tell him?' But I was afraid to go up. I remembered Fenwick's saying that it would just about finish him off. I wouldn't want that on my conscience ... now.''

There was no more writing in the book.

Although I felt I had come closer to Silva, what had happened on that fateful night of the storm was more than ever a mystery. Why had she taken a boat out when she had known she was risking her life?

There seemed one answer. She had been desperate. Could it possibly have been that after all that sudden and new-found happiness she had been bitterly disillusioned and she had made up her mind to embark onto the sea and let that fierce and entirely indifferent element do what it could with her?

My sad little sister! How I wished I could have been with her to listen to her story of joy and sorrow. I was certain that I should have been able to help her.

I put the exercise books into a drawer and locked it, for I did not want anyone else to read them.

Then I tried to piece together what I had read and ask myself why Slack, who must have known something of her story, had given them to me.

Was it some sort of warning? He was a strange boy. Sometimes I thought he was merely simple as most people believed him to be; at others I thought he was unusually perceptive.

Silva had disappeared on the night of the storm. Was he drawing some comparison between us? Silva went out in a boat presumably and the boat came back without her. One day perhaps another boat would be washed up. On its side would be painted the name Ellen.

She had gone to the mainland and he whose name she did not mention had been kind to her. He loved her, she had written. He had told her so. She was not the kind to imagine that someone loved her. In fact, I think it would be rather difficult for a man to convince her that he did. They had met; they had gone to the Corn Dolly together and he must have told her he loved her then. And yet she had gone out in a boat to face almost certain death.

Why?

In desperation? Had she, the child who had never felt wanted and suddenly found someone whom she believed loved her at last, discovered that she had been deceived? Had the discovery been beyond endurance? Or had someone lured her in some way to go out and risk her life?

A vision of Jenifry's face when she had seen me saying goodbye to Michael Hydrock after he had brought me home to the Island, rose before me.

Gwennol was in love with him; Jenifry wanted the most eligible bachelor in the neighborhood for her daughter. How strange that Silva's boat should have come back without her and that I should be caught in a leaking boat and fancy I saw dissolving sugar there.

I was beginning to feel very uneasy.

Jago rowed me over to Sanctuary Island.

"You haven't been on the sea since the accident," he said. "I've noticed that."

"I still remember it vividly. There were some moments of sheer terror when I thought it was the end of me."

"My poor Ellen! But you don't feel afraid with me."

"I've no doubt," I told him, "that if we overturned you'd bring me safely in."

"I only hope, Ellen," he said very seriously, "that whenever you need me I shall be at hand."

We came to the island and he helped me out of the boat. "Do you remember when we came here before?" he asked.

"Yes, it was then that we met the artist from Blue Rock."

"So we did."

"I've seen some of his pictures since in shopwindows on the mainland. I thought them rather fine. Do you like them?"

"Why yes. He's quite a good artist, I believe. Ellen, tell me, are you really settling into the life of the Island? Am I right in thinking you are getting rather fond of it?"

"I am very interested, particularly now that I'm getting to know the people. They talk to me and I find that appealing. I suppose it's because it makes me feel I belong."

"You *do* belong."

"Yes, I suppose so, but I've only just come here and having never known my father . . ." I frowned. "He doesn't seem to have been a very popular person."

"You're thinking of your mother's leaving him as she did. As a matter of fact, I knew as soon as I saw her that she would never fit into our way of life. She wanted more gaiety and a more lively existence."

"She didn't get much of that with my grandmother. My father didn't seem to care much for his children and that seems unnatural."

"He was a very sick man."

"I know he had a stroke, but before he was sick he didn't seem very fond of them."

"He was sick for a long time. He was never the same after your mother went, taking you with her."

"He still had my half sister."

"Silva was an odd girl and he never liked her."

"Why not?"

I didn't want to tell him that I had seen the notebooks. That was a secret between Slack and myself, and not knowing that, he could not understand why I had such a clear picture of my father.

He shrugged his shoulders.

"Silva was a difficult child. None of the governesses stayed. She was morose and liked to be left alone. She would go off for a whole day and no one would know where she was. But what's the good of going back over all that? It's the future I want to talk about."

"Your future?"

"And yours. In fact I hope they will be intermingled."

I looked startled and he moved nearer to me.

"Everything has been different since you came here.

Even the Island has taken on a new meaning for me. I've always loved it, always been devoted to furthering its interests and making it prosperous, but now everything seems so much more important."

My heart started to beat very fast. I had seen the implication in his manner towards me but I had not thought he would express his feelings so soon.

"You can't mean," I began, knowing very well that he did.

He put his arm about me and drew me to him. Then he took my chin in his hand and looked intently into my face.

"Ellen, I can't believe you're indifferent to me."

"Nobody could be indifferent to you, Jago. I'm sure of that."

"You mean they must either hate or love me. Which do you, Ellen?"

"Of course I don't hate you."

"Then you must love me."

"It was you who said that people must either love or hate. There can be a halfway feeling."

"I have no patience with halfway feelings."

"That is not to say they don't exist."

"I love you, Ellen. I want you to marry me, and I don't want any delay. I want to go straight back to the church and put up the banns. I think it has to be three weeks before a wedding. Come, we'll go right away."

He had sprung to his feet but I remained seated.

"You go too fast, Jago," I said. "Remember, it is only a short while ago that I was engaged to be married. I can't make a decision just like that. Besides, I'm not at all sure that marriage would be a good thing."

He stared at me in amazement. "Not a good thing! Between us! My dear Ellen, you can't mean that!"

"I do mean it. Everything has happened too soon for me. This time last year I had not thought of marrying anyone. Then I became engaged and my fiancé was shot. And now you are suggesting that I marry you in three weeks' time."

"What has this calculation of a year and weeks to do

with it? I love you. You love me. Why should we wait?"

"Because I'm unsure."

"*You* unsure! You know where you're going, Ellen. You're not some silly simpering female to be pushed in any direction the wind blows her."

"That's exactly so. I wasn't in love with Philip."

"Of course you weren't. You know that now because you realize what it means to love."

"Please listen to me, Jago. I will not be hurried into anything. I'm fascinated by the Island. I'm becoming more and more interested, but I have not thought of marriage and I don't want to hurry into anything. You must understand that."

He knelt on the traveling rug.

"You disappoint me, Ellen," he said.

"I'm sorry, but I must tell you what I feel."

"What do you feel for me?"

"I enjoy being in your company. I like to learn about the Island. In fact I find things here intriguing."

"Including me?"

"Yes, Jago, including you."

"But you don't love me enough to marry me?"

"I don't *know* you enough."

"You don't know me! After all this time!"

"It isn't very long."

"But I thought you knew all you wanted to know about me."

"I don't think one ever knows all one wants to about another person."

"Now you're being profound. I know enough for both of us. I know I love you. I know that nobody ever meant to me what you do, and I know that I wasn't really living until you came. Isn't that enough, and don't you see that our marriage would be the best thing that could happen to either of us?"

"Why?" I asked.

He looked at me incredulously. "You and I together for the rest of our lives on the Island. Together we'd make it into a paradise."

"Surely if two people are in love where they live is not important."

"Of course it isn't. But there happens to be the Island."

"Jago," I said, rising, "thank you for asking me but . . ."

"What do you mean? Thank you for asking me but! Why thank me for what you must know has been uppermost in my mind for weeks?"

He was standing beside me and he caught me and held me fast. Our faces were close and I could see the heavy lids had come down over his eyes as though he did not want me to see all that was there.

He kissed my lips then and I felt an immediate response to the passion which I sensed in him. It had never been like that with Philip.

I was aware of the screech of a gull overhead—jeering in a way.

I broke free. "No, Jago," I said, "I must think about everything. There's so much to consider. This has brought back what happened in London and I can't forget it."

"That was a fortunate release, my darling. That's how you are going to see it."

"It was not very fortunate for Philip."

"He's dead. Let the past bury itself. You are not going to mourn over that forever?"

"No, I suppose not. When I am sure, I shall be happy. All that will recede, but I must be sure first. Let me explain to you a little, Jago. When Philip asked me to marry him, a bleak future lay before me. I could have been very frightened if I had let myself contemplate it too clearly, but I always pretended to myself that it wouldn't happen. When Philip proposed it was like a miracle . . . too wonderful to be true. It was only afterwards . . . yes, before he died, that I began to have doubts and my childish belief in the future was considerably dimmed. Now I am here. I love the Island—yes, I do and I have so much enjoyed being with you and if we were to leave each other and never meet again, I should be unhappy. But I'm not sure if that's enough. Give me time to think, Jago. Whether you will give it or not I must have it. Let us go on for a little longer as we have been. Do this for me, Jago. When I'm with you I think I love you, but I have to be sure."

We were standing very close and he held my hands tightly.

"Dearest Ellen," he said. "I will do anything you want."

"Thank you, Jago. Take me back to the Island now. I want to think."

He picked up the rug and slung it over one arm, the other he slipped through mine.

As we went down to the boat the gulls shrieked their melancholy chorus.

He rowed me back in silence and when we entered the castle he said: "Ellen, come to the parlor. There is something I want to give you."

I went with him and from a drawer of his bureau he took out a necklace made of roughly hewn stones strung together on a golden chain.

He held it up. "It's been in the family for three hundred years," he said. "It's the Kellaway Island necklace. Look at these stones—topaz, amethyst, cornelian and agate. They have all been found on the Island. If you go down the shore at the right time you can pick up such stones. Mind you, they have to be looked for."

I took the necklace in my hands.

"It has been worn by Kellaway women through the centuries," he said. "You will give it to our daughter and she will give it to hers, and so it goes on—a link through the ages. And it's significant because it means the wearer belongs to the Island."

"I think it is too soon for me to accept the necklace."

"That's not so." He took it from me and fastened it about my neck. His hands lingered there and when I put up mine to touch the necklace his closed over it. "There. It becomes you. It looks as though that is the rightful place for it. Wear it, Ellen. To please me, wear it."

I hesitated, for I felt it was like a betrothal ring. I couldn't understand myself, for on most matters I made up my mind very quickly. What did I feel about Jago? If

I went away I would think of him constantly. I would be sad and there would be a yearning within me for his company. I wanted to be with Jago more than anyone I knew—and yet I was not sure that I really knew Jago.

I left him and went to my room and the first thing I did was to open my mother's sketchbook at the pages on which she had painted his portrait. There were two people there. I had seen the kindly protective Jago often, the guardian who had welcomed me so warmly. What of the other one?

I turned to Silva's picture and I thought: Oh Silva, what a lot you could tell me if you were here!

I turned the pages. The book opened easily at the one I wanted. The room—the homely, pleasant room; and even as I looked at it depicted so accurately there on paper, the feeling of doom which I remembered so well from the dream crept over me.

My eyes went to my reflection in the mirror and I saw about my neck the chain of Island stones.

I knew so little and there was so much to know.

# *The* Ellen *Is Found*

When I went down to breakfast next morning Gwennol was there alone. She smiled at me in a more friendly fashion than she had done for some time and I hoped that she realized that her jealousy regarding Michael Hydrock was unfounded. She asked me if I had fully recovered from my accident and I told her I thought I had.

"What an ordeal!" she said, helping herself to deviled kidneys and bacon. "It's enough to put you off going to sea for a long time, I should imagine."

"I went for the first time yesterday. Jago rowed me to the Sanctuary Island."

"You felt safe with him, I daresay."

"Perfectly. Oh, I shall get over it. I do wonder what happened to the boat and if it will come in."

"It seems hardly likely now. I expect it's well out in the Atlantic Ocean. It might be washed up on the coast of France though."

"It would be interesting to examine the leak."

"When you consider it, they're frail craft, these boats.

267

I wonder men ever trusted themselves in them."

"They wouldn't have got very far if they hadn't."

"Particularly those on Kellaway Island," she laughed. "I suppose one day you'll be taking a boat out on your own."

"I expect so. It doesn't do to give up just because something like that happens."

"It's a good day today. I noticed how smooth the sea was as soon as I awoke."

I wondered whether she was telling me she was going to Hydrock Manor and that I should, therefore, remain on the Island.

We chatted easily during breakfast and as we came out of the dining room and through the hall, Slack ran across the courtyard. He had a piece of paper in his hand.

Gwennol ran on ahead of me. "It's a message for me, is it, Slack?" she asked eagerly.

He looked uneasy. "No, Miss Gwennol. 'Tain't for you."

She looked bitterly disappointed and Slack stood uncertain for a moment. Then he said: "It be for Miss Ellen."

"For me?"

I took the paper. On it was written my name and then: "Fenwick found. I'll be at the inn this morning to take you to him. M.H."

Fenwick found! I felt the color rise to my cheeks. If Fenwick would talk to me about my father than I really would begin to learn something. I had forgotten Gwennol in the excitement of the news.

I said: "Slack, will you row me over to the mainland this morning?"

"Why yes, Miss Ellen. In half an hour I'll be ready."

"Good." I was about to go to my room to change into riding kit when I remembered Gwennol and hesitated. I wondered whether to tell her what the message contained and while I was pondering she turned and went off.

Perhaps I could explain later that it was not just an

ordinary invitation. It was too late to do so now. I went
to my room and changed.

Slack was ready with the boat and in a short time we
were at sea.

"Slack," I said, "you can go and see your parents at the
inn and row me back when I'm ready to go."

Slack was always delighted to have a few hours with his
parents and as we rode into the innyard Michael came
out to greet me.

"I've already told them to get a horse ready for you,"
he said, "so we can start at once if you like. But perhaps
you would like some refreshment first."

"I can't wait to see Fenwick," I said.

"Very well. We'll start immediately. It's about eight
miles inland, close to the moors. Ready?"

We rode out of the inn together. It was a lovely crisp
morning with a touch of frost in the air—which was rare
in these parts. The winter sun shone on the thin layer of
ice on the puddles on the roadside—it had rained on the
previous day. The bare branches of the trees stretched
upwards towards the sky like supplicating arms. I had
often thought that trees were even more beautiful in winter
than they were in summer. The leaves of the conifers
glistened and for me there was excitement in the air because I believed I was on a voyage of discovery.

"He wasn't easy to find," said Michael. "It seemed as
if the man was determined to hide himself. But he has
agreed to talk to you."

"So you have warned him of my coming."

"I felt that was necessary."

"Of course you are right. I'm so glad he will see me."

We had left the sea behind us and the countryside was
less lush here for there was a hint of moorland in the un-
cultivated stony ground.

And then the glory of the moors burst upon us. Bright
sun shone on the streams, which a few days before had
been trickling over the boulders and were now frozen into
immobility. We skirted the moor and came to the little
hamlet of Karem-on-the-Moor.

"This is the place," said Michael, "and Moorside Cottage is Fenwick's place."

The garden was neat and looked as though it had recently been made so; the cottage was small but charming. Ivy climbed its walls, against which leaned an old water butt to catch the rain. A small path of crazy paving ran from the front gate to the door across a miniature garden.

We tethered the horses to a stake and Michael led me through the gate to the door; and when we knocked this was opened by a man of medium height very neatly dressed in every detail.

"Mr. Fenwick," said Michael. "I have brought Miss Kellaway to see you."

"Come in," said Fenwick. "I understand you want to talk to me, Miss Kellaway."

"I should very much like to and it is good of you to allow me to come."

"By no means," he said.

Michael explained that he had business to attend to in the neighborhood and would like to take the opportunity to do that now. He would call back for me in about an hour. Would that be all right?

Mr. Fenwick said it would and I realized that Michael's impeccable good manners had made him realize that what we had to discuss might be of a private nature and therefore he had no wish to intrude.

Fenwick took me into a small room in which a fire was burning. There was a great deal of brass about the place and it was very brightly polished; in fact the impression was of complete cleanliness everywhere.

"Do sit down, Miss Kellaway," he said. "Sit near the fire. It's a cold morning."

I sat down and he took a chair opposite me.

"Now what is it I can do to help?"

"I think there is a great deal you can tell me. You see, I have only recently come to Kellaway Island and I had never heard of it before I came."

He nodded. "I know the story," he said. "I was so long

in your father's employ that I am well conversant with family matters."

"You knew my mother, of course."

"Yes and your father's first wife."

"And you knew my half sister."

"Indeed, yes."

"What sort of a man was my father?"

He hesitated.

"You knew him well," I prompted.

"I was with him every day and in his confidence to a certain extent."

"Then you must have known him as well as anyone in the castle. I can't understand why he was so indifferent to his family . . . to my half sister, to myself, to my mother."

"He was not indifferent to your mother nor to you . . . until she left him."

"But why did she leave him?"

"She could not settle down in the Island. She was constantly trying to get away. She wanted him to take her away but he wouldn't. He said he had his duty to the Island."

"But when she ran away he didn't care."

"He did. She had tried to go before but he had stopped her. He had ordered that no boat was to leave the Island without his permission. We never knew how she got away, but she did."

"Someone must have helped her then."

"It was something we never discovered."

"What about my half sister? What do you know of her?"

"She was a strange girl who gave a great deal of trouble."

"I've heard that. Why did she?"

"It seemed her nature to do so."

"Did my father not care for her at all, didn't he try to make her happy? After all she was his daughter."

Fenwick paused as though he were considering whether he should tell me what he knew.

I prompted him gently: "It's my family, you know. We're talking about *my* father. If there is anything strange about the family, I should know it, surely."

He said: "Your father was not sure that Silva was his daughter."

"Not sure!"

"She was known as such. Well, his first wife, Effie, was unfaithful to him. That was when things began to go sour. He went away on business and was sometimes gone for as much as three or four months. Silva was born seven months after his return. She was a perfectly well formed child but at first it was thought that she was a seven months' baby—and later people said that accounted for her ways. Whether she was or not is not certain. But your father discovered that her mother had had a lover and he half believed that Silva was the result of that liaison. Your father was not a forgiving man. He himself had followed a strict moral code and he felt it was incumbent on others to do likewise. There were violent scenes and during one of them Effie broke down and confessed that she had been unfaithful. She wouldn't admit though that Silva was the result of this. The fact was that your father was never sure and the sight of the child roused all his suspicions and he could not bear to look at her. Effie died of pneumonia when the child was quite young; she had never taken very much care of herself. Her life was unhappy but she did worry a great deal about Silva."

"Poor Silva! Couldn't my father see that whatever had happened wasn't her fault?"

"He could see that of course, but he didn't want to see her all the same. He used to say: 'Keep that child out of my sight.'"

"She knew it," I cried. "It warped her life. It was cruel of him."

"Self-righteous people are often cruel, Miss Kellaway. And I didn't think you'd really like to hear too much about your father's life."

"But I want to *know*. Then he married my mother. What of their life together?"

"He hoped for something from that. He met your mother on one of his trips to London and he changed a little when he brought her back to the Island. But she found the place oppressive. She felt cut off and was far from happy here. They weren't compatible and I think he was very disillusioned when he realized he had made another mistake. The fact is, Miss Kellaway, he was not a man for marriage. His temper was too short; he expected too much. It was the same with the Island. He was not popular with the people. He was too stern. He called himself just and he was, but people like human feelings in their relationships. If they get that, they'll forgive a little injustice now and then. As a matter of fact, the Island is a much happier place now—and oddly enough more prosperous—than it was in your father's time."

"Jago is for the Island heart and soul," I said.

"Jago is a very ambitious man—in a great many ways more suited to rule the Island than your father was. Your father resented Jago in a way because he knew this. There was often a sort of tension between them. Jago, on the other hand, believes himself to be so much more capable of running the Island—which indeed he proved himself to be—and I suppose naturally he felt a certain bitterness because he belonged to the illegitimate branch of the family."

"My father realized this since he left everything to Jago, I suppose."

Fenwick looked at me incredulously. "But by now you must be aware of the contents of the will."

"My father's will, you mean?"

"Certainly. *You* are the heiress of the Island. I know your age, because I remember the year you were born. You will be twenty-one next year and that is when you will come into your inheritance."

"*My* inheritance?"

"Certainly. Your father was a man with a strong sense of justice. You were his daughter. He was sure of that as he could not be sure of your half sister. Jago was to hold the estate in trust for you until you were twenty-one, when it becomes yours. If you died without heirs your half sister—because after all he was not entirely sure that she was not his daughter also—was to inherit. In the event of your both dying without heirs, everything was to go to Jago. So Jago now holds the Island until your twenty-first birthday."

I was astounded. I, who had thought of myself so often as the Poor Relation, had, all the time, been a considerable heiress.

"Your father was a very rich man, Miss Kellaway. Of course, his fortune is all tied up in the Island, but with the price of land as it is today and the prosperity of the Island —particularly in the last few years—you stand to inherit something in the region of a million pounds."

I . . . a millionairess!

"It's fantastic," I cried. "Are you sure this is true? I have heard nothing of it."

"I am astonished. Surely Jago informed you of all this when you came to the Island. I heard you were there and I thought you had come because of this."

"I knew nothing of it. I was invited to come on a visit because of something tragic which had happened in London."

He nodded. "Yes, I know. It was in the papers. It's most extraordinary."

"Are you sure you are not mistaken?"

"I may be, of course. I should be very surprised if I were though. Your father discussed these matters often with me. I was more than a secretary. I used to look after him personally. He trusted me. We were of a kind, and I understood his ways. He said it was unfortunate that he had not known you since you were three years old; he said that on his death you must return to the Island and learn about it and he hoped that you would come to love it. He knew how dedicated Jago was to the place and that he was leaving it in good hands, and he hoped that you would realize that Jago was necessary to the Island and to you. 'Of course,' he once said to me, 'she will marry no doubt and if she has a husband he might be able to do for the Island all that Jago does. That will be a matter for her to decide.' "

I was speechless. This had completely changed my outlook on everything that had happened. I, the heiress of the Island. I . . . a millionairess on my twenty-first birthday —and that but a few months distant.

I said at length: "I came here hoping to learn something about my father and Silva, whom I believe to be my half sister, and instead I learn this."

"My great surprise is that you didn't already know."

"I thought I was there as Jago's guest. I was sure he was what I thought of as Lord of the Island. Perhaps you have been mistaken."

"There is a possibility of that. I will give you the address of your father's solicitors. Go and see them and hear the truth."

"Shouldn't they have been in touch with me if this were true?"

"Yes. Perhaps they have been looking for you. It was only since there was this publicity in the papers that it was known where you were."

"My mother went to her mother and then I went to a cousin of hers when she died. I shouldn't have been so very difficult to find."

"It may be that they are looking for you. It's only just a year since your father died and mills of the law—like those of God—grind slowly."

"Well, I am quite bewildered."

"You must be to find yourself such an heiress."

"It is not that so much . . . although I have yet to consider what it will mean. It is the fact that I knew nothing. . . ."

He look at me covertly. "Perhaps Jago had his reasons for not telling."

I felt myself flushing. I was seeing Jago on the Sanctuary Island and remembering the manner in which he had kissed me. Why, of course he wanted to marry me! The Island would be mine, and I fancied he loved the Island with a passion he might not be able to give to anything—or anyone—else.

My chief feeling was one of hurt bewilderment. But the

scene was falling into place. How wise had I been to come
to Mr. Fenwick. He was telling me too much for my comfort.

"Your father was generous to me," he said. "He left me
enough money to live on in comfort for the rest of my
life. It is not settled yet—these things take so long; but I
had savings of my own and I bought a market garden
which was a going concern. But I realized it was not the
life for me, so I quickly sold it at a profit and bought this
place."

"You have settled down very quickly in a short time."

He had risen and gone to a bureau in the corner of the
room. He sat down at this and wrote on a piece of paper,
which he handed to me. On it was written "Merry, Fair
and Dunn"; and there was an address.

"Your father's solicitors," he said. "Why don't you
pay them a call. They will be delighted to see you if they
have been trying to contact you, which they must have
been since you are the main beneficiary of your father's
will. They will confirm—or deny—all that I have told
you. All I can say is that your father discussed his intentions very thoroughly with me and I remember the
representative of Merry, Fair and Dunn calling at the
castle. That was about a year before he died."

"How strange that, having made such a will, he made
no attempt to find me."

"He said he didn't want his life complicated at that
stage."

"And when did Silva disappear?"

"Only a few months before his death."

"Didn't he care that she had gone?"

"He didn't express an opinion."

"How cruel he was to her!"

"Remember—she always reminded him of her mother's
unfaithfulness. Perhaps if she had been a different child,
more attractive, more normal, he might not have disliked
her so much, but he often asked me why he should bother
with her and once he said that only the fear of scandal
made him keep her at the castle."

"Did Silva know that he doubted she was his daughter?"

"I don't think so. Few people did. I knew because he confided in me a great deal. He was too proud to speak of his doubts to anyone."

"I wish she were here now. I should so much have liked to know her."

"She was wild always. Once she threatened to throw herself down from the top of the castle tower. The governess of the moment said: 'All right. Do it.' And that made her change her mind. So no one took her threats seriously after that. I think she probably went out in that boat as a gesture, hoping to alarm people, and that it got out of hand. You can't play tricks like that with the sea."

"And her body was never found, though the boat was washed up."

"She was obviously drowned."

"It's strange that her body wasn't washed up somewhere."

"It doesn't always happen. There must be hundreds of people whose bodies have never been found."

"What a sad, tragic life! It is indeed a case of the sins of the parents being visited on the children. I am so grateful to you, Mr. Fenwick. You have told me so much more than I could have hoped to discover."

"It's information which you should know. But with regard to the will, you must see the solicitors whose name I have given you. As a beneficiary I was not present when the will was signed, but I feel sure that your father told me of his true intentions."

I said I would go to the solicitors that day if it were possible and when Michael returned and I showed him the address he said he would take me there right away. The small town in which the offices were situated was only a few miles out of our way and Michael knew the quickest route.

And so in the offices of Merry, Fair and Dunn, I learned that I was indeed the heiress to a considerable fortune which I should inherit when I was twenty-one and until that day this was held in trust, and that Jago Kellaway had the power to manage the Island estate and that my father had strongly advised me to allow him to continue to do so.

There was something else. It was true that in the event of my death without heirs, Silva Kellaway was to inherit the Island.

Since she was undoubtedly dead, it was explained to me Jago Kellaway was the next in the line of succession to the Island crown.

This last piece of news had set the alarm bells ringing in my mind since I had first heard it; but I didn't want to listen to what they were trying to tell me.

More than anything I was eager to confront Jago. I must know what he had to say when he heard what I had discovered and what excuses he would make for not enlightening me.

I was still bewildered and it seemed strange that the thought which was uppermost in my mind was not that I was going to be very rich but that Jago had kept me in the dark, and most insistent of all was the thought that if I were not there and since Silva was presumed to be dead it would all belong to him.

It was frustrating that he was not in the castle when I returned. Jenifry told me, when I asked if he were there, that he would not be back until dinnertime.

Impatiently I went to my room. I washed and changed, but it was too early to go down. I sat down and nervously leafed through the sketchbook. Inevitably I came to the picture of Jago.

I kept thinking of that moment when I had discovered the hole in the boat through which the water had slowly seeped. He had given me the *Ellen*. "You should have a boat of your own," he had said, when he had taken me down to the shore and proudly shown me the jaunty little craft with my name painted on her side. How delighted I had been—not only with the boat but because he had given it to me. Why was I thinking of all that now?

I could hear the cool voice of Mr. Dunn. "Should you

die without heirs the estate would go to Jago Kellaway."

There were long shadows in the room. An air of menace had crept in. But perhaps it had always been there.

At last it was time to go down to dinner and my heart beat uncertainly because he was there.

"Have you had a good day, Ellen?" he asked.

"Very interesting, thank you."

Gwennol was watching me closely, her eyes cold and hard. She was wondering whether I had been with Michael.

"I went to the mainland," I said.

"What? Deserting our Island again!"

Our Island, Jago, I thought. You mean *my* Island. At least it will be . . . or should be . . . in a few months' time.

I wished we were alone. I could scarcely wait to speak to him. How long the meal seemed, how difficult it was to make conversation with my mind running on one theme.

As soon as it was over I said: "Jago, I want to talk to you."

Lights of speculation leaped up in his eyes. Was he thinking that I had come to a decision? And being the man he was, who could not imagine he could ever be defeated, he would be thinking that I could no longer deny the fact that I wanted to marry him.

I faced him in the parlor.

"Today," I said bluntly, "I have made the most extraordinary discovery. It was a shock to realize that I am heiress to great riches."

He did not seem in the least embarrassed. "You were certain to discover it sooner or later," he said easily.

"Why was I not told?"

"Because you would know all in good time."

"I had a right to know."

"It was better that you shouldn't."

"Whose idea was that?"

"Mine of course."

"I feel . . . cheated."

"My dear Ellen, what a strange thing to say. No one

shall cheat you while I'm around to protect you."

"You told me that my father had made you my guardian until I am twenty-one."

"That's true."

"But you didn't say what would happen to me when I became twenty-one."

"That was to be a pleasant surprise."

"I don't like it, Jago."

"You don't like the idea of inheriting the Island?"

"I don't like being kept in the dark. Will you please tell me what all this is about."

"I thought you had discovered that. Tell me who was your informant."

"I have been to see my father's secretary, Mr. Fenwick, and he gave me the address of Merry, Fair and Dunn. Mr. Dunn explained to me the terms of my father's will."

"Well, then you know everything. How did you find Fenwick?"

"Michael Hydrock found him for me."

"Oh? Is he interested in your inheritance?"

"What do you mean?"

"I meant that he goes to a great deal of trouble to do what you ask."

"It was a friendly gesture. You aren't suggesting that he is interested in my inheritance, are you? He is very rich, I should imagine. He would not want what I am likely to get."

"Don't be too sure. Often those who appear to be rich are in urgent need of money. The richer one is, the more disastrously one can accumulate debts."

I thought: He is sidetracking me. Attacking when he should be on the defensive, which of course is what I would expect of him.

"You knew all this when you came to London," I accused.

"Ellen, let us not be melodramatic. It is not very long since your father died. All the formalities concerning his estate have not yet been resolved. I was appointed your guardian. That was why I took matters in my own hands.

I wanted to see you and inspect the man you were proposing to marry. His death made it possible for me to ask you here. I wanted you to see the Island, to get to know it, to love it before you knew it would one day be yours."

"Why?"

"Because, my dear Ellen, if you had heard that you were to inherit a remote island which could, if sold, represent a great deal of money, what would you have done?"

"I should have come to see it, of course."

"And very likely have sold it at once. Some unknown person might have bought Kellaway Island. That was something I dared not risk. I wanted you to come here, to see it for yourself, to grow to love it while you remained in ignorance of your father's will."

"And you thought I would marry you before I knew that the Island was mine."

"That has nothing to do with our marriage except that it will be convenient for you to have me here to look after it and work with you to make it an even more desirable spot than it is now."

I looked full into those heavy-lidded eyes; they held secrets, I knew. And I felt wretched because I could not trust him and it was becoming more and more clear to me that whatever he had done, my life would be dull and meaningless without him.

"Oh Jago," I began, and he came swiftly to me and put his arms about me, holding me so tightly that I thought he would break my bones.

His lips were on my hair. "Don't fret about it," he said. "I'll look after you, Ellen. You've nothing to fear with me beside you."

I broke away from him. "It's all so unnecessary," I said angrily. "Why did you have to make it so mysterious? Why did you come to London without saying who you were and then come to that house in Finlay Square . . . why?"

"I wanted to see you . . . to get to know you . . . before you knew who I was."

"I can't see the reason for it," I insisted.

"I wanted to know about this family you were marrying into, and what would have happened if I had presented myself to you? You would have introduced me to them, would you not? I did not want them to know that I was around, because, Ellen, I was making inquiries about them."

"About the Carringtons? They are a well-known family not only in England but internationally."

"Exactly. Then why should they be so happy about their son's marriage with a girl who was, as far as it seemed, penniless?"

"They had so much money it was not important."

"I'll tell you this, Ellen. Money is about the most important thing in the Carrington ménage. I believe they knew of your inheritance and that was why they were so eager for the marriage. They wanted that money. The Island would have been sold and the proceeds would have very comfortably and conveniently backed up the Carrington Empire."

"This is wild speculation."

"No. I leave that to the financiers of this world. Things are not always what they seem, my darling. I'll admit I love this Island. It's true I did not want to see it pass out of my hands. It was the greatest joy I had ever known when I met you and loved you on the spot."

"Your joy would have been slightly less intense if I had not been the heiress to the Island."

"Of course. But it would have made no difference. I was determined to have you for my own and I would have found some means of saving the Island too."

My common sense was telling me not to accept what he was saying, but common sense had no chance against that magnetism which was no less potent than it had ever been.

He went on: "Now, my dearest Ellen, you will look at the Island through different eyes. I will initiate you into the bookkeeping. The archives go back over a hundred years. You'll be fascinated. We'll work together. We'll have children, and we'll bring them up to love the Island as we do."

"You go too fast. I have not yet said I will marry you."

"This is perverse of you because you know as well as I do that you are going to."

"I think at times you believe you are not a man but a god."

"It's not a bad idea to have a high opinion of yourself. If you don't no one else will. Where is the Kellaway necklace?"

"It's in my room."

"Why don't you wear it?"

"The clasp is weak. I shall have to get it repaired."

"I like to see you wear it, Ellen."

"I will," I said, and thought how weak I was with him, I who had always felt myself to be strong and self-reliant! I had come demanding an explanation and because he had given me one, which I knew when I considered it alone I should find far from plausible, he had somehow talked himself out of a difficult situation.

What had happened to me? I *wanted* to accept what he said. I wanted to be with him.

It would be different when I was alone.

I said I was very tired. I had had a long day and would say good night. He held me against him and would not let me go for a time.

Then he said: "Good night, sweet Ellen. Don't be afraid of your emotions. I never thought you would be. Don't be afraid to love. It will be a wonderful experience, I promise you."

I said very firmly: "Good night, Jago." And I went up to my room. Immediately the uneasy thoughts were with me. I could hear the wind rising and I went to the window and looked out on a sea just visible in starlight. The waves were beginning to have that white-crested ruffled look.

Could I believe him? I asked myself. Could it possibly be true that the Carringtons had known I was heiress to a large fortune? Not Philip. I would not believe that of Philip. They *had* accepted me almost eagerly, it was true.

I was sure Philip was without guile, but would his clever family use him?

It was inevitable that night that I should dream the dream. There was the room again—more familiar than ever now that I had seen it so often in my mother's sketch-book. I could hear the whispering voices and my eyes were fixed on the door. It was slowly opening and there came to me the terrible realization that doom was just on the other side of the door.

The next day I avoided Jago. I told myself I must be alone to sort out my thoughts. The cool practical side of my nature must take command and assess the situation as an outsider would, unaffected by emotion.

That side of me summed up the situation. He came to London without saying who he was; he came to the house in Finlay Square; when Philip died he asked you here. That was reasonable enough, but why did he not say I was heiress to the Island? Perhaps he feared I would sell it. He wanted me to love the Island. And he had not said who he was because he did not want the Carringtons to know. It seemed wildly implausible when he was not there to look at me so earnestly with such love in his eyes. He had asked me to marry him, implying that it was purely out of love for me, but how much was love for the Island?

Then Ellen in love—for I had come to the conclusion that that was what I must be—took over: He likes to do strange things. He can't bear to act as ordinary people do. He wanted to see me and came to Finlay Square because he was curious about the sort of house we were getting perhaps, and most of all to talk to me alone. Rollo came and interrupted us then and cut short that interview. When Philip was killed he asked me here, which was natural enough, and it was possible that a girl who had lived mainly in London would very probably consider selling a remote island which she had inherited. It was true that the place grew on one; it had grown on me.

Yes, yes, said Ellen in love. I *can* understand it in a way.

I came out of the castle and climbed to the top of one of the hills from where I could look down and see most of the Island. How beautiful it was—very green touched with the gold of the gorse bushes; the houses with their orange roofs were enchanting and brooding over it all were the stone walls of the medieval edifice which had housed Kellaways for hundreds of years.

And this would soon be mine.

A man was slowly climbing the hill. There was something familiar about him. It couldn't be. I must be dreaming. But how like . . .

"Rollo!" I cried.

"Yes," he said, "you're surprised. I thought I'd find you somewhere."

"How did you get here?"

"By boat from the mainland. I'm staying at the local inn on the Island for a night or two. I have business in Truro and I thought I'd look you up on the way down. Esmeralda gave me the details."

"I see."

"I've come to ask you to forgive me," he said. "I'm afraid I was quite obnoxious the last time we met."

"I think we were all distraught."

"It was so sudden . . . so unexpected. I've suffered many a qualm of conscience. After all, it was worse for you than for any of us."

"There was never any light on the matter?"

"Nothing. Now I look at it more calmly. I just can't believe he killed himself."

"I could never believe it. I think the gun must have gone off accidentally when Philip was cleaning it."

"There was no evidence that he was cleaning it."

"There must be a mistake, but I don't suppose we shall ever know."

"I had to come and see you, Ellen, because I wanted to ask you to forgive me."

"I do understand. I know what a great shock it must

have been to you. Please don't worry about what you said to me. It was absolutely untrue. There were no quarrels between us."

"I was more and more sure of this as time passed."

"So do forget what you said. I am so glad that you no longer believe that I am responsible. How is Lady Emily?"

"Just the same as ever. She often speaks of you. We don't see a great deal of your cousin's family now. Esmeralda is on the point of becoming engaged to Frederick Bellings. She seemed very happy and contented when I last saw her. I understand you had an accident not long ago. I was talking to the landlady of the inn and she told me."

"Oh, how these things go round. I suppose the servants talked. Yes, my boat overturned."

"How did that happen?"

"How do these things happen? I suddenly noticed the boat was leaking. A boy from the castle fortunately saw me and came to the rescue and then Jago Kellaway came out and completed it."

"Did you discover what was wrong with the boat?"

"There was obviously a hole in it."

"How did that come about?"

"It's a mystery and was nearly fatal to me. I don't swim very well and was hampered by my clothes. I don't think I stood much chance of reaching the shore."

"What a terrible thing! I see it has little effect on you though. What about the boat? Was that brought in?"

"The boat hasn't come in yet."

"I suppose it won't now."

"I should hardly think so."

"So I have to congratulate you on your escape. My dear Ellen, you are not accident prone, are you? I remember something about your falling from a cliff. That was just after Philip's death. I expect you weren't as careful as you should have been on that occasion. It was at Dead Man's Leap, wasn't it? A dangerous spot."

"That was a terrifying experience. Yes, it does seem as you say that I might be accident prone."

He smiled and laid a hand over mine as it lay on the grass.

"You must take greater care obviously, Ellen. Examine your boats before you go out in them and for heaven's sake don't go near the edges of cliffs. Tell me, do you like being here? Are you going to stay long?"

"It seems to have become my home and I never had a real home before, you know. I could hardly call Cousin Agatha's house that. This place grows on me. I like it more and more every day."

"It's a rich island, I imagine. The agriculture seems in good form. A very profitable little place. The view from the highest peak is superb. I've been up there to have a look. I was going up there now. Come with me, if you have half an hour to spare."

"I'd like to."

"I plan to leave today. I did try to find you yesterday. My main idea was to apologize to you."

"It's good of you to come out of your way. I daresay you are very busy."

"As always," he answered, and seeing him there made me think that Jago's notion that the Carringtons were after my little fortune was absurd. "I thought I'd take the opportunity this Truro trip offered and I'm glad I did."

"I'm glad too. If you see Esmeralda please tell her that I often think of her and that I expect to hear all about her engagement."

"I will do that."

We had started to climb and now we were high above sea level.

"You should be careful here," said Rollo. "One slip and you could go hurtling down."

"I'm very surefooted."

"You weren't on another occasion."

"That was when the rail gave way. Nothing to do with being surefooted. In any case I'm extra careful now. Look, there's old Tassie down there. She's gathering limpets, crabs or something to make her concoctions."

"She looks like a disreputable old crone."

"I hope she hasn't heard that. She'd ill-wish you. Oh, she's seen us." I waved a hand.

"Good day to 'ee, Miss Kellaway," she called. "How be you then?"

"Very well, Tassie," I replied, "and you too I trust."

She nodded and went on her way.

"Whatever she's gathering will go into a love potion for some love-sick girl," I said, "or perhaps it will cure someone's warts or sties."

"It seems to me you lead a very colorful life on this island. Did she see me with you, do you think?"

"Certainly she did. Old Tassie sees everything. I think, probably, that's why her prophecies come true. She keeps her eyes open."

We went down the slope to the spot where I had seen Rollo. He took my hand in his and said: "So I am forgiven? I can go on my way with a good conscience."

I nodded. "Thank you for coming," I said. "Would you like to call at the castle?"

He shook his head. "No. I have to leave shortly. I just came to see you. If I have time I might call again on my way back."

"That would be pleasant," I said.

As we went our different ways—he to the inn, I to the castle—I thought of Jago's suggestion that the Carringtons needed money to bolster up their empire. That seemed quite ridiculous. What a strange day it had been! And Rollo's coming had taken me right back to the days of my engagement to Philip.


It was two days later when Slack came to me in a state of great excitement.

"Miss Ellen," he said, "she have come in. The *Ellen* have come in."

"Where is she, Slack?"

"She's in the cove. I dragged her there and hid her like."

"Why hide her?" I asked.

The bewildered look came into his eyes. "I don't rightly know, Miss Ellen. 'Twere like I were *told*."

"Does nobody know the boat has come in except you?"

He nodded. "I were watching for her. I saw her out there bobbing on the water and I swam out to her and brought her in. I brought her to my special cove where nobody goes much. She's there now. Come and look. I have something to show you and it's something I don't like. But we got to look at it, all the same."

He led the way down to the shore. It was a spot I had not been to before and I guessed that it was often cut off by the tide. There lay the boat.

"That's not the *Ellen*," I said at once.

" 'Tis and all."

"Where's her name? This one has no name at all."

He looked suddenly sly. "I painted her out," he said.

"Why?"

He scratched his head and looked lost again. "I can't rightly say. It seemed best."

"Why are you so mysterious, Slack?" I asked.

"Look 'ee here, Miss Ellen."

He directed my gaze to the bottom of the boat. A hole was bored there.

"How could it have got there?" I asked.

He seemed to read my thoughts, for he answered: " 'Tis only one way her got there, Miss Ellen. Someone bored a hole in her. You did talk of sugar. Well, if a hole were bored and packed tight with sugar 'twould take a little time to dissolve and that's what it did. 'Tis clear as daylight on a summer's day."

I can't bear it, I thought, as I tried to shut out the suspicious thoughts which kept coming into my mind. Someone had bored a hole in the boat—*my* boat, which only I took out. Someone knew I was not a strong swimmer, someone took a chance that I would go out in that boat alone and would not come back alive.

I stood there staring at the hole and then I was aware of Slack beside me gently laying a hand on my arm.

"Miss Ellen," he said, "if you do be in trouble will 'ee come to me? Maybe the Power will let me help you. Miss Silva used to talk to me. Will you, Miss Ellen?"

"Thank you, Slack," I said. "I'm glad you're my friend."

There was no turning away from the fact which was staring me in the face.

Someone wanted me out of the way so badly that he or she had attempted to kill me.

# In the Dungeons

Fear was stalking me. I was certain now that my life was in danger. One possibility occurred to me and it seemed the most likely. Illogically I refused to examine it; I conjured up all sorts of reasons why it could not be true and I refused to listen to the voice of reason within me.

And there has to be a reason, hasn't there? If some person unknown wants another person out of the way it can only mean that the removal of one brings gain to the other. Could this beautiful, fertile Island be the answer? It was mine—or soon to be—and someone else wanted it. I wouldn't accept that.

You fool, said my practical self, you mean you don't want to accept it. You won't face facts. If you were out of the way it would be his.

But he loves me. He has asked me to marry him.

Yes, and you want to. You want to so much that you deliberately shut your eyes to the truth.

If he married me, he would have a share in the Island. If you died, it would be entirely his.

It's nonsense, I thought. Just because I went out in a boat . . .

Then I pictured Slack's face, his eyes bewildered and anxious. Slack knew more than he would admit and this was his way of warning me.

I could not get Silva out of my mind. Was her story in some way connected with mine? What had happened to her? If she were only here and could tell me!

I went to that room on the ground floor which led from the hall and which my mother had used and in which I had found her sketchbook. There was a certain comfort in sitting on the old settle and thinking about my mother, who had run away, taking me with her—and thinking of Silva too.

How unhappy Silva must have been when she took the boat out! Was it really a gesture, as the threat to throw herself from the castle walls had been? It was frustrated love. I gathered that much from the notebooks. For the first time in her life she was loved . . . or deceived into thinking she was.

Could it have been that someone had pretended to be in love with her . . . perhaps because she was her father's daughter . . . his eldest daughter, who it was thought would inherit the Island; and had that someone discovered that my father doubted whether she was his daughter and had left the Island to someone else . . . myself?

Jago's face rose before me, intense, passionate, those heavy-lidded eyes which were not always easy to understand. He fascinated me and excited me; I wanted to be with him, to learn the truth about him—no matter how dangerous that might prove to be. I had always been adventurous and never one to take the safe road; and now it was as though Jago was beckoning me to go to him, to discover how far my suspicions were rooted in truth, to find the vital answer to the question: Does he want me or the Island? The answer to that might be that he wanted us both, which I knew he would freely admit. The real question was: Did he want to be the sole possessor of the Island? What did I really know of Jago except the overwhelming truth that he was exciting to know!

I almost wished Slack had not found the boat. How much more comfortable it would have been if I had dismissed the idea that I had seen grains of sugar and there had not been the evidence of that drilled hole.

Don't be a fool, I admonished myself. What's the good of being in love and finding life exciting if someone is planning to remove you from it?

As I deliberately refused to think of Jago as the one who had drilled that hole in the boat, hoping that I would not return, my thoughts went to Michael Hydrock, who had been so kind to me and seemed to enjoy my company so much. What if Michael had been the one with whom Silva had fallen in love? Then I thought of Jenifry and Gwennol, who had shown so clearly that my friendship with Michael did not please them.

Gwennol was a passionate girl. She would love fiercely and hate in the same way. They had the Devil in them, this branch of the Kellaway family—Jago's branch. That was how the legend went. Jago might want the Island but Gwennol wanted Michael Hydrock.

It was all too mysterious and complicated—but I could not rid myself of the thought that I was in danger.

If only my mother had talked to me! If only I had come to the Island earlier, I might have met Silva.

I pictured my mother here in this room, going to the cupboard, taking out her painting materials and then going out to paint a scene of the castle or the Island, or perhaps to do a portrait. Where had she seen the dream room? That was yet another mystery.

And as I sat there brooding I heard a sound and such was the state to which I had reduced myself that immediately a cold shiver ran down my spine. I stared at the door, which was slowly pushed open. I don't know what I was expecting. My fear was due to my conviction that someone was planning to murder me, I supposed, and was therefore understandable. But it was only Slack standing there.

"Oh, it be you, Miss Ellen," he whispered. "I did wonder. I knew someone was here like. It be a good spot to be when there's trouble about."

"What an odd thing to say. What do you mean by that, Slack?"

"Oh, just that it be good to be in this room like."

"What's so special about this room?"

"Miss Silva, her did come here. Her'd come and sit on that there settle, just as you be sitting now. I could shut me eyes and it would be like you was Miss Silva sitting there."

"How did you know she came here?"

"Me eyes did tell me so."

"My mother used to come here too. It seems that it's a sort of refuge."

"What be that, Miss Ellen?"

"A place you come to when you're pondering about something, when you're not quite sure what you ought to do."

"Aye," he said. "It be such a place. . . ." He paused and wrinkled his brow. It was as though he wanted to tell me something and did not know how to express it.

"Yes, Slack," I prompted.

"You be watchful, won't 'ee?"

"You've said that before, Slack."

"Aye, 'tis so. I know you should be watchful."

"It would be easier if I knew what to watch for."

He nodded. "If you be feared sometimes, Miss Ellen, you come here. I'll be watchful for 'ee."

"Come here? To this room?"

"Come to me first and then come to the room. Then I'd know you was here. That would be best."

I looked at him intently and again wondered if people were right when they said he was "lacking."

"Why, Slack?"

" 'Tis best," he said. " 'Twas what I told Miss Silva."

"So she came here and you came too."

He nodded. "Miss Silva, her trusted me, her did. You trust me too, Miss Ellen."

"I do, Slack."

He put his finger to his lips. "Here," he whispered. "In his room. That would be best."

"Why?" I asked.

"When the time do come."

Poor Slack, I thought, I really believe he is a little mad.

"Isn't it time to feed the pigeons?" I asked.

" 'Tis five minutes off feeding time."

"Then let's not keep them waiting." I stood up.

He smiled and repeated: "When the time do come."

The sea was being roughened up by a wind which was blowing straight in from the southwest and a boat was bobbing about on the waves which were threatening to envelop it. I left the cove and climbed the cliff, where I found a spot among the gorse and bracken. It was easier to think up here away from the castle.

I was wearing a cape of greenish hue which could be a good protection against the wind and if the sun came out could throw it open; so it was a useful sort of garment. Sitting there, in this green cape, I merged into the landscape.

I watched the boat coming in and as a man stepped out into the shallow water the fancy came to me that there was something familiar about him. I was sure I had seen him somewhere before.

Then I heard Jago's voice and seconds later he rode into the cove and down to the shore.

He cried out: "How dare you came here like this? What do you want?"

I couldn't hear the man's answer. He evidently lacked Jago's resonant voice. I could see that Jago was very angry and the notion that I had seen the man before was stronger than ever.

The wind had dropped for a moment and I heard him say: "I have to talk to you."

"I don't want you here," said Jago. "You know very well you had no right to come."

The man was gesticulating and the wind had started to moan again so that I could not hear what he was saying.

Then I heard Jago's voice again: "I have business to attend to. I'm late now. What can you be thinking of . . . to come *here*?"

The man was speaking earnestly and I was frustrated because I could not hear his words.

"All right," said Jago. "I'll see you tonight. Keep your self out of the way till then. I don't want you seen at the castle. Wait a minute though. . . . I'll see you in the dungeons. We'll be out of the way there. Make sure you're at the west door at nine o'clock. I'll join you there but you're wasting your time. You'll get nothing more. Where are you going now?" The man said something. "Go back to the inn then," said Jago. "Stay in your room there till tonight. You'll be sorry if you disobey, I tell you."

With that he turned his horse and rode out of the cove. The man stood looking after him. Then he looked up at the cliff. I shrank into the bracken but I was certain he had not seen me; but as he had lifted *his* face I saw it clearly and with a sudden shock I realized who he was.

He was that Hawley who had been valet to the Carringtons, the man who had made me uneasy when he had watched Philip and me in the Park.

I sat still, staring at the sea. What could it mean? What connection was there between Jago and Hawley—for I was sure it was he—the man who had worked for the Carringtons? I wondered about Bessie, who had been in love with him, and what had been the outcome of that affair. But most of all I wondered how the man was concerned with Jago.

There was no simple explanation that I could think of but a terrible uneasiness assailed me. I had not, as I had thought, turned my back on the old life when I had come to the Island—Philip's death, Hawley, Jago and everything that had happened since was connected with what had gone before.

Jago had certainly been angry to see Hawley. And Hawley? There had been something about his manner which had been a little cringing and yet truculent. That he was afraid of Jago was obvious, but on the other hand Jago was so angry at the sight of him that he might have something to be afraid of too. He must have known that he was coming because he had been at the cove to meet him; and the man was to come that night to the dungeons. Why to the dungeons? Because Jago was anxious that Hawley should not be seen. Not be seen by whom? By me perhaps. I was the one who had seen him before and knew that he had worked in the Carrington household. What would Jago say if he knew that I was already aware that Hawley had come to the Island?

Where is all this leading? I asked myself desperately. What had Jago to do with those horrifying events in London? What did he know of Philip's death?

Philip found shot. It was not by his own hand, I knew it. I was certain of it. Didn't I know Philip as well as it was possible to know anyone? Philip did *not* kill himself and if he did not then someone else killed him.

Why? Did Jago know the answer?

This was becoming a nightmare. I could not shut out pictures which kept coming into my head. Jago at the Carrington soirée. He had walked in without an invitation because he knew I was there. He wanted to see the family I was marrying into. He could easily have found out what he wanted to know about the Carringtons. For what purpose had he been in the empty house in Finlay Square? His explanations had not rung true at the time. Now they seemed more implausible than ever.

And Philip had died. Suicide, they said.

But it wasn't suicide; and if that was so, then it was *murder*.

And Hawley? What did he know about it? He had come here to ask something of Jago and they were going to meet in the dungeons.

There was only one thing to be done. I must be there, but neither of them must know it. They would talk frankly together and I must hear what was said, so I must be hidden there somewhere unseen. It was the only way in which

I could uncover the truth and begin to unravel this terrifying mystery in which I was entangled.

The day dragged past and it seemed as if the evening would never come.

I put on a dress of biscuit-colored silk and because Jago always looked to see if I was wearing the necklace of multicolored Island stones, I decided to wear it. Not that he would notice tonight perhaps; he would surely be preoccupied with his coming meeting in the dungeons with Hawley.

As I fastened the necklace I noticed once more that the clasp was not very strong, but it would hold.

Jago did notice the necklace. He said, at dinner, how becoming it was on that colored silk. He talked about the various stones which could be found on the Island and said that he thought it would be a good idea to start up an industry in cutting them and making them into ornaments. Even so, I sensed that his thoughts were elsewhere. It was ten minutes to nine o'clock when dinner was over. Gwennol and Jenifry went into the parlor to take coffee. Jago did not join them and I murmured something about having a letter to write.

I did not go to my room but slipped straight out of the castle and quietly made my way across the courtyard to the west door. A terrible fear came to me that Hawley might already be at the dungeons, in which case I should be discovered.

It was a bright night, for there was a full moon which touched the castle walls with an eerie light and I felt very uneasy as I hurried through the west door and down the spiral staircase to the dungeons.

I had been there only once before. It was not the sort of place one would make a point of visiting often. Moreover, there was something so repelling about it that even on that other occasion when Gwennol had been with me, my inclination had been to get away as quickly as I could.

I stood in the circular courtyard which was surrounded by doors and looked about me. I remembered from that first visit that behind each of the doors was a cavelike dungeon in which Kellaways had kept their captives of the past.

I pushed open a door and looked inside one. This was one with a small barred window high in the wall. There was a faint shaft of moonlight filtering through that window which was enough to show me the moist walls and the earth floor. It was very cold and smelled unwholesome. Nevertheless, I went farther in and half closed the door.

I waited for what seemed a long time and it must have been precisely at nine o'clock when I heard footsteps on the spiral staircase and the creaking of the courtyard door as it was pushed open.

Through the crack in the door I saw a faint ray of light. Jago was carrying a lantern.

"Are you there?" he shouted.

There was no answer.

I cowered into my dungeon and asked myself what Jago's reaction would be if he discovered me there.

Footsteps at last.

"Well, here you are," said Jago. "What do you mean by sending a message that you were coming here?"

"I had to see you," said Hawley. "Times are hard. I'm in debt and I need money."

"You were paid for what you did. What's your purpose, Hawley?"

"I just want a little something, that's all. I did a good job for you."

"You did a job and were paid for it. That's the end of it. I'm no longer employing you. You made a pretty good mess of it too, I must say."

"It wasn't easy," said Hawley. "I wasn't used to valeting."

"All good experience for you," said Jago.

"After all the trouble I got into . . ."

"That was your own fault."

"I might have been accused of murder."

"You weren't. There was a verdict of suicide, wasn't there?"

"It could have been different. Think what I had to do. I had to get friendly with that girl, the maid, and find out what your young lady was doing. Then I had to get the key cut for you. That was a tricky job."

"It was child's play," said Jago.

"I wouldn't call it that when a man was killed."

"You should have managed better than you did. Now listen, Hawley, you came here to make trouble. Or so you think. You're saying: 'You pay me or else. . . .' There's a name for that and it's blackmail, and that's something I would never accept."

"You wouldn't like the girl to know. . . ."

"There, you see. The blackmailer's talk! I won't have it, Hawley. I tell you I won't have it. You know what we do with people here who break the law? Offenders like you? We put them in prison . . . in these dungeons. They don't like it. There's something about the place. Perhaps you sense it. By God, Hawley, I tell you this: I'll lock you up here and hand you over to the courts for the blackmailer you are. You wouldn't like that."

"I don't think you'd like some things to come out, Mr. Kellaway. You wouldn't want that to happen. . . . The young lady . . ."

"One thing I wouldn't allow to happen," interrupted Jago, "is give way to blackmail. You've been on the mainland, have you? You know that Miss Kellaway is here. You've been hearing gossip. I hope you haven't been adding to it, Hawley. But if you think you can come here and try to blackmail me, you've made a big mistake. Remember what happened in Philip Carrington's bedroom."

"I was only working for you. . . ."

"You be careful. Things could go badly for you."

I felt limp with horror. I leaned against the wall, my fingers clutching unconsciously at the stones of my necklace. Could it be that Philip had been cold-bloodedly murdered by a man employed by Jago to kill him! There were such people as professional murderers. But why? The answer was clear. Because Jago knew that I was the heiress to the Island. He did not want me to marry Philip because he wanted to marry me himself.

There was a second or so of silence in the dungeons and during it I heard a slight clatter as though something had fallen.

Jago heard it. "What's that?" he cried sharply. "There's someone here. Did you bring someone with you, Hawley?"

"I didn't. I swear I didn't."

"I'm going to look," said Jago. "I'm going to search every one of these dungeons."

I crouched against the wall. I should have been numb with fear after what I had heard but somehow I couldn't believe it even now. There must be some explanation of all this. It was like some absurd masque in a melodrama and I could not—I would not—believe that Jago who had said he loved me could be the man my common sense was trying to tell me he was.

He would soon discover me crouching there. I would demand: Jago what does this mean? For God's sake explain. Hawley is your man. I know that. You sent him to London. Why? And then you came yourself.

I heard him say to Hawley: "You hold the lantern."

The light moved away and I peeped through the door. They had their backs to me and had started searching the dungeons on the other side. There was just a chance that if I were quick enough, and quiet with it, I might escape.

I waited for my chance, my heartbeats threatening to choke me, until they were as far as they could be from my dungeon. Then I slipped out silently, while their backs were still towards me, and in a flash I was up the spiral staircase. Luck had been with me. My escape had been perfectly timed and they had not seen me.

What now? I asked myself as I came out through the west door. If I could get to the main building and join Jenifry and Gwennol in the parlor I could behave as though I had not heard that revelation and have a little time to plan what I ought to do next.

I forced myself to look in at the parlor. Gwennol was reading and her mother was working gros point on a canvas. Neither of them expressed any surprise to see me;

they must have presumed that I had written my letter.

I picked up a magazine and leafed through it, my mind busy.

Oh Jago, I was thinking, what does it mean? Why did I let myself be so foolish as to fall in love with you? Hadn't I heard enough? He had paid Hawley to come to London. Philip had died. What had he said about Philip's death? "Remember what happened in Philip Carrington's bedroom."

Hawley must be a professional murderer. There were such people. The real criminals hired them to commit crimes for them and paid them well for it. Hawley did not think he had been paid enough and had come to blackmail.

It was too horrible. I could not believe it. I had misconstrued what I had heard and there must be some explanation. And yet a ray of hope here—if Jago wanted the Island, why murder Philip, why not murder me?

Why did my foolish heart go on fighting against my mind? Why did I go on trying to tell myself that it was a ridiculous mistake, a misconstruction? There must be a simple explanation and I must find it because what I had heard in the dungeons this night had brought home to me one overwhelming and undeniable truth: Whatever Jago was, whatever he had done, I loved him.

Could I, Ellen Kellaway, be such a fool? I knew he wanted the Island; he had confessed that much. But that was not all. He wanted me too.

He was coming into the room now. So he had got rid of Hawley. I kept my eyes on the magazine but I could feel his gaze fixed upon me. I knew that I was flushing as he sat down beside me on the sofa.

He said: "Have you lost something, Ellen?"

I looked at him in surprise. His eyes were gleaming and there was in them an expression I could not understand. There were mingling emotions there—passion, reproach and a certain amusement. The sort of amusement a cat might feel when playing with a mouse?

He held out his hand and I stared down at it in horror, for there lay the necklace and I knew at once where he

had found it. I knew what that clatter I had heard in the
dungeons had been. The catch was weak; I had grasped
the stones in my agitation and when I had released them
the necklace dropped onto the floor. Jago, searching the
dungeons, had at last come to the one in which I crouched
and there on the floor lay the necklace.

So he knew I had been there. He would know what I
had heard.

I took it from him and hoped my hands would not vis-
ibly tremble.

I heard myself say: "The clasp is weak."

"Where do you think I found it?" he asked, his eyes
still regarding me with that odd expression.

"Where?" I asked.

"You were wearing it at dinner. Just think where you
have been since."

I looked into space, foolishly trying to give the impression that I was trying to remember.

"You *must* remember, Ellen," he said gently. "It was
the dungeons. What on earth were you doing there?"

I laughed rather shakily and was aware of Gwennol's
watching me intently.

"Oh, I often wander about the castle, don't I, Gwennol?" I said.

"You're certainly fascinated by it," she answered.

"It takes courage to go to the dungeons at night," commented Jago.

"I'm not afraid," I said, looking straight at him.

He put his hand over mine and gripped it hard.

"I have a good deal to say to you," he said. "Will you
come into my sanctum."

"I'll join you shortly," I said.

"Don't be long."

I thought: I must act quickly and I've not time to think
what I should do. I must have time. I must digest what I
have heard. I must consider the implication and suppress
my absurd romantic longings.

Instead of going to my room I ran down to the hall and
out across the courtyard. Slack was at the dovecotes.

"You look proper scared, Miss Ellen," he said. "Have the time come?"

I thought of Philip in his room . . . shot. Jago had ordered that.

No, that was too wild. I couldn't believe it. I had to talk to him. I had to listen to what he had to say. But I had been listening to Jago for a long time and whenever I was with him I believed whatever he had to tell me. No. I must get away. I must consider everything calmly, coolly, and I could not do that when he was there.

Slack was saying: "Go to the room, Miss Ellen. I'll join 'ee there. Don't be afraid. It'll be as it was with Miss Silva."

Oh Slack, I thought. What are you saying? It will be as it was with Miss Silva who had gone off in a boat and the boat came back but not Miss Silva.

"Come quick, Miss Ellen," he said. "Maybe there's no time to lose."

He took my hand and we went into the castle. Slack picked up a candle as we came through the hall and lighted it.

"Hold this candle for me, Miss Ellen," he said. I took it from him and to my surprise he lifted the lid of the settle.

"Do you want me to hide there?" I cried in amazement.

He shook his head. "You see now, Miss Ellen. This ain't no ordinary old settle."

He leaned forward and to my astonishment he lifted the base, which came up like another lid. I could see down into darkness.

"Be careful, Miss Ellen. There be steps there. Do 'ee see 'em? Go down 'em . . . very careful-like. I'll follow 'ee. But do take good care."

I got into the settle and lowered myself down and sure enough my feet found the steps. I went down six of them. Slack handed me the candle and followed me, after shutting the lids of the settle. We were standing side by side in what appeared to be a dark cave.

"Where are we?" I asked fearfully.

"This be a great cave which do go right under the sea.

'Tis where I brought Miss Silva when she did fly away."

"What happened to her?"

"She did live happy ever after as she told me she would. It goes down deep. It goes down and down and up again. It comes out on Blue Rock."

"How did you know about it?"

"I knew from my mother. It's what they do call a natural cave, but the entrances was made in the old smuggling days. There was a lot of smuggling done here. 'Twas a hundred years ago and more. It weren't much used since then. My mother were the daughter of the innkeeper and she knew of it from her father, who knew of it from his. They used to store the liquor down here. 'Twere a good place for it. Ships could come from France to the Island and liquor would be unloaded and stored in this place until it were safe to bring it to the mainland."

"And when we get to Blue Rock, what then?"

"The artist will help us. He helped Miss Silva. He were very kind to Miss Silva, he had a real fancy for her. He helped her."

"So that was the way she went."

He nodded. "Her went away to live happy ever after."

"And the boat was washed up."

"That were a trick like. Her weren't in it. 'Twasn't till later on a dark calm night when she did cross."

"How do you know all this, Slack?"

"Well, I helped her, didn't I? Her talked to me, her did. Happy she were at the last. She were different from what her'd ever been before. She talked to me . . . like talking to herself, she thought it, but she liked me to be there. I was company, sort of. Her father had been cruel to her . . . terrible cruel . . . and she thought he'd laugh at her and try to stop her if he knew . . . so she ran away with her own true love."

"What happened to her? Where did she go?"

"That I never heard on, Miss Ellen. Be careful. The ground be rough going."

Down we went, down a steep slope below the sea. It was damp and cold and we passed little pools of water; at times my feet sank into the sand and the surface changed to rocks. Fortunately Slack was surefooted and it was clear that he knew the way.

"Now," he said, "we are beginning to go up. It's a climb now. 'Tis no more than half a mile . . . the distance between Kellaway and Blue Rock."

I said: "What will Mr. Manton say when he sees us?"

"He'll be ready to help 'ee get to the mainland if that be what you want."

I did not want to leave the Island. I only wanted time to think. I wanted to talk to Jago, to demand an explanation. But not just yet. I wanted a day or two to think clearly about everything, to make an attempt to piece together the evidence I had gathered, to try to stand outside the enormity of those emotions which Jago aroused in me and access the scene dispassionately. I wanted to discover how deeply involved I was with a man who was unscrupulous and might well be involved in the murder of Philip Carrington.

That was at the heart of the matter. I could understand his passion for the Island and his desire to possess it. To keep it he must either marry me or be rid of me. I wouldn't accept the fact that he didn't love me a little. He could not act as well as that. Perhaps in time he would love me even more than the Island, I promised myself, which showed how obsessed I was by the man, since I was so ready to compromise. But if he really were caught up in the murder of Philip . . . that must make a difference.

I was bemused and bewildered.

If he had hired an assassin to murder Philip what were his intentions towards me? What if he did not love me at all? What if I married him? I saw myself willing everything to him and then what would he do when he had no further use for me? What did I know of Jago? That I loved him. That was all. Is it possible to love a man whom one can suspect of murder? The answer seemed to thunder in my ears: "Yes, yes, yes."

But there was one thing he was unaware of. He thought

Silva was dead and Slack talked of her living happy ever after. What did that mean? She must have married the lover of whom she wrote and eloped with him. On the Island they had believed she was dead because the boat had come back empty. But if she still lived then on my death she was the next in succession. Jago did not consider this because like everyone else he thought Silva dead.

Where was Silva?

If only I knew.

"Can 'ee hear the sea now?" That was Slack. "We be nearly there."

We had been climbing steadily uphill while my thoughts had run on and now I could hear the sea. I could feel the fresh air on my face.

"We'm through," said Slack, and we were pushing our way through bushes and now were right out in the open. The wind caught at my hair, which escaped from its pins and streamed down my back.

"There be the house, look," he said. "There be a light in the window."

He took my hand and dragged me forward. As he said, there stood the house. The door was open. Slack went through calling: "Mr. Manton. Mr. Manton. I be here with Miss Ellen."

There was no answer. We had stepped into a small hall and Slack pushed open a door and we entered a room.

I felt my senses reel. There it was . . . the red curtains tied with gold fringe, the open brick fireplace, the rocking chair, the gatelegged table and even the "Storm at Sea" hanging on the wall.

In every detail it was there—the room which had come to me so often in my dreams.

This was a nightmare. It couldn't be real. I had strayed into the dream somewhere. The dungeons, the terrible suspicions about Jago—they were all part of it. It was a new form of the dream. I should wake at any moment.

Slack was looking at me oddly.

"Slack," I stammered, "what is this room . . . ? What is this place?"

He did not seem to understand. He said soothingly: "You'll be all right here. Miss Silva were . . ."

My eyes were fixed on the door. It was that door which had been the center of the dream. It was not the one through which I had come, for there were two doors in this room. The slow moving of that door which had never opened but behind which I had subconsciously known was the reason for my fear.

I saw the door handle slowly turn. I could not take my eyes from it. The door was beginning to open.

This was it—the moment in the dream when the terrible sense of doom had come over me. I was terrified of what the opening of the door would reveal.

Thoughts flashed in and out of my mind as they do in moments such as that one. It could only have been a matter of a few seconds, but time had slowed down. The fear had come to me . . . just as in the dream, but this was not a dream. I was now face to face with the moment of revelation. The artist! I thought. What has he to do with my life? I scarcely know him. Why should I feel this terrible fear of him?

The door opened. A man was standing on the threshold of the room. It was not the artist though. It was Rollo.

I was trembling with terror, but it was only the dream. Amazement was taking over fear. Rollo! What could Rollo possibly be doing at Blue Rock?

"Ellen!" He smiled. "How good to see you here. How did you come?"

I stammered: "I . . . I had no idea. . . . I thought . . . the artist lived here."

"He's gone to London for a few days. He lent me his place. You look scared out of your wits. Sit down. Let me get you a drink."

"I'm sorry," I said. "I'm so bewildered. I can't think clearly."

"Come and sit down."

Slack was staring at Rollo. I heard him whisper: "Something terrible have happened to Miss Silva."

Rollo had led me to the table and made me sit down in the chair which I had seen so many times in my dreams.

I just could not believe I was awake and this was really happening.

"You must tell me everything, Ellen," said Rollo. "What happened at the castle? The boy brought you, I see."

"We came through a kind of cave."

Rollo poured something into a glass and said: "Drink this. It will steady you. I can see you've had a shock."

He put the glass into my hand but I couldn't drink anything. I set it down on the table.

I said: "There's a tunnel from here to the castle."

He did not express any surprise. "I was concerned about you," he said. "That's why I didn't want to leave the place. I felt that something was going on there and that you needed looking after. I couldn't get that affair of the boat out of my mind."

"You think someone was trying to murder me."

He nodded. "I'm sure of it," he said.

Not Jago, I thought. I won't believe it was Jago.

"I want to get away to the mainland," I said. "For a while at least."

"Of course. I'll row you over."

"I think I'll stay at the Polcrag Inn until I've thought all this over."

"It's clear, isn't it? You're the heiress to that Island, a prosperous community. It's real wealth. People will go to great lengths for the amount of money that represents, Ellen."

I laughed weakly. "I'm sorry," I said, "but I feel so bewildered . . . so lost. Everything that has happened has been so strange. I . . . the Poor Relation to be so rich. I only recently discovered all this."

"Other people knew it and they acted accordingly."

"Why are you so kind to me suddenly?"

"I'm sorry for my past conduct. In any case, you were to be a member of our family. If Philip hadn't died. . . ."

I heard those words again: "What happened in Philip

Carrington's bedroom. . . ." No, Jago, I won't believe it of you. I can't.

Rollo seemed suddenly alert.

"What's happened to the boy . . . the one you brought with you?"

I looked behind me. Slack was not there.

"He must be around," I said.

Rollo went to the door. I heard him calling Slack.

Now I was in the room alone I examined it with a sort of awed wonder. I went to the window and touched the curtains. This was more vivid than the dream.

What was I going to do? I should have stayed behind and talked to Jago. I would go back to him and tell him I must know the whole truth.

My mother must have been here often, for she had re-created every detail in the room in her picture. Why had it played such a part in my dreams? I was baffled.

I had found the room but of what significance was that? I had lived through the moment of doom when the door had opened and revealed Rollo.

There was something unreal even about him—something which was different. He was not the godlike creature I had seen when we were young through the eyes of his adoring younger brother. There was something different about Rollo.

The door opened and strangely enough the old feeling of fear began to creep over me.

It was Rollo again. His face distorted with angry annoyance.

"I can't find the boy . . . the mad boy," he said. "Where can he have got to?"

"He can't have gone back to the castle."

"Why did he run off like that? What was he saying?"

"Something about Silva. She was my half sister. He was saying something terrible had happened to her."

"What did he mean?"

"I don't know."

"He's crazy, that boy."

"I don't think so. His mind works in a strange way,

that's all. He has what he calls fancies and powers."

"He's an idiot," said Rollo. "You haven't had your drink. You'll feel better for it, you know."

I took it up and sipped it.

"I want to go to the mainland," I said.

"I'll take you."

I stood up.

"Finish your drink first, and I'll get the boat."

"I've left everything at the castle."

"Why did you leave in such a hurry?"

"It seemed necessary then. Now . . ."

"You regret it?"

He was smiling at me and the room seemed to be dissolving about him. I could only see his smiling face.

"Yes, I think I was too hasty. I should have waited, should have talked to Jago. . . ."

My voice seemed to be coming from a long way off. Rollo continued to smile at me.

"You're growing very sleepy," he said. "My poor Ellen."

"I feel very strange. I think I'm dreaming still. This room . . ."

He nodded.

"Rollo, what's happening?"

"You're getting drowsy," he said. "It's the drink. A little sedative. You needed that—and so did I."

"You . . . Rollo?"

"Come. We're going now."

"Where?"

"To the boat. That's what you want, isn't it?"

I stood up and swayed unsteadily. He caught me.

"Now," he said, "it will be easy. Your coming like this. It couldn't have been better. Curse that boy, though."

He put an arm about me to steady me and we went out of the room and into the passage. The cold air revived me a little.

"What happened?" I cried.

I heard Rollo laugh softly. "All's well. I didn't expect

such luck. It'll be over soon. Come down. . . . Down the slope to the shore."

Something warned me. The doom feeling I had known in the dream was very strong.

"I don't think I want to go after all . . ." I heard myself say.

"Don't be obstinate. You're going."

"I want to see Jago first. Of course I must see Jago. I ought to have talked to him . . . asked him to explain."

I slid to the ground. I was lying among the bushes and I held on to these with all my strength.

"What's wrong with you?" Rollo was trying to pull me to my feet, but I clung with all my might to that bush. For a terrible realization had come to me. The dream had been right. My doom had come through that door, for my doom was Rollo.

The drink he had given me was drugged. I knew that now. This hazy sleeping feeling was meant to overcome my resistance so that he could do with me what he wanted. Why Rollo? For what possible reason could he want to kill me? He did want to. That conviction was with me strongly. Rollo had come through the door of doom and Slack . . . Slack had gone.

Even at such a time I was able to feel relief because I had been wrong about Jago. Oh, Jago, why did I run away from you? What is the answer to all this?

Rollo was dragging me away from the bush and I could retain my hold no longer. I was powerless against him and I could only delay him.

He had lifted me. "Don't struggle," he said. "It won't help you at all. It will only make me angry. Go to sleep. That's the best thing you can do."

It was rough going for him carrying me. I heard him cursing me under his breath. I could distinctly hear the waves breaking on the shore and I knew what he was going to do. For some reason it was important for him to have me out of the way and he was going to kill me. He was going to row out a little way and throw me into the sea and I should be unable to struggle because the drowsiness was increasing with every minute and I should soon be oblivious of everything.

I heard the boat scraping on the sand. He lifted me up.

A sudden flash of inspiration came to me. "It was you who tampered with the rail at Dead Man's Leap," I said.

"You've had a charmed life, Ellen . . . until now."

"Rollo, tell me why . . . why . . . what have I done to you?"

"You're in the way. That's all."

"But how . . . how . . . ? What can I mean to you?"

"Don't ask questions. Say your prayers."

"You came down here to kill me. Why?"

"I said don't ask questions."

He had put me roughly into the boat. I tried to scramble out but he was ready for me.

"Don't be a fool. I don't like violence."

"You don't mind murder," I said. "It was you . . . you who murdered Philip."

"If Philip had lived there wouldn't have been any need for this."

"Rollo, I know you are going to kill me. You owe me a little time. . . ."

"There's no time to lose. There never is," he retorted tersely.

This was the end then. I knew exactly what was going to happen. My sleepy body would receive the embrace of the sea and my heavy clothes would drag me down . . . down to oblivion.

But I was wrong. Indeed I had a charmed life—or was it that there were people to care so much for me?

There was a shout and I heard Rollo's furious exclamation. And there was Jago himself. He was on the shore, then wading out to sea. He had knocked Rollo aside and snatched me out of the boat.

"Ellen," I heard his voice through the waves of sleepiness which swept over me and I was filled with exultation. "My Ellen."

I awoke in my bedroom in the castle. It was daylight

and Jago was sitting by my bed. He bent over me and kissed me.

"All's well, Ellen," he said.

"It was a dream. It was *the* dream. . . ."

"No, it wasn't a dream. It was very real. He went off in the boat after I'd carried you back to the house. It was a rough sea and the chances are he didn't reach the mainland."

"Jago, I'm so bewildered."

"Important things first. I love you; you love me; although I must say you didn't show it last night. I was waiting for you to come to me as you'd promised. I waited and waited. Then I searched everywhere for you. By that time Slack came back in a state of alarm. He said you were on Blue Rock and that there was a man there who intended to harm you."

"How did he know?"

"He'd seen him before."

"He came to the Island."

"Yes, he did. He had the house on Blue Rock for a week or more . . . ever since Manton went to London. The artist had let the place to him during his absence."

"So he could have tampered with the *Ellen*. Why . . . why did he want to kill me?"

"It's a simple reason. With you out of the way his wife would have come into a great deal of money."

"His wife."

"Silva."

"But . . . she's dead."

Jago shook his head. "It may be that she is not. In fact it's certain she isn't, otherwise his actions would be pointless. That boy Slack . . . sly creature . . . pretending to be half baked all the time and knowing so much more than the rest of us!"

"Rollo wanted money. I can't believe it."

"I told you, didn't I, that their financial empire is tottering. They've seen it coming for some time. That was presumably why he married Silva. Then he discovered the contents of your father's will and that you came first. They were very ready for you to marry Philip which would have made them sure of the Kellaway fortune."

"Philip . . . oh Philip! What happened to Philip? I heard. . . ."

"Yes, I know what you heard. You were in the dungeons because you'd discovered I was meeting Hawley there and you knew Hawley. You hid yourself that you might eavesdrop. Then the necklace betrayed you. Ellen, how could you doubt me?"

"I had to know. I was afraid you might have done something. . . ."

"Which would have stopped your loving me?"

"The one discovery I made was that nothing can do that."

"Then it was all worthwhile. . . . But it was a near thing. If that devil had been five minutes earlier he would have had you at sea and then God knows what would have happened."

"Tell me everything that took place."

"I've had to piece a lot of it together myself. I haven't confirmed it. But this is what it seems like to me: Your father was not sure whether or not Silva was his daughter; he strongly suspected that she was James Manton's. So did James Manton himself because he and Silva's mother had been lovers. Rollo, who was interested in art, met James Manton in London, where he was having an exhibition, and he heard from him about the Island and the Kellaways. He came down and met Silva and as she lived on the Island and he had discovered that she was the elder daughter he naturally believed that she would inherit the Island. He had heard of course that there was a younger daughter who had been taken away by her mother and in whom the father had shown no interest. The rich spoils of the Island meant that it would fetch a high price if it were sold and the Carringtons needed a very large sum to bolster up their tottering empire. So he married Silva secretly and took her to London. Your father died and Carrington then discovered that there was one who came before Silva and that was you. If you had married Philip they would have persuaded you to sell the Island and invest as they advised, which would have meant their using your money."

"And you, Jago, came to London."

"To see you. To find out what was happening. I learned that all was not well with the Carrington interests and although I did not know that Rollo Carrington had married Silva and, like everyone else, believed her dead, I understood why the family was so anxious to welcome you. You were my ward—and still are, remember—and it was my duty to look after you. I engaged a private detective to make a thorough study of the Carrington affairs. He was rather a shady character; the nature of his work had made him so. By being in the household he found out more than I ever could through other sources. I came up to London and broke into the Carrington soirée, where I met you and promptly fell in love with you."

"I must have been very attractive with the Island to come."

"You and the Far Island, Ellen, were irresistible."

"The Island certainly is."

"And you yourself are not uncomely. How I loved your spirit right from the start. It was set off by that poor little Esmeralda."

"And Philip died."

"It was an accident. Poor fellow. It was a disastrous thing to have happened. Hawley was assiduously going through some papers in Philip's room when Philip disturbed him. Philip kept a pistol near his bed and he threatened Hawley with it, demanding to know what he was doing. Hawley lost his head and struggled with Philip to get the pistol away from him. It went off, alas, killing Philip. Hawley is a sharp character—very experienced in all kinds of adventures. . . . He saw what trouble he was in. He very skillfully arranged it to look like suicide and got away with it."

"Jago, you didn't hire him to kill Philip?"

"Good God, no. I was horrified by his death."

"But he was going to marry me, taking the Island with me."

"I was going to try to stop that. I was going to lay before you all the information I had gathered about the Carringtons, and I had a notion that you were not exactly madly in love with Philip and were at that time questioning the wisdom of rushing into marriage. I was counting on getting you at least to postpone the wedding for a while."

"And you got Hawley to have a key cut for you."

"Yes, I did. I wanted to have a word with you on your own in that house. I was seeking every opportunity to meet you. I thought that if we met there by chance I might be able to hint at something. . . ."

"It was a crazy thing to do."

"You'll find in the years to come that I often do crazy things. You're going to love some of the crazy things I do. I'd do a great deal to get you, Ellen, but I suppose I'd stop at murder. I was so anxious about you. I didn't trust those Carringtons. Then Philip's death changed everything."

"What will happen to the Carringtons now?"

"You'll be hearing about their collapse, I daresay, in a few weeks' time. But let's not worry about them. I want to talk to you, Ellen. There's so much to plan for . . . so much to say. Just think of it, Ellen . . . the two of us together on the Island."

I lay still thinking of it.

# The Outcome

I married Jago a month later.

Everything was clear to me by that time. Rollo's body was found a few days after that night when I had walked into my dream room and found him there. After his encounter with Jago he had had no alternative but to put to sea and try and reach the mainland; and the sea was not in a benign mood that night. Whether he had been unable to manage the boat or not I am not sure. It may well have been that he accepted defeat, for a few weeks later the collapse of the Carrington interests was announced in the papers. It was one of the greatest financial disasters of the century. Many people had lost their money in the crash and there was talk of a prosecution which might have taken place if Rollo had lived. It was presumed that he had deliberately chosen death by drowning.

I owed so much to Slack who, when he had seen Rollo, had recognized him as the man with whom Silva had run away, and he had instinctively known that he was there for no good purpose; so he had hastened back through the tunnel and brought Jago to save me just in time.

That seems to be all of our story.

Gwennol married Michael Hydrock eventually and they work together on the book about his family. Jenifry went to live with them. She had always been devoted to her daughter and had been afraid from the first that I might snatch some advantage from her even before she had been anxious on account of Michael. We are quite good friends now—though we could never be close—and I often smile to think of how I had suspected her of wishing me ill because of the reflection I had seen of her in a distorting mirror by candlelight.

And I have found Silva. Poor Silva, whose life was so tragic. I have tried to nurse her back to health and my main remedy is to teach her that someone loves her. Her brief honeymoon with Rollo had soon ended and when she realized that he had no love for her at all she had been more heartbroken than she had ever been before. He had kept her shut away with a nurse who was almost a keeper while he had sought to get his hands on her fortune; and then of course when he learned that I came before her, he had his motive for trying to remove me. Poor Silva, she had begun to believe that she was indeed insane.

It is my great task to convince her that this is not so.

I found her in a lonely country house which was Carrington property and I brought her back to the castle without her keeper. I call her my sister—and although it may well be that James Manton was her father, we both like to think it was otherwise. The artist is a kindly man and we often row over to his island, and have tea in my dream room; but he is really immersed in his work and although he is kind to Silva he cannot give her that special love which she needs.

It has not been easy. She was, at first, furtive and suspicious. Slack was helpful though, and delighted to have her back. He looks upon us both as his special protégées and I have often seen him smile with self-satisfaction when he looks at us.

When my first baby came—Jago after his father—Silva began to change. She adored the child and the others too. They love her dearly and I think that at last she is happy.

I never dreamed my dream again. I think I know why it haunted my childhood until its spell was broken by Rollo when he came through that door. My mother had lived on uneasy terms with my father and had wanted to go away. He, however, would not allow her to; but she was determined to escape. Mrs. Pengelly knew of the existence of the tunnel to Blue Rock and one night, so I later learned from her, they escaped through it. The artist was accommodating and he and my mother were already friends through their art so he was ready to help her. I was aged three at the time. My mother carried me through the tunnel and the impression made on my young mind by that room was clearly so vivid that it stayed with me through the years. I would have sensed my mother's fear that my father might have followed her and come through that door to prevent her escape, and I must have felt that fear so intensely that it haunted my dreams in the years ahead.

How I love the Island! How I love my life there! Jago and I are full of plans for the future.

Often we ride round it. The people come out to call a greeting to us. Old Tassie will be at her door with a new Malken purring round her skirts, regarding me as though by her special powers she has conjured up our contentment with life.

We lie on the cliffs and look down on the cove where I saw Hawley come in; we look up at the sky and see the pigeons now and then, perhaps carrying a message to Michael and Gwennol at Hydrock Manor; and sometimes we talk of the past.

"It's all yours now," said Jago.

"Ours," I reminded him.

Yes, I thought, ours, this fair Island, these beloved children, this good life. Ours.